ENDGAME

ENDGAME

A Harry One Sigh Novel

Gar Mallinson

This is a work of fiction. All of the characters, names, incidents, organizations, and dialogue in this novel are either products of the author's imagination or are used fictitiously. The town of Hammil does not exist in case you're looking for it. I needed a town, so I made one up.

Cover Photo ©Gar Mallinson
Cover Design © Mohammad Shawon

Copyright: © 2019 Gar Mallinson

All rights reserved.

ISBN: 9781708934668

1.

Jasmine Holmes and Jason Sanders had packed their water bottles and bedrolls, their pots and pans, their extra shoes and toiletries, their maps and freeze-dried basics, their inflatable mattresses and rain gear, their clothes, and their money. They left Toronto and the university around eight in the morning and rode the subway up to the 401, a super-highway that bisected the city. Hitchhiking was forbidden, so they tried, thumbs out, on the cloverleaf at Yonge Street.

    A commuter picked them up within the hour and they were on their way. He dropped them at the first rest stop on the 400 north as a favour, once he discovered from talking to Jasmine that they intended to cross the country. After lunch at the fast food counter, they found a family who'd give them a lift. The woman lectured them for hours on the perils of hitchhiking while she dug out as much information about them as she could. The kids, a boy and a girl, fought in the back seats of the large SUV all the way north. Jasmine and Jason were more than happy when the family dropped them by the side of the road at their turnoff to cottage country.

    They camped that night in the bush far enough off the highway that they couldn't be seen. In Ontario, it was illegal to camp anywhere but in a campground. The next day it rained, so they stayed put. By the end of that first week, however, they'd hitched all the way across the top of

Lake Superior and had hit the prairies. The weather had held. They'd been lucky.

In Manitoba, Jasmine began to understand the term "big sky". It was vast. It made her feel tiny. All the way across Manitoba and Saskatchewan she talked about that sky until Jason, frustrated with the constant references, told her to either find another subject or shut up. She shut up.

The other side of Calgary, the flat prairie highway began to undulate, and the foothills appeared. They mesmerized Jasmine, and she couldn't stop talking about them. Jason gave her one of his looks. Jasmine kept quiet. She was excited, but she kept her excitement to herself.

Rides were easy through the mountains. Drivers seemed to like picking up hitchhikers, and that was a nice change from the prairies where drivers seemed more suspicious. These were nice folk, and Jasmine became friendly with all of them. She liked people, and the mountains were spectacular. The road, where it hadn't been blasted out, twisted and turned looking for the least difficult passage. They got all the way to Kamloops with one man, a salesman who talked even more than Jasmine.

Their last ride took them down Highway 5 from Kamloops through Merit and down the Coquahalla. Jasmine couldn't take her eyes off the massive mountain sides as they descended. They skirted Hope and Highway 5 rejoined Highway 1.

Their driver took them across the flats all the way to Vancouver and left them on the side of the Grandview highway near Rupert Street. The intersection was a busy one with a gas station on one side and a huge superstore on the other. Traffic backed up for a few blocks in every direction around the lights. They were both used to busy cities and heavy traffic and enjoyed the change. They found a bus into the city proper and stayed in a hostel for four days to explore parts of the city. Then it was the express bus to Horseshoe Bay and the ferry to Vancouver Island to pick up Highway 1 once again.

They spent three days in Harbour City, a small place with not much to interest them. But they had to decide how far up island they were going to go. Originally, they'd intended to get as far up as t3he Queen Charlotte islands. Once they'd checked the northern tip of the island. That ferry would take them to the Queen Charlottes.

The highway north was full of stoplights. It was four lanes and modern, but neither of them could understand why there weren't overpasses. Who would build a highway and fill it with stoplights? And it wasn't called Highway 1 going north, only going south to Victoria. Going north, it was Highway 19, and hitching was forbidden.

Jasmine learned that from their first ride, a salesman who picked them up in town. He told them that there were fines for both the hitchhiker and the driver if they got caught. And that applied to all the intersections and lights all the way to Campbell River where the four-lane ended and a simple two-lane wound its way to Port Hardy. Jasmine and the driver talked all the way to Courtenay, their first stop. He let them out on the bypass part of 19, and they caught a ride with a trucker all the way to Campbell River. That first night on the road north, they splurged on a motel in the center of town.

In the morning, after a pair of Egg McMuffins and two Americanos each, they hit the road again. It took them two days to reach Port Hardy, and they were tired. Their last night before the city had been in the bush once again, and it had rained, hard, for a couple of hours. The morning had been miserable. They'd cleaned up a in a stream and had stood on the shoulder for what seemed like hours before a pickup stopped for them. Two rides later, they'd made it to the city called Port Hardy.

Now they were eating chicken they'd bought at a Colonel Sanders outlet on the outskirts of the city. In the grease-stained boxes they carried to a local park were limp French fries and handfuls of popcorn chicken, a favourite of theirs. These things were small, roughly circular, bubbly brown lumps consisting of bits of ground-up chicken breast deep-fried in batter. They'd arrived in Port Hardy late in the afternoon after the previous wet night in the bush. Their stuff was still damp, and the ride in the pickup had been uncomfortable. Jasmine had spent the time looking out the tiny window in the back of the pickup. They had been quiet and there'd been nothing to see but forests of conifers that filled the ridges and valleys, no farms, no houses, not even roadside restaurants or service stations. Jason had sat in the back with her, head down, his mood black. Jasmine didn't bother him and kept quiet. She thought he'd perk up once they got out of that truck.

They were tired, mostly from the excitement of being on the island at last, but also from the utter difference of the landscape. They weren't used to roads that passed through nothing but bush for hours. Even the prairies, as huge and flat as they were, had had more signs of human life than the towering forests of British Columbia. The passes through the mountains were one thing; there, they'd been distracted by the massive splendour of them towering overhead, by the frighteningly precipitous ravines that snaked through them, and by the warmth of the little settlements tucked in here and there where the land allowed. But here, the mountains were off in the distance, hardly noticeable; the forest, however, was like a silent threat that seemed to crowd in, pushing at the run of asphalt as if resenting the intrusion.

Jasmine ate her chicken slowly, sitting beside Jason, comfortable in the silence. She thought of what they'd been through so far. She remembered when they'd walked the ribbon of road, scuffing along on the shoulder in the gravel and bits of highway refuse: small chunks of tire tread; tiny pieces of red glass or plastic winking in the sunlight, the remnants of taillights; and occasionally, empty coffee containers mostly from thoughtless or uncaring drivers.

There wasn't much debris, not like Ontario where the sides of roads were littered with cast-off junk. There was just enough to provide the comfort of knowing the road was used, a human counterpoint to the silent presence of the great conifers.

They had crossed many bridges, but Jasmine remembered one particularly, a long curving bridge that never seemed to end. Glancing down she'd seen flecks of sunlight dancing off water largely hidden by the forest.

She now remembered nights black as ebony, the heavens shot through with more stars than she'd ever seen.

She remembered sun-ups as she ate her chicken, the times they'd packed up and begun walking the shoulder again. Cars had passed them quite often, and that had been disheartening, but rides had finally come, and now, here they were.

She remembered one guy, another salesman in a new car who'd explained the fences that lined one side of the highway down around Courtenay.

"It's for elk, you know, to keep them off the damn road. You hit one of those buggers, you got no front end left, let alone what happens to you. Sometimes, before the fence, people got killed; sometimes the mess on the road caused more accidents. So they built the fence. It goes up past Courtenay almost to Campbell River where I'm going."

Then he had explained that he'd have to let them out there. As they'd approached the city, they'd watched the four-ne highway reduce to two, then they were in.

"Can't let anybody know I gave you a lift, you know, new car and all, so sorry, but this is it. I'll drop you at that Tim Horton's in the plaza there; grab a coffee before I take it in. The dealership's just up the road a bit."

They'd gotten their backpacks from the floor and had gone inside with the salesman to get coffee. They'd thanked him for the lift and walked outside to look around and enjoy their drinks. Neither of them could understand the attraction Tim Horton's had; the coffee was weak and the sandwiches expensive with not much in them.

An old guy in an equally old pickup had pulled out of a dirt side road they'd just passed, had seen them walking, and had stopped for them. He had taken them up island a long way. The road had no fence to keep the elk at bay. It had only two lanes and curved around ridges of rock, dipped down through ravines, always searching for the easiest path. It went on and on. The old man had driven them a long way north from Campbell River, letting them.

They'd looked around Campbell River for a while, and as they walked, heavy rain clouds had rolled in. She remembered standing in a doorway with Jason, watching the water pouring down from the belly of a black cloud.

Twenty minutes later, the sun was back. They'd had lunch in a diner in the north end and by mid-afternoon were beyond the city in a sparsely populated area.

Jasmine and Jason had known each other for a couple of years, had lived together in the student residences at the University of Toronto for the last six months. It was an arrangement frowned upon by the university authorities but largely ignored by their rather lazy super. There were at least six couples pulling off the same thing.

Jason was naturally sullen. It was a kind of bad-boy quality that, Jasmine knew, had attracted her to him. She, on the other hand, was beautiful and outgoing. She'd been told she was. It was she who dragged him around most of the time; it was she who had the friends; and it was she who got the invitations. He'd finished his third year in Engineering, and Jasmine had finished her second in a split program of English and Fine Arts. This trip was something they'd planned and saved for. They had intended to hitchhike across the country, camping in the evenings when possible and staying in cheap motels when it wasn't. If they could manage that, they'd have enough to fly back. And, she thought, they'd damn near done it.

Jason was tall and thin with a mop of unruly brown hair and a charming smile when he chose to use it. Jasmine was petite with long, lustrous black hair falling sleek and straight half-way down her back. She also had a presence that drew the attention of every male in her vicinity, a kind of sensual grace that seemed to emanate from her like some provocative perfume. They made an attractive couple and assumed they'd have no trouble getting rides. But it hadn't been that easy. The ones who stopped for them were more intent on chatting up Jasmine. Jason was mostly ignored. He didn't like it much, but he'd realized that without Jasmine, he'd probably still be on the road.

Their plan was to spend a day or so in Port Hardy, in a campground if they could find one, and to take the ferry to the Queen Charlottes. They wanted to see the rain forest, experience the coastal waters, learn about the old villages, the totem poles, and the natives. They wanted to do all that in a week. First, though, they'd have to take a fifteen-hour ferry ride to Prince Rupert, stay overnight, then take another ferry to Skidegate on the Queen Charlottes. They didn't know how to proceed from there, but figured they'd find out when they arrived. On the map, the Queen Charlottes didn't look that big, not compared to Vancouver Island. They had enough money to cover the fares and any expenses they might incur. Coming back, they'd have to retrace their route one ferry at a time.

When they'd finished the Colonel's chicken and fries, they lay back in the sun for a while. They found the weather on the island so changeable that they took whatever sun they found whenever they found it. They'd had one day on the island's roads when they'd been hit by sun, rain, hail, sun again, more rain, and wind, lots of wind. Most days were less severe but rarely stable.

Once they'd found a trash container to discard the remains of the chicken and chips, they walked on into Port Hardy. Jason was a little distant with Jasmine, had been most of the day. She'd noticed it on the road. It hadn't been a hard day, but they had begun to argue while walking through town.

"I want to spend a few days west, on the coast, as close as I can get to the open Pacific."

"Why? We should stick to our plan and go to The Queen Charlottes, Haida Gwaii. That's what you agreed to do."

"Look, I'll do this, I'll stay in town for part of tomorrow.

"You'll see I'm right and we should go west to the Pacific. It's our chance to see something we won't get on the Haida whatever. We'll travel gravel roads west to either Cape Scott Provincial Park or Raft Cove Park. That's where we'll see the real Pacific. The trip to the Queen Charlottes can wait. We're in no hurry. I've come this far, and I'm damned well going to see the bloody ocean."

Jasmine wasn't having any. "But it's always what you want. We planned this trip together and you agreed: we travel the island north to Port Hardy; we cross to Prince Rupert; we stay there a day or so, then we take the ferry to Skidegate and spend a week on the islands. That's what we planned, and that's what we should do."

Jasmine was furious and a little frightened that Jason would suddenly change his mind like that and expect her to just agree.

"I don't want to see the Pacific now, and I don't want to spend god knows how long on gravel roads to get there, whichever park you choose. Besides, we'll see the Pacific on the Queen Charlottes for as long as we like. Right now, I want the ferry and a bed and some decent food and Prince Rupert. And what I want counts just as much as what you want."

Jason stopped, glared at her, dropped his backpack on the side of the road, and raised his voice. "You! This whole fuckin' trip you've been the center of everything, every ride, every place we've been, it's always you. I might as well be a piece of shit on some guy's shoe. It's really pissing me off. You pay any attention to me? Nooo, not you. You damn near make out with any guy who picks us up. Why don't you just fuck off! Just stick out your thumb, wiggle your ass, show your tits, and you'll get a ride, more than a ride. Fuck you, I'm gonna see the Pacific now! You can just bugger off."

She stared at him in disbelief, her heart racing. She was shocked at his anger. She realized that it must have been festering in him the whole trip. He was attacking her right here in the middle of the street. She looked at his mean, angry face as she backed away.

That's what he thought of her after all this time. The living together back in the residence, all the intimacy on the trip west, all of it must have meant nothing.

She turned slowly and began to walk.

Then Jasmine heard him yell, "Good bloody riddance!"

She turned and watched him walk the other way, repositioning his backpack. She stood for a few minutes watching him go, staring at his back, silently pleading he'd turn and walk back to her. Tears began rolling down her cheeks and her throat tightened.

She watched until he disappeared, then she turned to walk south. She walked slowly, the landscape blurred by her tears. Maybe he'd still catch up, she thought. But when she turned, all she saw was empty road.

The late afternoon sun warmed her, slid down her silky-smooth hair, throwing her shadow across the gravel as she walked. She wiped her face with the back of her hand. The sun was low in the sky but still warm. She'd have to find a place to stay. Fortunately, she carried her own money. The ferry tickets had not yet been purchased, so she had a lot more than she would have had if he'd blown up like that in Prince Rupert.

Jasmine walked on, still not believing what had happened. How could she have been so wrong about him? How could she have lived with him for six months and not seen the hatred? He hated her for what she was, what she did, who she knew, who her friends were, everything. Even when they made love, he must have hated her, even then.

She shuddered in disgust, as much at herself as at him. He was moody, sure, and she liked that quality in him. She should have seen what he was really like much earlier, should never have slept with him. She was a fool. The tears continued to fall, and she continued to brush them away. Her nose threatened to run.

The sun's warmth left her back and she glanced up. It was sitting now on the horizon, just going down over the Pacific, way beyond the island. Where Jason would be soon if he headed toward the coast.

Jasmine walked on until she reached a motel.

2.

The brothers had spent more than a month in the bush avoiding contact with anyone, especially the police, but they had grown restless and irritated during that time. They had left the stream they'd camped beside early in the morning and had worked their way over to the main highway south by mid-morning. By lunchtime they were parked beside a restaurant just south of Nimpkish. The older brother went in and brought their orders out to the truck: burgers and fries and fresh, hot coffee. Once they'd finished eating, they took the road south toward Courtenay, passing through Campbell River in the middle of the afternoon.

    The turnoff to Courtenay was a broad, curving cloverleaf sliding downhill. It fed them onto a two-lane blacktop that except for one long arc, ran straight east toward the sea. The road stopped at Courtenay's wide, shallow harbour. Another blacktop called Cliffe Street ran paralled to the harbour in both directions, separated from the water by a thin band of trees and a narrow strip of green grass. In places, the city had put flowerbeds in the strip of grass. Shrubs with a small yellow flower filled most of them. The left wing of Cliffe Street ran through a ribbon of commercial enterprises into the center of town. There the harbor ended and the river that fed into it appeared. At the union of these two, harbour and river, lay the bridge that fed traffic from Courtenay's main street across the waterway to the highway leading to Comox, a sister city, on the other side of the harbour. The brothers drove up Cliffe Street searching for a Walmart.

The store was part of a large plaza made up of the usual: a grocery, mall shops, and restaurants. Walmart anchored one end of the plaza, the grocery store the other. Walmart was a huge unit spreading out like a growth eating up the asphalt. It dominated the plaza, and it sold everything. The two brothers needed new clothes and camping supplies. Walmart had it all, and everything was cheap.

The older brother, who dominated the younger, chose the clothes for his brother and did the shopping; the younger one pushed the cart behind him. At the register, he paid with cash and the two left the store, stopping at the McDonald's that was joined to its side.

On the way into town, the older brother took the old truck they had through a car wash, spending a lot of time and numerous loonies getting the caked mud off the body. His brother stayed inside and watched him while he soaped and brushed and rinsed until the truck shone.

They parked the freshly washed truck in the town lot and walked up and down the main street. They bought a local paper and read it in one of the small parks with benches that dotted the shopping area. They needed a different vehicle.

The older brother found a public telephone in the library, one of the few still in service in Courtenay, and made a couple of calls. He arranged to see a four-year-old dark grey Ford Transit 250 low roof with all-wheel drive in Merville, a short distance up island. When they got there, the older brother struck a deal with the seller, an old guy in a plaid shirt, paid cash, and took the signed papers promising to register the sale the next day. Then the he drove ahead of his younger brother who was driving the old truck, back to Courtenay.

Around the city, like most of the cities on the island, there were Indian reservations, some with a fair number of inhabitants. Most, however, were small in population but large in area like the Puntledge Reservation Number Two. On one side of the long wooden bridge over the river were rows of townhouses belonging to the city. On the other, were the wooded banks of the western edge of the reservation. It was bounded in the south by the Tsolum River. In the north and east, however, its boundaries were simply marks on a map. The natives were always jealous of their sovereignty and didn't like strange vehicles with white people driving on their land, but there were so many badly kept roads running through reservations like this one, it was easy to lose a vehicle inside its boundaries.

The older brother in the Transit led the younger off Condensory Road into the reservation proper. He took roads that steadily degenerated from good gravel to poorly maintained gravel and finally to dirt tracks. On one of these, he pulled the Ford Transit into an open, grassy area beside a small lake and parked. His brother followed. Here they camped overnight. They lit no fire.

In the morning, as light mist stained with sunlight rose from the lake, they packed their goods into the Transit and left the old truck where it had been parked with the key in the ignition. It would be there for a few days with curious natives passing by on occasion. Then one of them would stop, see the keys, and take the vehicle. The papers would be inside, not the brother's papers, but the previous owner's, an old trapper who lived way the other side of Port Alberni back in the bush. The truck's new owner would discard those papers and drive the pickup only on the reservation where the local force had no jurisdiction.

The brothers had a full day to amuse themselves in their new vehicle. They cruised the town watching young women, then drove out to the main highway and into Cumberland to watch girls there. They learned quickly where the high schools were in each town and returned in midafternoon to watch again. They were searching for the right one. They didn't find her. Their hunger made them irritable. By late afternoon, they returned to downtown Courtenay and crossed the main bridge over the Puntledge River to the Comox side.

After a few tight turns to get around the city's largest park, the road they were on led up a long hill, past the international airport, and along the side of the town of Comox, which was huddled mostly down near the harbour. The brothers turned onto a narrow two-lane blacktop that led to the ferry docks at Little River, a tiny outpost beyond

Comox's northern boundary. Once they arrived, they waited for an hour in a long line of cars, watched the ferry enter the small harbour and dock, then followed the cars on board.

They sat next to a window, felt the rumble of the great engines, and watched the island and the ferry docks slowly diminish as the ship left the tiny harbour and began its long trek across the Salish Sea. They would be on the mainland in an hour or so, and their lives would begin again. The sea became a boundary between what they had been and what they would become. Their failures in Harbour City in their last days there would become as insubstantial as the great island now sliding into early dusk behind them.

The ferry docked right in the middle of the city of Powell River. The main highway south toward Jervis Inlet, Sechelt, and the ferry to Horseshoe Bay and Vancouver lay just beyond the terminal. To the north, the lights of Powell River's downtown glowed softly. The crossing had taken them from late afternoon to early evening, and the light had failed, a deepening dusk coating everything in a soft haze.

The older brother didn't follow the ferry traffic toward the center of the city, nor did he go south toward Sechelt. Instead, he worked his way across town, driving beyond the last straggle of houses and out into the foothills. He passed the municipal airport and the bottom edge of Haslam Lake. Then he drove along the side of Duck Lake and into the Smith mountain range, travelling back down toward the coast before turning up Weldwood Highway. That road took them up past Horseshoe Lake, Dodd Lake, and Windsor Lake, through heavy forest and around many massive rock cliffs. The two had driven a long way that day, and it was pitch black when they turned in-country part way up the side of Goat Lake, following roads that quickly degenerated to tracks. On one of these, they found the perfect place, eased the Transit into the bush and parked. It was full night now. They eased their seats back and slept.

Morning sun slipped into the truck through the partly open windows. The older brother woke first and lay back in his seat listening, the sunlight warming his arm. There was little wind, just the soft soughing of the conifers in the light breeze s that slipped through the forest. Birdsong floated among the great trees. A tiny brook near the car gurgled along, bouncing over stones and around moss-covered rocks in its course downhill. Over everything was the immense silence of the land. He felt it in his core, a brooding presence, a monumental pervasive power. He felt his own insignificance like a blow, and something in him recoiled even though the forest had been his home for as long as he could remember.

A little shaken by the experience, he woke his brother, and together they pulled out supplies, built a small fire, and made breakfast. Over coffee, feeling in control once again, he turned to his brother and said, "We have to have new names. We can't stay here, in the bush, the way we did on the island. We'll drive back toward the coast and look for a town that suits us. I'll coach you on the way. Then we'll hunt." His brother smiled in anticipation and nodded.

After they had cleaned the campsite thoroughly and themselves as much as they could, they repacked the Transit and made their way back to the two-lane blacktop. At an isolated service station, the older brother bought a map of the area and filled the tank. The two of them got coffee from the small store attached to the station and sat in the gravel parking area to drink and to talk.

"I'm going to call myself Vic Hunter and you'll be Able." He smiled at his brother. "It's who we should be given what we are. Now let's find a town."

He spread the map across their laps and studied it. "How about this one down here? It looks large enough. We'll drive there and take all the roads around the place until we're sure it'll do." The older brother had his finger near the bottom of Dodd Lake on a town called Hammil. His brother nodded and grinned, "Able, I'm Able. Able Hunter." He giggled with pleasure, his eyes bright, a grin plastered on his face.

He was still repeating the name as his brother took the van out to the highway and headed down toward the coast. The turnoff to Hammil was a dozen kilometers past the bottom of Dodd Lake. The two-lane blacktop veered off at a sharp angle and curved around a large outcropping. They followed it for a few kilometers of twisting road before they saw the town. It was nestled in a broad valley between abrupt hills carrying rank after rank of conifers up toward the mountains. From the vantage point of the last curve, they could see the expanse of the downtown, the fingers of suburbs, and the glassy surface of a small lake on the outskirts.

The road in smoothed out, straightened, dipped, and led directly to the main street after passing through a straggly line of suburban houses. Side streets branched off irregularly wherever the terrain seemed most accessible. The main street ran like an arrow right through the business district, and Vic Hunter drove slowly down it. Not too slowly, but like someone looking for an address or a particular store. He noted everything, especially the bulk of the city hall, a rather ugly stone building squatting behind a white picket fence and an expanse of green lawn and flower beds. The parking area in front of the white picket fence contained a couple of police cruisers and some reserved spots for cars that weren't there yet. Vic could see the word 'police' etched into the stone above a door on the ground floor of the three-storey building. The front steps were cement with stone sidewalls. The door to the police station was on the left side on the ground floor near the steps and the big wooden doors to the main building up top.

Vic drove on. Towards the end of the downtown area, he passed a feed-hardware store and a large restaurant painted yellow with a sign across the front in neon script spelling out the name Agnes. He wondered if Agnes really owned it and was present, or if it were like so many others, looking owner-operated but really a franchise run by a chain like Tim Horton's. There didn't seem to be any fast food outlets, at least not downtown.

The road continued into residential streets again, then led out of town into the hills. Vic took it a good distance until it turned to gravel and then to dirt before it dead-ended. He turned and reentered the town looking for another road he could follow. There were numerous ones to choose from. This he did for most of the day. One of those roads led past a sawmill and off that road were a few short tributaries. Vic followed them all.

The brothers spent the night in a motel off the main highway outside Hammil. In the morning, they drove the Transit farther on, passing between Little Horseshoe and

Beaver lakes and exploring roads that led off to the side. Most led into bush-covered hills and were short. The occasional one led to an isolated farm where there was enough flat land to carve a few fields out of the bush. They followed numerous roads in that area and on one of them found what they were looking for.

The farm, derelict and isolate, was at the end of the usable part of the road, if a rutted dirt road overgrown in most places could be called usable. The outbuildings had long ago collapsed. They parked and walked through the nearest field until they came to a scabrous two-storey clapboard house. It was out-of-true and leaned a little sideways, as if it were too tired anymore to stand up straight. Inside, as they had hoped, they found an old root cellar under the kitchen.

Then the brothers spent hours walking the periphery of the old fields. They worked their way into the bush for long distances searching, then retraced their route to the farm, took the Transit back to the motel, had a late dinner in the small coffee shop, and retired for the night in the same motel.

The next day, they were back exploring. This time with a detailed map of the area that they'd found in the service station's rack. According to the map, the road to the farm they'd discovered the day before went right past the farmhouse and continued inland until it joined up with another road. Vic realized it joined one they had already been on behind the saw mill up toward the town. He was already close to the turnoff for the old derelict farm, so he took the overgrown road about fifty feet farther than the cay before until he saw that it had become impassable.

Vic reversed and parked in the same spot he had the day before, and he and his brother began to walk the old road past the farmhouse. What was left of the road was the occasional indication of old tire ruts, especially in the sandy soil of the cuts in the small hills that rolled across its route and in the slight widening of the banks of small streams where the road had crossed them. The rest had pretty much grown in, covering any trace. The brothers, however, were expert woodsmen and had no trouble following the scant signs. Eventually, the road became more of a road again but not one anybody could drive anymore. There were too many saplings, too much sand, too much undergrowth.

The brothers rested for a few minutes, then explored the driveway following it to within a few yards of its terminus at a small house and garage perched on a ridge above what appeared to be the arm of a large lake.

They looked it over carefully, then retraced their route. Leaving the driveway, they walked back following the traces of old road to the farmhouse. In the whole of their journey, they had heard nothing except the calls of birds and the wind through the great trees. There was neither sign nor sound to indicate anyone lived close by, and that suited them perfectly.

Most of the second day was gone by the time they'd finished their explorations, so they returned to Hammil and stopped at Agnes' restaurant for dinner.

By dinner time, the restaurant was filling up. Along the windows were low-backed booths, most already filled with customers. In the center of the room, square tables held four chairs each and for the most part were still empty. Along the back wall ran a counter with a line of stools with red vinyl seats. A large serving window to the kitchen threw light into the room along with the odours of onions and hot grease. On the counter were round plastic pie trays all partly full. Behind the counter above the rear working area, glass shelves held the paraphernalia all restaurants carried. Against the side wall were more booths, and in one of these sat two policemen and one young woman. They were talking and eating supper. Vic took the booth next to them. The backs of these booths along the wall were high, higher than the heads of the people using them, so Vic and his brother had no difficulty hiding the fact that they were listening.

"Jenny, you got the schedules for next week done yet? I'm gonna need a copy for the meeting."

"They're on your desk, Herk, where they always are. You just never look."

"You remembered Bert's gotta go to the Powell River range along with Sam next week? They gotta qualify again like everybody else."

"I worked the schedule around that, the patrols are covered and so's the desk. You going too?"

"I was over there last week, did a couple rounds with Gordie. Don't have to qualify till next spring."

Vic listened for a while longer, but the conversation revealed nothing he was concerned with, just office trivia. He relaxed and ordered roast beef dinners for the two of them. Able remained silent.

3.

The two brothers had grown up in a small, isolated, fundamentalist community on Vancouver Island just outside Harbour City. Their father, a strict disciplinarian, ran his flock of fifty or so with an iron hand. The teachings were unorthodox, at the outer edges of even the most virulent fundamentalist sects. Members who questioned anything the leader said were first punished then reprogrammed, and during that period they were shunned by the entire group. It was the shunning that created the panic: the possibility of being thrown into an utterly foreign world beyond the community was intolerable to anyone in the small cult. All found their identity within the teachings and the close-knit community.

The two boys were punished often for leaving the confines of the tiny village and escaping into the heavy forest surrounding the isolated houses and the central meeting hall. Only two narrow blacktop roads led into the tiny community, and both were blocked off with home-made camouflaged barriers during meetings so that the roads appeared to dead-end. Meetings occurred every day and most evenings.

The boys usually got together behind the headman's house before wandering into the forest. They found their freedom from the oppressive rules of the community in that heavy forest but paid dearly for their escapades. When they were caught, which was often, they were thrown into a root cellar, dirt floored, dark and musky, until their father decided to release them. Their mother, a meek woman who never opposed her husband, fed them surreptitiously.

As they grew up in this repressive climate, they became more and more isolate themselves. The older brother always led the younger, whose dependence on him grew steadily until the older one became a dominant force in his life just as his father was a dominant force in the community. Slowly, the brothers began to develop rituals of their own which they practiced in the deeper parts of the forest away from the punitive atmosphere of the village. They became a cult of two, the older dominating the younger, their rituals controlling both.

As they passed through their early teens, these rituals became a perverse expression of authority over the creatures of the forest. Many were slaughtered, the blood exciting the brothers so much that the executions became as essential as the rituals associated with them. The feelings were visceral and exhilarating. The animal sacrifices preceding their times in the root cellar led inevitably to a connection as they lay in the dark hole between what they did and how they felt. It all coalesced in their union in the earthy, pungent cellar, a perverse coupling that fused it all together. By their mid-teens, the two were more of the forest than the community, and the obsessive fusion of sex and blood dominated their lives.

Very few escaped the tyranny of their father, and those who possessed the courage to leave were hunted. Often, they were taken back to the community, by force if necessary. There, they were closely guarded until their will to leave was broken. The few members who did escape did so by hiding long enough to change their very existence, developing new identities in places as far from the influence of the cult as possible. The brothers were two such survivors. They sank greedily into perversity, their obsession with ritual sacrifice and their own couplings the focus of their lives.

Whatever names they had had in their father's cult stayed there. They became whoever the older brother wished them to be as they explored new terrain. They became hunters wherever they were, satisfying their urges in the same way they always had: through the hunt and the blood that made possible their union in the darkness of the earth.

Vic was a psychopath, a charming, intelligent, successful man, well-liked in whatever community he became part of. He was a chameleon, a master of deception. He had no conscience, no empathy, and saw others as inferior creatures to be manipulated for his pleasure. He was clever and extremely disciplined. There was no succumbing to the pressure of the moment. Nothing triggered violent explosions of rage. He planned carefully, the twisted logic of his world always dominant.

The two left Agnes' restaurant in the early evening and booked rooms at the local hotel. It was a red-brick three-storey affair with gingerbread fretwork along its front with a recessed pair of front doors. The lobby was smallish with a highly polished floor of rich dark wood. The registration desk, also wood, shone with the patina of long use and great care. The man behind it was dressed in a dark suit and smiled as they approached. They chose adjoining rooms, registered, and were given access cards and a sticker for their vehicle which, they were informed, should be parked behind the hotel and not on the street since the town had an ordinance against overnight parking.

While Vic moved the Transit van down the side drive to the lot, Able waited in one of the chairs that were scattered around the lobby. He sat staring vacantly, the rich interior of the room hardly registering on him. Vic arrived a few minutes later and they took a tiny elevator to the third floor. The connecting door between their rooms was left unlocked, so they could sleep together in the dark as they always did.

They both unpacked and hung everything up. A laundry would be one of the first orders of business after breakfast. Vic would ingratiate himself with whoever he found, starting with the clerks he did business with. He could build a reputation quickly as a handsome, available, charming man with considerable life experience. He had sold himself so many times he was expert at it.

Able was another matter. He was reclusive and not very good at adapting to new places. Vic always had to coach him, but he was getting a little better at fitting in during the day. For the first few days, Vic would let him wander about the town so he'd be seen if not known. Then he'd begin the task of finding him something to do that would keep him busy enough, so he didn't stick out. Mostly it was just camouflage, a way of reassuring the public and whatever authorities took notice of him.

Able could hold down a part-time job if it were undemanding. Since his dependency on his brother was absolute, he couldn't function on his own for any length of time, and he needed constant reassurance. Earlier, in Harbour City on the island, Vic had kept him indoors in his apartment during the day when they were in the city. When they were not, he was left on his own at their cabin in the foothills of dense bush where he was more at home. But Harbour City had proven untenable, and they had had to leave rather hurriedly.

Vic knew their future lay in large cities where the hunting was better and camouflage easier. The transition for Able, however, was going to be difficult. That was the primary reason for starting in a small town like Hammil, buried in the back country, surrounded by bush. All Able had to do was look past the streets and there was home, the great coniferous forests and mountains of his childhood. Once they reached Vancouver, all that would change. The mountains would be too distant, the woods out of reach.

Able would have to master the urban forest, the canyons of the city gradually. Vic knew his brother, knew if they took long enough on their journey down the coast, he'd become more familiar and comfortable with daily urban life. The noise, the smog, and the legions of people all crammed into the city would unnerve him, but he'd adjust. It was just a matter of degree, a slow enlargement of his world. At least, Vic hoped that's how it would work. He had no doubt about their night life whatever the environment.

By late morning of the next day, Vic had met the girl at the laundry, had befriended the maid at the hotel, had visited some

shops, and had been charming everywhere he went. He was now ready to approach the head man at the local paper.

Just after noon, Vic crossed the street and entered a door under a sign that said "The Hammil Times." Vic looked around and after a moment approached the front desk. He picked up one of the newspapers and perused the front page.

The man sitting behind a large oak desk eyed the young man who had approached the office. He obviously wasn't delivering supplies or coffee. Derek, the proprietor, looked at him over the top of his reading glasses like an old professor who resented interruptions and waited. The kid was well enough dressed, had a good smile, spoke English at least, and didn't waste time on pleasantries, so he listened.

"Good Day. I'm looking for work, not full time. I know your operation's small and you've already got someone, so maybe freelance stuff. I'd prefer that anyway. I'd give you a resume, but I know you don't want one. I brought a few of the stories I've done recently for you to look over. I'll come back this afternoon if you're free, and maybe we could have a coffee and talk it over."

Vic handed the old man a file folder with some of his work from Harbour City. It wasn't that much larger than Hammil and the work was appropriate for a small operation.

"Three o'clock," Derek said, and turned back to his desk. He threw the file on top of the pile resting there and began editing copy.

Vic smiled, turned, and left him there. As the front door closed, the old man grinned and shook his head. He'd found his man after all.

Derek Manchester was an old-school newspaper man. He'd been around a long time and looked it. He'd started as a typesetter back when work like that had been an essential part of the business. Before that he'd been with the Sun for years. He'd left that end of the business and turned to editing where he had more control of language and numerous battles with the owners over content. He'd ended his career in the big city as day editor, and on retirement had moved north to this small community to run a newspaper the way he thought one should be run, free of the bias and the politics that infected the business in Vancouver and all other large cities.

In Hammil, he had one reporter who covered everything and none of it very well. His English was faulty and his nose for news was plugged. Derek didn't like him much and was always looking for someone better, but it was a small town with little local news and declining circulation thanks to the Internet, so the pickings were slim. He couldn't pay anyone what he'd like to, and that meant he'd only get incompetents like Ted Smith, his current imbecile. Still, there was enough of the older, print-oriented generation left to warrant running the damn thing. Besides, he liked it.

Able walked the streets for most of the day. He had enough for lunch and a couple of coffees. He liked the parks best, the ones with trees and benches. He sat in a small one in the downtown area and drank coffee both in the morning and the afternoon. He smiled at people and nodded as his brother had told him to do, but he didn't engage anyone in conversation. Vic had made certain he was well enough dressed, and he had his instructions: "Look for work you know you can do, something part-time if you can find it."

At three o'clock, Vic returned to the paper. Derek was waiting for him at the front counter, folder in hand.

"This is mostly crime reporting, and we don't have much of that around here beyond the obvious for a lumber town. Mines are pretty much moribund now. You have a nice touch though with the language and you know how to do a column. I'll take you on, freelance sort of. You give me one article a week as well as covering anything of any interest that happens, and I'll pay you minimum for the usual and per article for the special stuff. Can't do better than that, not with the circulation I got. You interested?"

"I'd be happy with that. Leaves me time for myself and gets you better coverage than you got now. I've seen the stuff you've
  been getting from whoever you've got, and I'm better."

"Anybody with half a brain and more than grade six English is better. But nobody like that wants to work for what I pay. And that makes me wonder why you do."

"It's filler for me. I don't need to work if I don't want to. But I like writing and I'm nosy. You already know I'll be moving on when I get restless. And you probably know I've got a brother who's not good at the social stuff. I'd be disappointed if you didn't."

The old man grinned. "You best get off your ass then and get me something. I'm putting the weekly together now, so you got a day or so. Bring your copy in before I close tomorrow, I mean normal closing, like five or so, not when I decide to leave."

"You want coffee or not?" Vic asked.

"Not," The old man said. "I only drink that crap in the morning early. You should have known that." He smiled at his new reporter, pointed at the door, and said, "Don't slam it."

Vic left, closing the door gently. The old man would do, he thought. He's the one, though, who'll give me trouble. He's too damn good, reads people well. He knows already I'm up to something, he just doesn't know what. And mostly he doesn't care. But I gotta be careful with him. He'll make connections I don't want made. Better to be on his inside than his out. I'll make him just as fast as he makes me, probably even faster.

He smiled to himself as he began looking for his brother and continued thinking. I'll have to decide where and when. It most certainly won't be around here, too small, too insular, but it'll be a great place to stick it to the locals, see how long it takes them, watch them bumble around with the case while I report it. Be almost as good as Harbour City. More of a challenge really, what with the old man to hoodwink, he makes it worth doing.

Vic met Able on the main street near the restaurant. He learned that his brother had spent most of his time walking and drinking coffee and hadn't tried very hard to find work. Vic knew it would take him a few days and wasn't about to push. It was just before five and the restaurant was crowded with teenagers from the local high school. A few workers, the ones who were either single with no inclination to fend for themselves or childless couples just off work, pretty much filled the front booths where the windows gave them a view of the street.

Vic and Able sat at their usual place. They could watch the rest of the restaurant easily from there. They looked always for the same thing: attractive young females who had something about them, something alluring. They looked for body language, the way they moved, their eyes. It was something the women couldn't help, something built into them, something that coloured the air around them and needed to be released. They'd find her.

The young ones left in dribbles as the two of them ate, and the restaurant became quieter as if something had leaked out. The ones remaining weren't interesting, so the brothers finished up and left. The town too had quieted as the dusk deepened, but for the brothers, pleasure grew. Dark was their time, and they reveled in it.

By seven that evening, they were cruising in their van, wandering the roads out of town, heading down toward the coast, toward the environs of Powell River, a few hundred kilometers away, and the coastal artery south. There they would find more opportunities in a richer hunting ground. They were hungry, but not yet obsessed as they had been when they left Harbour City. The pleasure of the hunt was what fed them now, and it would continue to do so until they found one of the special ones. Then everything would change.

4.

Jasmine stood in the doorway and considered the room. She let her backpack slide to the floor. The room was small and drab as most of them had been: light brown walls, dark brown carpet, brown chair, a desk with another chair, this one a kind of dining chair with a seat covered in dark brown fabric to match the carpet. The bed was a double with a bed spread in bright stripes of blue, green and red. At least the stripes appeared bright compared to the rest of the room. Jasmine turned on the bedside lamp, hauled her bag to the light brown bathroom, got out her kit, stripped, and climbed into the shower.

She felt better now. The shower made her feel clean even though it solved nothing. She stood in front of the sink and stared at herself in the mirror. She looked far better than she felt; she felt hollow, betrayed, abandoned, and the tears started again. She brushed them away, angry at herself because of them, turned from the mirror, and dressed again in her jeans and a fresh blouse. She lay on the bed thinking about Jason and Prince Rupert.

I won't let him, she thought, I won't let him ruin everything. He isn't worth it, not now, not ever. I can do this. I can just forget the Queen Charlottes and move south again, take the ferry to the mainland, and travel down the coast, maybe stop in one of the villages after the ferry across the Jervis Inlet. I can have a good time; I don't need him.

She got up, blew her nose, checked herself once again in the mirror, then left the room. She looked around the complex. There was a restaurant across from the front desk on the other end of the U-shaped line of rooms. There were a few people in the booths near the front windows. Jasmine shook her head. She didn't feel hungry, but she hadn't eaten since the chicken with Jason, and that had been mostly his.

It was dark enough now for the lights to show, for the restaurant and the motel sign to light up the edge of the highway and the front landscaping, leaving the huge conifers out on the edge dark against the night sky. She would eat, she thought, even though she didn't feel like it, then maybe read herself to sleep in a real bed for a change.

Morning sun slanting through the window of her room crept slowly up the spread, touching her hair and the side of her face. She woke slowly, felt across the bed for Jason, snapped wide awake, cursed, and rolled out of bed. In less than an hour, she'd packed, showered, had a light breakfast of toast and jam and coffee, and had begun her day walking south out of town toward Courtenay, a long way down the road.

It was a glorious day, bright sun, not a cloud in sight, and warmer than it had been. Jasmine took her time leaving the ribbon development along the outskirts of Port Hardy, stopping often just to sit and think about the days ahead.

She wasn't as comfortable travelling by herself, but she'd done it before. This was just a longer version, she thought. Besides, once she got across to Powell River, she was in tourist country all the way down to Vancouver, so rides should be easy. The way down to Courtenay, however, might be a little different. All they'd seen coming up were pickups, big ones, and pickups made her feel a bit uncomfortable, especially ones driven by guys with baseball caps turned backwards. She'd stay away from those if she could.

I'll look for real cars, she thought, and ones with more than a single guy in them. She cleared the city and its environs in about an hour, and she began to look for likely candidates, using her thumb when the traffic was right. By late afternoon, after a few rides in sedans, she'd reached Campbell River, found a cheap restaurant, had a small meal, and was now walking the shoulder on the newish four-lane bypass highway. She had just seen the sign that said hitchhiking was prohibited when a large, black SUV pulled onto the shoulder ahead of her and stopped. Jasmine grabbed the straps of her backpack and ran towards it.

The front door opened as she reached the rear, and the driver stepped out, the yellow stripe on his pants and the jacket and hat telling her that she'd flagged down the cops.

He was a nice enough young guy, but he made it clear that she couldn't hitchhike on this highway, and that he wouldn't advise it on any road. He asked where she was headed, where she'd come from, and Jasmine, a little relieved and feeling a bit guilty, poured out her whole story.

In the end, she got another warning about the dangers of hitchhiking and a ride into Courtenay. On the way down the highway, the constable whose name tag said R. Higgins, talked to Jasmine about the problems the force faced trying to educate young people, especially women, about what could happen to them. He told her about the highway of tears and the aboriginal deaths they had yet to solve: sixteen young women missing. He frightened her more than she would have liked, given that she had yet to get to Vancouver and a plane home.

Jasmine thanked him and said she'd likely stay overnight in town and maybe follow his advice and rent a car. Once off the main four-lane highway and down the long cloverleaf to the two-lane that led to town, she watched the forest slide by, the occasional dent in it made by a farm or dirt road, once by a working gravel pit. In town, as the SUV made the turn into the police lot, she watched the station grow in bulk. It was a one-storey block building in mostly white with a lot of windows on the second storey and large glass doors on the first. The flat roof bristled with antennae. She thanked the constable, listened to his instructions to the nearest rental lot, then walked down the sidewalk toward downtown Courtenay. She found the local Howard Johnston and picked up a schedule for the Powell River Ferry from the front desk.

The rooms there were too expensive, so she didn't register, but at the front desk, she learned there wasn't a ferry to the mainland until the next day. The desk clerk drew her a map to the local hostel on the other side of the downtown bridge across the Puntledge river and wished her luck.

Jasmine walked all the way downtown to the bridge, spotted a coffee shop on the corner, and had a latte and a

Danish. She sat at a window seat and watched the street as she ate her Danish and sipped her coffee.

She was tired even though it had been an easy day for her. She watched the traffic cross the bridge. It was steady, so she thought she wouldn't have a problem hitching a ride the next morning. After she finished her coffee, she got up reluctantly, stretched, left the coffee shop, and crossed over the bridge on the metal pedestrian walkway. She looked upriver and saw a dyke holding back the water. She walked along the length of it and through the park. She found the hostel a block farther on, a small two-storey cement block building servicing hikers and other travelers either on their way up island or like her, or on their way across to the mainland. After dumping her things in a private room, she left again for the park and the river.

The dyke path curved gently toward the bridge, following the curve of the river. She read a couple of the plaques along the way. One was about the damn she found, a small thing that held back a few feet of water, like a small step. The second one told her that the river was noted for the salmon run and the spawning grounds. She learned too that much of the river basin was ceded to Indian bands. Small reservations ran up its length on the side away from the main part of town.

Jasmine found a bench facing the river and sat for a long time. She didn't think about Jason. She thought about the Sunshine Coast across the Salish Sea and the ferry to Powell River, wondering what the town was like and how different the coastal area might be. The setting sun threw final flashes of light off the river, bothering her eyes, so she left the bench and returned to the hostel. She asked the young guy on the desk how to get to the ferry, got another hand-drawn map, and decided to retire early.

Her room was on the second floor of the hostel. It had one window with a harbour view. She looked out at a shallow, weed-filled estuary, with sand banks surfacing here and there. Farther out, the water deepened, changed colour, and spread out like a lake. She could just make out the harbour mouth and what she assumed was the Salish Sea. The water was still as a mirror, not a ripple across its wide expanse. A little bevy of red-wing blackbirds perched on the stalks of the reeds, their calls audible in her room. Slowly, the light began to fade. Jasmine sighed a little as if she regretted the day's passing. She turned toward the bed and sat, breathing slowly, her mind floating into nothingness. She sat until the room was dark, then she turned on her bedside lamp, unbuckled her backpack, opened her maps, and planned the next day.

Morning brought rain squalls and heavy wind. Jasmine watched the harbour: grey, dismal-looking water, white caps driven by wind expiring on the sand bars, the gusts bending the grasses and reeds as if they were nodding to her. There were no red-wing blackbirds. She shivered as she watched, rubbed her bare arms, and turned from the window to pack. She'd leave for the ferry around noon so maybe, she thought, the squalls would pass, and the day would brighten a little. She took the stairs down, asked the clerk, and learned about a McDonald's two blocks away.

By noon, the skies had cleared, streaks of high white cloud sliding across a sea of blue. Jasmine stood on the highway just up from the hostel, hoping for a ride to the ferry terminal far up the two-lane that rose up a steep hill toward Comox. She spent the empty minutes looking at the ribbon development that scarred the sides of the highway. There was no beauty here, only ugly shapes and garish colours. She got a lift from a man heading to the airport. He dropped her a few kilometers from the ferry dock, where the road to it branched off from the highway. This road was a narrow two-lane blacktop heading off at an angle toward the water. Jasmine walked slowly so that she could enjoy watching herds of cows in pastures near well-kept farmhouses and barns.

She'd just stooped to put down her backpack when a car slowed and then stopped up the road a bit. Jasmine waved, walked up as fast as she could and found an old man and woman in the front seat. The front window came down and the woman asked if she were taking the ferry to Powell River. Jasmine smiled and nodded, got in the backseat, and the car moved off slowly.

The woman was old, maybe in her seventies, Jasmine thought, but bright eyed and beautifully put together. She made Jasmine feel downright dowdy. "I'm Elisa, and he's Henry. And you are?"

I'm Jasmine, Jasmine Holmes. Thank you for stopping." Jasmine smiled, thinking how much she looked like an Elisa, all poise and confidence.

"Henry and I are going to Powell River for our daughter's wedding. You're welcome to stay with us for the crossing. It's a rather long one: an hour and twenty or so." Elisa looked at Jasmine over the seat. "You know, I've packed a lunch for the two of us, a large lunch, more than we need, so we'll share it with you. There's nothing on the ferry worth eating even though the thing is quite large and should have something. We'd like your company, so please say yes." Jasmine nodded and smiled.

The crossing was much longer than Jasmine had thought. She spent an interesting time with the couple, well, mostly with Elisa. Henry was a quiet, grey-haired man, also in his seventies, in a dark blue suit, white shirt with what Jasmine thought was probably an old-school tie. He smiled a lot, seemed interested in the conversation, but said little. Jasmine liked Eliza a lot and ran off at the mouth more than she usually did. They'd been discussing families what with the couple's daughter getting married.

"My parents were rather distant," Jasmine answered when asked about them, "but they always said they'd come to my wedding wherever it was. I lost them five years ago in a plane crash. My father was a pilot, and they went down in his Beaver in a lake in northern Ontario."

"Oh my god, I'm so sorry," Elisa said. "And here we are so happy about our daughter's wedding."

"It's alright, really. I was much younger and away at boarding school. They were both buried in Toronto, where mom had some family still left. It would have been harder had we been close, but I was always away, you see, always at school or at camp. My dad was a professor of Mathematics at U of T, where I go now, and my mom was often away on digs. She was an Archeologist. And most of her digs were in Israel and the Middle East. I was raised by a nanny on those occasions when I was home. I still miss them, but the house was sold and the money put in trust for my education. That's what my parents really cared about, that I got a good education, so that's mostly what I did and that meant that I was away most of the time. I guess I kept going for them as much as for myself."

Elisa asked about siblings, but just as Jasmine was about to answer, the ship's whistle sounded, and everybody began moving toward the exits. The question never got answered verbally, but Jasmine shook her head as she walked along, and Elisa nodded in acknowledgment.

The docking was uneventful. Jasmine waved at the couple as they drove off, and then turned toward the town, walking with the others up the grade to the main street. At least she thought it was the main one, but there was little to suggest any kind of downtown, just an ugly hotel, a couple of small restaurants, and houses spread out along the road. The town was a disappointment, really, and she decided to push on and not spend the night as she had intended.

As she walked through the straggle of houses lining the highway to Jervis Inlet and the ferry to Sechelt, she thought about her parents, then about Jason a little, then about nothing at all. She drifted along for a while before she began looking for a ride. The problem was that all the cars going south for the Jervis Inlet ferry had left the ferry she'd been on in a bunch, and they were long gone. There didn't seem to be much traffic. The few cars she did see either turned off on one of the side roads before they got to her or they simply ignored her and drove on.

Jasmine sighed, dropped her backpack on the shoulder, sat on it, and stared into space. She couldn't get her parents out of her head now, well, not so much they themselves, but the house, the neighbourhood, the street they lived on, and the good times during the rare times they all got together at the holidays. She sat for a while remembering, then sighed again, hoisted the backpack over her shoulder, and walked on.

She walked for over an hour. The road wasn't much to look at. It had a lot of curves, so she mostly couldn't see very far, and when she could, the road often disappeared into hollows. She could hear the water sometimes, but she couldn't see it. It bothered her that she couldn't see the sea because she'd had this vision in her head of little villages with tea houses and antique stores strung out along the coast close to the water. But this road ran through trees so that the Salish Sea was invisible.

She didn't think there'd be much at the ferry terminal, not if her map was any indication.

She heard the van before she saw it. She'd been walking down into one of the depressions the road followed. She turned quickly, stuck out her thumb, and watched the grey Ford pass, then slow and pull to the side. She jogged that way, her backpack slapping against her back. She saw the shoulder side door swing open, and she smiled. She'd make it across for sure.

5.

Alan Kim and Spence Riley belonged to the homicide division of the RCMP stationed in Harbour City. Alan had worked with Spence for more than three years and admired her, even if she was a bit feisty and always impatient. He more than admired her. He admitted to himself that he'd fallen for her rather hard. She on the other hand didn't suspect a thing, at least he didn't think They'd been ordered to Vancouver to work with the city police. There were some girls missing from Vancouver's East end and the she did.

Spence knew Alan had a thing for her, but she never said a word, at least not to him. She kept the relationship going in her own fashion and never let it interfere with work. For that matter, neither did Alan. He'd been divorced for a few years now, but still lived in the ratty condo down near the channel between the twin harbours. He'd meant to sell the place but didn't quite know how to do that without moving in with Spence. Since she hadn't suggested such a move, he held on to the condo, torn between waiting for something to happen with Spence and the need to get rid of the place and the last of the memories.

Their current case chasing a psycho killer had been troublesome. They'd almost had the guy and his sidekick, but the two had slipped away during a combined operation involving the homicide detectives and two private investigators from SHH Investigations. Harry and Sabina were still on the case, hired by the sister of one of the victims, and so were Spence and Alan. The brass suspected that the killers might be in the city now. The two detectives weren't so sure, but orders were orders, so here they were.

Alan and Spence presented themselves for duty at the offices of the Vancouver police at Main and Cordova. They'd looked around the area beforehand, especially the Main and Hastings corner, and were aware of the way the street functioned. They were still the leads in Harbour City's case of the murdered girls. The killers had barely escaped their efforts on the big island, and now, the city police thought they might be active on Vancouver's east side. Alan and Spence had been sent to help in the search for the girls on the assumption that they might be looking at the same pair of killers.

Brian Stevens was the senior detective, and on their first day in Vancouver, they reported to him. The squad room was huge compared to Harbour City, full of office flats that formed cubbyholes. In each of those, there were two back-to-back desks, standard issue, and a couple of keyboards and computer screens. Stevens' office, among others, was at the back and had windows. They could see light through the frosted glass.

Alan and Spence made their way to the back and knocked. The grunt they got probably meant come in, so they did.

Stevens was a big guy, over six feet and about as broad as a barn door. There was no fat on him, he was just big. He wore a grey suit with a white shirt and a dark blue tie, and when he stood to shake hands, both Alan and Spence had to look up. They were told to sit, so they sat and waited. Stevens studied them both.

"I think you guys got a bit of a raw deal on this one. You should have been left on the island to try again. As far as I'm concerned, you did a good job over there in a small-town department. If you hadn't lost the bugger, you'd still be hunting there, and I'd not have girls missing here. At least that's the thinking up top. I've got the case files here. Our IT guy's been keeping me up to date. We had our own screw-up with the pig farmer back in the day, so you'll get some sympathy for your case. What were you told about your assignment here?"

Alan picked that one up. "Our boss, Josie Atardo, told us we messed up using the two privates on our case, even if they were legitimately on the same cases. She's royally pissed that we missed the guy. Actually, we think there are two of them. She just sent us, said there were problems with girls here. Might be the same guys. And if the cases tied together, we should be here. She said we'd get our assignments when we got here. She also said that it was the brass thought there was a tie with your missing girls."

"How about you?" Brian pointed at Spence.

"I guess you could say we messed up our try, but we damn near got those two. And it was our op, so here we are. She told us to see Chief of Detective Stevens."

"About what I figured," Stevens said. "I need help with this. You're going with a couple of my guys. I think, given your experience with the cases over there, you can help us here. Maybe it's the same guys, maybe not. Either way, we've got you and we can use you."

He paused, looked down for a moment, then looked at each of them in turn.

"We got a problem with the hookers, both kinds. The strip's usually quiet, and we don't have many problems since patrol looks after them. But recently, we've had some not-so-nice incidents, beatings, some robberies, and what looks like abductions. Too many missing girls. It stirs up memories.

These girls, some have pimps, but most are independents and have no weight behind them, no protection. We're not sure what's happening, where they've gone, but we're treating them as abductions. We think maybe it's your guys operating on the strip over here. I'm gonna pair you two with Jake Kenney and Larry Sharp. They'll fill you in."

The phone rang. Stevens answered, grunted, and said "Do it." Then he turned to them again, anger flaring in his eyes.

"Everybody's real sensitive about missing girls since that prick, Robert Pickton. He raped and tortured the ones he took, then he fed them to his pigs. We took far too long getting to him, and we've paid for it. But not this time! We've either got a copycat like the psychos you guys chased over there, the ones who gutted the girls and left them in the bush, or else they're here now takin' our girls. I sure as hell hope it's something else. It took a lot of fuckin' around to arrange this op, what with two forces involved. You two and Jake and Larry'll be a kind of mini task force. You talk to Jake, he'll report to me. If it turns out it's your guys, then you're leads. Check with them for the files. They're on their way in for shift at four."

Alan and Spence left the station house and found a diner up Main that looked okay and wasn't crowded, maybe not such a good sign. They found a table, and Spence opened the Sun's section on rental accommodation again. Alan held up a cup to the waitress and she brought coffee.

"I've narrowed it down to two places that look big enough for the two of us, both two bedrooms. One's on Broadway, the other's out a bit on Nanaimo. That one's cheaper. We got time to check them out before we have to be back."

"The way you drive, maybe the closer one's better."

"I like the Nanaimo one, it's two hundred less and I drive fine. You just don't appreciate sports cars. Anyway, let's order and get on with it."

Alan signaled the waitress again and she came over. She was a bottle blonde twenty-something and pretty much ignored Spence. She wore one of those ubiquitous pink uniforms, and it was tight. Spence thought she and it belonged at a corner on the stroll. The skirt was short, the top low enough to be interesting. The way she wore it, the buttons that mattered would never reach the buttonholes designed for them. And she tended to lean over tables. When she did that, it pissed Spence off as Alan knew it would, and that wasn't good.

He smiled at the girl, held a finger up for Spence, and ordered a steak sandwich with salad. Spence went for a bigger salad and more coffee. But she wasn't smiling.

"You really need to look at that? Jesus, Alan, pay attention. We're gonna look at the Nanaimo one first, right? The other one's closer, but the street's mostly commercial and it'll be noisy, and the rent's a lot more. There isn't a lot of other stuff you'd want to touch. Some of those places are pretty scruffy."

"I guess what we're gonna do is what you want since you're driving. But I still think closer's better. We don't wanna drive to work every day, do we? I mean this isn't

Harbour City and the traffic's horrendous, especially in rush hour which seems to take most of the day here."

Spence was just about to start when the lunch arrived. She got hers first without much of a smile from the girl, but Alan got a close look at her superstructure and a smile full of teeth and the tip of a pink tongue. He appreciated both. Spence just grunted.

They argued over lunch about apartments and streets, but in the end, Spence had her way. The Camaro was red, flashy, and illegally parked on the street. But when they picked it up after lunch, there was no ticket. Spence grinned. "Day's looking up already."

She took off down Main, exhaust growling, made the light, and swung a right around the police station onto Cordova. She cruised slowly down the stroll to Campbell, stopped at the stop sign, eyed a thin girl standing there and got a little hand wiggle in return that made her snort in disgust. Then she drifted down the hill to the tracks, took her time going over them, and paused at that corner. They both watched a tall, black-booted, dark-haired girl wiggle her way up from under the overpass on Hastings, her heels making her hip sway more voluptuous, her short, tight skirt keeping her progress slow. She was very tall, mostly leg. Spence grunted, then took off. She took the corner down to Powell and turned right at the Chevron station. She had a clear run up the wide street and took full advantage. At Nanaimo, she turned right again and cruised along looking at addresses.

Alan had been quiet ever since the girl in the black high-heeled boots. Now he said, "You better get used to it, the stroll I mean, and the girls. There won't be any room for attitude on this one. What we got is maybe like what we had in Harbour City. Maybe our guys, maybe different guys. Everybody's taking this one very seriously, so you better can the judgments."

Spence ignored the lecture and asked, "That last one real?" she asked as she cruised. "Hard to tell, just the size is all."

"She's a tranny. Girls seldom go down that far. They stay up at Campbell. That seems to be the bottom end for them. From there down, it's CDs."

"There it is! Hang on!"

Spence slammed the Camaro into the curb, wedging it between a pickup and a panel van. She grinned at Alan who was still holding onto the dash and climbed out.

The building was a four-storey with two apartments on each floor. All of them had bay windows on the front façade. It was an older building, but it had been kept up. The paint looked good, the tiny front yard was neat with flower beds running up to the front door. The door itself had a shiny brass kick plate that had never been kicked, fresh varnish, and a polished brass handle.

"This looks promising," Spence said, and grabbed the handle. The inside had a small lobby-like area with brass mailboxes, also shiny, and a button marked 'super'. She pushed it. Nothing happened, so she pushed it again. Inside the inner door was the lobby proper, and from the hall on the left, a young, dark-haired guy appeared in a green twill uniform. He opened the inner door.

"You here about the apartment?"

"You got it." Spence said.

"Okay, it's on the top floor, we got no elevator, so it's stairs. Come on, I'll take you up."

The top floor was like the ones below. A short cross hall led to the recessed doors of the apartments on either side of the building. The one on the right was the one he opened, and they saw a kind of shotgun arrangement. A long hall led down one side with rooms opening off it. The living room with the bay window was first, followed by a large bedroom, then a bathroom with a claw foot tub, then another bedroom. At the back, the hall ended in a large dining room with an ample kitchen off to the side through a doorway. The kitchen had another door that led to an old-fashioned porch at the back of the building. The porch overlooked the asphalted parking spaces, one for each apartment, and a small garden tucked in on the side. A back alley fed the parking lot.

"Rent's a thousand a month, first and a damage deposit up front. It's been painted, and the carpets are new. I cleaned it myself, so it's good to go."

On the front of his twill uniform over the left pocket was a little sewn-on patch with the name Roy on it. Spence smiled at him. "Okay if we spend a few minutes looking around, Roy?"

"Have at it. I'll wait here."

Alan and Spence looked through the rooms. Everything was clean and fresh. The place smelled good. The bathroom was old fashioned like the rest of the place, but it was serviceable and large enough for the two of them. The baseboards and door and window frames were all old style, wide natural wood. Nothing stingy about any of it.

Spence grinned at Alan. "I think we got it in one. You good with this one?"

Alan grinned back. "I like it. It feels good. We're gonna need some stuff. Let's see what kind of lease we have to sign. If it's no more than a year, super, even better if we can go monthly."

Roy was waiting and he took them downstairs to the tiny office off the foyer. "We got a lot of interest in this one, but nobody's signed yet. If you're willing and can put down the deposits, it's yours, providing the credit check's okay, of course."

"I can write you a cheque now or bring you the cash tomorrow."

"Cheque's fine. You need to fill out this application and sign a lease for a year. You two together?"

Alan answered. "Yes, we're together. We're both cops, detectives, RCMP. This would suit us. I'll write that check. How much is the damage deposit?"

"Half a month, so that's fifteen hundred in total." Alan scribbled out the cheque while Roy watched. Alan handed it over.

Roy grinned at them. "I better watch myself then, eh? You bein' cops an all. You got a cell number I can reach you at? I'll fire this off to the agency and get back to you this afternoon."

Alan wrote out both their numbers on the back of a business card. "Either one will do."

Roy clipped it to the application and showed them out.

"We still have over an hour. You want to grab a coffee? We might not get another chance for a while. I saw a Starbucks back on the stroll where Cordova curls into Powell."

Spence glanced at him as she opened the car door, "Okay. You like the place?"

"I like it. It's just a lot of money up front. But yeah, I like it. I even like Roy."

Spence peeled out, drove up Nanaimo to Hastings, turned right and worked her way back to Campbell. There she turned right again and then left on Cordova where she took the curve too fast as usual and gunned the Camaro back up toward town. She looked over at Alan who was still holding the crash bar just in case.

"Thought I'd cruise the strip a few times, see what we can see."

Alan nodded, "Good idea, take it slow though."

She turned the Camaro at Main, then took Cordova back down, keeping to the south-side lane.

"You ever wonder why all the action's on this side? I haven't seen anyone on the north side."

"It's sort of industrial on that side, maybe that's it. Or maybe the girls like to be close to Hastings for some reason. The johns seem to go that way too, down here, over to Hastings, up to somewhere around Main, and back down. So that's gotta be part of it."

"Jeez, look at that one!" Spence indicated a girl on the street near Heatley. She was wearing a bright pink very short frilly skirt, a top with a vest, both pink with sparkles, and high-heeled pink pumps. On her head was a little pink cap, and she was wearing pink nylon thigh-highs that left a slice of thigh visible. Every step she took revealed a flash of pink panties. And she was tall, maybe five ten or so. A girl certainly, but a tall one with great legs.

Spence drove by slowly. The hooker looked over and realized a girl was driving. She smiled and stepped to the curb. Spence grunted and kept going. Alan grinned and shook his head.

The Starbucks was tucked into the little wedge where Cordova curved down into Powell. The lot was tiny. Spence slid the Camaro into one of the five slots beside a Harley and parked.

The place was equally small with six or seven tiny tables, two outside on the narrow walkway. The biker sat next to the front window, a chubby guy with the requisite beard and leathers. At the other tables were an assortment of people, two with laptops, two with papers, and at the rear table, a pair of working girls in shorts and tight tops holding unlit cigarettes and drinking coffee.

Spence and Alan ordered coffee and Spence bought a bun of some sort and a breakfast sandwich of egg, spinach, and cheese for Alan. They sat midway between the hookers and the biker and relaxed.

"So far, it's been an okay day. We got a nice place and a decent lay at the station. We meet those two detectives in less than an hour."

She was about to go on when her cell rang. She answered, listened, said thank you, and smiled at Alan. "We just got approved. The apartment's ours." She looked at the time. "We gotta roll."

They grabbed what remained of their coffee and eats, and Spence took the Camaro out to the street and up to the station. They tried to find a parking spot close by and ended up two blocks away on a side street. They finished eating and sat drinking the last of the coffee. Out of the car, they started up the street. At the corner in front of them, a large Anglican church rose into solidly into the sky. It was massive, more like a citadel than a church. And it was white, all of it. It dwarfed the fire hall that had been converted into a theater on the other side of the street.

They crossed Cordova and turned toward Main. Spence read the neon as they walked past the huge fire doors. "You know that play? That Godot thing? I heard all the two guys in it do is stand around and bitch."

"It's minimalist, yeah, but it's powerful. It's a lot more than bitching. We should go. I saw it in London's West End, and I'd really like to see it again. You game?"

"If you pay and supply dinner and drinks after, I'll keep you company, but if I think it's crap, we leave and eat. You agree?"

"To the dinner and drinks. But you gotta see it through, like it or not."

"Better be a fuckin' great dinner then." She grinned at Alan and picked up her pace. Spence could move when she wanted to. They walked back to the station and went up to the detective floor.

The place was full, men coming and going, some in suits; some dressed casually; some looking like bums. Those were unshaven, had long greasy hair, and they were dirty. They didn't smell too good either. Shift change was on full blast.

Alan and Spence walked back to Brian Stevens' office where they met the two detectives they'd been assigned to.

"I'm Kenney and this is Sharp." The one who spoke was tall and thin. His charcoal grey suit covered a crisp white shirt on a chest that seemed almost concave. The tie was blue silk. His partner was shorter and broader, dressed in a black suit that looked as if he'd slept in it. "You guys are the two from Harbour City, right?" Larry Sharp looked them over, especially Spence.

"Alan Kim, and this is Spence Riley. We've been assigned to you guys."

"We heard. You wanna come with us, we'll fill you in. You guys had a bit of a mess over there on the island, right?"

Larry Sharp took the lead, and they followed him over to a cubicle on the other side of the room. It was just big enough for the four of them. He didn't seem to want an answer to his last question, so Alan didn't give him one. Spence stayed quiet. Alan couldn't read her; he waited to see what kind of reaction she'd have. The cubicle was a mess, files covered the desks, the walls were papered with sheets of stuff stuck on with push pins, even the two spare chairs were covered. Jake cleared them off and they all sat.

"We've been over your case," Sharp said, "and to tell you the truth, we'd have done the same thing. You set up a good operation over there, and you damn near got those pricks. What those fuckers were doing was as bad as that Pickton prick we had. You'd have been set if it'd worked, but it didn't, so here you are on our turf helpin' with our mispers. On the assumption, of course, that your guys are now our guys."

The tall, cadaverous Jake Kenney picked it up. "What he means is welcome aboard. We're real happy you're here. We can use the help."

"Yeah, I meant that. So let's get you settled in and get on with it."

Larry Sharp was as abrupt as he was a walking disaster with clothes. The two of them were like fat and skinny with the clothes thrown in for emphasis. Alan and Spence smiled to themselves as they watched. The differences, they knew, were surface. These two worked well together.

The rest of the afternoon and early evening was spent on the files of the cases in Harbour City. They covered all the reports including the profiler's on the killers and the professor's on myth, rituals, and cults. Then they talked it through.

"The guy's a psychopath," Spence said. "He took girls from the stroll, only from there, and not just any girls. They had to have something special, some special quality. We wouldn't have known that without the two privates and their associates. It seems all these girls radiated something sensual, some aura like a strong perfume, you know, something that caught at every guy they met. And our perp had a helper, someone under his control. We're sure there were two from the last attempt when they tried to take two girls at once. They got them with a Taser strong enough to take them down, then tried to load them into an old pickup. When we rushed in to block them, they took off, plowed through a fence and some bushes, but they dropped the girls. We sent cruisers around to the street they broke out on, but they were gone. The two girls were out, the Taser'd dropped them where they stood. We learned later the pickup had taken train tracks out of town, so all our efforts to block streets got us nothing."

Alan continued. "The disposal sites were a problem. The area was huge; we ran a geographic profile to try to cut it down. All we learned was that the body sites, all of them way out in the bush, were related to where the perps probably lived. We scoured that area and eventually found their place way back in the foothills, but it took us days. In fact, it was the privates and their friends who did that job. We didn't have the manpower. They used topographical maps and a couple of guys from the forest companies that farmed the land to isolate probable sites, and it was in one of these areas that they found the place.

"The perps had a cabin for themselves, with a root cellar, that's important, the root cellar. They had another cellar they'd dug behind the cabin back in the bush, and as far as we can figure out, they kept all the girls they took sedated in that one. We know that from the one who escaped and from finally finding the damn thing, but these guys were careful, always careful, and we found it only after they'd blown it."

Spence added more. "We looked at the rituals a lot, finally. At first, we were just stunned at the savagery, the disemboweling, and couldn't understand what purpose it had. What else we couldn't understand was that there seemed to be no sexual molestation. If there wasn't any sexual motive, why take them? Especially them, you know?

The profiler suggested that there was a sexual motive, we just couldn't see it. I think it was the professor who nailed it down. He thought these guys were choosing these particular girls to save them somehow, maybe steal their power, by pushing them over into the next world, you know, by killing them all in exactly the same way, following rituals that made sense to them. We still don't understand what significance the rituals had for them, but we think we know now why they did what they did.

"The root cellar thing, though, that took some time to sort of understand. Here's what the profiler thought. These guys were brought up in a very strict environment, probably punished in a dark underground place like that, and somehow, it became part of who they are. She thought maybe the sexual part had to do with the two of them, and the girls were a necessary ingredient somehow. That part is guesswork, but everything else she said seemed to be right, so we figured we'd go with that until we caught them. Then, maybe, they'd clear up the questions."

When they finally finished with the files, it was almost midnight, and Jake and Larry showed them where to put the Camaro under the building. Both men walked back to the car with them and admired the ride. They coaxed Spence into taking them for a short spin before parking it underground. She followed Jake's instructions and had taken them around town a bit and down the stroll a few times. Jake was in the front with her, being tall and lanky, with Alan and Larry jammed in the cramped back seats.

Once underground and parked, Jake leaned over and said, "You're the driver on this operation any time we're together. You sure know how to handle this thing, and you're a whiz in traffic. Didn't know they grew them like you over there."

"Okay, enough with the damn chit chat," Larry chimed in from the back.

"Gimme a hand out of this thing. Jesus, it's so damned tight in here we're stuck together."

Jake did the honours, and the four of them walked over to the carpool and signed out an unmarked. It was the usual nondescript grey dodge that anybody who'd been on the street for more than a day would peg as a cop car.

"Yeah, I know," Larry said without anyone asking. "The fuckin' thing sticks out like a sore thumb, but it's what we get. At least it runs. Things get dicey, we take our own rides."

Jake added, "We're gonna cruise a bit, pick up a brew at Starbucks, fill you in some, then drop you on the stroll, let you walk it a bit, pick up some flavor that way. You need to cover Cordova and Hastings from Gore or Dunlevy down to Glen. That's the johns' circuit and the girls work both streets and all the crosses. So you get the crosses too, only the one block though. The other side of Hastings has some action on Pender, but not enough to worry about. We'll wait for you at the bottom around at the Chevron station. We'll show you where."

They took the unmarked out and cruised the east side. The two city detectives showed Alan and Spence the secluded spots the girls took the johns. They drove all the alleys south of Hastings, then the cross streets in the light industrial area south of Powell and north of Hastings, and finally they cruised Chinatown.

Larry added commentary as they went, so Alan and Spence knew a lot before they were dumped on the corner of Main and Pender in the heart of Chinatown.

The two of them stood on the street for a few minutes watching the action. What they mostly saw were druggies, alcoholics, and a horde of street people. The majority were gathered a block down at Main and Hastings at an outreach building, an old converted bank, where they were probably fed at specific times and maybe received some help with their addictions. That place and another mission run by a local church group were only a block either way from headquarters. On the corner where they stood there was some commercial activity, but they saw nothing to suggest it was hooker infested.

They walked east on Pender leaving Chinatown a block or so later and passed through a seedy residential area, houses on one side, a park on the other. They passed a couple of girls who were obviously working; both smiled at them. They turned north on Heatley, crossed Hastings, watched the girls on the north side of the intersection for a few minutes, then wandered down to Cordova.

In that short block, they passed five girls, two of them in short skirts and tight tops wearing high-heeled pumps. The clothes were not only sexy the way they wore them, but also seemed to be good quality. Both stood quietly on the edge of the sidewalk watching the cars. They made no move to attract anybody and didn't have to. The johns in the cars noticed and slowed. A few pulled in to talk.

The other girls, some obviously high on something were either crouched in doorways or sitting on the curb waving at passing johns without much interest. The upright ones walked the street slowly. The cars kept circling. The two who were reasonably attractive and better dressed were picked up before Alan and Spence turned the corner onto Cordova.

The corners were the most active spots. Girls stood at the cross streets or walked from one to the other on Cordova to show off their outfits and pick up trade. There was a lot of attractive leg on display and a lot of cleavage. What surprised Alan and Spence was the lack of anything on the north side: no hookers, no slow cars, nothing. And it was a one-way street, so both sides were equally available. It made little sense to them.

Spence was ignored as they walked, but Alan got some attention despite being with a woman. He spent some time declining offers. One or two were persistent until Spence took his arm and told them to fuck off. She didn't make any friends until they passed Campbell and went downhill into the tranny section. There, she got some attention from a couple of the girls, especially from one in tight, red short shorts, high-heeled black knee-highs, a lacy black top, and along dark wig. She was exquisite. Her makeup, her walk, her very presence was all female. Alan knew she wasn't, but she was so good he responded anyway. Spence also seemed intrigued with her and spent some time chatting until the girl caressed her cheek. That seemed to jolt Spence, and she backed off.

They walked down to Powell, saw the unmarked parked there, turned back and walked up to Campbell where they turned toward Hastings. They covered the stroll twice, walking every cross street and both main drags. Their second time down the hill past Campbell, short shorts waved to Spence and blew her a kiss. Spence tried to ignore her and scuttled around the corner looking for the unmarked. Alan grinned at the girl, and he too got a response, but a much more lascivious one with hips and legs.

Back in the unmarked, they both heaved a tired sigh, and Jake inched the car into traffic and took off up Powell. Neither detective asked how things had gone. They just waited.

"Those girls must get bloody sore feet walking around in heels all night. I got flats and my feet hurt. You gotta have some respect for that kind of tenacity." Spence leaned over the front seat addressing her remarks to the two Vancouver detectives.

Larry turned his head and answered her. "We check on them nightly, first to see if they're still around and second to check the traffic. Patrol watches them as well and a lot more thoroughly than we do. You gotta be hard to spend your nights on the street, johns or no, and some of those bastards have kinky tastes. Most of the girls are on something, and the pimps and dealers sometimes beat them. We like to know about that. Sometimes they get beat up by the johns too, and we like to know when that happens. But they won't talk to us, so we get most of our stuff from a few informers we pay big bucks to. The patrols are just so they know we're there and they can get help when they need it."

Larry squirmed around until he faced the two in the rear of the unmarked. Spence sat back. "Our big problem right now is the missing ones. The girls talk to us only when they know they're at risk. The johns and dealers are just part of doing business, and they accept the occasional beating as part of the life."

Jake kept his eyes on the road as they cruised. He added, "We know of three who've disappeared. We wouldn't normally be worried about that. The girls do move around, and some leave for a bit then come back. But what we hear is these three were regulars, depended on the street, and never missed a night. That concerns us. Either they got beaten so badly they're holed up somewhere healing, or it's worse. But if it's beatings that severe, we usually hear about it from the girls who help them, through our snitches of course. And three over a period of two or three weeks, that's not good. Beatings or not. Besides, we haven't heard."

Larry undid his seatbelt, adjusted his large frame, fastened it again, and threw an arm over the back of the seat, "We're thinking abductions now. It's been too long with nothing coming to us. And the girls, they're getting rattled. Word spreads fast down here. That fucker Pickton's still in the back of our minds and theirs too, at least the ones been around for a while. The new ones've been told the story dozens of times, and they know the street's a dangerous place. We fucked up big time with Pickton, and memories run deep. We gotta find out what's going on."

"We don't know the city," Alan said as he glanced out the window at the passing street, "and we don't know the strip. At least in our own backyard, we had a little knowledge of how things work. Here, we're blind. I can't see how we can help much."

Spence picked it up. "We had help there too, the privates got a hell of a lot more than we could from the girls. Hell, one of them, Sabina, used to live here, and she fit into the strip over there as if she belonged. Harry, the other one, he's got a history with Chinatown, and the last case they worked together had something to do with this area and with the girls. Here, we're where we were over there. We need help like that, and we don't have it by the looks of things."

"Well, we're not gonna get our asses in a sling the way you guys did. We're being watched close on this one with you two RCMP detectives involved, so any kind of set up isn't gonna fly even if we wanted it to. If you can get something useful by email or something, we're good with that. The brass here are happy enough with you two being seconded to us, but they know about the fuckup over there, so we can't rock that boat, not even a little."

Jake kept his eye on the road while he talked and threaded through the streets of Chinatown.

"It's well after one now. The stroll's pretty much shut down for the night. We'll take you back. You get some shuteye, and we'll pick it up tomorrow. Come in in the afternoon, say around two, and we can spend some time looking at what we've got again, see if we can find a way to get at the problem. It'll give you time to see what you can dig up from the privates over there. Give us time to work our contacts. That good with you?"

"We're good," Alan said. "We'll get what we can. Two's fine with us."

Jake took the unmarked down Pender, turned on Main, slipped across Hastings on an amber, and took the ramp down to the garage. Alan and Spence shook hands with the two detectives, got the Camaro, and headed home.

6.

Spence swung onto Nanaimo and found a spot near the building. "We still gotta get stuff tomorrow like a bed, two beds, somethin' to sit on, maybe a table for eating and things. We'll be sleepin' on the floor tonight."

"It won't be too bad, I brought two bedrolls in my bags, so we'll be warm and comfy. We can get breakfast out, buy the stuff we need, and get downtown in time. We need coffee and a maker first off. I gotta have coffee in the morning."

They walked into the building carrying the bags from the Camaro's trunk, and with some hesitation rang the super's bell. He came out in a set of scrubs and opened the door.

"I figured you two'd be late, so I've been watching movies. I got your keys here and your papers. You got the last spot in the back, on the right end. You can park there tonight if you want."

"We apologize for the hour. We got a late shift and had no chance to give you a call."

"It's okay, I understand about that. Don't worry, I'll find a way to make you work it off." He grinned at them and turned back to his door.

Alan and Spence went upstairs, unpacked, set up the bathroom stuff, and unrolled the bedrolls in the living room. By the time they'd finished, it was after two in the morning. They looked a little uneasily at each other.

"We'll figure it out in the morning. Gimme a few minutes, then you can have the bathroom." Spence shuffled past Alan, patted his cheek, then turned and left him there.

Morning found them curled around each other like two spoons in a drawer, the layers of the two sleeping bags between

them. Alan woke first, propped himself on one elbow, watching

Spence sleep for a little while.

He admired her as a cop, and as a woman just as much. They'd been together occasional nights back on the island. Spence had a condo in a row of ten on the edge of a quiet inlet north of the city. She could relax on the deck watching the moon on the Salish Sea out beyond the long arms of the bay. Their times together had started after they'd had viciously hard days and had gone up there to wind down with a beer and maybe an order-in pizza. They could comfort each other on that deck. Those times had started about a year after Alan was single again.

Watching her like this gave him moments of a peace he found in no other place. She was beautiful. And asleep, she was beyond even that, she could melt his soul. He carefully climbed out of his bag so as not to wake her and headed for the bathroom.

By the time he had finished his shower and shave, Spence was banging on the door. Alan knew better than to give her any grief. She wasn't the most pleasant of companions in the morning, and he'd learned early to give her space and feed her coffee as soon as possible. In that, she was like him. Coffee was essential, and without it, they both felt cranky. He got out fast.

Spence wasn't one of those women who spent a lot of time getting ready. She didn't use makeup much, and showers for her were necessary utilitarian functions, not luxurious indulgences. By the time Alan had rolled up the bedrolls and tidied the room, hanging up clothes and putting shoes where they could get them quickly, she was out looking stunning, one white towel around her torso, another wound around her head like a turban.

She smiled her 'don't bug me' smile and sorted through stuff for what she wanted to wear that day. The clothes had fared well for being stuffed in a bag for a day. Alan had on a pair of pleated pants and a jacket over a knit shirt. He watched as Spence chose a dark blue power suit: pants, white blouse, jacket.

They left quickly. Spence peeled the Camaro out of its parking spot and roared up Nanaimo. Neither one knew the neighbourhood, so the search for coffee was on.

She kept going up Nanaimo, cruising slowly past any retail strips. Both watched the street. Suddenly she cut into the curb, grabbing the one spot left on her side. A few doors down was a café called Bon's. They could smell the breakfast smells pushed out of the kitchen by the vent fan as soon as they got out: eggs, bacon, especially bacon. It was one of the numerous small, family-run greasy spoons that dotted most retail areas. But this one had a lineup, with people standing around outside, the line snaking into the interior.

Inside, the place was crowded and dark. The décor, if you could call it that, was mostly chrome and wood, old chrome and old wood. The carpet was something dark. The booths along the walls and down the center hadn't been changed since the fifties. The tiny vestibule had an old gum ball machine, and the counter carried a cash register that must have been part of the original fittings. As soon as one table emptied, it was filled. They got theirs about fifteen minutes later, time enough to see the constant flow of plates of eggs, ham, bacon, potatoes, and toast.

One of the two waitresses had coffee on the table before they'd finished seating themselves. Neither of the waitresses wore uniforms, pink or otherwise. They looked like customers in their jeans and tops. Their waitress, easily in her forties with frizzy blond hair and bright red lipstick, smiled at them, asked how their day had been so far, and proceeded to tell them how her last audition had gone. They both ordered bacon, eggs, home fries, and toast. The coffee was exceptionally good, and they finished theirs quickly.

Strangely, it wasn't the waitress who refilled their cups, but a customer who had walked over to the central coffee stand, picked up a pot, and refilled everybody's cup on their side of the restaurant. Both he and the waitresses seemed to know most of the customers, and he chatted a bit at each table. He said hello to Spence and Alan, asked if they had been there before, recommended the ham for next time, and gave them a short history of the place. It was weird and comfortable at the same time. It was a happy, frenetic place, a constantly shifting crowd of customers and plates. Both Alan and Spence could understand the appeal. This place was special. People came for the warmth as much as the food.

When they left the restaurant, the line was just as long with people chatting good-naturedly as they waited. They got into the Camaro and Spence booted it down Broadway. They watched for a retail area where they could get what they needed for the apartment. They couldn't find a department store in the area, so Spence fought her way through endless blocks of traffic, cursing most of it. They finally discovered some upscale shops in an area around Granville and Broadway. A bedding shop, a furniture store, and an electronics outlet took their orders for delivery the next morning. In a kitchen store around the corner they bought cutlery, china, pots, pans, a coffee machine, and some stuff they had never seen before. They placed it all in the Camaro and retraced their route.

Bon's was still busy, people still milling about outside talking and laughing. It wasn't a clean or a well-lighted place, like the one in Hemingway's story, but it had the same appeal. It was a place to be, a place to come back to, a substitute for home or maybe a place even better than home. Spence drove by slowly. They too would come back.

They unloaded their purchases from the car and took the stairs up three flights to the back porch and into the kitchen. Coffee and milk and some essentials went into the fridge, and somehow that made the place feel like home. They had enough for morning and lunch tomorrow while they waited for the deliveries of beds, chairs, a table, and a flat screen TV and DVD player.

Earlier that morning before Spence had gotten into the bathroom, she had called Telus for cable connections, both for the Internet and television, and Roy had let the cable guy in while they were out. After they set their purchases down in the kitchen, Spence noticed the modem router in the living room, the front indicators blinking.

She set up both their computers on top of the window seat in the bay window, typed in the code from the wireless router, and sent an email to SHH Investigations, the corny name the two privates in Harbour City had chosen for their business. She figured it was an amalgam of their first and last names, and even if it looked like a nice bit of double entendre, it was hard to imagine what their front-of-house girl, the caustic Isabella, did with that when she answered the phone. Someday, she'd have to phone just to find out.

The email reply was almost instant. Isabella was as efficient as ever. She'd sent the message on by cell to the two of them. Both were, as she put it, in that damned field again. She asked where she and Alan were and how they'd made out, so Spence sent on the information along with their cell numbers and new address.

When she returned to the kitchen, she found Alan still banging around filling cupboards with dishes.

"We've got Internet. I set up the computers on the window seat and fired off an email to Isabella. The two of them are out, no surprise, but she got them by cell and we should hear back soon."

Alan nodded and kept putting dishes away in the cupboards.

"Those two are always out somewhere. It's a much bigger business than it was. They get a lot of referrals from Will too. And with the renovated digs, the whole thing's a lot more impressive than Harry's old place."

Sabina and Harry had set up over a year ago after the last job they'd had in Chinatown in Vancouver. Harry's old friend, Will, who had helped them break the case and rescue Willow, Harry's kidnapped assistant, was part of the new operation, an associate with equal weight in the company. He still maintained his own thriving business run mostly out of his car. Will, along with his partner, Rory, a reclusive chameleon with street smarts and a pile of workers of his own, formed a wing of the new company.

Alan finished with the dishes, and they both retired to the living room and the computers.

"I got something here," Spence said, and opened an email

from Sabina. "She says we're not encrypted and should be, and she's offered to do it for us from her end. She says otherwise we're not secure. You wanna do that?"

"Sure," Alan said. "She's good at stuff like that, and we need her help anyway."

"Yeah, but I don't trust her. There's just something about her that's not right, know what I mean?"

"Oh yeah, you've been on about that ever since you met her. She's okay, you know, she won't screw us, never has, and she seems to get stuff nobody else can."

"That's what I mean, she gets stuff we can't. I don't trust her. She gets to put security on our computers, you can bet she'll slip in something of hers as well."

"Would that be so bad?" Alan asked. "She's on our side, after all, and since she can gather stuff from all over the place the way she does, we could really use being in the loop, and so could the guys downtown. It could be, you know, that the brass is right. That these missing girls are missing because our perps are over here now. Remember, Harry and Sabina are still on those cases, Mary and Kylie. They won't let it go until those two horrors are caught and they know why they did what they did. Besides, that lady in Chinatown won't let them."

"So how likely is it that our perps are here? I mean, we got no bodies, and that's part of their MO, the special sites and the mutilation. Since we don't have that, it's maybe not them. It's not copycats either without bodies and the rest of it. We need to concentrate on what we do have here. Do we really need to invite that pair in?"

"Well, you heard Jake, we need everything we can get, and they're not sure it isn't our guys, and the no-body thing? Remember how well those two hid the girls on the island? We wouldn't have found any bodies for a lot longer if we hadn't been lucky with the two hikers and those salal pickers. So we need to milk those two for what we can get, and if that means letting Sabina set up an encryption system, we gotta do that. She won't respond otherwise. Send her an okay for that, and let's see what we get. Lay out our problem and ask for any info she thinks is relevant."

"Jesus, Alan, I'm not your secretary. Do it yourself you're so intent on having those two in the loop." Spence glared at him as he knelt beside her. "My knees hurt, I'm getting a coffee."

While Spence stomped off to the kitchen to start coffee, Alan sent a reply to Sabina, then got to his feet and joined her.

As he entered the kitchen, he explained, "I sent off a message, gave her permission to set up the encryptions, and asked for any details we might be able to use over here. I know you don't like it much, but we need the contact. She's into Chinatown as well, remember, and that means she's got that old matriarch, Mamma Jing, to deal with, and that can't be easy. That woman runs Chinatown, she's got her fingers into everything, and she's stubborn. With Sabina, we get a network we can't get any other way."

Spence stopped looking at the coffee pot perking and turned to face him. She wasn't glaring any more, she looked troubled, and Alan felt his heart go out to her. He put his arm around her and just held her. She let him, for a little while, then she pushed him away.

"Coffee's just about done... You're right, we do need the connection. And, yeah, there's the Chinatown angle. Okay, I'm with you, maybe we'll get lucky. Look, I do admire Sabina and Harry. They're good at what they do, and they got ways we don't have, being strapped by regs and all. But I'd rather work alone, with you, and with Jake and Larry this time. Someday I'll talk to her, maybe get us over whatever it is, but until then she chafes, and their constant banter is irritating. It's like having a rash where you don't want it and can't get to it... What do you want to eat?"

Alan grinned at her, relieved that she'd agreed to the encryption. She was special to him, and he didn't like any friction between them.

"Surprise me. I'll check the computers."

In the living room, he knelt in front of the computers and saw mail on both of them. He opened his. The screen held an email explaining what Sabina had done and how the system worked. They shouldn't notice any difference on their end, she'd written, but the feed was now secure, and they were linked to a closed system involving Harry and her. Sabina also said that she was linked to Chinatown's computer installation in Horseshoe Bay and to her hacker friend Jim. Alan knew about Jim from their case with the dead girls and the escaped psychopath. But his knowledge was only peripheral since it was Sabina who worked the connection. The same was true of Chinatown's matriarch, Mamma Jing, whose link to the case was through one of the murdered ones, Mary Chan, a young Chinese girl from Singapore who was visiting relatives in Harbour City. What he and Spence knew of that connection was through Sabina as well.

Alan wrote back explaining that they were involved in searching for the missing girls from the stroll in Vancouver's east side. He asked for any information that might help the team of detectives working the case. He pointed out the obvious just in case: that active involvement from either of them was not possible given the politics and the parallels with what had happened in Harbour City. What Jake and Larry and the two of them needed was the connections Sabina had on the east side and the connections Harry had with Chinatown, the same sort of thing that had helped them infiltrate the tight network of working girls in the Harbour City case.

When Alan closed down and went back to the kitchen, he found fresh coffee waiting in their new coffee machine and a pile of sandwiches, crusts cut off, stacked on a large plate. On the side were two bananas.

"Some ham and cheese and some sliced chicken. Coffee's ready. We got maybe a half hour, then we need to see what Sabina's dug up for us, if anything, and get downtown by two."

They ate quietly, had a couple of cups of coffee each, then retired to the living room and the computers. Sunlight streamed in the front bay window. The cloud cover had broken as it often did during the day, and the rain had held off. October had been sunny and warm, more like August really, and winter rains had not yet hammered the coast the way they usually did. The bright light made it impossible to see the screens clearly, so they moved into one of the bedrooms and propped the computers on their knees.

Sabina had sent another email containing the name and address of a girl she knew from the stroll. The girl's name was Red because of her red hair, and she'd be available by evening. Red knew the night girls and the stroll since she worked it herself, and she'd be willing to act as a kind of liaison. All Alan and Spence had to do was leave their partners at home and take with them the requisite fee of two hundred dollars. Sabina warned them that Red could be acerbic, but she could be trusted. Also that Red had no love for Mamma Jing whom she'd met under unpleasant circumstances, so it'd be best not to mention any connections. Red's anger would limit her usefulness, Sabina warned, and sent a photo as an attachment along with a map. Alan opened both. He'd print copies tomorrow once he'd set up the printer.

7.

By two o'clock that afternoon, they were back in the detective bureau in Jake's and Larry's office. The place was as messy as it had been the day before, but the two detectives seemed less frustrated, calmer, and more inclined to treat them as partners and less as new arrivals. That stage of things seemed to be over.

"We got a kind of description of the guy we might be looking for," Jake offered, pointing to a sketch that was pinned over the papers on the partition. "We had a sketch artist draw this up. One of our contacts came in this morning with a little coaxing."

Larry added, "We know this piece of crap too. He's around sometimes, sometimes not. He's a pimp with a drug sideline, and he rides his girls hard. We don't like the son of a bitch, so we ride him just as hard when we can find him. He turned up last night and threatened one of our informants, beat her silly. So we're after him again. There's gotta be a connection. Otherwise, why pick on our snitch. We get that creep, we'll ream him a new one, dig it out of him." The metaphors held, sort of.

Jake looked at Spence and asked, "You get anything from your guys in Harbour City?"

She grinned at him. "We got a girl and an address, both available this evening. But she's cop shy, so we gotta do this one on our own or we get nothing. She'll talk to us only because Sabina, one of the privates on the island, vouched for us. There's a connection of some sort between the two of them. She might be able to help us out."

"Yeah, well, we can live with that. We chase both leads tonight. Let's go over everything again. Maybe if we do it this way, something'll pop that we missed before."

Jake reached into his drawer and hauled out a thick binder. Larry did the same and added, "We keep doubles, easier that way, so one of you sit with me, preferably you." He grinned at Spence.

The afternoon's replay proved fruitless, so all four of them left on foot to grab a quick meal before Larry and Jake hit the stroll to find their suspect, and Spence and Alan went off to find Red. The restaurant was a few blocks away from the station, in towards town, down on Hastings West in a much classier area.

On the street were banks, restaurants, high-end clothing stores, and one of the best classical music stores left in the province. Jake explained that he loved jazz, and that was another specialty of the place. The store was called Sikora, he said, but not even the clerks in the place seemed to know why. It was housed in the bottom of a neoclassic four-storey on the south side about halfway down the first block of the upscale section of the street. There were no big signs, no neon, no special lights, nothing, just the old front window with wooden racks of cds visible as they drove by. It was still open.

"I'd love to go in, but duty calls. Any of you guys interested in classics?" Jake leaned toward the window, eyeing the racks of cds there and glancing into the interior.

"Classic jazz, sure, you know that, and you know they've got great stuff, lots of Zoot Sims and Muddy Waters. I know, I know, he's blues, but hell it's all good." Larry joined Jake at the window, his hands shoved in the pockets of his jacket, pulling it down and off center. He bounced a bit on his toes. He turned toward Alan and Spence. "What about you two?"

"I like the real stuff, especially the Russians: Rimsky Korsakov, Borodin, Tchaikovsky, Scriabin, Rachmaninoff. Like that. Sometimes even Prokofiev." Alan leaned in, shaded the window with his hands, and sighed. "Too bad there's no time."

"Oh for christ's sake, we got a case you fools, let's go eat and get on with it. I'm bloody hungry." Spence slapped Alan on the ass and grinned. "Let's go big boy."

That got everyone's attention and a couple of raised eyebrows. Nobody said a thing, but everybody smiled.

The restaurant was farther down on the north side tucked in between a clothing store and a place selling so-called antiques for the tourists. It was only half full, so they found a booth easily. The waitress knew the two city detectives, and orders were fast except for Spence who couldn't decide which salad she'd like. She chose a large Caesar, no anchovies, and none of those stale bread chunks either. The waitress chuckled. "You got it Sweetie, no fish, no chunks. She sauntered toward the kitchen and slapped the orders on the rotating wheel in the serving window.

The four detectives talked about anything but the case while they waited and ate, but once the meal was over and the coffee orders in, the four of them set up the night.

"Just so we're clear," Jake looked around the table. "You guys are after this Red person and you're taking an unmarked. What you get we need to know, so maybe after, you come back to the station and fill us in. Larry and I'll get busy looking for our guy and do the same. Everybody good with that?"

Spence took a sip of coffee and nodded. "We're good. Don't know how late, but we'll be back. If we're lucky, she saw something we can use, like maybe our perps or yours. Even if it's just a vehicle, it'll help a lot."

The three of them finished their coffee while Jake settled the bill, then they walked back up the street, dawdling a moment or two in front of the cd store.

Back at the station, they signed out two unmarked cruisers, both grey, nondescript Dodges, both smelling of fast food, and both dinged here and there, but they worked. Jake brushed the dirt off one front fender and leaned on it. "Okay, these things represent the best the city has to offer. New anything is not likely this century, so please, don't damage them. They're fragile."

"They're both pieces of shit, but we'll be careful not to get them dirtier than they are. Jesus, we got better junkers on the island." Spence bent down and peered under one of them.

"What he means is we get crap, you get maybe better crap bein' mounteds and all, so we're maybe a bit jealous." Larry leaned against the side of an unmarked, didn't bother to clean anything.

"We get nicer uniforms too." Alan grinned at the city cops.

"Enough! Let's roll if these things start." Spence climbed into one of them and turned the key. The unmarked hesitated and grumbled, but it started.

They ran the ramp one behind the other, and both turned on Cordova.

Spence drove their piece of junk, grumbling about alignment and shocks and turned off Cordova at the bottom of the hill in the tranny section. She took Raymur, the street that ran under the Hastings overpass, and turned left at the T-intersection. After a short block she turned back onto Raymur. She crossed Prior and coasted along the side of Strathcona Park, a square block of green and gardens tucked into a warehouse area near the tracks. At the end of the park, she turned right onto Malkin and coasted along. This street ran a few blocks along the back side of the park with trees on one side and rows of semis and warehouses on the other. Red was supposed to be somewhere along this stretch.

The park side of the street was filled with community gardens behind a steep bank and thick tree cover, so it was good and dark except for the sparse light from the occasional loading doors on the other side and the parking lights of some semis parked in a line along the street.

The old Dodge crept along that section of the park. Alan looked closely at the park. Nothing. Spence took the car around the park again, down to the darker end. This time, just at the end of the community garden section where the park opened up, they saw a red-haired girl revealed by the feeble light from the park's toilets. She was leaning against the wall beside the door to the women's john watching the slow progress of the Dodge.

When Spence pulled into the curb, Red sauntered over. She was dressed for work in a short red skirt, a tight revealing top, and red high-heeled pumps. She took the asphalt path to the curb and waited. Spence backed up, and Red bent down to the open window.

"So, sweetie, what you looking for? Give you a good blow job for cheap, do her too if she likes." Spence snorted, and Alan looked straight at nice cleavage.

"We're the two from Sabina. You must be Red."

Red wiggled around until her cleavage was even more pronounced, grinned at Alan, and said, her voice dripping with sarcasm, "Jeez, how'd you guess? You're pretty sharp for a cop."

Alan sighed, shook his head, and said. "Sabina told us you'd be touchy, get in."

He leaned over the seat and opened the rear door.

"Sure, Sweetie, and show the whole street how much I love cops. This piece of junk is like a neon sign. Christ, couldn't you get something a little less coplike? No way I'm getting in that. Come on, park that thing and let's walk. Good cover here."

Red straightened up, kicked the rear door shut, and walked off a few feet. Alan glanced at Spence who rolled her eyes, and they got out.

Red stood there, her hands on her hips, one high-heeled shoe tapping impatiently, shaking her head.

"You even look like cops. Might as well wear a sign for Christ sake. Jesus, what the fuck were you thinkin'?"

Spence glared at her. "If it's so dark and secluded here and full of pretty boys with their dicks out, why the fuck do you care what we look like?"

"Okay, okay, Jeez, you're a feisty bitch aren't you." She turned to Alan, grinning. "You let the chick run things, you wimp?"

"She's Spence and I'm Alan. Cut the crap and let's walk."

"No fuckin' sense of humour either, Jesus! Okay, okay, you guys are way too serious, lighten up a little. Come on, we'll go this way."

They walked into the community garden part of the park away from the toilets and the flat green of the park lawns. The path was well marked and wide, so despite the poor light seeping in from the warehouses and crawling across the empty beds they could see enough to keep from stumbling.

"We can talk here," Red said, and sat on one of the retaining walls that marked out a plot of dirt. Her skirt rode up higher than any skirt should, and Alan wondered what was under it, there sure wasn't much room.

They sat on a raised bed close by and waited.

"So, what you want from me?"

"Well, we think there might be a guy we've been chasing over on the island who's killing girls over here now. He's a psychopath, so he's good at charming people, and he likes girls from the strip, takes them, tortures them, paints them up, and guts 'em. Then leaves them lying around here and there where you wouldn't expect to find them. Somebody always eventually stumbles on the mess and gives us a call."

Alan delivered this in a quiet voice as if it were just part of ordinary conversation and waited.

Spence picked it up. "We don't know if it's the same guy as the one taking girls from the stroll. Might be, though. And if he's here, he'll get girls easily. We got no mutilated bodies yet, but it's early days. What we want from you is anything you know about guys on the stroll and girls who've gone with them and not come back. We gotta stop this guy, if he's here, and if he's not, we gotta know that too."

Red shifted a bit, looked down at her pumps, the heels sticking into the soft stone path, and said, "I got nothin' like that. Like that guy you're lookin' for. What I got is a girl I work with sometimes. She's gone, and she shouldn't be. I mean, she really needs to work, you know, and she'd have told me if she wanted to bugger off for a while. So it's weird, I mean her not comin' back."

"Did you see her go? Were you there on the stroll when she got picked up? Do you know what the john looked like, the car, anything?" There was some urgency in Alan's voice now.

"I was like on the other fuckin' corner, okay? I didn't see who it was. I'd a seen that, I'd a been screamin' at the cops already. And it was just a fuckin' car, okay? I mean it was dark, you know, and he didn't stop long. She just climbed in, and he took off up to Campbell and over to Cordova. Who the hell knows where he went after that. I talked to a couple of the girls up there, you know, and they said it was a dark blue panel van, or maybe black, or maybe dark grey, a Honda maybe, or one of those things all look the same, an' Sugar, what she calls herself, just climbed in, no chit chat, and he took off. They didn't see who it was either, so no sense callin' anybody. We been watchin', but the creep's never been back, an' Sugar's been gone ever since. So that's what I got, a dark blue or black somethin' an' I got it second hand. How you gonna use that?"

"Better than nothing," Spence said and shifted her butt.

"Take us through the night this happened as well as you can, maybe something you saw'll pop out. Worth a try, don't you think?"

Red looked at Alan, sighed, and shook her head. "I been over it in my head, you know, 'cause we're close, like, I pair with Sugar, an' we make out okay, but I got nothin'."

"Try it again on us," Alan said and leaned forward to listen.

"We were standin' on the corner at Campbell for a time, then I walked down the hill and tried down there. I mean it's like tranny territory you know, but we split it sometimes, so it was okay."

Alan broke in, "What were you both wearing?"

"Jesus, let me tell it okay? We was just like me now. Okay, here's how it was: Sugar was wearin' a pink skirt and top an' pink nylons, thigh-highs, you know? An' she got on her blond wig, long, to her shoulders, and bangs. She likes pink, always pink stuff. That night she had black knee-highs, tall heels, johns like those, an' a small purse thing, you know, not a big bag like we have usually. Me, I'm like in a black skirt, lace top, pumps. I like pumps. An' I got no wig. Like my own hair. So there we was, her up there, me down the hill. Place is just starting to heat up, and down comes this thing, blue or grey or somethin'. Down Cordova like he's been circling, you know? So he pulls up at the corner, top of the hill."

"That's Campbell, right?" Spence asked.

"Jesus, 'course it is, I mean what the fuck else would it be? So there we was, an' he pulls in near Sugar, an' she just grabs the door an' jumps in. Didn't spend any time chattin'. That was weird that was, like she knew him or somethin'. So he comes down past me, does a uey next block down, comes back fast, up the hill an' he's gone. Like that. That's what I saw. Nothin' worth talkin' about. I was busy rest of the night, an' didn't think about it much when she didn't come back. Sometimes johns want an all-nighter, or maybe take us to a party over on Davie or somewhere. Or they dump us at another place an' we work our way back, sometimes that's how it goes. So I don't worry until the next night an' she's not there. I mean we live close to each other, sometimes together, but we don't keep tabs, know what I mean, so I was only lookin' for her on the street. She didn't come back all that week, so then I know somethin's off. She's got a kid her aunt looks after, an' she's gotta work, you know, got nothin' else."

Red looked at the detectives as if she hoped they'd find something in all that and get her friend back. She sat waiting, then shook her head, looked again at her heels digging into the crushed stone path, sighed, and got up brushing off the back of her short red skirt.

"You got nothin' right? So what the fuck use was that, then. She's gone is all, an' you guys got no clue. Fuckin' waste a time, this is. I'm gonna go back. You want any more find someone else, okay?"

"Hold up," Spence said. "I'll walk with you a bit. To the end of the park, that can't hurt, right?"

"Yeah, alright, but no further. I got my reputation to think of, you know, an' you don't look like no workin' girl."

They walked out of the gardens together and took the paved path toward Prior. Alan stayed where he was. Spence and Red walked together slowly, and near the center of the park, Red stopped and looked at Spence. "Whyn't you get some decent clothes, for Christ's sake, look like you belong down here. Isn't anybody gonna talk to you dressed like that, Jesus!"

"So how should I dress, then?"

"Get some different stuff, even jeans are okay. You got to do 'em right. You need a top shows somethin', I mean think where you are, for Christ's sake. An' those shoes, I mean their like fuckin' boots you wear to work in a store or somethin'. Get something with heels, you know, something makes you look like you wanna be a girl. What you look like now is someone who doesn't give a shit. You need to be one or the other, you know, be a guy if you want, whatever, but dress right, okay?"

Spence stood there stunned. She'd never even considered what she had on. The girl was right. If she wanted to get anything, she'd have to look like she wanted to be here. They walked on.

"Okay, thanks. What do you think will look good?"

Red stopped again. They were well away from the community gardens now and part way to Prior and the stoplight at Campbell. Beside them was a climbing rock for kids. On the other side was a circular cement something. Spence had no idea what that was for. Maybe a pool in the summer?

"Come here, let's sit by that cement thing. We can talk, no queers there, nothin' to disturb us. I gotta watch I don't get made with you the way you are, you know, I mean cop written all over you. So, what should you wear? Depends what you wanna do. Say you wanna talk to girls like me on the stroll, you gotta look like maybe someone who's new and wants to start in, so you sound innocent, like, you know? For that you gotta have somethin' shows some leg, more the better, okay? Then you need some kinda tight top, show a bit of stuff, you know, use a pushup."

Red looked at Spence's bust critically. "Yeah, a pushup, make you look like you got somethin' even if you don't, you know? Then you get some heels, don't matter boots or pumps or platforms, 'cause what you're tryin' for is a kind a walk, you know, like get some hip thing goin'. What you got now is worse than nothin'. Don't know what that guy sees in you. Shit, all the guys like leg and tit you know, so whyn't you give him some?"

Spence grinned at her. "You got a point, Red, but I got a job that makes me dress this way, sort of like a guy, you know. But I can change for down here, and maybe for him too. So can you help me? If we meet somewhere down here, show me how to dress? And you can show me how you work? Think I got a chance?"

"You wanna be on the stroll? You wanna work? That's bullshit. You don't wanna work."

"No, you're right, I don't wanna work. What I want is to look like I am and learn how things go just for a few nights. You can fit me up, show me how to dress, and sort of keep me near you so I can watch. It might help me catch the guy who took your friend. Hey, it'll maybe help me look sexier."

"Couldn't hurt, you wanna keep that guy you're with. Jesus, you don't look like much in that getup. I gotta work nights, you know, so you come down an' I help you out, you gotta look after yourself when I'm busy, you know, think you can do that much at least? I mean you don't seem very good at stuff like this."

"You teach me to dress, I'm gonna knock Alan's socks off. And yeah, as for the street, I learn fast, so I can look after myself. I just gotta get the feeling."

Red looked at her, slowly moving her eyes from Spence's head to her toes and back to her middle. It made Spence a bit uncomfortable, but it excited her too.

Red sighed. "It's not gonna be easy, but showin' you what to buy, tryin' it on, and showin' you how to walk, that'll be a gas. We can do it tomorrow, you want. Wanna meet in the afternoon sometime? Have to be down on Commercial somewheres, so we can hit the shops I like on Hastings. One place, we can use the back room to work on you. Get you dressed, let you walk, see how it goes. You good with that, I'm in. An' don't bring no fuckin' cruiser with you. You got a ride of your own?"

"You bet. Okay, tomorrow. You be anywhere on Commercial from Hastings down I'll find you, okay? Look for a red Camaro. Two o'clock on Commercial. Be there."

Red stood then, studied Spence, turned on her heel, and walked out of the park. Spence watched her go. Under the streetlight at the corner, her red hair glowed in the yellowish light. She walked up Campbell. One of the cars turned the corner and followed her.

Spence walked back into the park, the greens turned almost black in the sparse light. She could see the outlines of the tall trees that lined the edge, almost leafless now, etched against the lit sky of the city behind them; she saw the toilets ahead of her, the clerestory windows glowing with the muted light of a couple of dirty ceiling fixtures.

She made her way around the side, passed a couple of men talking quietly beside the building, little more than darker blotches against the wall. She found Alan sitting on the same wall she'd left him on.

"We got piss all out of that," he said as he stood up.

"We got a lot more than you think. I'm going shopping with Red tomorrow. She's gonna fit me out, teach me how to act, and take me on the stroll with her for a night. Maybe I can dig up more about the missing girls. There are three missing, aren't there? So if I'm down there and look like I sort of belong, I can get to talk to the girls all along Cordova, see what turns up. Somebody saw something, that's for sure. Nobody's gonna talk to us the way we are. Nobody's gonna talk to a cop, but a new girl who needs to learn, that's maybe a way in."

"How far you gonna go with this?"

"Well, I'm not turning tricks, if that's what you mean. Red says I'm about as interesting sexually as a tree trunk. She can't understand why you'd hang around me. She thinks I've got no tits, and I can't walk the way I should. Why anybody'd want to hump me is a mystery to her. From her perspective, I can see what she means. Can't hurt to get some instruction from someone who lives the life."

"There's nothing wrong with you, and you look fine the way you dress. I gotta say though, you look better undressed. Those few times I get to see that."

Spence grinned at him as they cleared the gardens and took the asphalt path toward the car.

"You're gonna love what I wear after tomorrow, and I'll get Red to teach me some of her moves. Of course, you can only look, you can't touch. After all, it's the job, so all you get is to admire what you can't have. No fraternization, remember?"

Alan stopped at the edge of the park and said, "You think you can turn me into a lust-crazed customer and leave me hanging, you're nuts. I get you home, and I'm gonna get what I've looked at all night, so get used to the idea. But remember since you're on the job, you gotta learn how to fend off the ones you've turned on. It's my job to make sure you can."

Spence snorted, walked around him, and got in the driver's seat. Alan sighed and grinned at the thought of Spence practicing hooker skills. He'd barely closed the door before she peeled out, startling a couple of guys walking down the side of the park.

The next morning, they were up early. All the stuff was supposed to arrive in the morning, and they wanted breakfast out of the way and the place cleaned up before the beds and furniture arrived. They had to be downtown at four, at least Alan did, and Spence had to meet Red at two.

By eleven, they were getting a little concerned. There wasn't a lot of time left. Spence was getting really pissed off by the time the trucks arrived. The drivers weren't happy either when they realized there was no elevator. Spence and the grumpy drivers got into it a bit before Alan smoothed things over with a few twenties. There were four men in the two trucks, so the beds and other items were inside quickly. Eighty bucks was a lot of lunches. He intended to make Spence pay for some of them. She'd calmed down by the time the drivers left.

They started with the beds since it needed two to get the frames assembled and the box springs and mattresses on. By one-thirty, the worst was over, and Spence had cleaned up and taken off to meet Red. The kitchen was functional, and Alan was happy to arrange the furniture the way he thought Spence would like it. To do otherwise wouldn't be in his best interest. Best to avoid conflagrations, he thought. He wondered if they should have rented, given how uncertain the posting was. But they'd decided to buy here and ship the stuff back to the island when and if. They could always use the pieces that Spence didn't want in his place, unless, of course, they finally got together, which he thought would be good, well, beyond good, bloody fucking marvelously good! He sighed, smiled, shook his head, then left for the station.

8.

Spence booted the Camaro down Nanaimo to the Dundas intersection, turned left, and wove her way down to Victoria. The name changed here to Powell, and once through the light, she hit the gas, dodging the occasional bus and hitting the inside lane when she saw a long enough opening between parked cars. She made the turn on Commercial just as it turned two o'clock.

Commercial Street began at Powell and housed a light industrial section that ran from Powell up to Hastings. It was four lanes, each two-lane side separated from the other by a median. Spence cruised up one side as far as Hastings, then down the other back to Powell. No Red.

Since she couldn't do a U turn on Powell or Hastings, she repeated the drive a couple of times, using the last block on each side to make a turn. On one of these, when she'd moved up Hastings a block and turned in again to make her way back down to Commercial, she spotted Red leaning against the side of a sleazy looking restaurant window talking to another girl, a thin brunette in a tight skirt and an almost nonexistent gauzy black top.

The restaurant window was just a single with the door inset on the side. It was dirty with the kind of dirt that built up through long neglect. You could hardly see what was inside. She could imagine what the kitchen looked like given the outside.

As she slowed the car, however, it became clear that the place wasn't deserted; at least three of the counter stools were occupied, although it was hard to tell through the filthy window whether they were male or female. Spence shuddered, and shook her head in disgust.

Red spotted the Camaro, waved, spoke to the girl for another moment, then sauntered over to the side of the road. Spence had already pulled in as far as she could. This street, running perpendicular to Commercial, was lined with mid-sized trucks on one side serving businesses and with cars and vans on the other. Spence was double parked, not that anyone here would notice.

Red ran her hand over the Camaro's front fender and gave Spence a huge smile. She was wearing what she'd call street clothes: a short skirt, red of course, a blouse also red, and a pair of heels a little lower than her night gear. Her hair was up, pinned with a tortoise shell comb, and her long neck made her look more graceful and taller.

She got in the Camaro, her skirt riding up, and stroked the dash. "This is one hot set of wheels you got here, one hot set. It's beautiful! And a course, I love the colour. You wanna run us down to Commercial then we can turn up Hastings. The shops I want are up a couple blocks, an' there's a place behind my fave where we can leave the car so it's safe. Man, a Camaro ragtop! Man." Red looked around the car, grinning.

"Why the hell weren't you on Commercial like we said? I been cruising the damn street for twenty minutes. Who was that anyway?"

"Bad day so far, or you just jumpy some?"

"Sorry, but I get this way when I have to wait for someone who isn't where she said she'd be."

"What's the problem with you? I was only talkin' to Jenny a bit. Shit, I was on that damn street for a half hour or so waitin' on you, so when I saw her comin' down the street, we sort of walked up a bit for some shade, you know? It's only like a couple stores in is all. I could see you went down the street, okay? Jeez, relax a bit, would ya."

"Oh screw it. It's good to see you. I'm just a little cranky, that's all, rough morning and all. Let's start over. Where we going?"

"Store's just up Hastings a little. Make a couple lefts one here, one there, and I'll show you. We're gonna go down an alley up there on the right, park in behind, leave the car where it's safe. Besides, that's the store we're gonna set you up in. I got a friend, gives me the back room to use when I need it. We trade favours, like, you know? First though, after we park, we walk a bit. There's a good shoe store just down the street. Guy carries a lot of heels and stuff. Good place and cheap too. It's just up here."

Spence wheeled the Camaro around a taxi that was double parked, and they entered a narrow alley running between Hastings and the next street over.

Red climbed out of the Camaro and pushed in a garage-sized wooden door set on a metal frame with a wheel on the end. She waved Spence in and closed the door to the yard again.

"We go in this way." She pointed to a dinged metal door set in the brick wall. There was no handle on their side, just a dead bolt lock set flush with the door. Red banged on the door, and they waited until it was shoved open from inside. The man who appeared was slim and olive skinned. He grinned at Red, gave her a peck, and motioned them inside. He took a quick look at the Camaro before he closed the door.

"Who's this then?"

"Spence, meet Artie, he's my man, he is." Spence nodded, and Artie stuck out his hand. She shook it.

"Nice wheels you got there. What year's that one?"

"Eighty-nine, fully restored. It's what I like to do when I got time and some bread."

"Artie, this's the girl I was tellin' you about. She's got a nice ride, yeah, but that's all she's got. She needs to work, okay, and we gotta shop for her. We're gonna hit up some stores, get some boots and stuff, then we'll be back an' we can set her up, see how she does, okay?"

"Anything you want, Red, you know that. Your friend's welcome anytime."

They left Artie's shop by the front door, and Spence got a look at the racks of clothes as they passed through. The front door had one of those bells that jingles when the door opens or closes. The building was old, and the bell, like the front door, was probably original. Artie's place was clean and nicely set up, though, with one wall scraped back to the raw brick and modern lighting used to highlight displays of clothing. The quality of some of the goods surprised Spence.

"That's an interesting shop, Red. He's got some nice stuff in there. Where's the stroll gear hidden?"

"He's got that in back for us girls, like, good quality stuff but made for show, you know, kinda stuff we can use. An' he's good about it. Let's us try on whatever, gives us space, never hassles any of us. Even lets us crash sometimes if we're, like, between places. I mean mostly just me and Sugar. An' he don't want nothin' either. He's not like some of those guys always coppin' feels and drooling all over you. Okay, we're goin' in here."

It was another single window shop with an inset door in an equally old building. Inside, it was all business. Flat-topped cabinets in rows were heaped with cheap leather goods, the walls lined with boxes. There wasn't any special lighting here, no scraped brick walls either, just fluorescent tubes and cracked plaster. The walls, when you could see them, carried a film of dirt years old that was highlighted by the light beige colour. The place smelled not unpleasantly of leather, and as Spence looked through some of the shoes piled on the counters, she realized that there were more than a few top brand names.

"Pretty nice stuff, huh? He buys up overstocks from all over, and just throws it in here. You search good, you find some real deals. Come on, I'll introduce you."

In the back of the store, a man with a nicely trimmed beard stood behind an old-fashioned wooden counter. He glanced at them over the top of a pair of wire-rimmed glasses and smiled. He had hand-written ledgers in front of him.

"Who's your friend?"

"This's a new friend of mine, Spence, she's needs some gear, so I brought her here. You got the best stuff around, Len, an' you like us girls, so we always come back, right?"

"That you do, Red, that you do. Good to meet you, Spence." Len smiled at her and nodded as if to say she'd do quite well. But Spence read his eyes and knew he wasn't fooled for one minute. She wasn't a street girl and he knew that perfectly well. Still, he played the game. He said, "So how can I help you ladies today?"

"Some boots and pumps, maybe? What ya think Spence, some knee-highs, maybe? Couple pair of pumps?"

"You're the boss, Red, whatever you think I need." She glanced at Len and smiled.

"You ladies take a seat and I'll see what I can find for you. What size and colour, Spence, and how high?"

"Give her fours, Len, and maybe up a bit more for the boots?"

"Size eights should do it. Maybe black and then red for the pumps." Spence smiled at him.

The two of them sat at the side where there were three old wing chairs with sizing measures on the floor and little stools for fitting shoes. Len had disappeared into the back of the store looking for sizes and colours, and heel heights specified by Red.

Red crossed her legs and tried to pull down the short skirt. It was futile, but she tried. "Len's sort of straight, you know, I mean, he likes us, but he wants us to behave, like, in his store." She nodded solemnly at Spence and yanked at her skirt again.

"You look good, Red, I meant to tell you that. I like your hair that way, for days anyway. Just keep your legs crossed. You'll be fine. You tell me if I'm getting the right stuff, okay?"

Red was about to reply when Len returned carrying an arm full of boxes.

"Let's try these," he said, and set the boxes on the floor. The first had a pair of red pumps, leather, good quality. The heels were about four inches, higher than Spence was used to on those rare occasions when she wore heels at all, but she gamely put them on. She walked across the limited floor area, glanced back at Red, got a nod, and sat down again.

"They're comfortable, I like them."

Over the next half hour, Len helped Spence try six different pairs, three each of red pumps and knee-high boots in black with slightly higher heels. The bill for her final choice of four was low, surprisingly reasonable. Len was a good man, she thought, and helped the street girls when he could, at least with the products he sold. He accepted them as equals as far as she could tell and was concerned with their welfare. That impressed Spence. They left the store with Spence's purchases in a large shopping bag.

"Len's a nice guy, you know, an' his stuff's real good. But he's a bit stiff, know what I mean? He always lets us know if we get too, you know, excited like. I only take good friends there. The other girls, some of them got no sense, an' I don't want to queer things with him. Okay, now we go back to Artie's and try on some clothes."

Artie was folding garments and organizing one of the sales racks when they went in. He smiled at them and pointed to the rear. "I put out some things for you to try, you too Red. I'll be in when you're ready, see how the fit is."

Spence had worn her best black bra and a pair of lacy black underpants, brief but not too brief. She kept her panties on, but Red pointed at the bra and off it came. Her legs were bare. It was a little unpleasant stripping down in front of Red, but she didn't seem to notice Spence's discomfort. She did, however, run a critical eye over Spence's body, lingering at the appropriate spots, especially at her breasts which were small and firm with large dark nipples.

"We gotta get you a pushup. I know a place got good stuff. What you've got is okay, but for tonight, I'll find you somethin' better, okay? Now try on that skirt maybe with the camisole top. No, that one, the lacy black one, yeah, that's it. Now put on some heels and walk for me... That's it, yeah, I like it... Okay, let's try the waist cincher over that see-through top, yeah that one. Come over here and I'll do you up. Don't worry about your tits, they're supposed to show, what you got at least"

The try-ons went on for a half hour or more, but by the end of that time, Spence had three outfits, three skirts, each cut differently, three tops, and the one waist cincher that could be used with any of it. Red picked the outfit she liked best and called Artie in.

He looked at Spence appraisingly, smiled broadly and nodded. "Oh, yes, my dear, you look ravishing, truly. May I see the others, perhaps with boots this time?"

They showed Artie all the outfits. While he was in the room, Red fitted the cincher over one of them, and Artie clapped his hands in delight. Spence understood now why he let the girls try outfits and use his back room. He got his jollies looking at the clothes he provided on the girls, and as far as Spence could tell, his pleasure was genuine both in the girls and how they looked.

Red tried on a new skirt and blouse, and Artie liked that too, but his greatest pleasure was the waist cincher. Somehow changing outfits in front of him, even for Spence, wasn't embarrassing. He seemed to know when to look away, and his pleasure was so innocent, any sensation of male lust evaporated like steam from a kettle.

Back at the counter, Artie tallied the bill, smiled at Spence, and reached behind him. He threw three pairs of black lace-top thigh-highs on the counter and said, "My pleasure, dear, you do look stunning in your choices."

Spence paid and thanked him. She used cash as she had at Len's place since she wasn't supposed to have much money and wouldn't have a credit card either that anybody would trust.

She and Red went out the back of Artie's place, got the car, and once out the gate and down the alley, Spence turned to Red and said, "You did a good thing for me today, I appreciate it. Let's get you where you want to go, and I'll meet you later tonight. Around eight good?"

"Eight's good, and you can let me out at the Starbucks on Powell. I need to eat somethin'."

"I'll go with you if that's okay, and lunch is my treat."

"Okay, but you gotta act like we was makin' out some, you know, because they know me and some of the girls'll be around. You got such a flashy car, you gotta act like a trick, sort a, okay? You'll be so different tonight they won't recognize you, so it's just for now."

"Jesus, Red, I'm no les, you know! I'll try but take it easy on me."

"You ought a give it a go sometime, double your pleasure, know what I mean?"

Spence snorted, damn near missed the turn, hit the gas and sped down Commercial to Powell, then along Powell to the Starbucks. The lot was almost empty: only one Harley in the corner and a pickup in the middle. Spence put the Camaro at the far end.

They got a table, ordered two large lattes and picked up a

couple of sandwiches from the cooler. Spence paid and they sat with the coffee and eats at the table near the front window. There were a couple of girls at a table in the back near the washrooms, and Red wriggled her fingers at them. Spence watched and wriggled hers too. The girls giggled, punched each other in the ribs, and wriggled back.

"See," said Red, "That's what I mean. They think we're together, and you did good wavin' like that. They seen the car when we come in, you know, so what else'd you be but a trick, a car like that?"

It was after four when Spence arrived at the station, having left Red back at the coffee shop with her girlfriends. The guys were waiting in their cubicle in the homicide bureau when she got upstairs, paper spread all over the place again.

"We been looking at the book again after wasting our time last night. We got nothing. Our guy didn't show, and our snitch won't talk, she's scared shitless. Don't blame her, that bastard's really bad news. Alan filled us in on your contact at the park. Get any further today?" Jake looked at Spence with raised his eyebrows.

"I'll be on the stroll with her tonight. We got some outfits I'll need, so we're good to go. Alan'll keep tabs on me and watch the johns. The contact's a girl named Red. She's not gonna talk to you guys, but I think she's starting to trust me some, so the next night or so should get us somewhere. She doesn't know what happened to her friend, Sugar, and I'm sure she thinks I might just find her somehow. I think that's why she's so cooperative. I'm a kind of a last ditch try for her."

Larry looked at her appraisingly. "You got outfits. With this Red character? Give us a description so we'll know you when we see you. Better yet, check in before you hit the stroll."

"Like that's gonna happen." Spence glared at Larry, and Jake grinned. "You're as bad as the johns. You can get your jollies when you see me on the strip, pervert."

"Ouch! Feisty aren't we."

Spence ignored him and talked to Jake who canned the

grin as soon as she turned toward him.

"So we take it from our end on the stroll, and you guys go in as heavies and find your psycho. That the plan?"

"Pretty much, that's it. We're known, so we can't work the way you guys can, but we got our own network out there, so between us four we're workin' both ends. Something should pop."

Larry looked at Alan. "You gonna watch her back?"

"That's the plan, not that she needs watching. I'll be cruising a lot, watching the girls and whoever turns up. I'll make regular passes, take off for a while, then go back to it. Anybody looks out of place, I'll call it in."

Larry nodded, "Still only the three missing. We got BOLOs out on them all, mispers are in, and we're pushing it."

Since it was almost five, they broke for the evening shift. Outside, Jake and Larry grabbed some food from a street vendor near the station's front doors. Spence took one look at the street, then at the cart, shook her head in disgust, and made for the garage.

Larry called after her. "Hey, you should try these. They're good. We all eat this stuff."

It all fell on deaf ears, and Spence marched on around the corner. Alan shrugged, looked apologetically at the two guys, then trotted after her.

"What's with you today? If they eat there, it's gotta be good."

"I'm not standing on the street chewin' on overdone sausage. We got a long time before we need to hit the stroll, so let's find a place we can sit at least. We can take the Camaro, maybe just go home. I gotta change anyway, so I'll cook something. Be better than that crud."

They walked down the ramp and into the service garage. Spence hopped in the car, started up, and backed out. Alan waited, got in the passenger side, and she drove out to Cordova and turned down toward Campbell. Once out, she looked over at Alan.

"What's it gonna be, champ, home, or a good place to relax and enjoy some decent food? There's a Cactus Club over on Broadway or an Earls, either one's good, and you'll like the waitresses. They all dress in black and they're all pretty.

Steaks are fabulous." She grinned at Alan, revved the car a few times and waited.

Alan rolled his eyes, sighed, and said over the engine revs, "You choose, you're doing the work tonight. Might be better if you didn't have to cook."

"Cactus Club then. They got great washrooms, so I can change there. I'll get one of the girls to help me with the cincher. They'll love that sort of thing, providing we've already paid the bill."

Spence grinned at him, shifted, and took off down Cordova to the bottom of the hill. She swung up under the Hastings overpass, made a couple of turns and took Prior down to Main. She turned left onto Main, followed a long line of buses up to the skytrain station, then shot up the long hill toward Broadway.

9.

The town of Hammil was named after Lake Hammil and stood about a hundred kilometers from that lake. It was way over near Dodd Lake and much farther inland. No one knew why it had been named after a lake so far to the west when there were certainly closer ones with better names.

The largest city in the area was Powell River; but it was at least a hundred and fifty kilometers away on the coast. Hammil, unlike Powell River, which was the economic hub of the region, had been a logging and mining town, so it had seen more violence, murders even, usually the kind that came from bar fights or so-called domestic disturbances. Even some from inebriated drivers, of whom there were many. But that was vehicular manslaughter, so it really didn't count. But these days, that sort of thing was so rare no one could remember ever having seen anything like it.

The oldest resident in town, Edna Myrtle, who was close on a hundred, couldn't remember anything like it either, at least not in the last thirty years, and if she couldn't remember, it hadn't happened. She remembered everybody and everything; she was the town repository of information, a walking history book. Okay, a hobbling history book. Every time Herk Burman checked in his data bases to see how far off on some incident or person she was, he found, when he could find anything, that her recall was not only vast but also accurate.

The town had decided some years ago to have its own police force; at least Mickey Patterson had decided. He had the most money, the most influence, and the biggest house, and had been mayor for so long nobody bothered voting much in the municipal elections anymore except for the slate of councilmen. The RCMP ostensibly covered the outside and assisted in the town when needed, but it was up to Herk to keep order, and he had done so with his five deputies and a couple of civilian assistants for the last four years, ever since his predecessor had accidentally shot himself in the foot with his new Glock and had to retire.

Herk was Chief Burman to his men when on duty and just Herk any other time. That morning, his youngest deputy, Sam, Harvey Reagan's boy, had screamed into town in one of the five cruisers, running the few reds and damn near taking out that little decorative picket fence in front of the town hall where the station was housed. He was so excited, he couldn't talk straight, and Herk had had to sit him down in his office and wait until he calmed down. Finally, though, he got it out.

There'd been a body found back in the bush, he said, way back in. Trapper Pete had flagged him down on his patrol to tell him. Pete was an old timer who lived in the bush and still made his living, such as it was, selling what he trapped. He had a shack he'd built himself and one of those new pellet stoves to heat it with every morning, except for summer, so he had to come into town every month or so to get bags of pellets to feed it. That's what he'd been doing when he flagged down Sam out near his place. Herk tried to get Sam to pass over the obvious and get on with it, but the boy was determined to leave nothing out. That's what he'd been taught to do, and he was damn well going do it.

Jenny Green, who was on the front desk, and Celia Farley, the file clerk and computer whiz, drifted in to hear as did anybody else who wasn't out on patrol. It was a little crowded, especially around the door.

"Okay now Sam, take it slow and give me exactly what he said. Start again with when Pete stopped you and keep the sequence clear."

Sam took out his little notebook and flipped through a couple of pages. Herk knew those ages would be filled with what he planned to do with Becky on the weekend. "Pete said, 'they's a body back in behind my place, other side of the spring stream, up that ridge back there and down near the big pond on the far side where that patch of pine is. I got traps along the pond, you know, and I was checkin' 'em when I smelled something from back in the bush, and it weren't small.'"

Sam paused here and looked up at Herk. "I used that shorthand I developed, so's I could get it verbatim, you know, just what he said."

"I know what verbatim means. Just get on with it."

"'I took a look-see up that short rise'. This is what he said. 'An' I found somethin' real strange. They's a girl there, what's left of her, under one of those pines, and a bunch of stones that didn't ought to be there all round her. She got funny stuff down one arm and up across the shoulder, them parts the scavengers left enough of to see. She's naked, she is, and somebody cut open her middle and pulled stuff out. Scavengers been at that too. She didn't get herself undressed and lie down there, so somebody put her there and did that. An' it was a while ago, it was, maybe three, four days. She's pretty ripe and bloatin' fast. You best get back there soon as you can.'"

"That's what he gave me, Herk, and I know how to find the place if he doesn't want to go in, but I think he does. He's comin' in to the feed store to load pellet bags. He'll wait for us. That's why I ran the lights."

"You ran the lights because that's what you like to do, Sam. No getting around that, but you were fast enough. Let's grab Bert and go look. Jenny, you get back on the desk and no media leaks. Celia, take what you can from that and see if there are any similars around. Go back a year or so and take it down to Horseshoe and Bowen and over to Comox and Courtenay and up to Port Hardy. Maybe even down to Victoria. Put the results on my desk. We'll be awhile."

Bert Graham was Herk's forensics expert. He came from a farm near the local lake, his daddy a woodsman working for the mill and his mom one of the local primary school teachers. Bert went to university in Vancouver for courses in Criminology and graduated with a degree in Forensics. Herk got him back with the promise of good pay and rapid advancement. He had no idea what he could advance to, but he got him anyway.

The three of them, Bert, Sam, and Herk, took Sam's car down to the feed store a couple of blocks away on the edge of downtown and looked for Pete's pickup. It was parked on the side in the alley near the loading doors.

Sam blocked the alley mouth with the cruiser, and the three of them got out. Pete threw the bag he was carrying in the back of his pickup and walked out to meet them.

"You get told what I saw yet?"

"We got told. Now what we need is for you to take us in, so we can see for ourselves. You know these two." Herk motioned behind him to Sam and Bert. "We'll help you load and follow you out."

He motioned Sam forward and waited while the loading got finished. The cruiser followed the old pickup out the town's blacktop to the side road and down to the one-lane that led back into the bush and Pete's cabin. He was in about four kilometers past the mill. The road was little more than a track in places, used enough to keep it open, but not enough for the town to expend much effort keeping it up. The old pickup was a four-wheel drive and sprung high, so it had no trouble. The cruiser was a rear-wheel Crown Vic with a heavier motor than the commercial version and a stiffer, heavier suspension. It had some trouble with the sand hills and had to maneuver carefully over the bedrock that in places was the road. The tiny streams in the hollows weren't bad, though, and the cruiser plowed through them after the pickup.

Pete's driveway was a different story. Pete had made it himself simply by driving over what was there after he'd cut down the smallest trees. It wandered around the big ones and up and down sharp ridges. Once in the drive to the cabin, Sam finally gave up and hit the horn. The three of them left the cruiser and perched on the load in the back of the pickup while Pete took it in to the house, a two-room place with a tiny porch sitting on a hump of bedrock that sloped down to the narrow arm of a large lake.

The water was deep, and the bedrock ridge the little house sat on was not very wide. On the far side of the arm was another hump of the same rock and rank after rank of fir and cedar as the ridge rose another fifty feet or so. The sun for most of the day came down the arm of the lake, so it was bright, and the water sparkled when it moved and was like a mirror when it didn't.

The three men got down from the loaded pickup bed, Bert with his forensics case, the other two adjusting their service belts. All three helped Pete unload and store his supplies. Then they sat on the tiny porch while Pete explained how to get in to where the body was.

"I gotta take you boys in," he said. "That there pond's a good ways beyond the lake, and there ain't no kind of path other than the route in I use myself." They'd discover that that route wasn't any kind of path either.

The afternoon was dry, the rains having held off. There'd been some a few days before and Herk knew that trace would be mostly gone by now, and wildlife would have messed up what was left. Still, they had to see what they could find.

"You best take us in, Pete, and we'll look around. Gonna have to call in the horsemen, you know that, but we'll do as much as we can. Let's go."

Herk stood, stretched, and they began walking. Pete led them around the end of the lake arm and into heavy bush. The salal was waist-high here, the footing difficult. This was mostly fir forest and cedar with a lot of widow makers thrown in. Pete worked his way around most of them, but they had to climb over a few of the smaller ones. Most of the dead trunks were old and decaying, but the storms last season had downed a good few more, creating walls of debris they had to go around.

After what seemed like hours in the thick bush, they saw the pond, first as a lighter spot in the bush as if sunlight had gathered there, pooling in the clearing in the trees the pond had made. Approaching it was the hardest part: the undergrowth was far more rampant and filled with shrubs and seedlings, and at the water's edge, it was soft with rot.

They skirted the bottom of the pond, and then Pete led them around to the far side and up a gentle rise of rock to a kind of plateau. Near the north end of this flattish area, they could see the grove of pines. The smell reached them then, rich and pungent and unmistakable. They all breathed through their mouths as they approached the trees. All of them glanced up, watching a few vultures circling.

"She's a bit ripe, she is." Pete said. "She's not gonna be pretty, that's for sure. She wasn't when I found her."

"Okay, Pete, you better hang back here and let us look. But I'd appreciate it if you'd stay close and take us back out when we're finished. We'll have to mark a trail when we leave." As they approached the site, vultures tearing at what remained of the girl, hissed and took off in awkward flight.

Herk muttered, "Bloody scavengers, I hate those things. He turned to Bert. "You okay with a ripe one like this? I don't think you've seen one this far gone before, so I need to know you're gonna be good with it."

"I'm good, boss, I've seen them this bad at the Mounties' body farm. But we won't get much, I don't think, not with one like this out here, not after those things got at her. Still, there'll be something, there always is."

But there wasn't. The girl, what was left of her, lay on her back in a tiny clearing beneath two of the largest pines, in a natural hollow with a sandy bottom that had been enlarged by whoever had put the body there. She was naked and badly mauled by scavengers, but it was clear she'd been eviscerated. They could still see the cut marks where animals hadn't gnawed at the entrails and the incision.

"Jesus, oh Jeez," Sam turned away and walked a few steps off. He wasn't sick, but he knew he might be, and he couldn't contaminate the crime scene. That he knew he couldn't do, or he'd never hear the end of it.

Herk and Bert knelt close in and examined what there was to see. "No clothes anywhere near, and she's in a sort of circle of rocks. They look water-washed, so they're not from the pond. Had to come from one of the streams. What the hell's on her arm? That bluish greenish stuff, looks like a pattern, what's left of it."

Bert moved in a little closer. He'd already put on gloves and booties and marked where he put his feet.

"It's something sort of painted on. There's not a lot of it left, but the shoulder's intact and the upper arm. There's the bloat and the discoloration from decomposition, so it's hard to tell, but I think it's mostly circles and stuff. Let me take some photos."

While Bert took the photos and sketched the scene, Herk walked back to Sam and Pete.

"We'll leave Bert to it for a bit. What I want us to do is look around in the bush for the clothes and anything that doesn't belong here. Watch for prints or tracks of any kind. So here's how we'll do it. Pete, you walk a circle round the place. Keep it out a ways, and mark anything remotely like a trail in. Sam and I'll set up a crime scene barrier, not that anybody's gonna be around, but it's what we gotta do. Then we'll look around a little closer in."

Herk and Sam watched Pete work his way into the bush.

"Anybody finds anything, it's gonna be Pete." Sam said. "He's been around here forever, knows every nook and cranny. He'll find a trail for sure."

"What we gotta do is mark it off. The Mounteds are gonna tramp in here and mess around. I'd like us to be as thorough as we can before I call in the Powell River guys."

Herk and Sam began to mark off the area with the yellow crime scene tape, winding it around trees and keeping it well out from the pine grove. All the bright yellow tape would do is draw the curious, but the curious out here would be Pete and maybe another like him. Hikers never came this way, and the pond was too remote for the town's kids to use. Still, Herk thought, crime scene tape was an open invitation, and he had never understood why it had to be so obvious a colour.

Herk met Sam in behind the crime scene and they tied off. They could see Bert still bent over the body.

The two of them returned to where they'd begun and watched Bert gather the evidence bags he'd filled with whatever he'd found and pack them in the case. Herk knew he'd record everything on his little hand-held recorder to add to the photos, sketches, and evidence bags. Some of those were plastic and sealable; some were paper, like lunch bags, for trace that the plastic would degrade.

Pete came out of the bush, saw the two of them and shook his head. He'd found nothing, no clothes, no tracks, no trace. He stood with Herk and Sam and watched Bert.

"There weren't nothing, Herk, but it's been a while. I can tell you though that guy is real good in the bush, real good."

"How do you mean, Pete?"

"Well now, he brought that girl in himself, I mean carried her like, she didn't walk in, I can tell you that for sure. A dead load like that's like carryin' a deer carcass through the bush. It's hard to do without leaving a trail. And there's nothing. Gotta be one huge guy or two guys, a load like that. Even after a few days, I'd a seen something. An' if he didn't use my road in, he's got a long way to go to get back here, a long way."

"Well, he had to come from somewhere. If it's such a long way, he must have used your road. We'll have to take a close look up past your place, maybe find some tracks in the streambeds. There's some sand up that way, more than we plowed through, maybe we'll get lucky."

"Could be you'll find track, but that there road's worse after my place, and it turns away toward the old Johnson place. Nobody goes back there, so it's grown in a lot. I don't think you'd get through anymore. Old Tom uses it, I know, but he don't drive now, and he don't trap much either. Takes in hunters sometimes, makes a bit that way. He's way up near Haslam Lake, though. Makes them guys drive down as far as they can get. Takes 'em in the other end around the bottom of Dodd's, down near Little Horseshoe, an' up that track to the old Johnson place. Could be this guy came that way. Be a hike, but the road's easier than the bush."

Herk nodded and thought about it. "If he came in that way, he'd leave his truck back in there somewhere near that farm just like Tom's hunters. We'll look around up there when we finish here."

He looked over at Bert just as he snapped his case closed and got up. "Bert's done. Anything else you can think of, Pete?"

The old man shook his head. "Nothin' else I can think of. Maybe I'll take a gander up the old road, see if I can spot where he come in, track 'em from there. I find anything, I'll let you know."

"Sounds good, Pete. If you'll do that, we'll leave the road to you and check out the farm from Tom's end. Find something worth talking about, Bert?

"I've got the trace, a sketch, photos. Those water-washed are interesting. I mean, why do it? I spent a long time on those marks tryin' to figure what he used and what the signs look like. Seems to be ink or something, and from what's left, it looks like a bunch of circles and curvy stuff running over the shoulder and down her arm. I think that's worth tryin' to decipher, but other than that, it's just weird, like it's staged for some reason. We need some help on this one, Herk."

"Yeah, we do. Let's get back. We gotta check up by the old Johnson place, then get back to town and give Gordie a call. If you're done, let's go."

Pete led the three of them back out, passing the pond on the other side where the footing was a little better. Sam put up markers, red tape on sticks he found.

"Bit longer this end, but not so many down, and the ridge's a little easier." There were far fewer trunks to maneuver around.

An hour later, Herk and his boys were on their way. Pete had driven them back to the road and the cruiser, and they were all a little ass sore from banging around in the truck bed as Pete wound his way around the big trees and up and down the ridges. It was a long driveway.

Back at the cruiser, Herk reviewed what Pete was going to do up the road and told him to come in when he found something and not to bother if he didn't. After that, Sam drove them into the station, took another cruiser for patrol, and Bert drove himself and Herk out to the end of Dodd and around toward Little Horseshoe. They left the Crown Vic at the side of the old road that Led to the Johnson place. Herk had Bert stop and walk the edge for about a quarter kilometer to look for sign, then walk the other edge back. He'd found nothing.

Herk and Bert could see the old abandoned farmhouse in the distance through the trees and undergrowth that had eaten up the few fields. The farm had sustained Johnson and his wife as long as they could work it, then when they couldn't, one of their sons had come back and taken them out. For a while, Herk and his predecessor had ferried in supplies to the old couple every couple of weeks as much to check on them as to make sure they were fed.

The old house was a clapboard two-storey, a bit out of true even when the family lived there; now it was a scabrous, rundown place, rotting into the ground. The small barn had already fallen in. The two men found where Tom's hunters had parked, and it was a lot farther in than they had thought. There were no tracks, but there was a hacked-out spot on the side that was sort of flat where a couple of trees had been chain-sawed off and the brush thrown aside. That spot, the two of them checked carefully for tire tracks, but the ground was too hard to show any recent activity.

They stood on the road and considered the possibilities. "We can't search the whole place," Bert said, "so why don't we check up and down the road again looking for a way in they might have used. If he carried the girl, he'd look for somewhere a little less rough, maybe a deer trail or something."

Herk looked at the road, shrugged, then nodded: "There'd have to be something all right, so we might as well, but if this guy is as good as Pete says, we're not going to find much. I was sort of hoping for tire tracks or maybe a bit of oil, so we'd know where to start, but what the hell, let's look."

They searched the edge of the old road as far back as they thought logical and then a bit farther, but there was nothing. They walked back in as far as the farmhouse and looked around. Inside, the floor was intact, but on one side, they found a rotted floorboard that somebody had stepped on, and the break was recent.

The two men moved carefully around the edge and saw enough to know that someone had been in the old root cellar. The old door in the kitchen wall had been forced back across the warped floor, and the stairs down, as decrepit as they were, looked as if they'd been used, at least on the sides where they were stronger. A thick layer of dust had been disturbed.

Herk was a little lighter than Bert, so he worked his way down first. He stood at the bottom of the rickety stairs and flipped his light around. When he put the beam close to the floor, he could see that it too had signs of disturbance.

He called up to Bert to get his kit from the cruiser and come down; he'd wait where he was.

Herk was sitting on the bottom step when he heard Bert working his way across the floor. He got up and turned to take the kit from him, so he could get down without the rotting stairs collapsing. At the bottom, both men squatted and shone their lights obliquely across the dirt floor.

Down here, there was a bit more moisture, and although the soil was hard, it looked as if someone had rolled around on it. Bert put on some booties and gloves and began a slow search of the dirt floor. Then he got out the camera and took some photos. He started on one side and ran a grid. Herk had seen him do this before. It was painstaking, slow work: up and down every foot, then across every foot, stopping and gathering trace as he went. And all of it was recorded.

Herk watched his head lamp moving and could hear him muttering into that little tape recorder he had. Though, as Celia had explained, those things didn't have tape anymore. They were digital, whatever that meant. Herk worked his way back up the stairs.

He heard Bert close his case and reached down to take it from him. Once they were outside, he asked, "What do you think went on down there?"

"I can't be sure, but it looks like there was some kind of tussle. Somebody was on the floor, lying down maybe. More than one maybe. Might have been sexual, don't know. I got some trace. There was a small fluid drop near one wall, could be anything from saliva to semen. I'll know better when I get back. There's enough to keep a bit and send the rest to the lab. Whoever it was tried to clean up a bit."

Herk nodded as they stood outside by the front door.

"We need to look around here, see if we can find where he went into the woods, maybe track him. We should look in the old barn and the sheds first, what's left of them, might find some clothes since we didn't at the scene. You could leave the case here. See what's what."

The search took an hour or so, but they found nothing more, no clothes, no indication that the girl or her captor had even entered the outbuildings. The two men walked the perimeter of the farm's old fields where they could. There were deer trails alright, but all they had were the occasional hoof prints in the soft spots. Finally, they gave up and returned to the cruiser, retrieving Bert's case on the way.

Back in town, Bert parked in front of the white picket fence beside Herk's Crown Vic. Inside, Herk made his call to RCMP headquarters in Powell River. As much as anything, it was a courtesy call. The crimes that occurred around Hammil were really looked after by Herk and his men. But Herk now knew this was a homicide and Gordie Parker needed to know about it.

Herk took the Hammil Lake Road to the Beaver Lake blacktop, worked his way around Ireland Lake and took Weldwood Road all the way down to the coastal highway. The rest of the couple hundred kilometers was a lot easier. Once in the city, he took Duncan over to Joyce, took that to Barnet, and swung into the lot that ran down the side of the police building. Headquarters was a two-storey, flat-roofed oblong, bristling with antennae.

Herk parked in one of the reserved spots, and because his cruiser was unmarked, threw his police card on the dash to keep from getting yelled at. At the main desk he talked to the constable and waited for homicide.

Detective Gordie Parker appeared on the stairs a few minutes later and Herk joined him part way up. They shook hands.

Homicide took up one full corner of the second floor. The room had four desks with Parker's office in a corner that had windows looking out onto the street. It had wood walls with glass half-way up. The door had glass in it too. Parker had a desk and two chairs with upholstered seats and backs. Two standard issue grey three-door filing cabinets stood against the wall. Gordie ignored the desk and sat with Herk in the chairs. Once Herk began to describe the nature

ENDGAME

of the crime, Parker called in his two favourite detectives, a heavy guy named Geoff Spurl and a tall, lanky, red-haired one named Frank Miller. They sat on opposite ends of the desk, one of their legs dangling, the other ones braced on the floor. Frank took notes. Herk had a passing acquaintance with both from previous cases.

In less than an hour, they were all heading back out to the site, Herk's cruiser leading the homicide guys in their unmarked. The Chief Coroner had already been informed and would follow later, along with the morgue wagon.

It was a long drive since it took them almost two hours to get to Hammil and another half hour to get out to trapper Pete's place. Herk stopped near the entrance to Pete's drive and honked a few times. While they waited, he described the trail to Parker and his guys.

They heard old Pete's pickup long before it arrived, so they backed the cruisers up and parked where they could at the beginning of Pete's self-made road. As Pete shook hands with everyone, he offered to go in to the site with them, but Parker declined. Herk suspected that Parker wanted his own men to see things fresh.

Pete loaded all the Powell River guys into his old pickup and set off back down the drive. Herk grinned to himself, knowing he'd hear about that ride once Gordie's crew was finished in the bush. He leaned against the cruiser and listened to the fading growl of Pete's old pickup. He stayed leaning on the cuiser's front fender thinking about other murders in and around the town. There'd never been anything quite like this one that he could recall. In fact, he thought, there hadn't been any of any sort for a long time.

He heard the light breeze sighing softly through the conifers and a bit of bird call, sharp and short, nothing he recognized. He looked at the ground by his feet, scuffed it a bit with his toe, took a deep breath and straightened. He walked up the old road a few hundred meters watching for anything out of the ordinary. It didn't take Herk long to realize Pete was right, you couldn't drive this sorry excuse for a road no matter what you had. Still, if anything was there, Pete'd find it. He was better than anyone. Herk knew.

10.

Herk turned the cruiser and went back to town to see what Celia had found. But first he stopped by the diner to make sure Agnes could keep some dinner warm for them all. They were going to be pretty late.

By the time Herk returned to the station, Jennifer had gone home, and one of Herk's men was manning the front desk. During his absence, Bert had been working on his trace, and he was a lot surer now that at least part of the sample he'd found in the old farmhouse's cellar was semen. They'd get DNA, so they'd have the guy cold if they caught him.

Celia was still on her computers as Herk knew she would be. She had three of them, one old one the station provided that she mostly laughed at, and two of her own. She was still combing databases. When Herk tried to talk to her, she shushed him, handed him a couple of pages of print over her shoulder while she fiddled with her keyboard and concentrated on her screens. It seemed to him she lived at the station. She was always there.

Herk didn't understand Celia. She didn't need to work; her daddy had lots. She did too for that matter. She'd said in her interview for the job that she'd written some successful code and sold it, something about encryption, whatever that was.

Once she'd seen the office equipment, she'd looked at Herk in disbelief and had insisted on bringing in her own machines if she got the job. As far as he knew, she still wrote and sold stuff on Her own time, what little there seemed to be of it. She got the job mostly because nobody else wanted it and partly because she had her own computers.

Celia hardly ever left the station. And it wasn't as if she were dowdy or anything. She had glossy dark hair worn long; she was slim but not skinny; she had a nice smile when she used it; and she wore the kind of clothes that made it very clear she had what it took. All his deputies had given it a go, but she just wasn't interested. Sometimes Herk wondered if she was maybe a girl's girl, but there weren't any of those around either.

What Celia had printed out for him got Herk a bit excited, and it took a lot to do that. She'd found two murders on Vancouver Island that were so similar they might have been copies of what he had. Both were close to Harbour City. She'd printed just the bare bones police reports, but that was enough. Herk got up again, opened the door, and walked over to Celia's station.

He was too impatient to wait, so he started right in, but she held up a finger, and he stood there grinding his teeth and fidgeting. Finally, she hit a key and swiveled round. Herk was about to open his mouth when she spoke.

"I know, and I'm on it. I've got the police stuff. That's the easy part and mostly it's through official channels, force to force courtesy. But here's the interesting part. I've broken some encrypted files, well, a little anyway, enough to know that this is a lot bigger than the cops over there. So far, I've got some private detective firm involved, and here's the thing. That bunch is linked with Chinatown in Vancouver. There's a lot of chatter going on between that Harbour City firm and some really big network. I'm not in yet, maybe won't be, but I know it's there and I've gotta tell you whoever's running it is beyond good. I'm gonna be awhile on this one. I'll print out what the cops got for you now. I wish you'd get with things, so I could just send you stuff. Print copy's slow and a pain in the ass."

There was a pinging sound that seemed to be coming from the computers, and Celia whirled around and started hitting keys. "Shit, shit, shit! They know; they're inside my firewalls. I gotta go. Go away!"

It was like the rest of the world didn't exist when stuff like this happened. Celia was gone and wouldn't be back until she
damn well felt like it. Herk sighed and went back to his office.

The printer in the corner had spit out a wad of paper. Herk picked it out of the tray and began to reverse the order. He never did understand why the machine had to print the last page first and made him do this all the time. It just seemed perverse. He sat and began reading. The reports were very thorough and well written, a hell of a lot better than anything the Powell River office put out.

Apparently, the Harbour City RCMP had a real mess on their hands. There were two killers who had murdered two young girls and had escaped every attempt to apprehend them. The cops knew a lot, knew there were two, knew that the girls were local and where the perps had found them. They'd been close, damn near caught them if you read between the lines. The cases were still ongoing, but cold now, and the manpower had mostly been redeployed.

A BOLO had been sent out, but just on the island. It was pretty useless anyway, Herk thought, the description of the vehicle and the two men was so vague it could be any number of either. Herk could think of at least three pairs of brothers in his own town who'd fit, and the vehicle, well, there were hundreds of those around. Then he thought of the murder he had and the lack of trace.

More stuff came spewing out of the printer and Herk got up to retrieve it. This batch had a lot more material. There was a report from a profiler with the RCMP, a report from a Professor at SFU in Vancouver on what the marks might mean, and the original forensics reports along with the autopsies for both girls. Herk started reading again.

The profiler had a pretty clear picture of who this guy was and confirmed a partner. The Prof guy had identified the marks on the girls and offered an explanation. And there was a report detailing background on the girls themselves.

One of them was Chinese and visiting Vancouver relatives. She'd come from Singapore. Herk would look that up. He had no idea where it was.

Now he was beginning to understand the connection Celia had found. Vancouver's Chinatown was a tight-lipped community run by a fat old woman if his sources were right and they usually were. She had a massive presence electronically he'd been told. At least someone in her employ had. It looked like Celia had disturbed her network. She wouldn't like that at all, Herk thought.

If the killers were going north, he mused, there's no reason they couldn't have left the island, crossing over at Courtenay-Comox or even going up to Port Hardy and shipping over on the Queen of the North to Prince Rupert. Then come down from there. There was a new ship, he knew, that replaced the one that had run aground because the crew on the bridge had been screwing around. He didn't know if the name was the same. But around here it'd always be the Queen. He figured the cops would have had that covered, and the airports, even the tiny bush ones, but maybe not fast enough or maybe not long enough. Herk knew all about budgets.

He took out his own notes and began to write up a murder book, at least his version of one. He spread all the copy out on his desk and started to set up a timeline from Harbour City on. He took into consideration all the variables, used a kind of flowchart to accommodate them, and added notes as he went. It was a time-consuming process, but it both clarified his thinking and gave him a sequential record he could refer to when needed. Besides, he had little else to do before Gordie Parker called.

He'd first met Gordie at the shooting range. There was only the one in Powell River, and Herk and his men had to qualify occasionally, and they had to do it there. Herk went in more regularly, and that's where the friendship developed. They shot together, and their scores were close. That was the cement in their relationship, the close scores. It became a competition, one besting the other a bit. And from there it went to dinner in town and a few beers, always at the pub since they were both single and had no interest in cooking. Whenever anything came up that involved the force, Herk tried to get Parker as the lead.

The call from Gordie came in around seven, just before the light began to fail. By the time he and his men got to town, it would be getting on to dark. He checked with Bert who was still in his tiny lab and as he passed Celia's little cubbyhole, he glanced in. He decided not to disturb her. She'd likely still be there when he got back from dinner, and maybe she'd have more stuff he could look at. After that, he'd kick her out, check with the night patrols, and go home himself.

Herk lived out on the lake in a small frame house painted green and trimmed in black. The town's lake, the one beside his house, was called Bass Lake, which was odd since it contained mostly lake trout. It was a small lake just big enough for a boat to make sense. Herk had a runabout at the end of a pontoon dock, and when he had the time, he fished for the trout. He didn't cook much, preferring Agnes's creations to his own. Mostly what he kept in the house were breakfast makings like eggs and bread and porridge. There was also a good supply of snacks and an even better supply of single malt scotch. It helped him unwind after shift, sometimes a little too much.

Herk had a small covered porch on the back of the house, and when it rained or when he just wanted to watch the water, he'd take a glass and a bottle out there and sit and drink slowly. He had a kid come in to keep the grass down in front and look after the small garden in back. It was mostly flowers and had been there when Herk bought the place five years before. He didn't quite know what to do with it, so he just left it. There was a boat house for the runabout, a sixteen-foot Lund aluminum hull, with a stripe down the sides. But that was for winter and the fall storms. Usually, it sat at the end of the dock where it was more convenient for runs to the trout holes. There were three he knew about, and he would sit in the Lund and fly fish.

Herk left the office and got to the restaurant just as the squad car pulled in. Gordie was driving. The three men got out of the car as Herk joined them.

"That was a hell of a mess, that was, both the route in and the body. The coroner and the morgue guys are still out there and he was royally pissed mostly because the body's way back in the bush, and he had to ride in that old pickup. He always wears the wrong shoes, you know, leather ones. Never learned to keep boots in the car. The morgue truck is stuck at the end of that bloody lane, can't get any closer, so the guys have to carry her out including out that damned driveway."

Gordie Parker sighed deeply. "It's a bad one, one of the worst I've seen. And whoever did this is one sick bastard. Let's go in. We need something to drink, then we'll see if we can eat. Jesus."

Agnes had set up a couple of tables in the rear and the four of them took seats and ordered beer. The detectives were tired and hot. The beer went down quickly, and Agnes brought seconds without anybody asking.

"Bert's gonna be here soon. He's just finishing up. I brought everything Celia got from Harbour City and the pair of murders they have over there. Lotta politics going on there, sounds like, it'd be nice if we could avoid that." Herk smiled at Gordie. "Not going to happen, is it?"

Parker shook his head, "If this one ties to those, and it probably does, the shit'll hit the fan pretty damn soon. We'll get the autopsy results from this one in a day or so, and stuff from the lab. Bert's forensics report should give us something too. This beer's good, but we better eat something." Geoff and Frank nodded when Gordie looked at them, so he stuck up his hand and Agnes came over.

"It's late boys, but I saved some good stuff for you all. You can have either roast beef with mashed and veg or some fresh trout the cook caught before his shift. He's got some stuff to go with it he's whipping up now. What you bunch don't eat, we will before we close. There's lots of pie left for dessert, and I made it myself. So what'd ya think?"

"Gimme the beef and mashed," Gordie said. Herk nodded agreement. Geoff and Frank both ordered the fish. "Oh, and some coffee with it if you don't mind."

"You all want some?" Everybody nodded. "I'll make a fresh pot. Gimme a minute."

Agnes walked over to the swinging doors at the kitchen and put in the orders. They could hear her messing with the coffee maker.

"We should leave the heavy stuff until we've finished eating. But let's talk ideas about this mess." Gordie looked around and the others nodded.

"I'll start," Herk said. "Me and Bert were first on the scene, so I'll tell you how it went. Bert can give you the details later. You know all about Pete, the drive in, and the body. Pete did a circuit way out. Couldn't find anything like a trail in. He also checked the road up past his place after he dropped you guys. Same result since he didn't call. We went in from the other end, way down the end of the lake, then over toward Little Horseshoe to the other end of the old road that goes up past Pete's. That end of the road's overgrown too, just like past Pete's, but old Tom Boakes takes hunters in there sometimes, and the upper part of it's passable. We found the cut out where they park, the hunters, but we couldn't find where our killer parked, and we looked.

"We think he came in that way, and I'll tell you why. It's what we found in the old farmhouse. It's rotting into the ground and isn't very safe to walk around in, but somebody's been in there recently. We found trace and disturbed dust, signs of a tussle on the dirt floor of the root cellar.

"Bert did a grid and got trace from one corner on the dirt floor. He thinks is either saliva or semen or both. He's pretty sure that there were two of them down there, maybe the girl as well. It's not hunting season, there are no fresh tracks anywhere, so it's gotta be our guys. We tried to find how they went into the bush, probably carrying the girl, but other than deer tracks, we got zilch. You guys need to go out there. It's the cleanest site I've ever seen. Nothing."

Geoff said, "Look, Frank and I can do that if you'll mark the map for us. Do we have any stuff from the site at all, I mean barring the autopsy and lab work, anything we've found personally?"

Herk shook his head. "No clothes, and that bothers me a lot, and so little trace. What bothers me even more is we can't find how they came in. They had to carry the girl, so how did they do that without leaving enough trace for Pete to figure out? He's the best we got around here."

"We'll bring in dogs if we have to, but the trail's so cold now, I don't think even the dogs'll get anything." Gordie looked at the other two who were shaking their heads. "Yeah, you're right, it's too damn late. They'll get piss all. Probably start after deer and run us ragged."

They all turned as the kitchen door opened and Agnes appeared with a whole series of plates running down both arms. The four cops watched her walk across the empty restaurant wondering how she was going to put the plates down.

"Here ya be guys, two beef, two fish. The red stuff on the fish is a special sauce. Hope you like it." Agnes slid the first two plates down on the table and somehow the next two were in her hands. Once they were down, she retreated to the counter for the coffee.

"Hey, this red stuff's good!" Frank looked around, "Really good!"

Geoff took a fork full of fish and dipped it in the red sauce. A bit reluctantly, he put it in his mouth. Everybody watched as he chewed. When he smiled and nodded, they all dug in and ate. Geoff was the one with the touchy stomach. Anything out of the ordinary, he usually refused to taste, and on the occasions he had, at least in their company, he'd made a quick trip to the john and come back looking a little pasty.

The four of them had almost finished with the main course before Bert joined them. By the time he was seated, Agnes had a plate of the fish in front of him, and he dug in. Bert came from a family that ate fast and he quickly caught up. Over pie and coffee, they once again began to talk about the body they'd found.

"The small sample I got is semen all right; that much I can give you. The lab'll confirm when the report comes back. I don't know whose, but it seems to me the only thing it can be is who we're looking for. It could be just kids, but then I'd expect more trace. The grid gave me just that one sample and some scuffing. I've got photos for what they're worth. That farm is remote, and what bothers me more than the lack of trace is how far out it is from the crime scene. We can't find any sign of how the girl got to where she was found. Not from the farm end or from Pete's end. Nothing. And no clothes anywhere." Bert took a bite of pie and looked around the table.

Herk said, "She had to be either sedated or dead when she was taken through the bush to where we found her, had to be. And I'd go for dead. There's no sign she was killed there, and there isn't enough blood around. Pete says this guy's very good in the bush. He can't find any trail in either. We're thinking we got two guys, same as on the island. Celia's found two similars near Harbour City and had a bunch of reports on them. Two guys, a girl whose identity we don't yet know, a kind of ritual killing it seems like, no evidence of how she got where she was, no sign of a vehicle, virtually no trace. We don't have much."

"Okay, we got zip from the scene. That's not too surprising given how old it is, but getting nothing about how she got there, getting nothing about a vehicle when we know there was one, that's just weird." Gordie sat back, put his fork down, and pushed the empty pie plate toward the center of the table. "And what else is weird is how staged the whole thing is. Even with the predator damage, that site was very carefully arranged. And we have no idea why."

"Well, we have," Herk said. "As I said, I've had Celia working similars and she found those others near Harbour City; here the site's near Hammil. I don't know if there's any significance in that, but there sure is some in where the girls' bodies were found and how they were laid out. We need to go back to the office, take the conference room and lay all this stuff out. Most of it comes from your headquarters over there, Gordie, so you'll have more than we have, but Celia dug up the connections and a bunch of other stuff. We need to look at it all before you guys go back. I've tried to work out a timeline. Let's go if you're done."

Herk stood to cover the expenses with Agnes at the register where she was smoking one of the two or three little wine-dipped cigars she allowed herself each day. She followed them out and locked up after them. By the time they'd reached their cars, the sign was off and the main room's lights were down.

They drove to the police building two blocks away. Herk took them to the small conference room where the rectangular table was covered with paper.

"Grab a seat, guys. Bert can you put on some coffee for us when you get your photos and sketches?"

Herk set up the overhead projector and slapped a page on it. Celia had been at him to get a PowerPoint program that projected from a computer but Herk had resisted. He dimmed the lights a bit, and the first of the reports from Harbour City showed on the screen.

They spent the next couple of hours going over what Herk had gathered together. Around eleven, they took a break. Herk's dispatcher had called out and one of the night crew brought some fresh coffee and donuts. They ate and drank standing up and wandering around the small complex of offices. All except Celia's, of course, which was still occupied.

They returned to the conference room a bit less sleepy. By one in the morning, the five men had reviewed everything that Celia had found and had talked over the site in question. They were so exhausted they could hardly see straight. Gordie, Geoff, and Frank waved from the cruiser and took off. Herk and Bert straightened up the conference room and left for home.

By the time he got to his house, Herk had gone from exhaustion to wakefulness, so he hauled out the scotch and a crystal glass and sat on the back porch watching the lake. It was like black glass out there until something disturbed the surface. There was just enough ambient light to see a suggestion of foreshore, then the sleek black of the water. The only sound was the occasional Canada Goose talking to its mate. The scotch was smooth and smoky and Herk sipped and sat and felt the quiet seep into him.

He fell asleep in the lounger, but the clunk of the bottle as it hit the wood floor brought him back. He retrieved the bottle, the glass still in his hand. Fortunately, it hadn't fallen. Or he'd have had one less piece of the Cross and Olive he kept for the scotch. Fine whiskey needed fine crystal. He took both in with him and went to bed.

11.

It was getting dark as Alan dropped Spence off on Powell just west of the Starbucks. She walked down the slight grade across the railway tracks and turned up Raymur. She was supposed to meet Red where Raymur crossed Cordova, but the girl was nowhere to be seen. Spence glanced up and down the street, puzzled. The whole stretch was deserted. It should be busy by this time.

A single car drove slowly down past her and turned onto Glen a block down. He'll likely circle and come back down the alley, she thought. There was usually at least one girl over on Vernon by the alley mouth, so when the cars circled round, they'd slow there and take their time coming back. Spence watched for the car while she waited, but it didn't reappear. Strange, she thought, where the hell is everybody? And where the hell's Red!

Spence walked back and forth until her temper began to fray, then she marched up to Campbell and looked around. When she found Red, she'd ream her a new one.

There was no one on that corner either. There were a few cars trolling, but only a few, and they weren't stopping. Spence didn't get it, there were no girls and no johns. She walked back down to Raymur.

She stood irresolutely on the corner for another few minutes, then turned and began walking down to Powell so she could walk up to the Starbucks at the junction. She hadn't gone more than half the block when Red stepped out from a deep doorway on the other side of the street and motioned her over.

"Sorry, sorry, sorry, but vice raided the place, and everybody split, me included. Pain in the ass, those guys. They don't do this often. Hardly ever, but they took a few of the girls in this time, so we all had to, like, get the hell out, you know. Must have been a dozen cruisers all came in at the same time, really messed things up. Me and some of the girls, we hid in the alley. One of the parking spots's got a fence, you can squeeze between the wood doors you know, so we just stayed there. I waited until it was clear and came back lookin' for you."

Red looked so apologetic that Spence's anger evaporated like mist on water. She sighed deeply and smiled. "Well, at least we're both here. I guess some of the girls'll be back. From what I've seen, though, we won't get much business tonight, not that I want any, but you know what I mean."

They stood on the corner for a while, watching the occasional car slow and look around. When one of them pulled up beside Spence, Red bent down to look at the driver, but he'd spotted a tall, leggy tranny coming back from the Hastings overpass and took off toward her.

Red shrugged. "Maybe that's why the cops came, you know, scare off the weirdoes like the one you're lookin' for. A big raid like that, we get sort of freaked about it for a bit, but you wait, in an hour thing'll start up again. Slow maybe, but they'll speed up. Let me look at you."

Red stepped back and ran a critical eye over Spence's outfit. She stood hip shot, one arm propped on the other elbow, one finger tapping the side of her chin, as if she were in a store looking at a mannequin dressed in something she wasn't sure about.

"Well, it's pretty good, you know, alls you need is some work up top. Jeez, that bra's not doin' you any favours. Look, I brought a real nice pushup for you. Come down here, we'll find a spot in the alley, you take your top off and try this on." She reached in her bag and pulled out something so lacy Spence could see the streetlight through it.

"Might as well wear nothin'," Spence muttered.

"You got nothin' to wear nothing for," Red said.

"What the hell, Red, I got tits, and they're not that bad!"

"Yeah, yeah, like a skinny fourteen-year-old. Look, you gotta have somethin' goin' on up there, and you don't. So when you're short a bit, you get some help. This'll help, trust me. Now get your top off, I seen'em before so don't go funny on me."

Spence rolled her eyes, stepped into a doorway in the dimly lit alley, and removed her top. She reached behind and undid her bra and made a grab for the flimsy thing Red was holding out. She dropped her bra in her bag and fussed with back hook of the new one.

"Jesus, Red, this thing's a couple of sizes too small!"

"Only the cups, Sweets, that's so's to push what you do got up and out where it needs to be. Here, let me."

She reached behind Spence and did up the bra. It was tight alright. Spence still had her top in her hand, so she slipped it over her head and tugged it down. Red wiggled the top, pushed up underneath the cups and stood back. She eyed the effect, did a bit more messing with it, stood back again, and nodded.

"It'll do okay. Gives you something to sell, anyways. I'm not sure I like the top much, though. You bring any of the others? Better yet, you bring the waist cincher? Man, that'll do it with that top."

Spence reached down to her bag, pawed around a bit, and yanked out the waist cinch. Red helped her on with it.

"Oh, man, that's it, that's perfect. Here, look at yourself. Come out here and look." They both picked up their bags and moved down the alley a bit.

She showed Spence her reflection in a glass door that caught what light there was in the alley. Red reached up and undid another of her buttons, then stood back admiringly. Spence was appalled. She looked like a hooker.

Shit, she thought, I am a hooker. Spence stayed in front of the mirror, not looking at her image, but musing over what Alan would think. She wondered if he'd still feel the same way about her if she dressed like this. Or would it turn him off? Would he hate the look and her with it? She wasn't sure he'd separate the two different girls.

Spence heard Red sigh behind her and tap her foot a few times. She turned and smiled, then turned back to the mirror-like door, thinking, I read somewhere that people respond to images. 'They become what they behold'.

Spence looked at herself once more, turned around, and checked her rear view. She stood hipshot, wriggled her fingers at herself, smiled.

"Okay, Red, am I ready to go?"

"Jeez, about time! You look good, babe, real good. You're gonna get a lot of attention in that getup. You just gotta think like us a little, you know?"

"Right, like that's what I want, to think like you, no offence. I got a job on the other side, sort of. I gotta admit, though, in this outfit, things do get altered a bit."

Red waved her hand around. "Whatever. At least you look like a girl now and not like some sort of mix. You gotta loosen up some, Spence, let it out a bit. I mean, your guy, he can't be happy with the getups you wear. I mean, it's okay, like, for when you're home and bein' sloppy, but you gotta show him some respect, give him somethin' to want. Jeez!"

They left the alley together and stood on the street. Little was happening, but they could see someone up on the corner at Campbell and a couple of cars coming around. So maybe the street was slowly returning to normal.

Spence turned to Red: "So what am I supposed to do here? Do I just stand around? And what happens when somebody stops? How do I look for this guy? How can I tell him from an ordinary john?"

Red stood looking at her. "How the hell do I know, you're the cop, you tell me. Alls I know is he's gonna be around sometime, right, I mean he's got three girls now, prob'ly all messed up or something, an' he's gonna be lookin' for more, an' you're here to make sure he doesn't get 'em. Especially me! An' you're supposed to find Sugar, right? So how you do that, that's your bag."

Red sighed dramatically. "The johns I can help with. Look, when they stop, you lean in an' be all friendly like, and ask what they want. Then when they tell you, you just say you don't do that if it's weird, and for the normal stuff you just keep your price high, okay?"

"So for the normal stuff, what's high?"

"Jeez, I'd a thought you'd know that already! Okay, here's how it goes. A blowjob's sixty, that's mostly what you'll be asked for, a regular screw's like a hundred, like that, okay? So you ask for more, sometimes a lot more, if the guy looks like he's got it. You act like you're classier than the rest of us, like you're slummin' just for kicks. So you can back off if you want to, right?"

"What happens if the guy agrees with the price, then what? I mean I'm not doin' it, you know."

"Tell him you have to pee or somethin' and take off. I'll watch you some unless I get busy, just don't get in a car, alright?"

Spence nodded. She wasn't happy with the deal, but at least she could watch the girls, see if she could spot the freaky one. She hadn't a clue how she'd do that. She could trip over him and she wouldn't know. And if it were the psycho they were looking for, the same thing applied. She wouldn't know him from any other john. Unless he tried the taser, she thought, then she'd damn well know.

The two of them walked up to Campbell, discussing things as they went, crossed over the T-intersection, and continued up to Heatley. They stayed there for a while along with some girls who spent their time wandering the sidewalk as far up as Hastings and back. Then the two of them walked on up the street to the Firehall Theatre at the corner of Gore. Here, they crossed over and sat on the steps of the Anglican church, that huge white building Spence and Alan had seen when they first got here. It had long, slit windows and looked more like a flat-sided, weirdly crenellated castle than a church, except for the cement steps and the monumental front doors. Its bulk dominated the street, but it didn't stop the action on the far side. Red left Spence there and walked back across the intersection.

Spence watched Red stop and talk to a girl in a short white dress and black pumps. The girl was svelte, moved gracefully, and seemed barelegged. She had her hair down so it covered her shoulders, and with her light brown skin, she almost glowed in that dress.

Cordova. Only the other side had girls, so that's the way the traffic flowed. Spence had a perfect vantage point.

She and Red had set it up this way when they'd finished talking it out down on Raymur. Red would work the street down one side and Spence would follow on the other. That way, she'd blend in as one of the girls, wouldn't have to fend off the johns, all of whom were on the other side trolling, and she could keep an eye on what was going down. From her side at each of the corners, she could see up the streets and cover the cross-street action as well. It was a decent plan, but it still left identification iffy.

Spence sat on the church steps and watched.

When Red left the corner and walked back down Cordova, she followed, sauntering along, trying to imitate the walk and the manner. The more she looked like what she pretended to be, the better her chances. Spence felt different. The longer she was here, the more she felt a part of it. She could almost smell the lust, almost taste it, as if it were a kind of effluvium that seeped out of the street itself.

In tandem, they crossed Dunlevy, then Jackson, both busy corners. The next one down had the mission on the corner and was crowded with the wreckage of the east end: the homeless ones, the habitués of the street, the druggies, and the drunks. Only one girl stood near them, but on the other side of the street. No girl would stand on the side where the groups of lost ones waited for the mission to open. Ironically enough, Spence thought as she stood on the north side of Cordova and watched, this street was named Princess.

Red didn't stop there long. She sauntered down toward Heatley where there was better action. Spence did the same.

Here, cars formed a long, slow line, feeding off Hastings and turning onto Cordova. There were a few girls along that block and three more on the corner to catch the trade coming down the one-way. Spence stayed on her side and watched. She didn't like being more visible here since there were no doorways to slip into and nothing on the side street but the blank paneled walls of small industries and storage facilities.

Cordova and Powell looking as much like a hooker as she could. Only the occasional car came her way, and none of the few that did even slowed. She felt a bit insulted. After all, she looked good, even Red said so.

She watched a dark van slow on the cross street and cruise along close to the girls. She couldn't make out the colour in the glow from the corner lights. And when the stop light switched to red, it was even harder to tell. The van crawled along, the driver's window down, a man's arm hanging out the side. He stopped three or four times to talk to the girls, but no one got in. Like the cars, he turned the corner and drove down Cordova.

Something about the van didn't sit right with Spence, but she couldn't put her finger on it. She'd wait to see if it returned. She'd call Alan if it did. He was circling the area in a sedan the force used for surveillance, one from a drug bust that didn't stand out here.

Spence had her cell handy in the bag slung over her shoulder and she watched intently. And now she saw the van again. She moved closer to the wall as she watched it creep along. The arm was still there. She was pretty sure it was the same van. She wondered what about it had caught her interest. The driver stopped twice to talk to some of the girls. Again, no one got in.

That's it, Spence thought. No one got in.

Spence crossed the four-lane and walked up the west side of Heatley. She caught Red's attention, and the girl sauntered over.

"We've got something maybe. That van, the dark-coloured one, it's been around twice now and nobody's interested. What's he doing?"

"Walk up to the corner and come back down my side. I'll ask, see if he's serious or just lookin'. Some of 'em do that, you know, just look, maybe for a couple nights before they pick up any of the girls. I think they look for a favourite, chat her up a bit, then come get her, you know?"

"I'm gonna give Alan a call. He's circling around somewhere, and he can swing by, do the lookin' thing and watch the van."

"Okay, Sweetie, you just watch yourself, you look so good, I'd pick you up myself, and you're gonna be on the right side of the street."

Red planted a peck on Spence's cheek and trotted across the road to join the others. As Spence watched, Red began talking to a couple of the girls, one of the ones the van driver had talked to.

She fished her cell out of her bag and called Alan as she sauntered up the street toward Hastings. She gave him her location and watched Red talking to the girls. Then she crossed with the light on Hastings and began to walk down the busy side of Heatley. Before she could get to Red, a large black car slid into the curb beside her, and the passenger window went down. Inside, she could see a man in a suit, dark hair, tie, and glasses. He leaned across the seat and Spence leaned on the doorframe and smiled at him.

"You're a pretty thing, why don't you get in and we can discuss things."

Spence chuckled. "Well, Hun, we usually do that first. What'd you have in mind?"

"Get in where it's comfortable. I don't like bargaining on the street."

"No way, Sugar, we do it this way or not, your choice." Spence raised her eyebrows and waited.

"I don't care about the money. Whatever you charge is fine. I need to get off the street here. I don't like cruising like this."

"A man with unlimited funds, I like that, but I'm not getting in until we settle things."

Spence was getting a little desperate. She had no idea how to get away from this guy, and she couldn't stand here like this all night. She was about to tell him no dice when Red sauntered up and stuck her head in the window.

"Hey man, you want a BJ? You don't want her she's lousy, me, I got a mouth you won't believe."

The driver stared at her. "Get off my car. I'm not talking to you, I'm talking to her. Take a hike."

"Hey, maybe you better just watch your mouth." Red stuck her head farther into the car.

The driver slammed the car in gear and hit the gas. Red whipped her head out just in time, gave the door a quick bang with her fist as he peeled off the curb. When the driver heard the thump, he slammed on the brakes and got out. He walked around the car, looked at the door, then started for Red. About four whistles went off as the girls blew for help. The guy stopped, turned, jumped back in, and took off around the corner.

"Pain in the ass, those guys. All they do is come around, make us feel like dirt, you know, like we're trash, then piss us off and leave. So we use the whistles. Scares the shit out of them and they go away. The rest of the guys, they're okay, all they want is a quickie. Those pricks want you all night for next to nothing. Screw 'em. You alright?"

"Yeah, I'm alright. Anything from the girls?"

Another car slowed, and Red was about to saunter over when Spence said, "It's Alan, let me talk to him, and then you come over again if you like."

"No, no, Sweets, that's perfect. You talk to him like you did with that guy, then get in and let him take you away for a bit, then drop you back. It'll look like you're working, and the girls'll like you better they think you turned a trick."

Red elbowed Spence in the ribs and chuckled.

The car sat at the curb, and Spence sauntered over. She leaned in the open window, grinned at Alan, and watched his eyes travel down her top. Red was right, he seemed to like what he saw. "So, big boy, what's it gonna be, you want a blow job?"

"Jeez, Spence, just get in, will you?"

"I dunno. Let me stick my ass in the air out here for a bit like we're bargaining." She looked at the discomfort on Alan's face and relented. "Okay, okay, hang on a sec."

Spence turned, waved to Red, opened the door and got in. Alan pulled away and turned the corner onto Cordova. He stayed on the street to the bottom of the hill, then hung a right and took Raymur down under the overpass. He pulled into the parking lot for the apartment complex just past the bridge and parked.

"I found the dark van you were talking about. He was up on Gore, pulled over, talking to a girl in a white dress. At least he was trying. She looked like she wanted to get rid of him. Couldn't stop there, so I went round again, but he was gone. The girl was still there. I drove the circuit again, but there's no sign of him. What made you focus on him?"

"I don't know. It's just that he was there, talking to girls, but no one got in. That's not so unusual according to Red, but there was just something about him."

"While I was driving around, I got a call from Jake and Larry. They got the creep they were looking for, so they banged on him for a bit. Their words. He's being booked for assault, but they say it doesn't look like he's the one taking the girls. He was jammed up in North Van on a disorderly last couple of weeks. So maybe we're looking for something like that van. And it might be our guys, so we gotta be extra careful."

Spence nodded. "Take me back to where you got me, then maybe expand your circle, take in the surrounding area, especially the alleys, and maybe the residential pockets. Also the park over there where we met Red, and that long street behind it. There were some bushy places along there. He could be around here. Any dark vans, grab the plate numbers and run them. I'll hook up with Red again, and we'll keep on with the stroll. Looks like the van's all we got."

"Already on it. I checked a couple of streets over, did a sort of grid. I'll expand it after I drop you. If that van's around, we'll find it."

Alan pulled out of the lot, went down to the T at Union, took a right, then another right up Campbell to Hastings. He turned left with the light, made a right onto Heatley, and dropped Spence where he'd found her. He also gave her sixty bucks in case anybody asked.

When Spence got out, there were only a couple of girls on the block, and neither of them was Red. She walked back to Hastings and sauntered up to Gore looking for White Dress. She covered the stretch down Gore to Cordova and up to Hastings twice and found nothing: no Red, no White Dress, no van. It was getting late and her feet hut.

She didn't know how these girls did it. She had more sympathy for them than she'd had before, and a much better understanding of how things worked. It was dangerous, tiring, and demanding in a different kind of way. The girls had to be good, they had to be attractive, engaging, they had to fake damn near everything from liking what they did to the guys they serviced. Still, the girls kept coming back to the stroll. It was a way of life for most of them. In many cases, not just money, she was sure. Maybe the ritual dragged them back night after night. Or maybe the flavor of the street, a mix of lust, fear, hunter and hunted, and the camaraderie too. There must be easier work she thought.

Spence leaned back against the wall of the building on the corner of Cordova and Gore, grateful the night was almost done. It was close to one, and girls who had been here all night were still leaning in car windows, smiling, and taking tricks. She found it beyond depressing. Spence waited for the light, then crossed Cordova and turned down toward Campbell once again. She took it as far as the bottom of the hill, then called Alan.

He picked her up at the end of Cordova where it teed into Glen, drove down to Powell, and turned back into town. They'd circle until they spotted Red, and when they did, Alan would pick her up while Spence lay down on the back seat so the other girls wouldn't see her.

"I cruised every street, did a grid, found a few vans, but only one looks promising. I took down the plates of any that weren't white, so I've got three we can run. But I found a dark-coloured van I think might be the one we're looking for parked over on Malkin behind the park where we first met Red. No one in it, but it's a possibility. There's no computer in this heap, so we'll have to call the plates in. Get Jake or Larry to run them. There's Red."

"Yeah, that's her. Gimme a moment here."

Spence flattened herself on the back seat, and Alan slowed the car and crept along following Red. They were on Gore again between Hastings and Cordova, and Red was on the corner talking to White Skirt. Alan stopped just short of them, and Red detached herself and sauntered up. She took one look at Spence curled up on the back seat, grinned at her, then got in the front with Alan. As they rounded the corner, she waved and said, "Hey Spence, good move, stay down 'til we're outa here."

She slipped her hand onto Alan's thigh and made him squirm a bit. "Jesus, relax why don't ya, I don't bite. Well, not unless you want me to. You gotta pay me anyways, so the kinky stuff's free just cause it's you, hun."

Red patted him on the thigh a little higher up, leaned over the seat, and said, "Jeez, Spence, you didn't tell me he's so much fun. An' here I thought the pair of yous was straighter than rulers."

Spence sat up, stuck her face in Red's and gave her a peck. "You don't know the half or it, Red, we're lucky to keep our lease the way we carry on. We just look straight for the job, you know?"

Red rolled her eyes, "Yeah, and cows got wings. You two could use some kink, but you'd need a manual to get it right, Jeez."

"Okay, enough you two. I found the van. It's over on the street back of the park. I'll drive by, see what you think."

"I got somethin' for you too. You know the white skirt girl? She goes by Glory on the street. She's seen this dude before, but not with a van. She thinks he's a short guy who walks the streets sometimes and stares at the girls. They all think he's a bit off, you know, like somethin's missin', so they try to ignore him. They think he's harmless, but this one time? She told him to grow up and come back when he did. Made him mad, that did. She's not sure it's him because she can't tell how tall he is in that van, but he looks like the guy. Problem is, Glory's not so hot on details, like, so she can't describe him very good. Just he's got this funny look and his hair's straight back, and his voice is kind a whiny, you know, like high pitched maybe."

"That's not too bad," Alan said, "Short and a high-pitched voice, can't be that many of them around walking the streets. Anyway, here comes the van."

He'd already crossed Prior and turned onto Malkin. Ahead of them lay the wide, flat, grassed area of the park and the toilets with their clerestory windows dulled with grime, throwing a feeble light into the night. On the street in front of them just down from the toilets was the van. There were no streetlights here, just the diffused light from the warehouses on the far side and the parking lights of the occasional semi idling on the other side of the street. The van looked dark, but the true colour was still indecipherable.

Alan parked behind it, and all three got out. He pulled a flash from the beneath the dash, and they looked in the cab through the driver's side window. The body of the van had no windows. There was nothing in the cab, just the usual crap on the floor and slips of paper thrown up on the dash.

Behind the seats, though, the van had a wall with a perforated panel in it and maybe a door. It was hard to tell.

Red had disappeared while Spence and Alan were checking out the van's interior, and as they walked down its side looking for telltale marks they could use to identify it if they saw it on the stroll, they saw Red sauntering out of the gardens on the path that led down into the park proper. The garden area behind her was pitch black.

As she reached the rear of the truck where they were standing, Spence rolled her eyes and shook her head. "Red, we don't know where this guy is, and if this is the van, the guy steals girls. You need to stay close."

"I had to pee, Jeez, lighten up can't ya?"

"We've got what we can get here, let's take off and check the plates, see what that tells us. Red, where can we drop you? You gotta be done for the night."

"You owe me sixty bucks, you do. I don't do this for nothin', gotta live you know."

Alan reached in his pocket, peeled off a series of twenties and gave them to Red.

"For services not rendered for which I'm grateful, no offence. We need to get rolling. Everybody in please."

"Let me off over on Glen. You wanna do this tomorrow night, Spence, you meet me the same place at eight, okay?"

"If I'm there, we're on, if I'm not, you'll know we got other stuff to do. Okay?"

"Sure, be nice to see what you put together though. You did pretty good tonight."

"My feet hurt, my back's sore, and I need a shower. I don't know if I can take many nights like this one."

"You get used to it, an' then it's kinda fun, you know, an' the money's good most nights. Let me out here."

Alan had turned on Prior and then made a left at the ice-cream parlour on the corner. They were two blocks further down when Red told them where to stop.

"I got a place down there," she said, pointing down a short street ending at the rail tracks and a high chain-link fence covered in what looked like ivy and fronted by a thicket of blackberry bushes. Across from the little row of two-storey houses was the wall of a commercial business of some sort, one of those light industries the city was so gung-ho about these days. Beside the plant and the railway tracks was an alley that ran down its side and curled around its back. Alan turned in to an overgrown dirt track on Red's side of the street to let her off.

Red pointed at the alley beside the plant on the other side. "This's hooker alley this is. Girls doin' short tricks use it. There's a couple of them around here, the other one's down a block. It goes around some houses leads to garages, an' comes out like this one on Glen. Both good places, the cops don't bother us. You might wanna look 'em over some, see if you can spot that van messin' here. Thanks for the lift, see ya tomorrow Spence."

She thumped the door with her palm, waved to Spence, and sauntered off. The two watched her turn up the walk leading to the last house, a two-storey clapboard that looked tired in the dim shadows of the streetlight.

Alan backed up, turned, and took the surveillance car back to the station. On the way, it started to rain.

12.

When Herk walked into the station in the morning, Jenny just rolled her eyes at him, no hello, no where the hell've you been, and no donuts. He knew something was up.

He entered his office and saw Mickey the Mayor grinning at him.

"You got a problem here, Herk, my boy, a big problem, and I need to find out what you're doin' about it. Got some flak from the townies on this one, so here I am. Why don't you set a bit and we'll discuss it?"

"You're in my chair. But nice to see you up so early." Mickey didn't move.

"Must be that jerk Harvey Couch you're talking about. He's always up in arms about something. Why do you care? Just because he's a lawyer doesn't mean squat to me and shouldn't to you."

With a sigh of reluctance, Mickey levered himself out of Herk's chair and came around the desk. He was a head shorter and a good bit heavier than Herk, but he had a presence, you couldn't deny that. It was part of his success and part of what kept him mayor, and he used it with a razor-sharp, cunning intelligence even if he did sound like a hayseed.

"We gotta take this one seriously, Herk, the bugger's gone and done it again. He's talkin' to his cronies in Victoria. So now it's political, and I've got to do some sweeping. Let's decide how to shut them up, him too."

Herk took his desk chair and the mayor pulled a chair from in front of the desk around to Herk's side and sat facing him. This way he could talk without feeling he wasn't in charge. Even though he wasn't, not in a murder investigation.

"So what's the problem, Mickey, I mean other than the obvious? You got a burr up for some reason other than Harvey?"

"Well, now that you mention it, I surely have. Election's coming up next year again, not that I have any worries about that, but I got that prick Elton, our good ol' district MPP, makin' noise again, and I don't need that right now. He gets goin' and we'll have the same mess we had with those two fires and that body couple years back. I gotta have something to shut him up with, and as I understand it, you got piss all."

"Your understanding's wrong, Mickey, I got a lot of stuff, I just don't have a way to use what I've got just yet. And here's what you don't and shouldn't know. Gordie Parker and his crew are on it too because we got links to other murders like it on the Big Island. The Mounteds are already involved over there and now they are here. You're the only one outside the force who knows about that link. So you've got the power of their brass in your corner; I don't see how either Harvey or Elton can hurt you much as long as they don't catch on. Unless they do, we're fine."

"Didn't know that, Herk. I probably should have in spite of what you said. You're holdin' back a bit on this one, aren't you? You're usually up front with me on things, so why not here?"

"The Mounteds' brass is putting a kind of equal and opposite pressure on Victoria. That's what I hear, and that's probably why Harvey's foamin' at the mouth this time, and why that prick Elton's down your throat. I got asked to keep it down, so that's what I've done. Nobody knows anything about the links except the guys in Powell River, me and my crew, and now you. And that's against the rules, so I gotta know I can trust you not to blow this one, or we're both gonna be steppin' in more than we can scrape off."

Mickey sat perfectly still for a few moments, then sighed and nodded. "This is gonna turn into a ripe pile of horseshit, isn't it? We gotta keep the stink down some. How're we gonna do that, Herk?"

"First off, we let the Mounteds take the flak. Let them make the press releases, and the more they step in it, the less of it gets on us. Beyond that, use whatever threats you can on that asshole Harvey. Let him grumble all he likes but keep him away from Manchester's loony Ted. He never gets anything right, but he can do a lot of harm to both of us in that crummy paper. Derek'll publish it after he cleans it up some. He's like that, and he's always been opposed to having you as a kind of perennial political force in the town, you know that."

"Yeah, but he's been fair with it, never screwed me too bad. Still, with this one, you're probably right. I got some stuff on Harvey I've been saving for emergencies, and I guess this qualifies. I'll look after him. Elton, though, he's another can of worms. If the Mounteds can't shut him up, we're gonna have a problem. You gotta keep me in the loop from now on, though, fuck the brass."

"You're in now, and I'll make sure you stay in, but it's gotta be between us. Just us, not my crew, not the guys in Powell River, just the two of us. If we keep it that way, we'll make out okay."

"Okay, you best get back to it, and I'll be moseyin' along. Any time you want a beer in the evening, gimme a dingle." With that, Mickey sauntered through the outer office, out the door, and across to the hardware store. Jenny watched him go, shook her head, and walked into Herk's office.

"You gonna tell me why that blowhard's been in here again?"

"I know you got a bug about him, but he's good for the town, stable and fair mostly, so be nice. I can't tell you what I don't know. He was in here bitchin' about being bothered again with a case that's getting some notice upstairs. The usual political stuff, and Mickey's getting old and less willing to bend sometimes, that's all it is."

Jenny stood in the doorway leaning on the frame as she always did. Herk could tell she didn't believe a word of it, but she'd live with it as long as he didn't treat her like a secretary, and he always made sure he didn't. He'd have to be extra careful. She had her radar out, and any little misstep, she'd call him on it. He hadn't lied to her yet. Just a few evasions and no tells.

"Can you get Celia for me? I need to know what's happening with the misper report."

"You can get her yourself; she's where she always is. I'm not your gofer, Herk." With that, she left, head up, a sense of hurt pride radiating from her like heat from a woodstove.

Herk shook his head. Didn't take me long to fuck that up, he thought.

He walked down the corridor to Celia's room. The computer screens were lit as always, and stuff was streaming across one of them. Celia was totally absorbed. Herk knocked softly and she turned, looked at him for a moment while her eyes adjusted, smiled, and waved him in. That was unusual; mostly she was too distracted by what she was doing to bother until he made himself a nuisance.

Herk leaned in the doorway and asked, "You got anything on that misper? The girl we found out at Pete's?"

Celia leaned back in her chair. "If I had, you'd know, Herk, I always slip that stuff along as soon as I get it. So why are you here?" Herk sat in the one chair that didn't have piles of printer paper on it.

"Well, this one's got some heat behind it, so I thought I'd check just in case."

He smiled at her. She wasn't hard to look at what with the long black hair and a figure to go with it. Her clothes were always top quality, stuff that looked simple and easy but was anything but. It was also revealing without being what he'd call obvious. She wore heels and he could tell they were the best. She was a gorgeous girl all right and he couldn't understand why she wasn't batting off the guys with a big stick. Not the girls either, he was sure of that.

Celia smiled back, a twinkle in her eyes. She always knew what he was thinking when he looked at her like that, and she found it amusing. "I sort of gathered that, what with the constant activity I've been looking at, especially between Powell River and Harbour City. And then those privates and the guys in Vancouver. Something's bubbling away, that's for sure. I can give you a little more now than I could before but not about the misper. Nothing there yet and I've been looking. I can send you the rest or I can just tell you the gist of it."

"Okay," Herk said and waited while she sorted stuff in her mind. "The crap's hit the fan in Harbour City. Two of the lead detectives on the murders, the similars I sent you, have been sent to Vancouver East detachment. As far as I can ferret out, they're there to help the local force with some missing girls. Everybody's afraid it might be the same killer or killers. The RCMP cops think there's two of them. Seems the two cops used two private detectives and a citizen in their last attempt to get the two killers. They got close, but since they lost them in a botched surveillance over there, and the killers might be here, they've been reassigned."

Celia took a sip of coffee and turned to Herk, continuing, "It's political, there's tons of press. There's also some connection to Chinatown and some encrypted stuff going back and forth that I haven't been able to break yet. Unfortunately, they know I'm there snooping, so I'm not going to have a very easy time getting in, but I'll keep trying. They know who I am, but not how to get at me. I'm going to write it all up tonight and print you a copy. I'll work offline, so no trace."

But Celia knew there could already be. She knew the Chinatown computers had already registered her probes, probably sent a spider out, maybe riding a program inside her firewalls. They probably had ones that not only caught stuff in its web, but also renamed files and sent them back, whether incoming or outgoing. Those programmers could own her computers and install a keystroke program through a back door along with other devices that cloaked anything they did. She'd run diagnostics for sure. She'd be careful, but even diagnostics couldn't find what really good guys hid, and the Chinatown programmers were the best she'd ever seen.

Herk thanked her and walked back to his office, sat in his chair, and thought about things. If his murder was linked to those in Harbour City, and it looked like it was, the perps had to be around here. Unless, of course, they'd just dumped the body and moved on.

There were still no answers as to why they'd disemboweled her and marked her the way they did. Well, if these were the same guys, there were some ideas. That professor from Simon Fraser seemed to understand what those marks meant, at least he had an opinion which was more than anybody else had. And the profile, that nailed down what kind of animal he was dealing with. Add to something homemade, not commercial, and there was a chemical analysis attached to the report. But there wasn't much that they knew that did them any good.

Their perp was a psychopath, big bloody deal. From what he'd read, Herk knew those guys were like everybody else except they had no conscience. He'd read in the profiler's report that they were successful in the communities they lived in. Well, that let out most of his friends, him too, but included people like the mayor and such. So basically, it could be anyone who made money and was good at what he did. Owners of companies, stores, stuff like that. The only sort of lead he had was that whoever it was, if he was still around, he'd be new in the town, and there weren't many of those, maybe only two or three in the last while. The problem with that was these guys could go dormant for long periods if they wanted, at least that's what he gathered from what he had. That seemed to be the current idea anyway, so looking at just the new ones wouldn't get him very far.

But if they had any sense, he thought, they were long gone. That's what he would do, dump the body and get out. But he wasn't a psychopath and didn't think like one. He knew they had their own logic. No matter how bizarre what they did seemed to everybody else, it seemed perfectly reasonable to them.

"I gotta dig that damn report out, and the one from the prof." Jenny stuck her head around the door. "What?"

"I didn't call, just talkin' to myself."

Jenny rolled her eyes, muttered, "Weird", and said to Herk, "You gonna do that all day? It's distracting is what it is. I can hear you out at the desk. Can't you do that under your breath like everybody else?"

She was still pissed over his conversation with the mayor, Herk thought. She had a long memory for stuff like that. He'd have to call her in and give her something that didn't matter, just so she'd stop tryin' to listen in on everything he said.

"Maybe you oughta take a seat for a bit, or better still, put somebody else on the desk and come to lunch. There's some stuff you oughta know."

Jenny grinned at him, stuck up her thumb and said, "Be right back, don't you leave without me."

Herk knew calling someone in would make her feel important, more than the receptionist she was. Still Herk liked her and didn't want to lose her. Throwing her occasional bits and feeding her lunch was a small price to pay for office harmony.

They left together for Agnes's place just as a cruiser rolled in. From the other side of the street, Herk watched Sam climb out and head inside. He smiled to himself. Sam could drive, and he could help with investigations, but his telephone skills were something else. Usually he just cut people off. Then Herk had to smoothe some ruffled feathers, especially from the old biddies who called regularly to report nothing much.

At Agnes's they got the usual booth in the back, and Agnes brought them coffee. Over lunch, Herk gave her the bare bones of the case they had. Nothing about the connections Celia was working on and nothing about Powell River's connection with Harbour City and the murders there. He trusted her, but she wasn't the craftiest girl, and a good reporter could worm stuff out of her. It'd happened before, and on this one, Herk was determined to avoid leaks.

Once they were back in the office, Jenny relieved Sam before too much damage had been done and sent him back to patrol. Herk sat thinking again, quietly this time. He rummaged through the files he had and dug out the profiler's report and the one from the professor. He laid out the autopsies on both girls from Harbour City and the background investigations. Then he just sat and looked at it. Sometimes his best hunches came from just looking over what he had.

He pulled out his timeline sheets and put them on the side. The autopsy from his own vic wasn't in yet nor were the detectives' reports from Powell River. He could understand Gordie's reluctance to forward half-baked stuff, but he needed what they had to add to Bert's forensics report. He grabbed the phone, hesitated, put it down, and sent an email. Safer than the phone, he thought, what with the big ears around his station.

Herk studied the reports in front of him. Then his phone rang and Gordie said: "We've got some activity on the net, so you won't get anything over email except polite fuck-offs. Our guys are working on who the hell it is and how he got in, but to be safe and to keep reports between us, it'll be phone and personal from now on. You good with that?"

Herk glanced toward Celia's office. He'd have to tell her about this asap.

"I'm good," he said to Gordie. "We need to talk though, so how about one of us comes to the other, probably be me, and we can go over everything again. I've got some questions and I'm sure you have too. Can't hurt to talk. Anything on the misper yet?"

"Zip in BC, and everywhere else." Gordie said, "Yeah, we need to get together, and I need to get out of this madhouse, so how be I come there, we can grab some dinner and spend the evening at your place. Bring what you got home with you. I'll bring the stuff from here. We got the forensics report now and the autopsy results have been promised for later today. I can be there by six, that work for you?"

"Meet me at Agnes's. I got some real old scotch at my place needs drinkin'. You can stay over. Spare room's ready."

"Best offer I've had in months. Be good to get the hell out of here for a night. See you at six or thereabouts."

Herk grabbed his hat, walked over to Celia's cubby hole, told her about the probe on the computer system at the Mounteds. When she looked at him with big eyes, he asked, "That was you?"

"Shit!" she said, "Yeah, I'm in there, but I was sure they didn't know. I got some fixing to do before they find their way back here. Go away."

Herk watched her from the door for a bit, decided there was nothing he could do. Then he told Jenny he'd be out for the remainder and to leave any messages on his desk.

"Anything I can help with?"

"Nope, I just need some time to myself, sort out what I got and decide where to go next. I won't be in till tomorrow, so you handle the office. Schedule's posted, so it shouldn't be too bad. Appreciate it, Jenny."

"Have a good one, whatever it is."

Herk thought her tone was okay, so he didn't feel bad about leaving her in charge or about skipping out. He'd like to get in a spot of fishing before dinner. Besides, he thought better in the boat out on the lake where nobody could get at him.

The afternoon sun had a sort of quiet haze in it that softened the bird calls and turned the water by the dock a kind of copper colour. It was unnaturally still out there, kind of hushed as if the day were waiting patiently. The air was saturated, heavy, and the rushes in the shallows were upright and unmoving, like green spears stuck in the mud. Herk sat with his coffee, wondering if he'd bother getting the boat out. Seemed a shame to disturb something so peaceful.

As the afternoon moved on, the lake stretched out in one clear, glistening, copper sheet. The haze got so thick, Herk felt as if he could walk down to the dock and grab handfuls of it. Nothing moved.

The afternoon stumbled along, the air grew fat and pressed down harder on everything. Herk dozed off. The rumble of distant thunder roused him, and he looked at his watch. Five thirty already. The water looked listless, flattened. The thunder came again. Herk looked off past the lake toward the mountains, but they were gone in a blanket of heavy cloud.

He went inside and threw some water on his face to wake up, took his rain gear off the peg in the hall, and drove into town. By the time he got to the diner, the wind had picked up, gusts throwing bits of paper and a lot of dust around the street in scooting, swirling eddies. The thunder rumbled almost constantly now.

Herk took a booth by the window so he could watch the wind and the swirls. When the rain began, it danced off the asphalt like corn popping and was soon moving like a thick cloud through the streets. He saw Gordie's car turn in, water cascading out from the front tires. He parked as close to the front steps as possible and Herk watched him dive from his car to the stairs, holding his hat against his head.

Gordie hung his wet jacket on one of the hooks on a post at the edge of the booth. He put his hat on top and wiped his hands across his face as he slid in. Agnes brought coffee and set fresh cream packets on the table.

"It's a son-of-a-bitch out there. The road in is damn near covered. I had to take it easy in the big dip just before town. Must be nearly a foot deep on the road. Didn't want to stall."

"You boys need more time or do you wanna order now?" Gordie looked up at her and smiled. "I'm good, gimme the beef again if you got it. Herk what're you having?"

"He's having the beef too," Agnes said. "It's the only thing left now. Had a run on everything else over lunch. Still some pie, though, so we're good to go." With that, she turned and headed for the kitchen.

Gordie grinned. "The pie makes everything worth the effort, especially hers, best damn pie around, including the River. I'm gonna enjoy this, screw the storm. We'll just wait it out, have more pie, see which peters out first."

Herk grinned back, nodded, reached out a hand, shook with Gordie, and said "It's good to see you. This mess lets up tonight, we'll get in some good fishing in the morning."

The storm took its time leaving the town, grumbling ominously. Herk and Gordie waited it out, polishing off the pie in one of the round plastic pie trays that lined the counter. The rest were already empty. They sat back then, watching the rain turn to drizzle. They paid up and left.

The lot was still covered in water for the most part, but it was way down, and they could see the pavement through it. In a few minutes, it would be just wet, glistening asphalt. Gordie followed Herk out to the house, and they sat on the covered rear porch up near the back wall where it was still relatively dry. They drank old scotch neat over ice.

The evening had calmed nicely, the wind just a memory. The lake was still a bit roiled, waves sluicing in and shifting. The air was clear, the heaviness gone along with the heat. It was a lot more comfortable both inside and out.

About an hour later, they went inside and spread the reports out on the floor in the living room, pushing the chairs and the coffee table back to make room. Gordie had brought the autopsy and the forensics reports. They compared them carefully with the ones from Harbour City. The similarities were unmistakable.

The problem was that none of the reports had anything that helped them with the identity of the killers. That there were two killers was now a certainty. Who they were was the big question. They both pulled out Roberta Cannon's profile.

"How'd you get yours?" Gordie asked.

Herk sighed. He'd hoped Gordie would ignore the fact that he had a copy. "Celia's better than good at this stuff. She got it, and the prof's report on the marks. I don't ask her how, I just take what I get."

"Yeah, sure you do."

Herk grinned at him, shrugged, and Gordie said, "Who the hell cares how, you got 'em that's all that matters. Let's look. See if anything pops. Oh, and you better tell Celia we're on to her. Don't worry, I'm not gonna spill the beans, but the guys are good at our place, and they know someone's screwing around."

"I already did that. I've been reading till my eyes hurt. Can't see anything useful. But maybe we can talk it out, see what we get."

Almost an hour later, they had more detail but nothing they could act on.

"Son of a bitch, we're gonna look just as stupid as the guys in Harbour City, even stupider, we haven't even had a chance to chase them. We got shit."

"I think it's a one-time hit. I think they're long gone. But I don't think like them, you don't either, Gordie, so who the hell knows. It's what I'd do, you too, but if they're gone why be so careful? They left us nothing. We still don't know where they came in or how they got the body where they did."

"No, wait, Herk. That's not true. You remember the old Johnston place? We know they were in the root cellar there, and they did leave some trace. They broke a floorboard in the living room, and they left marks in the dirt floor of the root cellar. And then Bert found semen. It's just there's nothing about what they left that tells us who they are, where they came from. It's that we still don't know how they went from the farm to the bush, the site. Because there was no sign even though they'd have to have carried the girl."

"Okay, let's talk through the profiler's report again. Even simple stuff. It's got a few things. The profiler's some woman named Roberta Cannon. She's a criminal behaviour analyst, a fellow, that's what they call her, certified by the International Criminal Investigative Fellowship. She belongs to you guys. You got two and the Ontario guys, the OPP, they've got the other two. Only four of them in the country, I guess."

Gordie nodded and said, "I'm way ahead of you, Herk, I already know about her and she's damned good. So, paraphrase, maybe we'll catch something we missed."

"Okay, here she says serial ritual crimes like these are very rare. And this guy is even rarer because he's very controlled, hasn't escalated, doesn't make messes, leaves nothing behind except victims. She goes on about how rare this guy is because of the control he has, and says he'll have no criminal history, but he'll have a hunting ground, a specific one he goes back to, and a disposal area that's so huge, he'll be hard to pin down. Hmm. She's sure this one has a partner. And she says a lot of these guys get their vics from a specific ethnic group usually, but that's not the case with this one. She says psychopaths like this one, have an area they hunt in that's special, either one they know well or one that's likely to contain the type of person they're searching for. Okay. Here she thinks the disemboweling has a sexual basis, and for reasons she doesn't know, our guys gain power from doing that, apparently."

Herk shifted on the floor, redistributing his weight on his thighs. "She says here it gives the top guy dominance in some way, and he'd have to repeat the rituals exactly step by step if they're to work, so he'll be really finicky about things like that. And he might return after the cops are finished to make sure everything is as it should be."

"Shit! We should have put someone on the scene."

"Wouldn't have helped, Gordie. If we'd put a guard in, he'd have seen him and just waited us out. Okay. There's more. She says he's between twenty and thirty-five, probably on the younger side, very intelligent, lacks any empathy, is Caucasian, had a strict upbringing that isolated him, but he'll look good, be attractive, seem just like the rest of us. She says he'll stick close to the investigation, and he'll get his jollies from our bumbling around trying to catch him."

Gordie nodded, "Yeah, so if that's true, he's still here, and he'll stay here and watch our progress. That's something we missed. That's good. Maybe we stand a chance of getting this guy if he sticks around."

"Here's something else. She says the second guy will be submissive but a willing participant, under the thumb of the other one, sort of like a cult of two, she says. The more the top guy does this, the more powerful he feels, so he'll keep doing it."

"Okay, what we've got we didn't have is he sticks around. He wasn't here before because this is our first case, so he's new, in the last month at least. That's something. We need to focus on that."

"Let's see what pops up in the prof's report." Herk picked it up.

"Read it like you did that one, maybe something else'll jump out."

"Okay, a lot of the same stuff here. Our guy's controlled, the rituals are important to him, have to be repeated the same way each time, probably goes back to fix the scene when we're finished with it."

Herk read on in silence for a bit, then started again.

"Here's the dirty on the inky drawings on her arm. They represent a kind of threshold between this world and the next, the one the soul enters after death. There's something about duality and the wheel of life... Okay, this is good. He thinks our guy's intent on delivering the girls he takes to the other side through a repetition of the rituals. The circular symbols, he thinks, represents circular time, the concept of death and rebirth central to western religions. He thinks the guy wants to move them from one world to the next to fix something wrong about them. He talks about the colour and says it fits too. This bluey green. He thinks the symbols are a kind of shorthand that has a message, but we can't read it because we don't understand his reasoning. But he thinks the ritual both isolates the two of them and creates a new reality for them. It's pretty academic stuff as you'd expect from a guy with a doctorate teaching at a university. There isn't much here that helps us, except our killer's got to repeat everything exactly. So he's got to stick around and repair what we mess up. Same thing the profiler says."

Gordie sat quietly considering what Herk had read. Finally, he said, "There's something there though. Look, if our guy is sort of delivering the girls and he needs a certain type, and he needs to do this ritual stuff all the time, he's gotta have a job that gives him leeway to search and find them. That's a limited market, don't you think? So we can maybe make something of that. Look for new guys, two of them, who get jobs that give them a lot of free time. If they haven't gone, then maybe we can find them."

They discussed what they had to do and who to contact the next day and how to go about checking anyone who was new to the area. Finally, after midnight, they gave up, had a final small scotch on the back porch where they watched the stars and listened to the night calls.

Morning crept in without waking either of them. It was only when the sun slid over Herk's face and threw red light through his eyelids that he woke. He sat up groggily and winced a bit. The headache was one of those throbbing ones, and he regretted that last scotch.

He shuffled out to the kitchen, put on some coffee, and grabbed the aspirin. While the coffee perked, he went to the small bathroom and splashed water on his face and brushed his teeth. When he got back to the kitchen, he saw Gordie bending over the perking coffee pot, studying it as if it were some strange specimen he hadn't seen before.

"It's a coffee pot," Herk said, "It makes coffee. The bubbling sound, that's the stuff inside getting ready."

Gordie turned slowly. "You're a wiseass. Jeez, my head hurts, we didn't drink that much. Must be the cheap scotch you buy. Got any aspirin?"

"What's that little bottle next to you on the counter, the one with the cap off?"

Gordie grabbed a couple of the tablets and dry swallowed them. "You want some of this, or you just gonna make snappy remarks?" He was waving the pot around; some of the coffee slopped out of the spout and made a crescent of brown on the linoleum floor.

Herk glanced down, said nothing, looked back up, and grinned. "You're supposed to put it in a cup. There are some of those right above your head." He pointed at one of the cupboards.

Gordie sighed, mumbled something about mornings, and got out two. He poured, added milk to one, and handed the other, black, to Herk. They sat at the kitchen table, blew quietly on the hot cups, and sipped.

"It's after eight, there any sense getting the boat out?"

"It's a touch late, and it's sunny, and it's pretty still. We'd get a tan if we went out and it'd be quiet. Still, wouldn't have nothin' to cook."

"Great, no fuckin' fish. What've you got for breakfast?"

"Burnt eggs with coffee or Agnes. Got no bread, forgot it."

"Agnes then, probably better for us anyway."

They carried a second cup out to the back porch and sat looking at the morning. It was clear and still. They could hear something messing around in the cattails, and there were the sounds of a few Canada geese out on the lake having a dispute. The sky was cloudless and the sun warm, so they moved their chairs out a bit and sat in the sun, sipping.

Agnes's place was busy, the smell of bacon and eggs heavy on the air inside. Herk and Gordie got their usual booth in the back, and Agnes brought them more coffee. She stood waiting; the two men looked up and mumbled "Eggs" at the same time. Agnes nodded and left.

"What the hell did we just order?" Gordie asked.

"Three eggs over easy, hash browns, whole wheat toast, double order of crisp bacon."

"All that?"

"Yup. You know I was thinking on the way in, we got no idea how these two guys get the girls to go with them willingly. I mean, why would they? And if they didn't, how the hell did they manage that? Not one of the autopsy reports notes any defensive stuff, and there were no marks on the bodies to indicate the use of any kinds of restraints. So how did they get them?"

Gordie said nothing for a while. He just sat looking past

Herk's shoulder. Then he looked directly at him. "Think. What could you subdue someone with that made him immobile immediately and left only a tiny trace that you could hide easily with, say, cut marks?"

Herk sat up and after a minute or so said, "A bloody Taser!"

"I'll bet you breakfast that's what they used on the girls. I mean, look how easy it'd be. Just walk up and nail them. And if you did it carefully, you could place the marks where you were gonna cut later, especially with what girls wear now. Keep 'em out that way till you got them where you wanted, then use something else or maybe Taser them again. If you knew what you were doing, you'd leave nothing on the bodies, and you'd have the dose just right, enough to incapacitate but not enough to kill."

Agnes returned with small plates of toast and larger ones of bacon, eggs, and hash browns running up and down her arms. She slid them all on the table. While they ate, they left the case alone. When they were finished, they got coffee to go, paid up, and went out to the lot. They sat in Gordie's unmarked and went on with what they had.

"Okay, say they Tasered the girls. What then? If they kept that up, they'd probably kill them, so how about this. They use a Taser to get them into the car or whatever, then they sedate them with something like Ativan or whatever, maybe even roofies, keep them down that way. No marks, no nothing, and they could do whatever they liked to them. What gets me is no evidence of sexual interference. Why take them if you don't want them for that? I know, I know, the ritual stuff, next dimension, and all that. But nothing sexual, no penetration, nothing. Why not?" He sipped his coffee, grimaced, and put it in the holder.

"Maybe the whole point is to get them over to the other side, fix 'em that way. Maybe there's no need for sex. But if I remember from what you read out last night, Roberta, the profiler, said there had to be a sexual motive. And if there was, why no signs of anything sexual. Is there some sexual thing they could do that didn't leave any sign at all?"

Gordie paused and rubbed his chin. He added: "Then again, we always find them late, like the one here, days afterward, so much is degraded, the bodies're so far along, maybe there's nothing left to find, especially if they used condoms. How the hell would we know if there'd been anything like that? Even the autopsies might not find anything. It doesn't necessarily mean there wasn't anything."

"You got a point. There could have been something, and we wouldn't know. Both coroners found nothing, though, and both thought it unlikely there had been anything other than the ritual stuff, and I guess they'd have a better idea than we would. Still, you might be right. But even if you are, where does that get us?"

"About where we were. Look, we can't solve anything the coroners can't, so let's concentrate on the other thing we talked about. We know these guys stick around to see what we're doing. Both reports said that. If they're right, we need to get going with looking at newcomers and tourists. Here for sure, but maybe the River as well. Didn't the stuff we got say these guys use a huge disposal area? If they do, then we'll have to look near or in the city as well as outside. There'll be literally hundreds of possibilities, everywhere from Hammil to Powell River and all the tourist places in between. That's a lot of acreage. Shit!"

Gordie took a sip of his coffee, swallowed, and poured the rest of the cold drink out the door.

"I've gotta get back today, and it's already near noon, so let's go to your office and set up some kind of plan. We start, even if it's not much."

They took both cars up the street. Both Jenny and Celia were in, the deputies were out on patrol. Herk stopped at Jenny's desk, said good morning, and told her he'd want everybody in later in the day. He'd let her know when.

They sat in Herk's office and set up a search grid. They'd start by investigating all new arrivals in Powell River and Hammil, then they'd have to check all the new arrivals in the hotels and camps as well. They divvied up the search area, Gordie taking the larger chunk since he had more resources to throw at it. It would take weeks to run everybody down. Since the killers would appear normal, all they had to narrow things down with were that they were new to the area and that there were two of them.

Gordie left an hour later. Herk asked Jenny to call everybody in, then run over to Agnes's and get a tray full of coffee. Squad cars pulled in over the next half hour or so, lined up at the picket fence like so many piglets. Deputies gathered around Jenny's desk until the place was overcrowded. It didn't take many. Glancing out his office door, Herk got up and went out to the front desk.

"Okay, all of you into the conference room. Grab a coffee from the tray and sit. Quietly."

Once everybody was down with a cup, Herk filled them in on what he and Gordie suspected. He laid out the big picture, indicated what search areas had been decided, who was doing what, and assigned patrols for town and for the surrounding countryside. Their job was to stop any suspicious vehicles containing two males, roughly twenty to thirty -five, who were new to the area and if anything seemed off, to haul the occupants in for questioning and impound the vehicles.

"Use any kind of violation to pull them over. Invent one if you have to. If you suspect anything once you know how long they've been around, find something to keep them, broken taillight, whatever. Bring them in. We can always apologize later if they get the wind up and we're wrong about them.

"Try to be nice about it. Lots of yes sir's and no sir's, but get them in. Use whatever pretext seems likely to work. Last thing we want is a lawsuit, so be on your best behavior. I don't expect much of anything from this, but we gotta try. And no cowboy stuff, no sirens, no lights, just a friendly violation stop. That's the way to do this. Just be vigilant, okay? These guys are killers."

"Are we supposed to know what to look for?" Arnie asked.

Herk shook his head. "There isn't anything in particular. What I'm askin' is for you to use your best judgement. It's not likely you'll stop anyone who raises your hackles. You have to keep in mind that one of these guys is a psychopath. He'll be charming, cooperative, nice as pie, just like everybody else. That's why this exercise isn't gonna get us anything much, but we gotta do it, just in case."

13.

Sabina was in her part of the office on the second floor of Harbour City's old firehall when Harry got back. He'd spent part of the day with a client in Duncan finishing up a fraud case. Isabella was at the front desk.

"You're back already? Not much goin' on in that field of yours?"

"That field, as you know, is our bread and butter; that's a mixed metaphor, isn't it? I'm sorry if that's hard for you. I'm a detective, so I understand them."

"Harry get in here and leave Izzy alone, she's got enough to do without you bangin' around out there."

"Detective, now there's a misnomer. You can't find your mail half the time."

Izzy jerked her finger behind her, glanced down at the keyboard, and began to type, ignoring Harry.

"Hey, big boy, you get that case settled? You been at that one over a week, and I got something much better for you."

"Of course, it's settled. Izzy's invoicing it as we speak. So, what've you got that's so interesting?"

"Murder most foul. Actually, I don't mean to be cavalier about it. We really do have a murder, another one by our two escapees looks like."

SHH Investigations had been formed over a year ago after Harry and Sabina had gotten together in Vancouver s year ago during a fraud investigation that turned into a murderous manhunt. A bunch of thugs were determined to stop them from investigating by whatever means possible.

ENDGAME

Harry had been on his own until he'd gotten mugged in an alley. Sabina and a girl named Red, habitués of Vancouver's east-end stroll, rescued him by screaming their heads off at the alley's mouth.

Sabina, it turned out, was anything but what she appeared to be both in terms of sex and vocation. She was a transvestite who loved the flavour of the stroll but not its customers. She was also an expert computer programmer. As a sideline, besides her love of the effluvium of east-end nightlife, she drove motorcycles in competitions. Red, her friend, was what she was, a hooker with a temper.

Sabina had gotten caught up in Harry's case because she'd found an envelope Harry had dropped in the alley when he was being beaten by the company's thugs. Later she looked for him on the stroll to return it, not knowing she was being watched. After that, both Harry and Sabina were on the run.

They finished that case with lots of help from Chinatown, a hacker, and the cops, and virtually destroyed the large construction corporation that had been responsible for everything. The prime mover, however, the head of the whole thing, managed to leave the country before the cops got to him. In the ensuing uproar, several political heads had rolled.

Harry brought Sabina back to the island, his home and the location of his old business, and reopened the office in the old fire hall, this time with Sabina as a second operative. Together, they started a larger operation, SHH Investigations. Sabina and Harry were partners and two others from the island, Will, another PI, and his sidekick, Rory, joined them as associates.

Isabella, a brassy blonde who manned the front desk, didn't take crap from anyone. As far as the phone was concerned, Isabella called the place S and H Investigations since saying SHH on the phone was, as she pointed out, bloody ridiculous. She thought Harry a lightweight and Sabina a classy broad and wondered just how permanent the job with them would be. Time didn't mellow her, but it changed her impressions. She knew they were good together even if Harry seemed like a bumbling fool.

Harry and Sabina hadn't been in business a year before they became involved in the hunt for a psychopath who was murdering girls, leaving them posed in the bush in ritual positions no one but the killer understood. The finds were gruesome, involving severe mutilation and strange painted symbols. Even though the bodies were posed, they would not have been found quickly had it not been for hikers in one case and salal gatherers in another who stumbled on them. There was no logic to it.

The local RCMP detachment assigned the case to Alan Kim, a quiet, dedicated homicide detective, partnered with Spence Riley, a fiery dark-haired beauty. They joined forces with Harry and Sabina and finally trapped their suspects. They got very close to an arrest, but the suspects escaped.

"It's the same guys, Sweets, same kinda bush site, same circle of rocks, same markings, same mutilation. But it's over near Powell River on the mainland, back in the interior. Some place called Hammil, it's around Dodd Lake somewhere. Local cops and the Powell River detachment are on it, and I've got the dope."

"You sure? Sort of hoped that pair had given up, but of course, they wouldn't, would they? Better call Will and have him tell Rory. We'll have a meeting, and Izzy can get donuts, cinnamon ones. Where the hell are Alan and Spence?"

"Vancouver, H, remember? Their helping the locals over there on a missing girls case in the big city. Might be our guys there too. I set up a link with them. I know where they are over there and what they're doing. I set it up so we can keep them in the loop on this one if they aren't already and so we can mine whatever they get. Still, you know what the forces are like. They never talk to each other. Turf, I guess. And if it weren't for Jim in Van and keeping my own check on things, I wouldn't know either. The missing girls on Van's east side, that's what Alan and Spence want info on. It sounds like it might be a separate matter, but who knows. The brass is going apeshit again over the one up near Power River. Add all that to the Pickton episode that's still on everyone's mind and you can understand the panic. There's already talk of a task force forming, and you know how useless they are."

"But you have hacked everything I assume, and you have Jim and by extension Chinatown mixed in, so we're good aren't we? Better still, nobody knows you got your fingers on their privates except us, so we're like inside traders or something. Did I mix my images again? Print everything you've got, and we'll spend tonight going over all the stuff, among other things of course, then let's hook everybody up and see what happens."

"Fingers on their privates? Jesus, H, that's gross. It's gonna take me a few hours, so you go play with reports or better still, dig up all our paper and our copy of the old murder book, and we'll piece it all together tonight."

"I'll make fresh coffee and get Izzy to round up some grub. We're gonna be awhile."

While Isabella was out to lunch, Harry started on the filing cabinets they still kept in the back room. Even though the office was run electronically, Harry liked paper and kept records of every case. Well, Isabella really kept the records since Harry couldn't file his mail let alone anything else. Under Izzy's watch, the records were immaculate, and Harry found stacks of stuff. He hauled it all out and piled it on his desk. Most of it would go home with them, and with the help of a good scotch, they'd cover it all.

While Sabina mined her spiders and various electronic webs and printed out the threads of data, Harry put together a sequence of paper records from their connection with the local missing girls case. Along with their copy of the murder book that Alan Kim had kept, he had all the printouts of the electronic traffic and the reports from Will and Rory, the two associates the company now had on the payroll. It was a large pile.

Isabella returned with fresh donuts and a couple of beef sandwiches from the Modern, the town's best and brightest reasonably new café. She'd also brought a couple of salads for which the place was famous.

Sabina and Harry ate at his desk. Sabina'd brought the records of some emails from the coroner in Powell River.

"Succinylcholine, H, it's a drug they use in operations. It leaves virtually no trace in the body after use, very short half-life. Here's the downside: it's gotta be used with a respirator and some other narcotic because it paralyzes muscles, all of them, even eyelids, but it does nothin' about pain, no narcotic effect at all. Jesus! If that's what they used, it's beyond evil. Sue Patterson, their new coroner up there, thinks it could be what their creeps are using, if so it's probably what our creeps used here. If she's right, the girls would suffocate. Here's the horrible part: they'd be conscious while it happened, not able to move anything. And this stuff has no narcotic effect. So if there was any pain involved, they'd feel it."

"Jesus, I hope she's wrong, that coroner, if those girls were conscious when they died... We know the disemboweling is post mortem, thank god, but who knows what else was done to them. Lying there dying like that, Christ! That stuff should be banned. How the hell would anybody get it?"

"That's part of the good news, if there is any in this mess. It's carefully controlled, and any missing would be reported immediately. So that, combined with the fact that it's only available in hospitals, means our guys would have a hell of a time getting any. Still, there's always the Internet. You can get anything if you try hard enough."

Harry chewed thoughtfully on the last of his sandwich. "How many substances are there that would leave no trace like that? Not a single tox report found anything, and those guys looked. Have they done a tox screen up there in Powell River?"

"Yup. They tested for that stuff on the advice of Doctor Sue. The report's in now and there's nothing. The problem with testing for it is that the test itself is unreliable and any findings inadmissible; it's a controversial test and it's expensive. The fact that they've done one at all is an indication of how seriously they're taking the possibility that our guys used this stuff."

Harry pushed his paper plate aside, put one foot on the edge of the open bottom drawer in his desk, and rocked back and forth.

"You've already tipped that damned chair a couple of times, H, you sure you want to keep doing that?" She shook her head. "Okay, Sweets, it's your ass. You got all the stuff from our case? I got all the latest from the current one. It's time we got Will on side. Rory, well, let's leave that to Will. The guy's so reclusive, I doubt he'd even come in."

"You talked to Jim, yet?"

"He's up to date and so's Chinatown. Mamma Jing's still frothing at the mouth for these guys because of Mary, the Singapore girl those creeps killed. She gets anywhere near them, the cops won't have to worry about a trial."

"Can we reach Alan and Spence too, I mean without screwing up their careers?"

"I'm gonna try to get them to agree to include us again, but after the mess over here, I don't know, the homicide bureau over there might take offence. The brass sure will, so I gotta be careful how I do this."

"Best you get at it then. I'll organize this stuff, so it makes some kinda sense. You find out who's doing what where. If we can fit, good, if not, then we'll do what we always do, go our own way. We got anybody funding any of this?"

"There's Olivia Chang, Mary's sister, she still wants these guys caught. Given what they did to Mary, she'll be onside. I can talk to her. Otherwise, nobody yet."

Harry's and Sabina's home in Harbour City was in an old building on Stewart, the main drag that led to the ferry running between Vancouver Island and Horseshoe Bay on the mainland. The building was a two-storey flat-roofed brick structure with a hair salon on the ground floor. Harry and Sabina's reached the second-floor apartment through an entrance under an arched opening beside the hair salon. The door was heavy wood and set back from the street. Stairs led up to the second floor, the stairwell pierced by small vertical windows every so often to throw light into an area that otherwise was a bit dark.

At the end of a short landing, another heavy wooden door opened directly into the living room, a large space with a series of arched windows running along the front. The light from these windows with their stained-glass tops threw patterns of colour across the floor in the late afternoon. The bedrooms were off to the side along with the bath, and the kitchen was at the back with a view over the main harbour framed by two islands: Protection with its houses and docks, and Newcastle, a provincial park with one dock. The inner harbour was always busy.

Newcastle was run by the local Snuneymuxw natives, if one still called them that, and was serviced by a couple of small boats that ran across the harbour during the summer. Their main aim was to service the Dinghy Dock, a floating restaurant on Protection. But they crossed to Newcastle when there was enough demand. Sailboats were everywhere in the harbour, from single-rigged small ones to sea-going schooners and ketches. Some of them wintered over. From Harry's kitchen window, he could see Gabriola Island's huge cliffs out in the Salish Sea way past the inner islands. On sunny days in the late afternoon, those cliffs glowed with rich amber light.

Harry parked the car in the gravel lot at the side of the building near the hair salon, and the two of them walked past the salon's front windows and climbed the stairs. Both were carrying boxes filled with paper from the office. Once inside, Harry dropped his near the door and made for the kitchen and the scotch bottles. He loved single malts and always kept a few good ones on hand, both here and at Sam's bar. Sabina dumped hers on the living room floor and hit the bathroom.

Harry was drinking a small one and looking out the at the harbour when Sabina sauntered in fresh from the shower wrapped in a robe.

"Where's mine, Sweets?"

"Still in the bottle. The stuff evaporates if it's left out, and it's one of the better singles. Your glass is on the table with ice; pour the melt out first."

Harry turned from the window, admired the loose bathrobe, smiled appreciatively, and picked up the bottle. Sabina gulped the ice water and held out her glass. Harry poured.

They both stood at the window watching the activity in the harbour for a while. Two sea planes came in, taxied to the dock, and disgorged a few passengers. A large private ocean-going motor launch appeared a few minutes later. As it tied up down further at the town dock, they stared at the thing. It rose four-storeys above the water. The town had two docking areas for craft under sail, and one for ridiculously large motor yachts like this one. The commercial docks were even farther down beside the rail yards. They watched a freighter down there load raw logs for a while, the yellow loaders scuttling like beetles back and forth from the yard to the vessel.

"Let me get dressed in something comfortable, then we'll unpack those boxes, okay?"

"Wear something interesting. It helps my concentration."

"Anything short and tight seems to do that, so I've got lots of choices. Any specific colour you'd like, boss?"

"Any colour at all as long as it's black. Henry Ford said that, I think, but not about girls."

"I don't imagine it was, but then he was a man and so are you, so anything's possible."

They spent part of the evening sorting through what they had, the living room floor covered in piles of papers. Sabina had her bare feet tucked under her and was wearing a mini and a lacy black top she knew he liked. Harry had changed to running shorts and an old tee. He too was barefoot.

He looked over at Sabina. "Okay, we've got stuff sorted and we've started fresh files on the Powell River case. Pardon me, the Hammil case. We got anything new?" Sabina pulled her legs out from under her.

"The usual, forensics, tox, profile, autopsy, email traffic between the locals and homicide. We've got a picture of things alright, but it's about the same as the ones from here. So nothing much new. No indication of where the girl came from yet, who she is, or why she was around there. They've got mispers out all over the place, BOLOs, and the usual search patterns. They've even got a copter messing about. There's just so much bush and so many possibilities. They're doing what needs to be done. Their budget must be huge, but we know that these guys will seem perfectly normal, so the cops likely won't know even if they stumble on them."

"We weren't much better off here when this mess started. If it hadn't been for the lumber companies and Rory's crew, we wouldn't even have found the cabin or the pit."

"Interesting that, they found a pit over there too. In an old abandoned farmhouse, a root cellar. And it'd been used. And it wasn't that far away from the dump site." Sabina showed Harry the report and pointed to a paragraph. "What got to me in our cases was how they could get the bodies from that pit to the site where they eviscerated the young women without leaving trace. They gave us nothing, and those sites were a long way away. How the hell did they do that? Go that far and leave nothing?"

She shuffled through the papers some more and said, "Here it is. The new M.E. thinks they might have been naked when they carried the body. She thinks there's no other way they could transport without leaving trace, and even then, she's doubtful that it could be done without leaving at least some sloughed off epithelials. Maybe they used the same paperish suits we use so we don't contaminate crime scenes. I wonder if they thought of that. And I wonder if those things leave any trace."

"I don't suppose they would, would they? After all, we wear them to keep scenes clean, so they can't shed much of anything.

What the hell are epithelials?"

"Skin cells. You know, the suits make a lot of sense, and they're easy to get. But I dunno, wouldn't you compromise the damn things carrying something on your shoulders?"

"The forensics guys wear them, and they carry stuff, don't they? Why don't they just call them skin cells?"

"Epithelials sounds so much more learned than skin cells, don't you think?"

"Harder to spell though. I like skin cells better. And wouldn't there at least be a trail of her skin cells if they did that?"

Sabina handed Harry the report. "What she's on about's in the last paragraph. And she might just have something with both the drug and moving the bodies. We should ask about the suits and skin cells. See if there were any at the site. Of course, there would be. There'd be hers at least. Since we don't know where they brought the bodies through the bush, and since the sites were so old when we found them, trace of any kind would be negligible. I think I just ruined my own argument."

"Forget the cells and check on the suits. At least it's a possibility, and we don't have much else."

They spent the rest of the evening reviewing the old cases and comparing the new one, but nothing new struck them.

So they left the crime reports and began to plan an approach to Alan and Spence in Vancouver. Nobody over there had anything on the missing girls yet.

"I'll email Spence and see if we can figure out a way to integrate what we get with what they get without screwing things up. Can we go over if we get invited in?"

Harry thought about that. "I don't see why not. Izzy can hold the fort. If anything comes in that's urgent, we can get Will to handle it unless we need him over there. He's more useful here though. He knows the island. Vancouver's foreign territory for him. He could help more from here anyway. You got any idea how we're gonna get in?"

"Not a clue, Hon, but we'll get in somehow. Let me start with Spence. I bug the hell out of her, but she'll come through. One day I'll have to take her aside and reveal myself, I guess."

"I thought you only did that for me! That's upsetting that is, and she's a girl too."

"Well, you didn't seem to mind Sally, and she's a girl."

"Sally's Sally, Spence is a cop. It's sort of like cavorting with the competition, isn't it?"

"I cavort with Sally; I discuss with Spence. Jeez, H, she's stuck on Alan anyway. But Sally now, maybe you should worry a little. Be good for you."

"It's not in my nature. Besides Sally's super. So maybe you should do the worrying. I could move in and queer your chances, no pun intended, well, maybe only a little. Wasn't something in there alliterative?"

Sally only likes girls and me, so your chances are slim to none. But if you wanna try, I'll coach you. And yes there was."

"Didn't you try that once before, coaching? Then you reconsidered. I think you fell for me and didn't want competition."

"Yeah, right. But you're a sweetie, and I won't give you up even if your puns are terrible. Let's leave this stuff for tonight. What's in the fridge?"

"Some beer and a couple of eggs. Why don't we get dressed, hit the Modern for dinner, then shop? By that time, we'll need another scotch, so we better get some ice too."

14.

Herk sat on his back porch watching the early morning sun turn the mist over the lake into a pure white layer, like long strips of cheesecloth floating in the air. As he finished his second cup of coffee, the mist slowly dissipated, and all that was left were a few wisps over in the reed beds near the trees on the far side. The lake itself was like a sheet of glass in the morning sun, and he could hear the occasional ticks from the warming metal of his runabout as it sat at the side of the dock.

He thought about breakfast and whether to make his own or to drive in and let Agnes make it for him. The restaurant was usually open early and not very full until close to nine.

Now, it was just past six on an October morning, still far too warm and sunny for this time of year. The fall rains were late. The land was still parched even though they'd had the occasional downpour, and the grass, usually green by this time, lay baking in the heat like the thatch left in fields. Even the trees looked a little tired, as if their leaves were getting too heavy for their limbs. The deciduous ones had only now begun to change into fall colours. Most were still a dusty late-summer green, but in a month, the leaves'd be gone and the trees nothing but bare, black limbs lifting into dark skies. To Herk, even the legions of conifers seemed listless, their deep colour bleached by the sun. He got up, rinsed his cup in the sink, looked in the fridge, and grabbed his hat. He'd let Agnes feed him once again.

As usual, the restaurant was almost empty when he got there, only a couple of tourists bent over plates of bacon and eggs in one of the front booths. Herk sat in his usual place, and Agnes brought coffee. He nodded his thanks and ordered his own plate of bacon and eggs with toast and home fries.

He sipped quietly. He could see out the front window from where he sat, and even this early, the day had begun to look coppery and brittle. Could be rain before nightfall, he thought. And that would make the search for the killers a bigger pain than it already was. Agnes arrived with plates in both hands. Herk smiled. The bacon looked crisp, and the eggs were sunny, just the way he liked them.

"I got fresh rhubarb and berry pie, just out of the oven, by the time you're finished that stuff it'll be cool enough. You get first cut. Want the rest to take to the station?"

Herk grinned at the thought and nodded. Jenny would try so hard to resist and would last about thirty seconds, then blame him for the rest of the day for making her fat. Celia wouldn't even notice. The rest would be gone as soon as his deputies walked in the door.

"That'd be real nice Agnes. The girls won't be able to resist, and my men, at least the first one or two'll have it gone before the pie plate's cool. Stick it on my bill, and thanks."

Herk's deputies, all five of them, had been pulling drivers over, gathering names, and interviewing likely pairs of men recently arrived in the area, but had found nothing in the last few days. There were two new guys in town, one doing freelance stuff for Manchester's paper, and the other picking up odd jobs here and there. At least Derek was getting better stuff now. The last article on the murder and the slow pace of the investigation was at least well-written. The younger guy seemed a bit slow, but people liked him because he smiled a lot. Herk decided to keep an eye on both of them just because they were new, but he didn't think these guys would yield anything.

There were four other possibilities in town, and all of them had been interviewed. Two had done nothing but fish the lakes around Hammil and could account for every day of their two-week and the other two were developers for a consortium down south interested in finding property on one of the larger lakes suitable for building a lodge to provide conference space to city-weary businessmen. They too seemed unlikely candidates for murder, especially of young girls. Both were rather portly and avuncular and didn't look very able.

Agnes brought another coffee, this one to go, and a Pyrex pie plate wrapped in plastic along with the bill. Herk paid and took the cruiser to the office, parking it with a couple of others by the white picket fence in front of city hall. He took his coffee and went around the car, gingerly lifting the pie from the passenger seat. It was still warm enough to cloud the plastic wrap.

Jenny wasn't in yet, but Celia was, the screens of her monitors visible through her office door. Herk didn't bother her. If she had anything for him, he'd either find it on his desk or it would come spewing out of the printer in his office when she sent it to him. He set the pie squarely in the center of Jenny's desk, walked to his office, and settled at his desk.

He pulled out the grid map and marked how many lodges, inns, and fishing camps remained to be checked. Gordie and the crew from Powell River would check Powell Lake and everything down past Lois Lake as far as Jervis Inlet, the body of water that sliced into the land all the way up past McCall's Landing. The inlet cut off their coastal area from the Sechelt area to the south, and you had to take a ferry from Saltery Bay to Earl's Cove to get farther south. That still left hundreds of square miles to check, and innumerable camps hidden away on the lakes. It was almost impossible, but they had to try. He could smell the pie cooling on Jenny's desk.

Herk made a list of the day's checkpoints and took it out to the desk. She'd radio the cruisers that were going out to the checkpoints when she came in and assign search areas to the two constables patrolling the town this morning. Then these constables could help check out of town as well. Back in his office, he stood at the window. The coppery cast to the air was still there. Something was coming, he thought, and coming soon. Herk heard Jenny come in and walked out to say good morning.

"You're in early today. Who're the two who left the cruisers?"

"Pie, damn Herk, that looks good. Sam and Jerry, I think. Let me look."

She rummaged around in her desk and came up with the roll call from yesterday.

"Yeah, Sam and Jerry had some town stuff to do at end of shift and left the cruisers here. They'll be in shortly. I shouldn't, but I better get a piece of that before they wolf it all."

"I put the search grid assignments on your desk for today. Get Sam and Jerry out for a bit, maybe get someone else to cover town."

"Okay, Herk, other than bringing the pie, what's bugging you? I do this every day, you know, and when you mess around out here, I know something's going round in there." She pointed to Herk's head with one long index finger.

"Nothing to worry about, Jenny. It's just this search area. It's frustrating for everybody and gives us damn little. Too many people, too many inns and fishing camps. And Powell River's got the worst of it, for sure, all the way down past Lois Lake to Jervis Inlet. All we got to do is Dodd and Horseshoe, and maybe Lewis and Nanten too. But there're still a lot of camps to check let alone campgrounds. And we don't have a lot of time."

Jenny nodded. This murder was bothering everybody, especially the guys who were doing the canvas. It was like looking for the proverbial needle in one bloody huge haystack, and nobody held out much hope they'd catch these guys. Hell, even she knew they could question them, clear them, and never know they'd let the creeps go.

"I'll be out for a bit Jenny, goin' over to the paper to talk to Derek, see what that new guy's doing. You mind the house, especially that pie. Anything comes up you know where I am."

Derek was in the back room when Herk walked in. He came out to the front desk shaking his head. "I got nothing for you, you know that, so why're you here?"

"Got to talk to that new fellow writing for you, Derek, he around today?"

"He's not an employee, I already got one of those and he's no damn good. He's freelance, Herk. He comes when he likes and leaves the stuff and we dicker about what it's worth."

Derek turned around and went back inside, leaving Herk to fend for himself.

Herk shook his head and thought, the crusty old bugger's a bigger pain in the ass than usual. Of course, he's got diddly squat to report on the murder of the decade, must just bug the hell out of him too. Even the stuff Vic Hunter's writing for him doesn't cover more than the basics. His story was fair and pretty accurate, but it went nowhere.

Herk took the unmarked cruiser out to the highway and began to go through his list of inns and fishing camps. Since two of the inns were right on the highway, he'd do those first, then hit the secondaries and the three fishing camps up around the lakes. It wouldn't take all that long. It was late in the season. Even with the good weather, there wouldn't be many people to question.

The first inn was on the edge of Lake Ireland just below Dodd. It looked like a large log cabin with a restaurant tacked onto the side and a gravel lot out front. There were three cars, all SUVs, nosed in towards the restaurant.

Herk entered the main doors of the inn and asked for the manager. The clerk made a short call, and a tall man with a barrel chest and enough belly to roll the top of his pants over his belt came down the stairs. He took Herk into his tiny office.

"You know why I'm here, Mr. Smith, don't you?"

"Reggie, just Reggie."

"Reggie it is then. You've heard about the murder of the girl, haven't you? We're looking for two men been here maybe a few weeks, no more than that, though."

"Yes sir, I figure it was somethin' like that. I got Harold out there to pull the registrations and credit receipts yesterday, so I got them here. We only had two couples, guys I mean. Both fishermen. Weekend ones anyway. Got the credit card stuff and their registration cards for you. I took Xerox's for our records, you got the originals, I know that's what you need, originals."

Reggie handed Herk a brown envelope, the kind you could fit a large sheet of paper in. Herk nodded and opened it.

"You remember these guys at all?"

"Not me personally, no, well only to see them mornings in the restaurant sometimes, but Jimmy and his son work the dock, and Jimmy Farrell, he took them out on the lake a few times. He'd know most about them. I'll take you down to the bait shop and introduce you. Jimmy, he doesn't say much, so I'll go with you. I know how to get him to open up a bit."

"Good, let's get it done then, and I appreciate the help."

The dock lay down a grade directly behind the inn and was reached by a wide, crushed stone path that curled around the trunks of a stand of Douglas fir. The lake stretched out from a wide dock with a bait and equipment shack perched on it. Opposite the shack, along the deep dock, lay a series of runabouts and a couple of larger cruisers. Ireland was a relatively small lake, but it was deep and protected by high cliffs on three sides. Jimmy and his son were both there, the son cleaning the boats, the father in the bait shop reading a paper.

Reggie led Herk into the shop.

"Jimmy, this here's the police chief from Hammil. He needs to ask you about the guys you took out last week."

"Which ones?"

"All of 'em, I guess."

"Only four or so."

"Well, all of those, then."

Jimmy put his paper down on the counter and waited, looking questioningly at Reggie. Reggie pointed to Herk.

"Talk to him, Jimmy, and don't make him drag it out of you." Jimmy looked at Herk, nodded, and waited.

"Tell me everything you remember about them, how many there were, where you took them, for how long, what they looked like, how they acted, things like that. You just tell me the stories for each of the pairs starting with the first. Think you can do that, Jimmy?"

"Yup, I suppose."

Herk waited, Jimmy waited. Reggie finally said, "Well, do it then, Jimmy, the man's got a lot to do."

Over the next half hour, Herk got a pretty fair description of the four men Jimmy had taken out. The time frames were clear, and all of them had been out every day of their stays all day. They didn't seem likely killers to Herk, but he'd have to have Celia check out the credit card information. She could mine a lot from that. Herk thanked Jimmy and followed Reggie back up the path through the Douglas firs.

His next stop was down the highway on Nanton Lake, another inn made from logs, but smaller and more family-run than the one on Ireland. Herk questioned the owners, a husband and wife pair who lived in the inn like Reggie. They'd had no one in the last few weeks and had virtually closed down for the season in spite of the good weather.

The next inn was a bit of a hike. Herk had to drive down the highway toward the coast a good distance before turning inland again up Spring Lake Road, a rough blacktop that curled around every rock outcropping. It went way past the very small Spring Lake, curling over to the much larger Haslam Lake and running down its side until it reached Larson's Landing. There it stopped. Herk had to swing off well before the big turn and take a secondary over to Lewis Lake. That road was mostly gravel and near impossible to travel once the rains came.

The lake was a decent size, though, and the fishing was good. The inn was tucked in at the edge of a small but deep cove. Mostly fishermen stayed here and flew in by seaplane from Powell River. Supplies came in the same way. Herk parked in the large gravel lot and went in.

The interior was anything but rustic. It boasted a modern sort of bar on the side and a rather posh restaurant. Already, there were three or four people in the bar, and the restaurant looked busy. Herk approached the reception desk and got a glowing smile from the uniformed young woman.

"I'm the chief of police up in Hammil, miss, over by Dodd Lake, and I need to see your manager or the owner. We're checking every inn and camp in the area looking for two men. We've had a murder as you probably know, and my men and the RCMP in Powell River are talking to everyone in the area, especially anyone from outside who's been around for the last couple of weeks or so."

The young woman's smile faded fast, and she picked up the house phone.

"Bill, there's a policeman from Hammil here at the desk asking for you. It's about our guests during the last few weeks, and that murder you were talking about yesterday. She glanced up at Herk, smiled again but couldn't hold it, and said, "He's here now and he needs to talk to you... I don't think he'd like to wait for Mister Grant. No, he didn't show me one. You need to come talk to him." She listened again and Herk could hear a raised voice coming over the phone.

"He'll be right out," the young woman said. "He's my oldest brother and he runs the business for the owner, Grant Hughes. He's out on the lake with a very important client."

The girl pivoted and pointed toward the back of the large foyer where Herk could see through large French doors as far down as the lake itself. "We can't reach him out there, so Bill will have to fill in. I hope that's okay?"

"That's fine, miss. I'll wait here for him. What's Bill's last name and yours, if you don't mind?"

"Oh, of course, I'm sorry. My name's Grace, Grace Noble, and Bill's my brother. So we have the same last name."

The man who came out from the hall beside the reception counter was tall and a little heavier than he should have been. The frown of annoyance on his face told Herk this guy wasn't going to be very cooperative.

"I'm William Noble, I manage the inn. Do you have a warrant for this sort of thing?" He stood there, legs spread, hands on his hips as if he were addressing a recalcitrant child. He was trying for stern and unapproachable, but it wasn't very convincing. Herk decided he'd play this one straight. He was a bit tired of this sort of bravado, tired of the 'what the hell do you want' sort of thing.

Herk stood there looking at this officious jerk, then said, "I'm Herk Burman, chief of police in Hammil, and I don't need a warrant. If you'd prefer, I'll have the homicide detectives in Powell River question you. Of course, you'd have to come down there for that to happen. Your choice, Mister Noble. You can talk to me or you can talk to them, but you will talk to one of us."

Herk crossed his arms over his chest, leaned against the reception counter, and waited.

"I can't give you any information about our guests. They have a right to their privacy, and you do need a warrant to get it."

"Look, Mister Noble, I'm investigating a murder, and I'm gatherin' information about everyone who's come into the area in the last two weeks or so. I'm not arresting anybody, and I'm not threatening anyone either. I'm asking politely for your help. You don't want to give it, I'll just ring up the Mounties and you can deal with them. They'll send a cruiser for you and take you back to the station. I'd as soon avoid that, but if you want to make this difficult just because you can, they can deal with you. I have neither the time nor the inclination."

Herk kept leaning against the counter and waited. The manager waited too.

"Right, I'll make my call. They'll bring you your warrant and your transport. Good luck to you."

Herk turned, walked out, and went to his unmarked cruiser. He was annoyed, called Gordie in Powell River and explained.

"I've got a horse's ass up here on Lewis Lake, manager of the inn, won't give me the time of day. I'd like to shoot the bugger, but I know it'd make more work for you. He wants a warrant and he wants to deal with you guys. So give him what he wants, and don't be nice about it. Yeah, a copter'd be a nice touch. Sure, I'll hang around."

Herk grinned to himself and stepped out of his unmarked just in time to see William Noble approaching. He still looked belligerent.

"I've talked to our lawyers, and they told me you've no right to ask for anything pertaining to our guests."

Herk leaned against the door of the unmarked, smiled at the man, and said. "You'll be happy to know the RCMP are on their way with a warrant to search the premises and to talk to you. They tend to be a bit short with uncooperative people like you. I'm here to make sure you're here when they arrive. We can go inside and wait, if you prefer. It won't be long."

Herk smiled at the man and waited.

"I'll be inside. You can wait out here."

"My job is to secure your presence, sir, so either I go inside with you, or you wait here. If you refuse, I do have the authority to restrain you."

Herk reached behind his back and pulled out his cuffs.

The manager rolled his eyes, shook his head, and started to walk away. Over his shoulder he said, "You can deal with the lawyer, he's on his way too."

Herk followed until they reached the steps at the front doors of the inn. There the man stopped, looked at Herk, and said, "No further for you. You're not welcome inside."

As he reached for the door, Herk stepped close to him, grabbed his wrist, and snapped on a cuff. The other he put around his own wrist. He said, "I'm sorry you chose to do things this way. My orders are to restrain you if you tried to leave."

At that moment the roar of rotors rose above the inn as the helicopter came in over the trees, circled, and began to set down in the gravel lot. The turbulence buffeted the two men, so they had to lean into it to stay upright. Once down, the copter disgorged two men and rose again, flying back the way it had come.

Gordie and Frank ducked and ran to join the two on the steps. Once the copter had vanished over the trees and they could be heard, Gordie looked at William Noble and said, "You the uncooperative individual that forced us to come up here?"

"That he is," said Herk, and undid the cuff from his wrist. "I'm afraid I had to cuff him to guarantee his presence."

Gordie looked at him and said, "Get inside. We'll wait for the cruisers and the team with the warrant. Your boss, I understand, is out on the lake with a client and will be in forthwith. You best tell your help to secure a room for us. We'll be awhile. Frank, take him in. I want to talk to the chief here."

Gordie could hardly hold a straight face until the two had gone inside. He turned away from the door and grinned at Herk. "That makes my day, that does. I'm up to here with people who think we're less than shit. No biggie with the copter. We were near here and have been in it for hours checking chalets, places that can't be checked any other way. I got a couple of cruisers in the area to come up and join in the fun. Stupid, arrogant prick. We'll make sure everyone knows he refused to help. We do need the info. Not that it'll help much."

"He called the in-house lawyers."

"Good, it'll be nice to see how they handle the threat of an obstruction charge. I'm pissed enough to do it. If you're almost finished for the day, you can take me back to town, and we'll grab some dinner. I won't be long here. Hang around and watch the fireworks."

Gordie slapped Herk on the shoulder and went inside.

Herk went to the unmarked to check in with Jenny. He'd finish the fishing camps tomorrow. There were only three of them, and they were all sort of in a row, so he could finish by noon or so.

As Herk was making the call, a black Crown Vic pulled in and a man in a dark blue power suit got out. Right behind him two RCMP cruisers roared up, light bars throwing colour, brakes leaving long scars in the gravel. A constable, paper in hand, climbed out of the first cruiser and trotted into the inn, ignoring the man in the suit. The men in the second cruiser walked over to Herk.

"You guys came in along the side of the lake, so you see anything out there?"

"One cruiser. Looked like one of those new Chris craft things tyin' up to the dock. Looks like it just got in. Nice looking thing."

"That'll be the owner with his client."

Frank appeared at the inn door and waved them in. "You two stand down. Herk, you come with me."

As they walked across the lobby toward a side hall, Frank said, "We got a room. The owner's here now and we're getting the records we need. Everybody wants to get this over with, especially the manager. The owner's ordered him to give us whatever we want. The lawyer's checked the warrant and is just observing, so he can bill his time I guess. We're not serving the warrant if we get some cooperation, and it looks like that's happening now. Gordie'll be done soon. We've got the paper trail on any pairs of guys or singles been here the last few weeks. There're only four altogether. I think there's one guy we gotta talk to, but that's it. He's being called in now."

The room was a small conference room and there was coffee. The owner had a cup in his hand and was blowing on the surface. He looked none too happy. Gordie was talking to an older man, probably the guide. William Noble, the blowhard manager who had started all this, was sitting at one end of the table looking uncomfortable. His head was down and he seemed to have shrunk into himself. A constable was taking notes. On the table near Gordie was the paperwork. The lawyer sat on the other side of the table listening.

Gordie was being polite for the lawyer's sake. He addressed the owner. "I want to thank you for coming in so quickly, sir, and for the information you provided. This helps us eliminate people and narrows our search considerably. And you, sir," Gordie said looking at the lawyer, "I want to thank you for keeping this simple. We have what we need now and can let everybody get back to work." Gordie ignored the manager.

The lawyer nodded, got up, took his briefcase and left. The guide got another cup of coffee. Gordie took the files he'd been given and came over to Herk who was leaning against the wall with Frank beside him.

"Let's go. We've got the stuff for what it's worth. We'll talk in the car."

The manager was still sitting in his chair at the end of the table when they left the room. Herk stopped at the registration desk to thank the young woman for her help, and then they walked out to the lot. One cruiser was still there. Everyone else had cleared out.

"Frank's goin' back to town," Gordie said. "He's got family stuff. Me, I'm like you, got no family to worry about, so let's go to Agnes' and have a bite. I was gonna stay over anyway, so we can compare what we've got. And maybe Agnes'll have pie."

Herk drove them back to town. By the time he'd cleared Spring Lake road and reached the highway, Gordie was asleep. Herk drove slowly; there was no real hurry. The sky had turned dark since they'd left the inn, not only because of the early dusk this time of year, but also because there was a heavy cloud layer up there. Herk turned on his lights. He had barely cleared Lake Ireland when the first drops hit the windshield. By the time he reached the road into town, the rain was steady with occasional heavy downpours. Gordie was still sleeping.

15.

As Herk entered the town, Gordie lay still, his head against the cuiser's door. The rain was pelting the car and forming huge pools of water. Herk slowed for the hollow where heavy rains usually left a long, deep pool, and tonight was no exception. The wipers were on full blast, and still it was difficult to judge just how deep it had gotten.

He eased the cruiser through enough water to send a wave out from the front bumper. Every year, it was the same: heavy rain, a deep pool on the damn highway, and a bunch of calls for stalled cars. He had to talk to the mayor again.

The lights ahead of him were blurred by the downpour, but the reddish glow of Agnes's place tinted the darkness. Herk took the cruiser in slowly, parked in the lot up near the restaurant, and reluctantly woke Gordie.

Herk watched him struggle to the surface, peer around himself sluggishly, then everything in him seemed to focus, and he said, "Thank God for Agnes. I'm damn near starved. I hope to god she's got pie."

"Why else would we drive all this way?"

"Damn straight. Let's get in there!" Gordie pushed open his door, slipped his feet out into about two inches of water, and made a clumsy dash for the door. Herk followed, grinning.

Inside, it was bright and dry, and almost empty. The dinner rush was over, and only three couples sat in the booths next to a window that resembled a miniature waterfall. Gordie made a beeline for the one they usually used near the back on the side wall.

He had barely slid in before Agnes was there, pad ready, and a scowl on her face.

"You're too late for dinner, you two, but I can scrape up something. I got one pie left, so you're luckier than most. I was saving it for me and the boys, but for the cops, I'll make an exception; you can have some, not all mind."

"What kind?"

"Why do you care, you'll eat just about anything."

"If it's pie and it's yours, you got that right."

Herk slid into the other side while this exchange was going on. He waited expectantly for Agnes to tell them what was left besides pie.

"You get that last, fella. I'll scrape up what we got. You both get the same whatever it is this late." Agnes sauntered back to the kitchen, and they both heard her as she went through the spring-loaded kitchen doors.

"Hey Jimmy, what's left? I got two cops to feed."

Gordie looked around slowly and sighed. "That was a useless day. Like you, we found nothin' which is about what I expected. Still, the inn was fun. The brass's throwing a lot of money at this, so it's high profile around town. Add that to what went down over in Harbour City, and we get helicopters. The overtime's good, but hell, it's like looking for two pine needles in the bush."

Gordie paused, stretched, and rotated his head from side to side. Herk could hear it cracking. "I went in to talk to the coroner before we left this morning, and she had some interesting things to say once we got past the usual bitchin'."

"She?" Herk said. "What happened to the old guy?"

"Resigned, didn't he, said he had family problems. I thought the old bugger was long past that sort of thing."

"So what's this she like?"

"Well, she shouldn't be a medical examiner, not with her looks; you end up lookin' not listenin' the way you should, and it pisses her off. She's somewhere in her thirties, looks like, and she's sharp.

Once the usual unpleasantries were out of the way, she had a lot to say. She's been bothered by what bothers us: not so much who these guys are, but how their victims end up with no marks on them except for the cutting and the painting. She told me again that the girl had been murdered where she was found, but her heart had stopped before she was cut."

Gordie counted off what they knew on his fingers. "Lividity matches the position of where the body was; no defensive wounds; no trace under her nails or anywhere else; not even much from the site sticking to her. So how did they do it?"

Gordie waited. Herk shrugged, "Been bothering all of us, that has."

"Here's where the new Dr. Sue Patterson got interesting. She says the girl died of asphyxiation and maybe what we're lookin' at here is something that incapacitated her, left her unable to respond, like that date rape stuff. But something that maybe also caused the asphyxiation because the girl did asphyxiate, and she wasn't strangled. She was thinking some substance like an anesthetic. Something that leaves little if any trace after a while. Remember, after a while is always when we find them. And she had a suggestion, but she said I wasn't going to like it. Succinylcholine is what she said."

Gordie waited. Herk shrugged again. "So what is this stuff?"

"Okay, here it gets brutal. It's a neuromuscular paralytic; it paralyzes all your muscles. If that stuff got used on the girls, ours and the ones in Harbour City, they all suffocated while those fuckin' psychos watched. And the girls'd know, they'd know they were suffocating, they'd be terrified, and then they'd fuckin' die. We gotta get these pricks."

Gordie stared at Herk, his eyes hot with fury. Then he looked down at the table while the moments passed. Finally, he seemed to deflate.

"We talked about where our girl was found, and she had something to say about that too. Our two guys had to carry her, and they had to do that very carefully, and probably they'd have to be as naked as she was. Otherwise, there should have been some fiber trace even after all the time she lay out there, and there wasn't. She thinks the reports out of Harbour City were right, that the girls were Tasered.

She thinks it's possible the Tasering went on every time our girl regained consciousness, and in the same place, so there were no marks when she was eviscerated."

"But if that stuff's a paralytic anesthetic, that's like a sedative, right? So she wouldn't be conscious while it happened, would she?"

"According to the coroner, there are no narcotic effects. There are very few possibilities where you end up with a body and no trace at all, even with the most exhaustive testing. And Doc Sue says the testing she ordered would have found anything else. So our girl would be as conscious as we are while it happened. Think about that. She's conscious, and she can't breathe, and she can't move anything. We ought'a just shoot these fucks when we find them."

Herk did think about it. If the new coroner was right, this was the worst thing he'd ever heard of. It was beyond inhuman, it was evil. And if that's what happened, Gordie was right, they had to find these guys and exterminate them.

"Here's the thing, though," Gordie said, "if they used this stuff the way she said, it'll be impossible to prove, from the body at least. Testing results are iffy. In every case history she's read, the tests were discounted because they were suspect. She said it was just one suggestion, but given the lack of trace, either it was something like that or it was that."

"If we can't nail these guys with the tests, maybe we can get them another way. They had to get this stuff, and that can't be easy."

"That's another thing she said. It's very carefully controlled, so any missing drug would be reported. It's impossible to get any other way than through hospitals and clinics where it might be used."

"The Internet?"

"She says not, but who the hell knows these days. Oh, and she raised another problem. Sux, what anesthesiologists call this stuff, is usually given intravenously in controlled doses, so our guys, if they used it, had to know the right dose and had to have some way to get it into the girls' systems. Not one of the coroners working on the murdered girls found any evidence of injection."

"Maybe she's wrong, then, maybe it's something else. I mean, if it's impossible to get, if you need to know about doses, then our two guys'd be unlikely to either have it or know how much it'd take. And if it has to be injected and nobody's found any marks, then this stuff isn't it."

Agnes appeared with two plates heaped with fries and thick sandwiches. Neither man had much of an appetite, so Herk asked Agnes to pack it up to go. She didn't ask any questions; she just looked at the two of them, turned on her heel, and walked back through the kitchen doors.

Herk paid and tipped her, and they left. It was still raining but not as hard. The lot had drained a bit, so they weren't wading to the car. Not that it mattered given what they'd run through on the way in.

Herk drove them out to his place by the lake, put the boxes in the kitchen, poured two generous shots of scotch, and carried them to the back porch where Gordie was already stuffed into one of the Adirondacks. They sat quietly, sipped the scotch, and watched the rain pock holes in the surface of the lake. Herk got up at one point, went in, and returned with the bottle. The two men continued to sit and listen to the rain.

An hour or so later, Gordie turned to Herk and said, "We gotta start again in the morning. We gotta cover the rest of the fishing camps. Then I gotta go back and write the damn reports. We gotta justify the expense even if we get nothin' and nothin's what we're gonna get."

Herk sat quietly nodding and refilled his glass. After a while, he said, "I'm getting loaded. I'm seeing two lakes. Maybe we should eat that stuff Agnes sent."

Gordie leaned over and added a bit to his glass. "This stuff's so good it's a shame to dilute it with food, but you're right. There are two lakes."

It took a bit of effort to get out of the Adirondacks without spilling the scotch, but they both managed. Herk undid the boxes, shoveled the thick sandwiches onto plates, dumped the chips into the microwave to heat, and slid the ample slices of pie onto others. He put all four plates on the table, waited for the microwave to ding, slid the chips out, and put them on the table as well. The two of them ate quietly.

"S'good," Gordie said. "Needed it."

"Finish your scotch. We gotta be up at five if you wanna get to the chopper on time."

At four the next morning, the birds started as they always did, but this time no one heard them. At five the alarm went off in both bedrooms, and the two men walked groggily toward the bathroom.

"Aspirin's in the medicine cabinet," Herk said. "Don't use it all up. And don't dawdle. I'll make coffee. That's all we got time for."

Gordie nodded and wished he hadn't. "Be out before it's down."

By five-thirty, the two were in the cruiser and on their way to the chopper. The rain had stopped, but the sky was low and dark. They hit the highway and headed west toward the copter station.

"If Doc Patterson's right about that stuff you talked about, that succyl stuff that paralyzes muscles, we gotta find out where they got it. That's mostly a records search. I'll call in and get Celia on it. If it's out there she'll find it."

"I fly anywhere in that damn bird this morning, I'm gonna puke. You got any more aspirin?"

"Glove compartment."

"About the stuff..."

"Yeah, yeah, I got it. I already got the good doctor to send on her thoughts to homicide here and Harbour City. It's just a suggestion, and I hope she's wrong. Shit, I dropped some." Gordie popped another aspirin in his mouth and looked at the floor, shifted his feet, bent down a bit more.

"Forget it, I gotta get the damn thing washed and vacced anyway. Besides, It's just aspirin, can't hurt anything."

They both thought the doc just might have something, and they should start searching for the stuff as soon as they could. They knew it wasn't a sure thing and they might not find any source online. They also knew they'd be derelict if they didn't try. Herk called through to Celia at the station while he drove. He could hear keystrokes in the background.

Gordie nodded as he listened to the exchange and said he'd talk to their researcher as soon as he reached the chopper.

"You got one more flight, right, so you'll be done by noon. And I got three camps to talk to, then I'm done. I'm not goin' back, I'm coming down. Why don't we get everybody together, take another look at everything we've got." Herk glanced at Gordie then back at the road.

"There's a conference call setup goin' on this afternoon between the heads in Harbour City and our guys, so, yeah, come on down. We'll see what comes out of that, if anything."

Herk turned off the highway and took the two-lane to the heliport. They could see the field from the road, the far side lined with broadleaf trees glistening in the pale light, the pad and machine shiny with rain as well. The copter was obviously waiting, the pilot standing beside it running a check. Herk dropped Gordie at the small office and took off. His fishing camps were a good distance away, and he wanted to be done with them quickly.

Herk was well down the highway when he heard the rotor pulse, and the copter roared by overhead. It was raining again, but it was one of those misty soft rains that would make all the greens in the bush pop and soak everything by day's end. He didn't mind driving through this feathery light stuff. No run-off problems like you got with the heavy rains: no downed trees, no rockfalls on the road, no washouts along the ridges where the water cascaded down damn near everywhere. It'd be a pleasant enough drive.

Two of the fishing camps were over on the west side of Horseshoe Lake way south of Nanton Lake. From the highway, Herk had to navigate a narrow ribbon of blacktop over to the lakeside. Neither camp had guests and neither had had any male couples in the last month or so.

The last camp was down at the base of Horseshoe on Tony Lake, a much smaller lake with a large campground at its base and the fishing camp halfway up. Herk knew the owner of the camp and stopped long enough for coffee and a sandwich at the small eatery attached to the office. Kevin Taylor ran the place along with his wife, Barb, a dark-haired woman with one of those cheerful bouncy personalities. Kevin was the opposite, taciturn and reserved. Together, they made the place work. They still had guests, two of them. They were new and didn't interest Herk. But the couple they had had until a couple of days ago sure did.

Barb leaned on the counter, slid a mug of coffee over to Herk, watched him wolf down the second half of the ample beef sandwich, and said, "That pair we didn't like much, too full of themselves, they were, and secretive. Like they knew something we didn't? They spent most days just driving around. They'd disappear after breakfast and turn up sometime in the afternoon. I think they went out once. Never caught anything, but we didn't expect them to. They weren't fishermen, that's for sure."

"What'd they drive?"

"It was a van of some sort. Kevin'd know more. More coffee?"

"Sure. So what'd they do other than drive around that you know about?"

"Couple of times, they came back pretty scratched up. Been in the bush looked like and didn't do too well. But we didn't see much of them, you know? They kept to themselves a lot, drank some in the bar nights, but nothin' extreme. Sorry, Herk, I can't give you more than that except that we didn't like them much."

"Okay, I better get their registrations and check 'em out. Can you run copies for yourself? I'll need to take the originals. I'll get 'em back to you." Herk glanced at his coffee cup. "And once I finish this one, I'll have another coffee while I wait."

"Help yourself, you know where everything is. I'll dig out the paperwork. They paid by credit card at the bar, so I'll get those copied as well. Back in a jiff."

Herk drank his coffee, refilled his cup, and waited. When she appeared, he took the paperwork Barb gave him, thanked her, walked down to the dock to say goodbye to Kevin, and was on the road shortly after that.

The rain stayed a kind of fine mist for most of the trip down to Powell River, and Herk made good time. The two at the fishing camp didn't seem likely, not with their obvious problems in the bush. Herk was certain his two wouldn't have a scratch on them. But it had to be checked. He called Celia again and gave her the information.

Powell River had sun, not much, but some. The sky was kind of murky as if it couldn't make up its mind, and the sun, what there was of it, was that weak watery kind you got when the weather was changeable.

Herk drove into town and parked in the station lot down at the end where nobody would bitch about it. He'd used his cell to call Gordie on the way, and the man was at the front desk talking to the desk sergeant when Herk walked through the doors. They shook hands and Gordie pointed up the stairs. "You know where stuff is, so help yourself to the coffee, I gotta take a leak. Be right behind you."

16.

In the Vancouver station, the homicide floor was busy when Alan and Spence arrived in the morning. There were briefings on some cases that needed so much manpower, they were held in conference rooms. There were partners in cubicles all over the floor setting up the day's activities. Add to all that the general buzz that rooms like this one had at this time of day, and it was like walking into a huge betting parlour just before a race.

Jake Kenney and Larry Sharp were in their cubicle on the far side of the room even though they weren't on duty till four. Spence and Alan made their way over. The four of them were a bit squeezed, but Kenney had managed to get the flats pushed back a bit and another pair of desks installed. The extra chairs were gone. Jake looked as if he'd just stepped off the cover page of a style mag. He wore a bespoke light-grey pinstripe, a crisp white shirt, and his standard blue silk tie. By contrast, Larry looked like a fugitive from an all-night bar. His black suit was creased everywhere, his shirt, an off-white light grey, was a wilted mess, his tie was black and off center. Everything was clean; it just didn't look like it.

"Brian had a word with us this morning, and it wasn't a good morning. He's pissed we're not getting the girls sorted out. But he's pretty unpissed we got that fuckin' pimp off the street, so we get no more complaints about beatings. All in all, not a bad start."

Larry grinned as he paused and added, "And how about the digs, eh? Housekeeping got it done last night. You got your desks and you got your one filing cabinet, actually one of ours, and you got your pair of terminals about the same age as the building. All in all, a fab office for four."

Jake sighed and shook his head, "It's the best we could get. And Brian wasn't that bad. He's concerned about the girls is all. Larry has a tendency toward the flamboyant."

"Jesus, Jake, you're about as stiff as your shirt. All I'm sayin' is we got nice digs here for a cop shop. And anything more than your deadpan delivery is only flamboyant to you. You got the energy level of a corpse. Sort of look like one too."

Spence threw her bag on one of the desks settling who got what, and the action killed the repartee between the two.

"Spence, you get anywhere with the stroll and Red?"

"I'm goin' back tonight. Takes time to get accepted down there, but I'm in okay. There was a raid went down. You know anything about that?"

"One of the sporadic invasions by the vice squad. Political really. Makes them seem concerned with the public good and all that. It doesn't mean much and accomplishes next to nothing. Mostly it's just noise."

"It emptied the stroll, scared the shit out of the girls, and it took most of the evening for things to get back to what passes for normal, so I didn't get much. That happen often?"

"Too often for me, but pretty irregular and sort of spread out most of the time unless there's some sort of pressure from somewhere."

"There is some good news," Jake added. "No new girls have disappeared, and we have a line on a van and driver. Seems this guy harasses one girl in particular, and it pissed her off enough to call it in. The van's a dark colour, the driver's got a weird voice. No description beyond that."

"Yeah, so that's like half the clients out there." Larry yanked on his tie. "Big fuckin' help, a dark van and a kinky voice. Still, we'll watch for him. You guys get anything at all?"

Spence grinned. "You got the van right. We found the thing last night, or we think it's the one. It was parked over behind the park. And if it's the same one we saw talking to a girl up on Gore across from the Firehall Theatre, then we got somethin'. Alan ran the plates."

"I got an owner okay, but he's deceased." Alan glanced at his notes. "His old lady said the van got sold years ago, she doesn't remember to who."

"Whom," Larry said and grinned.

"My, my, very polished with agreements and such. Can't say the same about the suit though." Alan grinned at him and ran his eyes up and down the length of the offending garment.

"You wanna be careful makin' snap judgements, books by their cover an' all that. And you a cop." Larry looked suitably indignant.

Alan shook his head and the grin got bigger. He looked down at his notebook. "The van got sold alright. But the plates're the same old ones. Whoever bought it paid cash and never changed the ownership. So that gets us nowhere. Except we do have the plates now. I've already put out a BOLO with the instruction to observe and follow but not apprehend."

Alan thought for a moment, then added, "I also requested any sighting be relayed to one of us. That way, we can take over the surveillance. If the driver hits the stroll, we can follow him, maybe find the girls."

"Good. We got our piece of shit locked up. Had to lean on him a bit. Resisted don't you know, so we're good to help with this one. If we get this prick, and he's the one who guts girls, god forbid, everybody's gonna love us." Larry sat back, a satisfied smile on his face.

"And we'll make sure you two get credit for all of it. No skin off our noses, and you get some of yours back." Jake nodded and smiled too. "We've been digging up background on the three missing girls. We have street names. Might be them, might not."

"Yeah, and we got some hits." Larry shoved both hands in his suit jacket pockets. "All three've been talked to one time or another and wound up in the data base. If it's them." He shrugged his shoulders to get the suit coat back up on his shoulders where it felt more comfortable. It immediately slipped down again. "So we put together dossiers. Let's grab some coffee and go over them, see if anything clicks with you guys."

They were about to leave the cubicle for the cafeteria a floor down when Brian Stevens appeared in the opening. "You four, my office. We got something you need to see."

"So much for coffee," muttered Larry, yanking his hands out of his pockets. All four trooped along behind Brian.

Brian's office was damn near sterile compared to the office they'd just left. There weren't any papers tacked up, no messy files on the desk. And they could smell coffee.

"Pot's back there on the credenza, help yourselves."

Brian settled behind the desk while they helped themselves to coffee—porcelain cups, silver spoons, sugar, and real cream. They juggled back to the chairs arranged in front of the desk and waited.

"There's been another bush murder. This one's up in the Powell River area. Some trapper found a body out near his trap line near a town called Hammil. That's near the lower end of Dodd Lake. Here I'll show you."

On the corner of Brian's desk, was a small black unit with glowing buttons. He pushed one of these, and a map appeared on a large TV panel off to the side. The coast of the BC mainland from Jervis Inlet up past Powell River filled the screen. He picked up a pointer, and a red dot followed the highway up to the lake and moved off to the side.

"It was about here, back in the bush. Let me enlarge this section." Brian hit another button and the area expanded to three times the size.

"The same MO as the murders you guys had over in Harbour City. Young female, disemboweled, funny blue marks all over her shoulder, body sitting in a ring of stones. She'd been there a while too. I've got the initial report, the crime scene photos and sketches, the autopsy report, and all the forensics. I've also got a special note from the coroner up there. She seems to think she may have an idea about the method and cause of death." Brian turned off the overhead, reached in a drawer, and handed Jake a thick file.

"All four of you are on this, especially you two." He looked at Alan and Spence. "You've got a feel for whoever did this. You need to be the movers on this one. Jake, you take charge as always, but these two are gonna run this thing. You're all off anything else.

Liaise with the Powell River guys and see what pops. They've just begun an area search, so we're a bit late getting in. We're gonna need a crew on this asap. Jake, I'll expect to hear from you on what you need by shift end. Oh, and keep the missing girls from the stroll. Might be a connection. Work 'em both. Get on it."

All four of them rose, coffee virtually untouched, and filed out Larry looked back longingly.

"Real cups, shit, that coffee was the best I've had in years, shit!"

"We'll get you another one from the caf." Jake grinned, "Don't want you jittery from lack of caffeine."

Back in the cubicle, all four pulled chairs around the desks and spread out the files. They spent an hour or so reading what they had before they began to discuss the case.

Spence handed the forensics report and the crime scene photos to Jake. "Take a look at the shoulder. You can just barely see it what with the decomp, but those marks are identical to the ones we found on the island vics. So the prof's report on what they mean still holds. If you haven't read it, I've got it on my laptop. Let me print some copies."

While Spence was doing that, Alan filled in. "The gist of the report was that these two guys took the girls to transform them, send them over to the next world, and presumably that cleansed them somehow. All the symbols are symbols of transformation, the zodiacal ones and the circular ones.

"The profiler agreed with him and added one interesting thing. She was certain there was a sexual element to the killings even though there was no evidence of sexual molestation. We still don't understand that part, but the profiler was convinced somehow sex came into it. Here's something else. Every case involved a cellar, a dirt room underground. That's where the girls were kept. The report from Hammil says there was a root cellar in an old farmhouse. Sex, dark cellar, transformation. The one girl who escaped near Harbour City confirmed the root cellar thing. She was kept in one. We did a bush search and our guys found the remains of a cabin with a root cellar out behind. There was another one under the cabin itself. The notes from the forensics guy in Hammil say that that farmhouse root cellar was used by the killers up there. It is our guys."

Spence came back with copies of the professor's report and handed them around. "This guy is a world-respected mythographer and he's an expert with symbols and cults. We found him at Simon Fraser. He came over during our cases on the island and visited the sites. He also sat in with the profiler and the two of us. The result was interesting. The two of them, Prof and Profiler, fit together perfectly."

"Something you need to know about the girls too. Every one of them had a quality that attracted our perps. The one who got away has it too. It's a kind of sensual aura. They radiated a kind of sexual innuendo. You know, that thing some women have that every guy within a mile responds to? Even women see it. It's in the way they walk, the way they move, everything. You can't miss it."

"Wish my wife had it. I'd get home more often." Larry grinned at them and flicked his eyebrows.

"She left you a year and a half ago, so if she had it, you missed it." Jake stared over the tops of his reading glasses at Larry.

Larry ignored him. "So what else you got we should know that isn't in this pile of paper?"

"They're all young; they're all dark-haired; and they all had an interest in the stroll. So maybe there's a link to the girls we're looking for here. And if there is, we're not gonna find them in a hurry. They'll be in the bush somewhere just like the pair we had over there and the one they found in Powell River." Spence looked at Alan and he nodded.

"How long was that one lyin' there?" Jake asked.

Larry rifled through the initial report, stuck his finger on a paragraph, and said, "Three days or more. Nothing from Hammil or Powell River until the autopsy was done. Then they seem to have made the connection. Coroner estimates she'd been there longer: four to five days before she was found. So we're talkin' a week or so since the killing."

"It's possible they could be here. But it's unlikely our three are a part of it. They've been missing longer."

"It's still possible," added Alan. "Our guys might have gotten off the island, come here, and started with the three girls here. Then moved north up the coast. And if that's the case, we're gonna find bodies stuck somewhere out in the bush here, maybe up in the mountains on the north shore, or even in one of the bigger provincial parks. There are a lot of possibilities in close range."

"We get bodies turnin' up around here, the shit's gonna be so deep, we'll have to wear waders. That happens, all four of us'll be on patrol in fuckin' Cranbrook." Larry didn't look happy.

Jake gathered up the reports, looked at the other three, and laid out the day. "Spence, keep your date with Red tonight and see if you can get anything out of the girls. Alan, find that damn van. Link it to the driver. Larry, you and me'll set up with Powell River, get something organized with them and Harbour City. Take us most of the day. So we get together late afternoon, see what we got?"

Everybody nodded, and Alan and Spence left the two detectives arguing over who'd do what.

On the street outside the department, the same food cart stood in the same place. Odours of fried onions wafted over them, and Alan turned towards it.

"Not on your life. Look at that thing. It hasn't been cleaned since it was built. And look at the guy running it. He hasn't either."

Spence hooked her arm in Alan's and pulled him along.

"But he's got fried onions! Nothin' like fried onions on a dog or burger. We could save time and money."

"I'll settle for the Starbucks down on Powell and Cordova, but no way I'm eating from that thing."

She drove. They were down Cordova and at the coffee shop before much else got said. Spence drove the grey unmarked dodge the same way she did her Camaro, fast. The effect wasn't the same, though, the ride was too soft, the cornering lousy, and the engine underpowered. Still, Alan grabbed the edge of the door with one hand and the dash with the other.

They ordered large coffees and sandwich wraps. The place

wasn't busy. There were two girls at a rear table, both too skinny with that vacant stare the hooked ones had. They were in minis and tops and none too clean. They were, however, aware of Spence and Alan, and seemed to make themselves smaller somehow.

"Jesus, we been made by that pair," Spence whispered to Alan.

"We need to be less obvious somehow. Maybe it's the shoes." She glanced down at the regulation lace-ups on their feet. "The damn things make us walk different."

They took their coffees and sandwiches to a front table. Spence sat with her back to the girls and Alan added cream and sugar to his coffee and milk to hers at the little counter. When he turned, a cup in each hand, he almost collided with the two girls clattering out the door on their high heels. He put the cups on the table and sat beside Spence so they both had a view of the narrow lot.

"They seemed a little concerned."

"They were both high. Probably shot up in the bathroom. After the other night, everybody's still a bit gun shy. We're cops and they know it."

"You're right, we gotta get better shoes. What do you think about the latest? Are our three missing ones here part of the island mess, you think?"

"I'm not sure. And I'm not sure I agree with you about their starting here in the city. It makes one kinda sense, but I think they went north after Harbour City. Everything down here was so damn tight with patrols, I don't see how they could have moved anywhere without someone spotting them."

"If they started again up north, then our three aren't part of it, and we need to focus on the van and driver. There are two killers in our cases over there and only one guy spotted here, at least that's what everybody says, so you might be right. This could be a separate thing. If it is, I gotta find that van and its driver. You're off till tonight when you meet Red, so we can cruise together. See if the damn thing's around the park first off, then grid the place until we find it. If he leaves the van behind the park a lot, all we have to do is wait until he shows."

"Suits me. I'm meeting Red at seven, so if we hit our place

about five, I can make dinner and still change and meet Red. When do we get together with Jake?"

"Around shift change. Let's get back by three-thirty."

Once the sandwiches were done and the coffee gone, Spence hit the john while Alan got them both a Pike Grande to go. He waited for her in front of the small store, the coffees sitting on one of the two small tables that were jammed into the tiny cement raised space between the store front and the curb of the parking lot.

"Those girls were definitely shooting up. The john's a mess. Couple of needles in the waste bin, toilet paper all over the place, and a sink you wouldn't wanna wash in. Jesus, I hate washrooms like that. They make me feel dirty just going in." Spence was still rubbing her hands together as if they needed cleaning.

"Just milk in that one," Alan pointed to the closest coffee cup. Spence wiped her hands on her pants and picked it up.

"Thanks. Let's drink in the car. I want to get out of here."

Spence drove them to Strathcona Park, slid around the far end, and cruised slowly along its length. The van wasn't there. She parked close to the raised area containing the community gardens, and they drank their coffees while they considered their next move.

Spence sipped slowly. "We should extend what we look at. Include the part of the stroll on the other side of Clark."

Clark was a main feeder to the Powell east-west artery, and along with the ramp to the docks that rose up over Powell and fed the big rigs into the restricted port areas, Clark effectively split the hooker area into two halves. The half Spence was referring to contained blocks of light industry and warehouses, and after dark and even in the afternoon, the girls used Franklin Street, a block up from Powell, for trade. The johns would make the circuits off Clark and Powell numerous times watching the girls. Trade was slow during the latter part of the day, but at night, it was brisk.

"I met Red up there on Commercial, and there was some action even in the afternoon. Not much, but some. We can grid the whole thing in a half hour. I don't think we'll find anything until tonight, but it's worth a try."

Alan slid his coffee back in the holder. "He's gotta park

that van somewhere. If he's not here, could be he's parked up there. You're right, we better do the whole area, and we need to check between Powell and the docks, see if he's holed up back on one of those alleys behind the shops."

"You know this is pretty useless, don't you? I think Larry and Jake wanted us out of the way so they can get the liaison stuff done and have a plan ready for when we meet at four."

"Well, it beats sitting around reading reports in that rabbit warren. At least we're out and doing something. We can go past the house anytime you want, get your stuff. You can change at the station. Save messing around in rush hour that way."

"Sounds like a plan."

Spence put the unmarked in gear and slowly circled the park. She took Prior, which was what Venables had become Parkside, back to Raymur and cruised down under the Hastings overpass where the tranny stroll was. She hit Powell, passed Clark, and took the unmarked over to Franklin, then to Commercial and began the grid. There weren't many streets between Hastings and Powell, but they were long. The whole area was a patchwork of warehouses, the occasional small restaurant, the occasional bar, industrial shops, and a couple of small four-storey hotels.

The van wasn't anywhere in that grid, so Spence took the unmarked back to Campbell and Hastings, and they started another grid there. The result was the same, no van.

"Fuck it," Spence said. "Let's go home for a couple hours. I can see what's' goin' on in Harbour City, make some snacks to take with us, and change for tonight. We can still be back before three-thirty."

"All we're doing is burning gas, so sure, let's head home. Why is it this feels just like patrol?"

"Because it is like patrol. It's make-work. Like I said, it gets us out of their hair while they set up with Harbour City and PR. They want time? Let's give it to them."

Spence swung the unmarked around and headed out Hastings to Nanaimo. A left at the corner took her to the alley that ran through the middle of the block and led to the small lot behind their apartment building. They took the back stairs up to their unit.

The place looked a lot better now with stuff in it. They'd moved things around until the rooms felt right. Alan wasn't sure what that meant, but Spence seemed to know, and it was she who'd decided when that had happened.

The door from the back porch led directly into the kitchen with its old-style, hexagonal white tile floor and its Quaker-style cabinets. The stove, fridge, and dishwasher were new and white as well. The door in the right wall at the end led into the dining room.

Spence had set up the computers on a small table in the living room, and she punched them on as soon as she got there. She sent off an email to Sabina and Harry, then moved a room down into her bedroom and picked out the night's costume: the required miniskirt, a lacy red top, quite tight, black thigh-highs and black high-heeled knee-high boots. The bra and panties, both black and lacy, she put on under her street clothes. In her large bag were the usual items along with some mace and a blackjack. She wasn't taking shit from anybody.

She checked the two computers, saw nothing from the privates, shut down, and took her gear to the kitchen.

Alan had made more coffee and a bunch of sandwiches. They ate quickly and packed up some snacks for the night since Alan would be her cover while she worked with Red. Then they headed for the station.

Jake and Larry were where they'd left them earlier in the day. The rest of the room was filling up with returning detectives finishing paperwork before shift change. The office was a mess. Papers were strewn all over the place including the two desks assigned to Alan and Spence. There were crime scene photos tacked to the fabric flats that separated their space from the other detectives, and a new addition, a white board. It was stuck in the corner, making the space even tighter.

"Ah, the wayward twins, finally." Larry looked at them over his shoulder.

"You said four. It's three-thirty now. You two got rid of us for the day so you could do whatever you were doing, so stuff it."

"Ouch, prickly, aren't we?"

"It's been a frustrating day so far, and it's going to be a long night, so if you've got something going, tell us."

Spence threw her big bag on her desk on top of whatever the other two had covered it with, dumped more paper off her chair, and sat.

"Okay, lighten up Spence. We need to go over what we got while you were out looking for that van." Jake smiled at her and Alan and gestured to the white board.

"We've got some structure now, some coordination between the detachments, and we've got some principals lined up in all three places. So we've got a kind of task force of homicide detectives in all three cities: Harbour, Powell, and here."

Alan looked at Jake. "Who?"

"In Harbour City, we have you two back on the case workin' from here. Josie Atardo's in the loop. In Powell River, we have Gordie Parker and Frank Miller, homicide, and in Hammil, Herk Berman. Then for Vancouver, the two of us. Your boss told us you're to decide where and how we pull this all together."

"Wonder why she decided to grab control from there?" Spence looked at Alan who shrugged.

"It's political. She's been told."

"Let's put it to them then." Spence glared at everyone. "Let's get what we need: that pair of privates from Harbour City. They know the old cases backwards, and they have a super-connection to Chinatown and that woman who runs the place. I never thought in my wildest dreams I'd ask for them, but that's what I'm doing." Spence looked at all three of them starting with Jake.

Jake shrugged, "No skin off my nose, get 'em if you want 'em."

"Larry?"

"None off mine either."

"Alan, you on board?"

"I've always been on board with those two." He looked at Jake and Larry and added, "They're very good, and they have connections we just don't have. They're also about as bad as you guys with the jokes, but they're capable. They helped get us close to catching those creeps."

"I'll add 'em to the list." Jake picked up the marker and waited.

"Harry and Sabina, partners. Office is called SHH Investigations. Silly, but it's what they chose. Last names I've never been sure about. Hargreaves or something."

"So now we got two more," Jake said. "The two of us, you two, two from Powell River, one from Hammil, two privates from Harbour City. Nine in all."

"The brass'll leave us alone until we either fuck up or solve it. Then they'll be there in droves. We'll have to be careful not to get trampled." Spence grinned at the others and stretched.

"We gotta center this mess somewhere. We should probably move it up to Powell River. That's the latest. That's where the search is going on, not that I think they'll find them. If there are more, god forbid, we'll move with them. We need to settle who's running the show and get started." Alan looked around.

"Brian's already put us at your disposal, and now, so has Josie Atardo. Since you carried the first cases, it's your baby. You two are leads as you so gracefully put it, so if you fuck up, the rest of us just shrug and let you get creamed." Larry grinned at them.

Jake stood at the board looking reasonably happy. "All we've done so far is get the ducks in a row. All the permissions are in place, everybody who matters knows, task force has been okayed, budgets are in place. Word is we get whatever we need to catch these guys. Overtime's been authorized. So if you want to start setting up who does what when, everything's good to go."

17.

At six, it got dark enough for him to start. He always dressed in black: black shoes, high top runners; black elastic-top pants made of soft, noiseless fabric, the kind that joggers and old men wear; a black t-shirt, short in the body; and a hoodie, one of the lightweight ones with an elastic waist.

It was already October, but the rains hadn't really started yet, and it was still warm, so cruising was a rich experience for him: long soft nights with colourful prey all over the place, so easy to take, like stealing apples from a cart.

These girls, he wondered why they weren't more aware of him. He walked in their midst, hoodie up like every young guy in town, completely ignored while they concentrated on flashing legs and tits at every car that went by. Only the occasional one looked his way, her smile glued on, but he ignored them, passing by in silence.

Those weren't the ones he wanted, not the ones he had to transform. He looked for the laughing ones, the strutting ones, the ones who thought they were somehow special because they were noticed more, picked up more, and by virtue of that, were more convinced of their appeal to the unbridled lust of their prey. The sirens of the streets.

He'd remove them from the equation and diminish them bit by bit until they were bled of the arrogance, they thought they possessed by right. This night he'd take one he'd been watching, the one in the tight white dress, the one who glided like liquid down the sidewalk, her long legs swinging, her arms swinging, her knowing eyes focused on the street. She was full of herself.

She had laughed at him the one time he stopped to look at her and had thrown out her hips in that way she had, telling him to come back when he was big enough.

He was a short man, he knew that, and seemingly skinny, and he looked very young. But he wasn't young, and he wasn't skinny. He was strong and sinewy; he was like a well-oiled machine, and he could move very fast, faster than the kid she thought he was. And unlike kids, he was patient; he could keep it all inside where it couldn't be seen. He only looked impotent; he wasn't at all.

He left his dark blue panel van on the far side of the square of parkland with the community gardens. He walked along the unlit path that cut through its center, the night turning its greens to blacks. He crossed Prior at the light and walked up to Adanac. He turned on Adanac and walked through the tiny garden up to Main, then to Hastings, then down to Campbell, passing the many restaurant supply houses, the steam bath where the girls sometimes took their tricks, the outreach mission churches, and the little convenience stores shoved in here and there. He had time.

The scenario in his head was detailed and rich. It had been sent to him; it repeated itself over and over day and night; he knew his task was to improve with each one he took. The vision shimmered in front of him in perfect clarity, more real than the grubby street or any of the girls who infested it.

At the corner of Campbell and Hastings, he paused. The light changed in his favour, but he remained standing at the curb, swaying slightly as if he were high on something other than the pictures flowing though his mind. The light turned against him and he waited. When the light changed again, he crossed Hastings, turned on the other side, and walked back up toward Main.

He put the visions flowing through him away and watched the street. He discarded the working people, the drunks, the homeless, and the drugged. He saw only the girls, and these he noted carefully, evaluating each one as if he were in a market, picking over the offerings of various stalls.

He turned the corner on Main, walked along the side of the police headquarters building, stepped around two men in plain clothes just leaving through the double glass doors, and turned again onto Cordova. He passed the ranks of police cars lining both sides of the one-way street like long links of white sausages streaked with blue.

He walked by the Anglican church on the next corner across from the Firehall Theatre, its vast white bulk rising ponderously into the air. A block before, he'd passed the wasteland the city called a park, a dirty oasis dotted with the shambling wrecks of men and tired women. In one corner was a playground, an incongruous splash of bright red and blue and yellow tubes and swings and slides. The irony of the juxtaposition was lost on the park's inhabitants but not on him.

He walked on down the slight grade past the mission on the other side. Men shuffled about near the door in a large messy group, like a litter of discarded husks. On this block across the road, the houses stood back in the growing darkness, mute and neglected. He continued walking down to Heatley, to the stop light. He stood on the corner and leaned against a pole watching the three girls on the other side. A single straggly tree fighting a lost cause rose from the tiny patch of earth near the corner.

One of the girls propped her back against its trunk and watched the cars stopping and turning at the corner. When one seemed to slow more than the others, especially if the driver's window were down, she'd stand up, smile provocatively, and wriggle her fingers palm out, arm crooked at waist level. When the driver failed to respond and the car turned the corner, she'd slouch back against the tree, whatever light had been in her eyes dimming to flat and dull.

He waited for two lights, watching, then crossed the street and continued his walk. This one was a long drab industrial block relieved only by the ambulance station. He crossed Cordova to the other side where the girls were. Way down, on the corner ahead of him, he could see a few girls.

This corner was one of the girls' favourites. They were always clustered on the sidewalk or in the doorway of the building that stretched along the side of Cordova.

He paused when he got there, scanning the gaggle on the corner for White Skirt, but she wasn't in the group or on the cross street. He watched most of the cars swing into the curve to Powell, then walked across the intersection following the smaller flow of cruising cars down to Campbell, the drivers turning their heads so they could see the girls on the sidewalk more clearly. White skirt wasn't on this block either.

From Campbell on down the hill to where it ended at a T-intersection two blocks further on, Cordova Street became the tranny track. Here, the girls' skirts were just as short, their outfits just as provocative. Most of them, though, were much taller.

He hesitated at the corner, shrugged, and walked on down the hill and across the train tracks. He glanced up under the Hastings overpass, but there were no white skirts. He didn't think there would be, but sometimes the girls mixed in just for laughs and made the night even more confusing.

He turned back, walked up the hill to Campbell, turned left back to Hastings and repeated his movements. He would continue this way for the rest of the evening following the seven-block long one-block wide rectangle until he found White Skirt, or the stroll closed down. If this night journey proved barren, he would return to the other girls and continue his work until the darkness came back.

The old refrigeration room still with its functional, heavy, insulated wood-and-metal door lay at the rear of the derelict building. It had no windows, of course, given its function, and it was heavily insulated with thick internal walls and even thicker external ones. It had belonged to a fish company that once ran trucks of frozen imported fish to various Vancouver businesses, especially those in and around Chinatown, and to upscale restaurants all over the city. The business had suffered from a downturn in the economy caused by a change in the governing party, one that was more favourable to unions. Not that the fish company had a union, it was staffed entirely by hard-working immigrants from Asia who had no knowledge of such organizations and were, therefore, easily exploited. As profits declined because of that change, however, the company that owned the building and imported the fish simply abandoned it and moved its operations south of the border.

So the building stood, the few windows in its facade boarded up, its truck lot empty and weeds sprouting everywhere. Although there was water, there was no power and no heat.

The small man in black clothing didn't care. To him it was both home and a place to perfect his vision, a place to transform his girls. He kept them in the old freezer and fed them when they deserved to be fed. Otherwise, he left them water, a few flashlights, and a portable toilet. Once a week, he gave them enough soap and water to clean themselves in the large metal tank he'd found in another part of the fish plant. He took them there one at a time, locking the others in, and watched for signs of transformation as they bathed themselves.

There were three of them. One was named Sugar, at least she had been until he took the name from her. Now, none of them had a name that mattered. Whatever identity they had formerly possessed, however shaky, was gone. They were now just his girls, responding only to him, rarely anymore to each other. His intention had been first to break down who they were and then to reform them according to his vision. In the first of these, he had succeeded; in the second, he was less successful. But he had patience and a calling. He would reform them.

The girls lived mostly in darkness unless their prison door was open, and that occurred only when the man in black was in during the day. Even when he was, the light was limited to the suffused and feeble glow from two filthy skylights. Since the man worked as a cleaner in a small church close to the tenderloin on most of his days, he was not in residence much during daylight hours. It was the darkness mostly that robbed the girls of their identity and broke their ability to communicate with each other. They became remote, even from themselves.

The church pastor where the man worked was a good man who cared more for feeding the indigent than holding services. He operated his outreach program with the proceeds from a meagre fund provided by city services in recognition of his dedication to the homeless of the city's east end. What little he had, was augmented slightly by his congregation's contributions at Sunday services and by the bingo night each Tuesday for which there was a nominal charge per card. On occasion, he found businesses sympathetic to his cause, and they too contributed. Still, it was hard times for the church and its mission. When he could, he paid the man in black in cash.

On Sundays, sometimes, the man sat in a rear pew and listened to the pastor speak of a higher power, one who cared for least among them. Especially for the least of them. On one of those evenings after the service ended and the man was left alone in the church to clean and close up, a voice spoke to him. It was soft, whispery, and came from everywhere in the small church, like a musical note floating on air. At first, he couldn't understand it because he couldn't hear it clearly no matter how hard he tried, but Sunday after Sunday, it returned when he was alone. He felt it as much as heard it, and over time, it became a part of him. Eventually, he carried it with him beyond the confines of the church, an ever-present whispery sensation that seemed to require something of him. And then one night as he walked the streets, the vision formed, and he knew what the voice wanted.

The small man had no success finding White Skirt that night. He walked slowly back to his old van and drove to the derelict fish plant, the vision shimmering, almost translucent, floating through the hardness of the street, never entirely obscured by the dark bulk of the buildings or the black shadows between them. This time of night, the streets were silent and empty, the city sleeping. He left his van on the street behind the fish plant as he always did when he was tending to his flock.

He had no work at the church for the next two days, and in that window of light, he felt he must recreate his girls and bring them back transformed. Then he would release them to the night once more, chastened, aware, and grateful to him for the revelation. He must find White Skirt. She would be his finest achievement. There was so little time and so much to accomplish.

The next evening, the man parked his van behind the gardens at the rear of Strathcona Park where he sometimes left it. He'd look for White Skirt, and if he found her, he'd return for the van. Most of the girls wouldn't get in with him, but unknowingly they helped him look for the bad ones, the ones who needed correction, the arrogant ones who shouldn't misuse their power the way they did. He could help them. He could take the power from them and make them to what they really were and should be. He'd almost finished with the ones he had, only White Skirt eluded him. Once he had her and gave her back to herself the way she should be, he could rest. He was tired; it was a difficult task he'd been given, but he had no choice. The voices were more insistent now. They never left him. He knew what they wanted, and he knew his time was short.

He locked the van, checked everything twice, and walked back toward the stroll. He did his usual circuit, consumed once again by the vision.

He floated up Hastings and down Gore and there she was, White Skirt, alive with the power she so misused. She was beautiful, the most beautiful of any of them. She glowed with power. He slid past the intersection, turned up Cordova, turned again at Main to the other side of Hastings, towards the park and his van.

He started the van, drove slowly up the side of the park to Prior, turned toward the city, found Gore. She'd wait for him, she knew he was coming. She'd see his state of grace, and she would enter the van as had the others. He stopped at Hastings, crossed when the traffic allowed, and there she was on the corner: White Skirt, a shining temptress, alone and waiting.

He slowed and rolled down the window. She saw the van and sauntered over. She smiled up at him, climbed on the passenger side running board, and leaned in the open window.

"Hello there. You want some company?"

"You want to come inside, miss? It's warm in here and dry."

She froze suddenly, and he wondered what he'd said. He tried again.

"You look lovely in that white dress, I'd like to take you home with me, I truly would."

Glory knew that voice. But it didn't go with the van. It was a voice she'd heard before. She hadn't liked it then and she didn't like it now. It gave her the creeps.

She couldn't connect the van with the short, thin man in black, the boy she'd sent packing long ago. A little shaken, she climbed down, and muttered, "Fuck off."

She walked back to the corner and it followed slowly. She ignored it. If he didn't move away soon, she'd walk down Cordova and the traffic would force him on. She stood hipshot again, her long, lovely legs on display, her tight skimpy top promising pleasure beyond measure. She almost shone, her colour was so striking against the white of her short dress.

The drivers of the cars on Cordova slowed as they passed her. The man in the van watched them, saw their lust drawn out of them by the succubus in white. He knew her power over them. After all, he fought it himself every time he drew near. She would burn him, destroy him in the flames of his own lust for her.

Without the power of his vision, the whispers of the voice, he would be as lost as they were in the hands of the temptress. Out of the endless flow of traffic streaming down the asphalt, one drew to the curb. He watched her work her magic, open the door, and disappear inside. Another lost soul, he thought. She'd suck up his essence, gorge herself on it, and grow even more powerful as she diminished him. With each of them, she grew more dangerous.

He had no choice. He must take the power from her. Soon he would have the greatest of them all as the vision promised. That battle would be epic, he knew.

He started the van and drove into the flow of traffic down Cordova. He had lost her tonight, but only for the present.

The dance of power between them would continue until he succeeded in taking her.

18.

The little man in black slipped through the opening in the rotting plywood panel that covered the rear loading doors. They were heavy steel roll-ups that had been left unlocked and up about four feet for some reason, perhaps by someone else who had used the place. The outside edge of the loading bay entrances had been covered in plywood, but the weather, especially the rains, had compromised the panels.

He'd pried one sheet loose when he'd first found the building and discovered how many of his needs the interior met. It had running water and lots of space. It even had skylights. He discovered the great wood- and metal-door of the freezer that opened on a large dark space. Inside, he could hear nothing and see nothing. It was as if the outside didn't exist once he entered this room. It was a special magical place. Now with his vision, it had become even more special. It was a waiting room for his special girls, the dark womb of rebirth. It seemed to him that the voice had led him here to this perfect place.

Once inside the loading doors, the man waited for his eyes to adjust to the gloom and then walked slowly around his home. He pushed through the large swinging doors at the end of the wide corridor into the main room. The great wooden freezer door at the end of the building was closed, and he could hear nothing. His girls were inside and quiet as he knew they would be.

The man pushed up the locking handle and pulled the door open. The three girls barely reacted. They were all huddled on cushions, which he had taken from discarded sofas left on the curb and pushed together in a corner to make a kind of bed. The room stank of chemical toilet and unwashed bodies. The girls' clothes were dirty, and they were ripe with the odours of neglect and fear. He shook his head. He'd cleaned the toilet only a few days ago, but the girls had little appreciation of all he did for them. They no longer screamed at him, no longer tried to get out of the freezer when he opened the door. They were broken now, so he was gentler with them than he had been. All he needed to do now was to infuse them with the vision and release them. The voice would tell him when they were ready.

He kept what food there was in a series of lockers he'd found in a room close to the loading docks. All of it was processed and bagged or canned. He didn't trust bottles. The water he got from taps, and he had plastic plates and cups and cutlery from the church. He'd return all of it when his work was done. And he was close.

Lately, the voice had filled his body with a constant whispery sibilance and his head with a glorious shimmering vision of transformation that was all light and shifting colours.

He watched the girls for a few minutes in the beam from his light. They were curled up together on their cushiony bed, but they knew he was there. He could tell from the way they shifted when the light hit them.

I'll feed them something special tonight, he thought, they deserve something good. They're almost ready. All the arrogance, all the slyness had gone, and in its place, he saw an acceptance that warmed his heart and pleased the voice. I'll even let them bathe a few days early, he thought. They need to be as clean now on the outside as they are on the inside.

Once done bathing, he'd wash their clothes. He considered the order of things. "Those two first, then dinner. I have tins. I'll give each of my girls one. The brown beans, I think" He muttered to himself. "I have some bread left from yesterday." The girls didn't hear him. They'd faced away from him and huddled together in the corner on the few cushions he'd left them.

He rubbed his hands together in pleasure and closed the door to the refrigeration unit. He hesitated, then reopened it, smiled at the backs of the girls, and left it that way. They would stay. He'd removed all the bad from them. They had no reason and no desire to leave. They'd been redeemed, recreated, they were pure. He was certain of it.

The voice swelled inside him, rapturous, colours erupted in his head, pushing out into the dark space until they filled it, turning the darkness into a wondrous shimmering vision. His girls. They will shine on the street, he thought, glow with their redemption, they'll be examples of the perfection waiting for White Skirt.

Inside the locker, Sugar stirred, opened her eyes, and whispered, "He's left the door open. He thinks we won't leave."

Rose, a tall black-haired girl, turned her head toward Sugar. She blinked a few times and muttered, "He's right. How would we get out? We can barely crawl after what he's done to us. And he keeps that fuckin' door closed and locked most all the time." It was more than she'd said in days.

The blond girl behind Sugar, whose name was Blue, looked at Rose and said, "I don't think I can walk very far anymore, and I hurt everywhere. He took my shoes."

Sugar stared into the meager glimmer of light coming through the filthy skylight. "He took all our shoes days ago. So what? We can go barefoot. We're all wrecked from being in here and putting up with his shit, but we got a chance to go, and we should take it." Sugar looked at the other two. "He thinks we're done. We can't let him win."

"I am done," Rose said. "We can barely walk across the floor to the tub when he lets us get a bath without we help each other up."

All three girls were addicted to drugs of one sort or another, and the withdrawal had been hard on them. The man's general mistreatment of them had taken a toll as well, and they'd all lost weight.

The little man in black smiled to himself. All that remained was to inject the vision. The voice would tell him how.

Tonight, he would finish with his girls, at least the three he had. White Skirt was special. He understood that, understood why he had failed to capture her. She was there, but he wasn't ready yet. When his girls were put back, shiny and new, then he could take her. The voices whispered. His path was clearer now.

He turned on the upper faucets to let the tub fill while he inspected the lockers. He took out four cans of kidney beans, part of a loaf of stale bread, and some bags of chips, vinegar and salt, which he liked best. He carried the items back to the little kitchen area he'd constructed from some old crates and had covered with a plastic tablecloth.

He opened all the cans, got out some plastic spoons, cut up chunks of bread, and opened the chips. He put everything on a board he'd found and carried it back to the area near the big tub. He turned off the water and got out some blankets. He put one on the floor, put the board with the food in the middle, and placed the other blankets around it. He stood back, looked critically at his arrangement. Then he went to get his girls.

When he shone his torch into the blackness of the freezer, he couldn't believe his eyes.

He flashed the light all over the freezer. His head hurt. Suddenly the voice was muttering insistently, louder than before. He felt the urgency as a living thing inside him and bolted into the main area of the fish plant. They had to be here, maybe by the big tub? He ran that way and swung the light wildly around. There were no girls. Not in the tub, not on the blanket, not eating, nowhere. He ran back to the freezer, ran inside and swung the light around. Nothing. He was sobbing now, and he hurt. The voices were angry, tearing at him, demanding, implacable.

Rose picked her way gingerly across the rough wood floor, her arm on Sugar's shoulder. Blue was behind her holding on to the waistband of her mini. They'd left the freezer only minutes ago, had kept close to the walls, and were at the far side of the main room now. They all knew where the man was and avoided any stretch he'd be likely to cross. His light was a problem for them in one sense and a benefit in another. If he swung it their way, he'd find them; if he didn't, it became a beacon telling them where not to go.

Walking was hard. The real problem was no shoes. They tried to move fast, but the floor was rough wood with lots of splinters. Added to that was the darkness and the difficulty finding their way. And they didn't know how to get out. They had no plan except to go as far and as fast as they could. What kept them moving was their fear of the man and their desperation to avoid the black nothingness of the freezer.

Sugar led them past piles of debris stacked along the walls, letting her hands do the seeing. The fish plant had a row of rooms down one side, dressing rooms, a canteen, and offices for the clerical staff. They got trapped inside the first of them until Sugar found the door again. Now, she felt her way past the open doorways.

In the main room they saw the light bouncing around behind them, heard his rapid, anxious mutterings. Their fear of discovery drove them on.

Sugar discovered a pair of large doors when they got past the row of rooms. When she felt her way across them, they bent outwards. Swinging doors, she thought, and pushed one open slowly. She led the others through them into a long wide corridor she sensed rather than saw. Rose still had her hand on Sugar's shoulder, and Blue still held on to the waist band of Rose's mini.

Sugar sensed there was something less opaque about the darkness. She slid her hands along the wall, felt the boards that ran horizontally about four feet up. They were rough with chips and gouges, but they led her steadily on. They could no longer see the man's light or hear his desperate mutterings.

Sugar's heart was racing. She continued to feel her way down the corridor, patting the horizontal boards as she went. She recognized them. They were like those wide boards she'd seen in the storage areas of the grocery stores she'd worked in. Those boards kept the carts that carried boxes from the storeroom to the store proper from gouging the walls. And she knew that there were loading doors somewhere close by, just as there were in the grocery stores. She closed her eyes and prayed. She knew the boards she was feeling now would lead them to those doors in the back and to freedom.

With the other two in tow, Sugar moved as quickly as she could. She needed to get them out of there.

Suddenly she heard a loud bang. The man must have burst through the doors. She saw his flashlight flicking off the walls and ceiling. She stood still, using her right arm to motion the other two down. She felt her breath in her throat as he stumbled past them. Sugar knew he would see them if he lowered his light even an inch.

The man wasn't seeing much. Panic drove him. The voices were roaring in his ears. They screamed at him, and the colours were angry too, like great flashes of lightning blasting through his consciousness.

He ran down the corridor slamming into the great metal overhead doors. He muttered incoherently, the volume rising and falling. He didn't know what to do. He turned to retrace his steps back to the main part of the plant.

The girls heard him yelling in the large room beyond the swinging doors. Sugar struggled to stand again and help the others up. Once she had managed, she moved as quickly as she could down the wall. She'd seen the huge loading dock doors in the man's light, seen the four-foot gap at the bottom and the plywood beyond.

Her heart was in her throat as she felt her way along. Her fingers found the corner, then the corrugated surface of the great doors. She traced down until her fingers found the opening. She felt the plywood at the edge of the loading dock, pushed on it as she moved along the gap until she felt one panel give.

Sugar pushed hard, saw the opening widen, and with the others in tow slipped through. The three girls stood on the narrow platform of the loading dock, breathing hard and filling their eyes with the pale darkness of evening. In the distance, they could see the lights of the city.

They could hear the cars on Powell. They took deep breaths, their hearts pounding. Sugar wasn't sure that they were free yet. He could still find them. She shuddered. They had to get away. She led them along the narrow platform to a short metal ladder leading to the broken pavement of the lot, and the three climbed down.

They ran clumsily across the cracked pavement in their bare feet. All three were silent and breathless as they reached the street. They crouched in the doorway of the building next door and pulled more air into their lungs. Blue began to cry. Sugar shushed her and stood. She had to pull the others up.

"We can't stay here. He's gonna come out and take us back. You want that? Let's get to a bigger street. Come on, move!"

The three girls stumbled down to the corner, Blue still holding onto the waistband of Rose's mini. She was limping now, blood from a cut in her foot leaving a trail of little splotches behind her.

Sugar led them to Commercial, then up a block to Franklin. They knew where they were now, and their hearts pounded. At the corner, she turned and took them across Commercial to the blocks of Franklin leading toward Clark. This area of warehouses was familiar territory. They needed to find someone with a cell phone. All their friends on the street carried them. They saw no one and hurried toward Clark.

Rose stubbed her toe on the edge of a cracked piece of the cement sidewalk and yelped. "Shit! Oh fuck, that hurts, shit!"

She stopped, leaned on the wall of the building they were passing and examined her foot. Blue let go of her waistband and leaned too. Sugar turned toward them, glanced back and looked at Rose's foot.

"Can you still walk? We gotta get past Clark if we can't find anybody here. Should be someone, but I can't see anybody. Test it, let's see if you can keep going."

Rose put her foot down gingerly, stood on it, winced, but nodded. "I can keep going, but the fuckin' thing hurts. Slow down some."

"Me too," Blue said, holding up her foot. Both girls turned to her. Blood was still dripping off the ends of Blue's toes. Sugar took a close look, felt the pad, and shook her head.

"How long you been walkin' on that?"

"It got hurt in the big room. It still hurts. Is it okay, you think?"

"You've cut the part behind your big toe, and it looks deep. Can you still walk on it?"

"It hurts, but I can walk, sure, like I been doin'. Can I hold on to you, Rose, please?"

"You've been holdin' on to my skirt so hard my gut hurts. Gimme your hand instead, yeah, like that. Okay, let's go."

Sugar led on, but not much slower. She was driven to get away. She squinted down the street, but there were no girls. She could see the cars passing on Clark a couple of blocks down and headed that way. It was strange. She knew it was late, but maybe if they headed down to Powell toward the tranny circuit somebody'd be there.

The girls walked on, crossed Clark at the Powell light, passed under the bridge when the traffic began to flow, and moved slowly up the street toward Raymur. There was enough traffic to light the way.

Sugar knew they were at the edge of the stroll when they passed Vernon and Glen. Just as they got to the Chevron station at the corner of Powell and Raymur, Sugar saw a cruiser in the lot and ran as fast as she could.

Sugar got to the open window and bent down. "We need help. We just got away from a crazy guy been holdin' us in some old plant over past Commercial. My friends are hurt. We got no shoes, he took 'em. We been walking' barefoot for blocks. Please just get us out of here. We're scared he's comin' after us."

Both cops watched as the other two girls approached, both limping badly.

The female officer had gotten out of the cruiser while Sugar was talking through the window. She'd walked around the rear end and was looking the girls over.

Rose turned her head and watched her. Neither cop smiled. Blue started to cry.

As Sugar tried to explain more, Rose joined in. Even Blue stopped crying and began to explain. The female constable tried to listen, but she couldn't understand her. Finally, the driver got out of the car and yelled, "Quiet!"

The girls jumped.

"Okay, you, yeah, you in the pink, you start. Take it from the beginning and do it slowly so we can understand you. You other two just shut up for a while, okay?"

Blue started to cry again and slid down to the pavement behind Sugar. Rose stood beside her, and Blue slumped against her bare legs.

While Sugar talked to the female officer, the driver knelt beside Blue and talked quietly to her. He helped her up and put her in the rear of the cruiser. Rose just stood and watched. When he turned toward her, she nodded and got in beside her friend.

Sugar told the woman about the man in the fish plant.

"He collected us, you know, like off the street. We thought it was just a trick, you know. He had some stuff he gave us. We thought we'd get high. But it put us to sleep. We couldn't move or talk. Maybe roofies? Whatever, we couldn't do nothin', and we all ended up in that shitty freezer. An' he took our shoes and locked us in. I mean, all that was about me, but Rose and Blue, they got the same. He's weird, lockin' us in that damned freezer. We had nothin', just what he fed us and some cushions and a stinkin' toilet, you know, one of those kind sits on the floor you don't gotta empty? And it was dark. All the time. We talked just to keep from goin' nutty, you know, but we was in there a long time, and soon we couldn't talk much."

Sugar stopped and shook her head, her eyes watering up. "You gotta go look you don't believe me. You gotta look."

The cop nodded. "We'll do that for sure. You get in with your friends. Here, I'll open the door. Watch your head."

She put Sugar in the back seat with the other two, leaned against the trunk, and talked it over with her partner. "We gotta call this in, get some more guys down here and take a look at that place. They look pretty bad."

"Let's get some of the guys first. Call it in after we see what's going on. These might be the missing girls we heard about. If they are, an' we get the guy as well, we're golden. I'll make the call."

Within minutes, two more cruisers, lightbars flashing, sped into the station lot. Motorists filling their tanks took their time and watched the action. The three cars stood hood to trunk while the occupants talked, then the original car flipped on its light bar and all three peeled out of the station, the one with the girls leading.

Once on the street, they shot up Powell in a line, blues and reds throwing rippling colours across the building fronts, traffic pulling to the sides of the street. They crossed the intersection at Clark and sped down to Commercial. All three made the turn, then slowed and separated.

The cruiser with the girls went up the slight grade toward the fish plant, the second moved down Commercial a block and turned in, the third followed. All moved slowly, light bars off. Once up the steeper part of the hill, the second and third cruisers separated, one moving slowly down to the front of the fish plant, the other approaching from the other side. All three cruisers slid quietly to the curb. The girls in the back of the first cruiser watched and stayed silent. Sugar pointed to the empty lot and the loading bays covered in plywood.

For a minute or so, nothing happened. Then the cruiser doors opened, and five cops gathered on the sidewalk. The woman officer in the front passenger seat of the original cruiser stayed with the three girls. The remaining five split up.

Once on the bays, they could hear someone yelling inside.

One of the them slipped through the rotting plywood, a second followed. The third remained on the platform. All three slipped the restraining straps on the tops of their holsters, freeing their side arms, and took their heavy mag lights off their belts.

The two inside waited in the dark for a few minutes, listening to the muttering and yelling that came from the other side of the swing doors at the end of the short corridor. As their eyes adjusted to the darkness, they could make out the doors as shadowy rectangles, revealed by moving light flickering around inside the main room. They approached the doors slowly and quietly, hands on their pistol butts. One of the two pushed open a door and slid through. The second followed.

In the main room, the two could see the beam of a flashlight moving erratically around the space. They could hear the voice of a man presumably yelling at someone, then muttering to himself. They waited, watching the source of the light. When it moved toward the front of the large room, they simultaneously flipped on their two Mag lights, holding them high over their heads and out to the side.

The man in front of them didn't hear them. Didn't look at them. He was screaming and nodding, then he stopped and seemed to be listening to something the constables couldn't hear.

The two bright mag lights pinned the figure to the spot. The two cops approached him carefully, their lights focused on the wild, muttering man.

One moved behind him, the other slowly to his side. They tried talking to him, but he didn't respond in any way. Didn't even look at them. The cop behind him shut off his light, and pulled the man's arms behind him, dropping him to the floor. The man screamed and struggled as the cuffs went on. Both cops pulled him to his feet and dragged him screaming as if he were being beaten toward the loading dock.

The cop they'd left outside had removed the one rotting plywood panel, exposing the partially open overhead door. He'd attempted to push it further up, but the door was jammed. Instead, he knelt at the side and waited. He saw the swinging doors open and his fellow officers appear as they approached with the struggling man. Then he helped them get the man under the frozen loading door and off the deck. In the weedy parking lot, he became more violent, so two of the officers had to drag him to a cruiser and put him in the back.

The three girls watched silently from the security of the cruiser. The female cop spent some time with the other uniforms outside the car the man was in, then returned and called the dispatcher. All three cruisers left the fish plant together. One turned toward the local hospital with the apprehended man thrashing around in the back seat; one returned to its beat; and the third, with Sugar and her two companions, took off for the detention center at the east-end station on Main.

19.

The next morning, it rained hard, the kind of rain that soaked everything. Spence turned from the apartment window and considered what to wear.

Alan wandered into the kitchen in his housecoat, his hair wet from the shower. He joined her at the back window. "Great, rain, just what we need."

He gave her a peck on the cheek and turned to make coffee. Spence stayed at the window until the coffee was ready. Then she too turned, filled a cup, added some milk, and wandered into the bedroom to dress.

When they arrived at the station, the floor downtown was busy as always in the morning. Alan and Spence threaded their way through the controlled chaos to Jake and Larry. The place was a mess, also as usual, but there was a big grin on the faces of both men. The four back-to-back desks were jammed in, but they'd found room for a few chairs against one of the flats. All of them were filled with files.

Jake folded his tall lanky frame into his desk chair, pushed back a few inches, and waved his hand at Larry who had deposited himself on the edge of Spence's desk. He was wearing another of his suits, this one a kind of sharkskin colour, with a pale grey shirt, and a tie that sort of matched his suit. The suit coat was undone, the pockets sagging a bit from his habit of sticking his hands in them. The suit might have looked good on someone who cared, but on Larry, it looked like he'd worn it for days and slept in it. He always seemed to look like that.

"We got good stuff and bad, but the good stuff is really good! I'll give you that first, make you feel better. The bad stuff's just what it is anyway. We found the girls, well, they found us. Here's how it went down.

"One of the patrols on the stroll was parked in the lot at the Chevron station on Powell drinking coffee, and while they were sitting there, along comes this blond in pink towin' a couple of others. They were all hobbling 'cause they had no shoes."

Larry paused and looked at Jake. Jake picked up a couple of files at this point and handed them to Spence. He didn't say anything, just nodded to them and flipped his hand at Larry to continue.

"Anyway, the cop and his partner were pretty dubious at first, but when the one in pink started talking, they called in couple a of cruisers, left patrol, hit a fish plant, and caught a guy."

While Larry was telling the girl's story, Alan opened the file he'd been given and set out three pictures on the desk. Spence recognized the pink one called Sugar. She was Red's friend.

"So this creep picked her up and promised money and drugs, said he had a place. She thinks he gave her Rohypnol in some Vodka. Doesn't remember much after that."

Jake took over. "Three cruisers set up around that fish plant. They could hear the guy in there yelling. Two of them went in through a loose board they found on the loading dock and caught the guy. He was out of it, so they took him the Psych ward at Van General."

"That's the good news," Larry said. "Now the bad. The shit's hit the fan over this murder up in Powell River. We got a lot of political flap goin' on, and Brian's getting a load of shit thrown at him. Sort of like you guys in Harbour City. But this is worse because of Pickton. Nobody wants another mess like that, so the brass are shitting bricks, and it's all sliding down the shute to us. We're gonna be swimmin' in it."

"That's some picture, shitbricks and all." Spence shook her head and smiled at Larry.

Jake said, "What they want is some action from the task force they can feed to the media so they can look good. And we haven't really got it off the ground yet. I mean, the guys up there know now, Powell River and Hammil, and so does Harbour City, but we are still sorting it out. And we all get covered in crap if you two screw it up again."

Larry grinned at Alan and Spence and shook his head in sympathy. "You poor shmucks. This one just seems to follow you around like it's stuck to you."

Spence grinned at him. "It's not just us wadin' in it. You two better get some tall boots too, and the guys up north. We all need to get together on this. But we're still cleanin' up the three girls' mess, and I need to talk to Red tonight, so she can spread it around the stroll. Everybody's a bit freaked out there."

"I've been talking to Powell River already today. Gordie Parker and Frank Miller especially think we should center up there, maybe even up in Hammil." Jake smiled and sighed. "They've stopped messing about with copters and drones searching the camps, but there's still a lot of pressure, probably from the same source as here."

Larry nodded. "Yeah, there'll probably be some leaks here with the task force, so Hammil sounds good. Let's move it. We can get it set up while you get settled with Red. Maybe have more on the nutcase by then too. We wanna go talk to him and the girls again anyway, tie it up, file the reports, and get it done with.

"So far, we're golden here: we got that pimp beatin' on everybody in custody, we got the three girls back, at least we get credit for it seein' as it was our case, we got the nutter committed, and we got the task force the way we want it since we gotta have one. It's all gonna help, and Brian'll spin it for us, keep the crap at a low level for while at least."

"Good. We'll go with you to talk to the girls before I see Red tonight." Spence turned to Alan, her eyebrows raised in question. He nodded.

"We get the girls' story straight, we file that one. We need a psych report along with the medical. We need to make sure Josie Atardo on the Island gets a copy. I'm hoping

Brian will do that for us. We could be in Powell River in the morning if we can get this mess cleared today."

"I don't know about the psych stuff. We'll ask if they have a profile. Anyway, the girls are out of holding, been sent to emerg, and are out of there and in isolation until the tests are done." Jake glanced at his watch, a frown on his face.

"And we need to get to the loony bin out in Coquitlam. Find out what that nut has been up to. He was transferred there a few hours ago from the general psych ward. There should be an evaluation by now too, and we'll need that to close out the case. Brian can look after the press."

All four of them left the station and grabbed an unmarked from the garage. It was a reasonably clean one, but it smelled of antiseptic and grunge, the way they all did. Spence drove. When she got up on Twelfth, she slipped into the hospital's parking garage and parked in one of the reserved slots.

At the General, the isolation ward they needed wasn't the one used for regular patients; it was a secure ward they needed with a guard on the main door. There were four rooms, and they were often full. Three of them were full today too, but this time with one girl each. Since Sugar was the only one who seemed to have any clear idea of what had happened in the fish plant, they all felt that Spence should talk to her. Girl to girl seemed the best way to go. The three men split up with Larry talking to Rose and Jake to Blue. Alan waited outside Sugar's door. The two of them were, after all, the prime investigators looking for Sugar.

The room was better than Spence expected. It was institutional, but someone had tried to make it look a little homier. There was an easy chair in the corner, a TV on the wall high up so it was easy to view, and some half decent framed prints on walls that had been painted a soft peach colour. Sugar was sitting up in bed and looked a lot better than her photos. The nurses had cleaned her up, and she'd been fed and was resting comfortably.

"Hello Sugar. I'm Spence Riley, a detective with the RCMP. I know your friend Red. I've been working with her for the last little while trying to find you. She won't stop until she knows you're safe.

"That's Red for ya. She's stubborn and mouthy, but she's my best friend ever. I miss her a lot. She know I'm here?"

"Not yet. I'll see her on the stroll tonight. We were gonna keep lookin', but now I can give her the good news, and she can spread it around."

"You guys got that creep locked up, haven't you?"

"Good and solid. He's not going anywhere."

"He didn't really hurt us, you know, he just wanted to help us, something we didn't understand about. And he locked us up in that fuckin' freezer. That was the worst thing he did. That hurt us inside, the dark, you know?"

"Yeah, I got no idea how you guys stood being locked in the dark. It must have been like a deprivation chamber, you know, one of those boxes they lock you in so all you can hear is your heart pushin' the blood around? You got a lot of guts. I don't know if I could survive that in one piece. Look, Sugar, my partner's outside. He's been looking for you too but mostly for the guy who took you. I'd like him to sit in while we talk if you don't mind. If you do, it's okay, just say so and I'll let him wait outside."

"Naw, he can come in. I got no problem with a guy tried to help me."

Spence cracked the door and motioned Alan in. "This is my partner, Alan Kim. He's interested in what happened to you, what this guy did to you, what he wanted from you. All that stuff. We've got him, and he's not getting out. He's in a hospital where they can maybe help him a little. He won't get out. But we need to know who he is."

Spence and Alan spent over an hour with Sugar getting as many of the details as they could from her. When they came out, Jake and Larry were waiting.

"We taped the two girls, Rose and Blue. Neither one could give us much, but the gist of it is on tape. How'd you two make out with Sugar?" Larry had stopped in the hall and was looking questioningly at Spence.

"I had mine running in my purse. I didn't tell Sugar or she probably wouldn't have talked as freely, so it's probably worthless except for the reports. Yours probably is too. Anyway, it's what we expected, but now we've got the details, and that'll help with the report on this guy."

"On that note," said Jake, "let's get out to Coquitlam and see what's happening there."

The psychiatric hospital in Coquitlam was off Colony Road, a narrow two-lane blacktop that ran from the Loughheed Highway across the flats toward the Fraser. Spence drove slowly. Potholes pitted the surface of the road like tiny bomb craters. Water-filled ditches ran along both sides, overgrown with rushes. Flat, neglected meadows of grass and small shrubs spread out on both sides edged by fences that lined the ditch tops. Clumps of blackberry cascaded down the fences in places. The only trees visible were way down by the river and around the hospital buildings they could see in the distance. The rain that had started that morning had changed to a misty drizzle, so the landscape looked like an eerie, desolate Friedrich painting.

The hospital itself didn't improve things much. It consisted of two low-rise buildings, both finished in an earthy colour so that they seemed more a part of the ground they rested on than anything else. The first housed an evaluation center for the marginally affected along with a floor of administrative offices. The patients in this one were primarily people the local force found wandering on the streets. There were a lot of those. The second was the true hospital. It treated the worst of the psychologically damaged, people who had been committed by the courts or by their families. The rooms in both buildings were safe secure rooms with locks on the doors and bars on the windows. Even though there were trees and meadows outside and glimpses of the Fraser, the bars made both buildings feel like prisons.

Following Jake's instructions, Spence parked the unmarked in one of the spaces reserved for police vehicles. The lot lay off to the side of one of the buildings buffered from it by a thin line of vertical oaks.

They headed to the front and up a wide cement sidewalk to a pair of glass-front doors. Inside, they identified themselves at the security checkpoint and passed through without a problem. They had left their weapons locked in the gun vault in the trunk of the unmarked. The guard buzzed them through a pair of doors painted a rather nasty green on the far side of the room. Beyond those doors, a long hallway stretched ahead of them with more doors opening off each side, just like any hospital corridor.

The evaluation center was on the first floor, and its hub lay directly ahead of them about half-way down the corridor. A tall willowy blonde psychiatric nurse manned the circular desk. She seemed as out of place in this environment as a morbidly obese girl in a Victoria's Secret store. She was expecting a pair of them, not four, and expressed concern about a bunch of cops in the room with the patient at the same time. Her solution was to move him to a secure room with a viewing room attached, so that only two of them would be in the room with him. The other two could watch. She made a couple of calls and handed a copy of the patient's initial evaluation to Jake.

She led the four down a side corridor to a closet-sized room with a glass wall that overlooked a standard hospital room. The guy who'd done the evaluation, a doctor named Sinclair, met them there. He was short, dark, and harmless looking, wearing dark trousers and an open-necked shirt. He handed Jake a sealed brown file-sized envelope.

The four had agreed ahead of time that Alan and Spence would take the lead, whatever that turned out to be, and Larry and Jake would sit back and observe. This situation was perfect. The nurse took Alan and Spence in, and the doctor stayed with Larry and Jake in the viewing room to watch the patient's reactions and to add what he could to what the detectives already had in the evaluation report.

When Alan and Spence walked in, the patient was in bed and a little out of it, having been medicated. Spence was disappointed, though she understood the necessity. The nurse had told them he was given to violent outbursts that seemed to be directed at some imaginary beings, likely not at the people around him. The medication was to avoid such outbursts and to give the man some relief from what seemed to be intolerable pain associated with flashing bolts of colour.

The news wasn't very reassuring, especially since the ties on the bed weren't being used, and the patient could get up and wander about the room if he wished. But once they tried to talk to him, they relaxed a bit. He seemed harmless enough, and he answered their questions as well as he could. He seemed surprised that Alan and Spence weren't aware of the voices, and he rambled on about what they expected of him and how the streets shimmered with light when they spoke.

The two detectives were gentle with him. They learned that his name was Jack Lucas and that he hadn't harmed the girls physically except for the deprivations, hadn't abused them sexually in any way. His intention was only to help them, to put them back on the street cured and cleansed. That way the girls could receive the vision the voices promised.

"I put them in that dark room so they could get rest and get away from the streets and all that temptation. And to make them safe. That dark room was perfect for that."

The voices, he said, had told him to do that, except they didn't tell him how exactly. But then they agreed that the dark room was perfect, and the voices were happy. But once the girls escaped, the voices got very angry.

Jack Lucas was far more lucid than Alan and Spence had expected. But once he described the escape and the angry voices, he became more agitated. Then he began screaming and holding his head. The nurse rushed in and asked them to leave.

Alan and Spence rejoined Larry and Jake and Doctor Sinclair, and they all repaired to a lounge to talk. In the end, the doctor could add little but a diagnosis that involved a latent Schizophrenia. It wasn't that simple, but that's what the four of them understood. The four detectives thanked him and waited for the nurse to fill in what she could. From her, they got some idea of the timeline. Jack Lucas would be with them for a full review, and that would take weeks. After that, the decision on how to treat him would rest with the hospital. They'd be informed of the man's state later, and of the treatment the hospital personnel decided upon. She checked to make sure they had the initial evaluation forms.

In the car going back to the city, the four divided up the paperwork. Larry and Jake would prepare the reports on the girls, Spence and Alan, the one on Lucas. That work would carry them into the evening shift and Spence's meeting with Red.

Once all that was underway, Jake and Larry would get Brian's approval to connect with Powell River, and set up an HQ, probably in Hammil. They'd also arrange transport for the morning. The budget they already knew was almost unlimited since the media had begun to hint that the case here might be connected to the murders on the big island. The brass were covering their asses almost every hour.

Larry and Jake went happily to work requisitioning everything they could think of that might help before the money dried up. Spence and Alan, once their paperwork was finished, went to the apartment to pick up some clothes for Spence, returned to the station, and got out the least offensive unmarked they could find. They headed for the stroll.

Alan wanted to see the fish plant on his own, especially the freezer, and Spence agreed to meet him at the Chevron station after she'd talked to Red. The car was blue this time and freshly washed, so it wasn't quite as obvious as it might have been. Of course, the girls would make them right away, the johns probably not. She took the unmarked straight down Cordova.

Spence wasn't sure she'd please Red with her choices for the night, but she felt she was getting the hang of things at least a little. She'd decided on a pleated black mini, a sheer red top, and black lace waist cinch she'd found. She's put her four-inch heels on when she got out of the car.

Alan eyed her appreciatively while she drove. "You look good, not just good for the stroll, I mean you look good, you know. It's maybe not so much what you're wearing, as interesting as that is, but more in how you move now. You seem to change everything about you: how you walk, how you carry yourself, how you act. How do you do that?"

Spence smiled. Whatever Red had shown her, by example if no other way, seemed to be working. And she felt she had changed and not just in how she dressed.

"You live around these girls even for a night or two, you feel different about them, and you lose some of your preconceptions along with what makes you a middle-class straight, I guess. Anyway, I'm learning something; I just don't know what that is yet."

She pulled into the Starbucks drive-through and picked up a couple of coffees, then peeled out to Cordova again and followed the curve onto Powell. She turned right at the Chevron station and cruised up under the Hastings overpass on Raymur. She stopped there, turned the car over to Alan, put on the heels, and taking careful sips from the Starbuck's cup, sauntered back toward the corner. Alan turned the car around so he was facing Powell, kept it in idle, and watched her go. She'd meet Red in an alley between two warehouses on Glen.

20.

Herk talked to Gordie on the phone about the four Vancouver detectives who'd suggested setting up in Hammil where the latest crime had been committed. "Two of the four are the original RCMP detectives from Harbour City. They lost the killers over in Harbour City the first time when they tried to trap them. You know about that?"

"Okay, I got that." Gordie switched the receiver to his other ear and motioned to Frank with his free hand. Frank grabbed a notepad and picked up another receiver on the same line.

"Okay," Herk said, "we got these two, Alan Kim and Spence Riley from the Harbour City Mounteds, and we got Larry Sharp and Jake Kenney from Vancouver City Police, and then we got you and Frank from Powell River, and from here, me and probably Bert, my CSI. I guess we can all go to the hotel, or maybe put five up there and you come bunk with me. That suit you?"

"Long as you don't cook and the scotch is good, bunking with you sounds a hell of a lot better than a hotel. But that probably won't fly with the guys from Vancouver. The two from Harbour City are runnin' this thing, so I guess they'd have the last word. We'll try it on and see how it goes. They'll be here in the morning, so you'd better have a word with whoever owns the place."

"How sticky's this gonna be, you think?"

"Six cops, not counting you guys, from three jurisdictions all approved by their heads and the heads in touch with the brass on every move? You gotta ask?"

"You know we're not gonna get anywhere, don't you? What the hell could we accomplish in a group up here that we haven't already got goin' where we are?"

"We got a big budget and a lot of antsy politicians who all have elections comin' up sometime. They gotta look good and so do we. Nobody can afford a couple of loonies running around killing people. So a task force it is, an' we better damn well get these guys or we're all history."

"Okay, so we go through the motions and pray for a break. We have any word at all on who the girl is yet? How can we not know that at least?"

"We got mispers out all over the place, right across the country now, and all the northern states. Somebody's gotta know who she is. What I think is she was on vacation over here and nobody's missed her yet."

"A young girl and she doesn't call home? You'd think the parents'd be up in arms by now."

"We gotta worry about this task force first off. Maybe they want to be out in the sticks so they're harder to get at, and we both know the brass, the bloody politicians, and the sneaky press are gonna be all over this. We'll be sendin' in updates every damn hour and then the press conferences'll start. It's all bullshit, of course, but it's necessary bullshit, I guess. This's gonna be one big clusterfuck with us danglin' in the middle."

"There's an image for you, danglin', in the middle of a clusterfuck. Seems a bit lascivious somehow. Look, you two get up here tonight if you can, and we'll be ready for the Vancouver bunch in the morning. I'll get the hotel reserved."

"Three hours, we'll be there. Get Agnes to make some pies."

Herk put the phone down, sat back, and stuck his foot on the open bottom drawer. Yeah, he thought, one big mess is what it'll be, and it'll get us nowhere we haven't already been. Might be good to meet the guys from Harbour City though. With a sigh, he pushed the drawer closed, got up, and wandered out to the front desk.

"Jenny, I'm gonna be over at the hotel for a while. We're getting invaded tomorrow, and Gordie and Frank'll be here in a few hours. If you got nothin' on, come with me and you can get the setup down now."

Jenny shut down her computer and looked at him. "And who's on the desk if I do that, huh?"

"Call in Sam. He's close by, and all you're doin' anyway is playing Solitaire and looking on Facebook, so it's not like there's an avalanche of activity."

"Sam can mess up just sittin' here, Herk, you know that. But I'll come if you buy me a coffee." The two of them walked down the street to the hotel, a three-storey, red-brick building gussied up with a long porch and gingerbread fretwork on the front. By the time they reached the doors, Sam's cruiser had pulled in by the white picket fence in the front of the city hall building.

The hotel lobby was small but beautifully kept. Dark hardwood floors shone, and the front counter gleamed with polish. You could smell the lemon oil. Along the other side of the room sat a couple of stuffed easy chairs fronted by an old Persian carpet, a little threadbare here and there, but rich with deep blues and reds. A large green palm in a large ceramic pot in an even deeper green stood in the corner. The whole room reeked of comfort and a slower lifestyle, as if you'd suddenly been dropped back fifty years. Herk liked the place.

Burl was on the desk. He looked as old as the lobby, and he was dressed to fit the room. Today, he wore a black double-breasted suit with a fine grey stripe, a starched white shirt, and a black tie with tiny red dots on it. Herk smiled at him and nodded.

"Burl, you're gonna get invaded tomorrow morning. A bunch of city folk're comin' up to look into this murder we got. We're gonna need at least five rooms and probably one of those little conference rooms. They'll be settin' up some phones and computers. Probably need breakfast and snacks too. You can bill the department unless you hear different from me."

Burl's only reaction was a pair of raised eyebrows. He smiled at Herk and flipped the registration book around to face him. "We have those two young men on three and a couple on one, so floor two is theirs entirely. I'll block it off. Both conference rooms are available too, and the kitchen can handle the load if Mable comes in to help out. Can you give me any names, Chief Burman?"

Herk grinned. "Just Herk, Burl, just Herk is all. So far, I've got Alan Kim and Spence Riley, detectives from Harbour City RCMP, Gordie Parker and Frank Miller, those detectives from Powell River RCMP you already know; and I got Jake Kenney and Larry Sharp from Vancouver City Police, they're detectives too. So there won't be any uniforms around, except maybe me and Bert. If you can keep the pairs together, that would be appreciated, I'm sure."

Burl had been writing rapidly through all this. He still kept a hand-written ledger on the long counter and the room keys in one of those old-fashioned wooden key racks on the back wall. The three or four vases of flowers spread around the room were fresh every morning from the beds out the back beside the parking area. Off season, the florist down the street provided them. Today, the vases contained fall mums.

Jenny had watched the first part of this exchange as she always did when she came in with Herk. The formality and dated décor amused her, especially Burl. By the time Herk had given Burl the names, however, she'd wandered into the small breakfast room on the far side and ordered some coffee for both her and Herk. She sat at a table by the large front window, looked out over the porch that ran along the hotel's front into the street, and watched the patches of shadow sliding across the pavement. She didn't get breaks like this very often, and she liked to enjoy them when she did. Herk joined her a few minutes later.

While they were finishing their second cup, the rain started. It wasn't gentle either. It came straight down, dancing off the pavement and drumming on the covered porch outside the window.

"I should've known. With those clouds so thick, I should have changed my shoes. Shit!" Herk suppressed a grin. Wouldn't do to set her off.

"I could go get a cruiser if you like. Save your shoes at least. Sam's still parked out front. I don't mind, you know, I like rain."

"Herk, you lie like a trooper, you do. You don't like getting wet any more than I do. But I appreciate it. These are new heels. So go get the cruiser, you Sweetie, and I'll get you another coffee for the office."

Herk heaved himself out of his chair and headed out. On the porch, he pulled up the collar of his shirt and sprinted across the road. He ran up the street to the city hall building and hit the office door hard, startling Sam who quickly closed a magazine. Herk grabbed the keys off the front desk where Sam had thrown them, sprinted back out, and grabbed the cruiser, flicking on the light bar. He plowed in right up to the hotel's front porch. the blue and red strobes throwing pulsing patterns of light through the deluge.

Jenny came out in her bare feet, shoes in one hand and a Styrofoam container in the other. Herk leaned over and opened the passenger door. Once in, Jen shook out her hair and smiled at Herk.

"Shit boss, right up to the door with the reds and blues. Let's go back the same way!"

Herk hit the siren a short one, peeled back out, and ran up to the station. Jen was already braced for that one, but Sam was up from his chair and out the door, his mouth a big O. Once he realized who it was, his expression turned sullen.

Herk sighed. "I suppose I've gotta do something nice for him now. He's gone sulky again."

"He'll live, and you gotta admit that was fun. Let's go in as if nothin' happened. See what he does."

Jen entered still carrying her shoes, Herk with his collar still up. Neither one said anything. Jen handed Herk the Styrofoam cup and motioned Sam out of her chair. She thanked Herk for the lift. Herk just nodded and walked into his office. When he opened the carton, there was a small coffee and a large piece of pie. It wasn't Agnes', but it'd be good. He grinned broadly and glanced up to see Sam leaning on the doorframe.

"Can I have my cruiser back? You want I should go back out on patrol?"

"You've done some desk duty, Sam, and what with the scare, maybe you should take a break. Not much happenin', so go get yourself a snack somewhere, then go back out. Take your time, rain's heavy enough you couldn't see much anyway."

Herk threw him the keys, and Sam left the office with a nod to Jen and a smile on his face. It didn't take much to make Sam happy.

The rain stayed heavy through the morning. When Gordie Parker and Frank Miller left Powell River, it was still dancing off the pavement and flooding the streets. Frank drove his own four-by-four rather than a cruiser. If they had to go anywhere off highway, they'd need it. The drive up was slow, especially around the lakes. By late morning, after a couple of stops for coffee, they were plowing through the foot or so of water in the hollow on the outskirts of Hammil. They made straight for Agnes' restaurant. Herk had figured that's what they'd do and was waiting inside for them, one empty pie plate pushed to the center of the table.

Gordie grinned at him, shook off as much as he could, and the two of them sat.

"Do you think you could get someone up here to fix that damn road? We had to practically float over that hollow you got out there. Used the tires like paddles to get across. Nice deep treads on that four-by-four. You eat all the pie yet?"

"You already know that hollow out there saves us from the great hoards wanting in. Besides, the town's got better things to do with its money than fillin' holes. The pie's fresh and it's still hot, so watch your fingers. Agnes's already on her way over. How about you Frank, pie for you too?"

"I do and Brenda'll have my hide. Says I'm looking a bit too round. Nah, I'll pass on the pie and have a cheeseburger instead. No fat in those things, no sugar either. They make 'em out of veggies somehow. I read that on the Internet."

Agnes heard it all and said nothing as she passed the table. She hit the kitchen door, and they could hear her yell at the cook. When she popped back out, she had a couple of pieces of pie still runny and steaming. She set the plates down and said to Frank, "That burger'll be a bit. Cook had to hack up the veggies first. You want fries with it, he'll have to hack some more."

All during lunch, the rain pounded down. Then it began to taper off. By the time the three left for the hotel, it was little more than a light shower. The depressions in the roads were still water-filled, but the rest had run off. They took the four-by-four down the street and parked it in front of the station. On the way, Herk asked about the guys from Vancouver.

"On their way already. Left early this morning, but they got two ferries to take and in this stuff there're probably delays. They should be here by midafternoon. We got everything set up here?"

"One full floor and two conference rooms. Won't matter how big this gets, we got the space. You comin' out to my place or are you stuck here?"

"It'll probably be wise for the two of us to stay with the group, at least for tonight. Maybe we can find some excuse to do somethin' else tomorrow. The guys from the city are bringin' up a coms truck. Probably set up one of those conference rooms today so we're operational by morning. I got no idea what the hell we can accomplish doin' this, but I guess it keeps everybody happy. At least the press can't get to us. All the releases are bein' handled by the brass out of Powell River. We ship to them, they tell the press. And on the off chance we actually get somewhere, they're all set to take the credit. Give us the blame. Let's get Celia to intercept everything. Keep things in order."

Herk was about to protest, but Gordie expected that, grinned, and held up his hand.

"I already know you're doin' it. You hacked us and you hacked Vancouver. You got your fingers burned a bit, but you got in. I expect that girl's hacked those privates too. So let's make sure she knows she has our blessing and turn her loose."

Herk nodded. "You're gonna build up some serious karma, you are. She hardly ever leaves anyway, and with you egging her on, she'll attack everything. And she's good. Let's go in and put it to her."

Celia was in her office as she always was. When Herk and Gordie came to the door, she held up a finger, entered something, watched her screens for a moment or two, then turned, a smile on her face.

"Wow, the big guys from Powell River! What a thrill! Herk, get out of the way so they can get in. You come to arrest me or something for cracking your lousy security? You guys really need to fix that. I got by your firewalls easy and your encryption sucks big time. I know, I know, I was sloppy and you caught me, so not all bad."

"Actually," said Gordie, "we want you to hack everything in sight. Especially Harbour City and Vancouver. Even the privates if you can. We need to grab it all and see if we catch anything worth having. But, and this is a big but, you can't get caught. You can end up in the can. It'll be a kind of black ops thing, complete deniability on this end, complete vulnerability on yours."

"Gotcha. I already have you guys. I got spiders in your structure, and trust me, you won't find them. Your guys think they cleaned me out, but I'm still in there. These little guys catch everything and spin it back. The other two, Harbour City and Van, they'll be a bit of a challenge, but I'll get them. The privates, now, that's a different story. Whoever's running their stuff's good, and they're linked to servers on the mainland that I can't get a fix on. So no promises there. You guys, though, I can have fun with you, but only if you leave, so shoo!"

All three backed out of Celia's office and went into Herk's.

The unmarked cruiser from Vancouver, one of the newer ones, was stalled at the Earls Cove terminal. The ferry was berthed at the dock in front of them and would stay that way until conditions on Jervis Inlet improved. There'd been two cancellations so far, and the next scheduled run was a toss-up. And once they got across to Saltery Bay, they still had a long run up to Hammil. So far, the trip had been a nightmare. Highway 1 out of Vancouver had been slow because of the torrential rain, and once at Horseshoe Bay, they'd found themselves part of a huge backup.

Nothing was sailing to the Island, and the smaller ferries to Bowen and the Sunshine coast were delayed. They'd lost the better part of two hours there, and now they'd lose another two or more here. Alan and Spence were wandering around the terminal buildings and the coffee shops. The rain was still heavy, but the wind had dropped.

'This is a bitch." Spence turned from the window she was looking in and glanced at Alan. "We've been on the road most of the day already and we haven't cleared the damned

Inlet yet. It'll be nightfall before we're in. Seems to me it's a sign of how the rest of it's gonna go. This a boondoggle."

"Sure, but it's their boondoggle not ours. The brass insisted on this one, and they're not stupid. It's political, and they'll spin it to their advantage whatever we do. Still, you're right, we're in charge, and if we screw up again, we'll probably be out. It'll be okay. We just have to use everything we've got."

Spence shook off her cap, glanced up at the sky, and stuck it back on. "The rain's let up now. You think we'll be good to go soon?"

"It's not the rain so much as the wind, and that's dying down too. No idea what the open water's like. I doubt Jake and Larry's flight made it either. Those small float planes don't like heavy wind and chop. Bet we beat them in."

Jervis Inlet was a wide cut into the land that narrowed as it went inland. The cliffs farther in created a kind of wind tunnel, so the mouth was often subject not only to the swell from the Salish Sea, but also to a chop from the crosswinds streaming down the cut. And the ferry wasn't large enough to withstand either very well, so crossings were often delayed during the rainy season.

Alan and Spence and the truck full of electronic gear got across around three on the first ferry available. The roads south of Powell River were wet, but there was little more than mist as they drove north. The road moving inland toward the lakes was another matter. The earlier deluge had dragged forest trash onto the road, especially when the road curved around headlands. In a couple of places, they had to stop to remove branches and debris that had washed down.

They came into Hammil just after seven, the cloud cover still solid and the light failing rapidly. But the road, other than the hollow just before the town, was clear. Alan pulled the unmarked in at the white picket fence in front of City Hall. The comm truck followed.

Jenny saw them coming and called Herk, "Hey boss, it's those guys from Vancouver. You wanna come out, or should I send 'em back?"

"Send 'em in, Jen, then maybe run over for coffee and grab some coffee and donuts."

Alan pulled open the glass door, introduced himself and Spence, and asked for Chief Burman.

"Straight back. You'll find him in his office with some detectives from Powell River." Jenny jerked her thumb over her shoulder and bolted for the front door.

"Pretty girl, but where the hell's she goin'?"

They ran into Herk at his office door, introduced themselves and met Gordie and Frank. They all went to the small conference room.

"Sorry about the mess," Herk said ushering them in. "We've been tryin' to pull things together. Grab a seat and we'll get ourselves organized. Gordie and Frank've brought their material from Powell River, and we've been tryin' to find connections between here and Harbour City. Same guys, it looks like, but we can't find them, and we've looked."

Gordie said, "We've covered the area the best we can, lakes, camps, and the like, by both car and copter, but it's huge and we could miss them easily. I'm sure you guys already know how that goes."

Spence nodded. "Once these guys get back in the woods, it's like lookin' for a single needle in a bunch of pines. We sympathize. What we really need is to see the site and whatever else you've found. Have you fill us in on what you think."

Frank grabbed a pile of folders from the center of the table and flipped one each to Alan and Spence.

"This is a compilation of what we've got up here: site reports, forensics, autopsy, search parameters, and a synopsis combining your profiler's report and the info on cults from that SFU guy. We've added our conclusions for what they're worth. We can visit the sites tomorrow when you guys are set up."

"You said sites," Alan asked. "What do you mean?"

"Well, we think there're two," Herk said. "There's the actual body site and then there's an old farmhouse we think they used. It's got a root cellar."

Alan nodded, "Our psycho's pattern alright. We gotta see both sites. Let's read the files, and you can fill us in."

All five of them were reviewing what they had in the reports and discussing what else they might have when she returned with what was supposed to be donuts.

Everybody stopped work and leaned back, while Jenny distributed things, opening wedge-shaped containers. "Alice makes the best pie this side of heaven," she said, "and the coffee's good. If you want more, let Jenny know, and she'll have some ready when you go to eat dinner."

Herk looked around the table. Got nods from everyone. "Good, Jen. Please set it up."

21.

Highway 1 was water-covered when Vic and Able Hunter drove from the ferry docks at Horseshoe Bay to downtown Vancouver. Traffic was slow, the spray from the transport trucks cutting visibility so much, no one tried to pass. On the hills, everyone slowed. The feeders from West Vancouver simply made matters worse, and finally, the inevitable happened: someone attempted to pass one of the large transports and rear-ended another vehicle hidden in the spray.

That event stopped everything, even the police cars sent to investigate the accident. Two of them were edging slowly down the shoulder, squeezing past the stalled cars and trucks. Vic could see the light bars flashing way down the road behind him.

By this time, the rear windows of the van were fogging from the humidity so that the flashing reds and blues threw blankets of colour into the interior as the cruisers passed. Mixed with those blunted colours, Vic could make out the blips of amber from the following tow trucks.

A half hour went by before the damaged vehicles were off the road and traffic began to move. But it stalled again at the approach to the Second Narrows Bridge. Marine Drive West, carrying most of the traffic from West and North Vancouver, led onto the highway just before the bridge, creating another long snarl that only unraveled on the other side of Burrard Inlet.

In frustration, Vic turned off just under Hastings and took McGill into the east end. Many other drivers had done the same thing, so another snarl developed at the Nanaimo-Dundas intersection. The van inched along. Vic had no real plan. He knew they needed somewhere to settle and find work. Able, he knew, would have a problem adjusting, but he'd done it before in Harbour City and again in Hammil, so he might manage here.

He edged the van down Dundas past the light at Victoria where Dundas turned into Powell, then on into the city proper. He turned up Main and passed through Chinatown. The lights at Terminal left him wedged between a long string of cars and a line of buses at the skytrain terminal.

Edging back into traffic, Vic drove up the hill on Main and around a curve onto the Kingsway. After a few blocks, however, he began to wonder if they'd find anything suitable. The street was filled with commercial operations interspersed with small residential neighbourhoods.

He drove along the Kingsway as slowly as he dared, looking for a motel rather than a hotel. He wanted something with a ground floor, so he could leave privately if he wished. On one of the curves, he saw a long, low building and pulled to the curb. A large unlit sign with black letters on a white background identified the place as the "Moonlight Motel". It was stuck incongruously in the middle of a string of commercial businesses, everything from clothing stores to pizza parlours.

The motel was a large, L-shaped place painted light green. It sat well back from the street and backed onto a residential neighbourhood. A line of trees poked up behind it. The lot was over half full, a good sign. Small grass areas holding numerous small trees were scattered about around the parking area.

The office was at the front and looked toward the street. Vic asked for a room at the back on the long arm of the L and got the one double left, the last room on the end. Maybe they'd stay for a period, depending on what sort of work he could find. He bought a map of the downtown core at the front desk and took the van to the end of the lot.

Able sat quietly looking out the window. Vic knew he wouldn't question the choice of places or the reason for bringing them to the city. His brother would follow him wherever he went. But Vic also knew the constant traffic made Able uneasy, that he had a fear of big cities. His brother had never been strong. Able would obey him as he always had, but in a place this large, only reluctantly. And that made him a liability.

Vic smiled to himself. Cities were good places, good for what they needed, especially at night. But even the much smaller Harbour City had confused Able with its streets and rows of houses. Hammil, where they had last lived, was a little better: small, with the forest pushing down the slopes. But for Able, even Hammil had had too many people doing too many things.

The motel room had two beds and a bathroom. There was no kitchen, but there was a big television bolted to the wall. Vic knew Able would like that, especially if they could get the Nature channel. The room was the usual pale beige with darker brown accents, but there were contrasting bedspreads in stripes of red, green, and orange that helped. Able could maybe do odd jobs again. There weren't any woods anywhere close, but at least there were some trees and maybe a small park.

Morning found them on the street at a restaurant that served breakfast. Vic watched Able closely and he could see his brother's tension.

Vic leaned over the table and took Able's hand. "You don't like the streets, do you? Just try to hold on. We'll find somewhere tomorrow. We'll find a place outside the city. You can handle that, can't you? Then we can hunt in our special places just like we did in Harbour City."

Able didn't smile, just nodded hesitantly and looked out the window at the traffic. He'd eaten almost nothing. Eggs sat on his plate filmed over with grease, strips of bacon beside them. One piece of toast had a bite out of it. That was all.

Vic looked out the window, wondering what to do. He knew his brother, knew that the last time he'd been okay was back on the island. Damn, he thought, we almost had them, the damned girl detective and her stringy friend. Just another minute and we'd've had them in the truck. He's not adjusting to anything here, he didn't even in Hammil. He's like a bloody cancer. They left the restaurant and walked. Again, Vic watched his brother. The noise, the honking, screeching brakes, the sirens, all seemed to shrink Able into himself. His shoulders were hunched, and his walk was stilted. He flinched when trucks went by.

"Can we go somewhere today do you think? It's too big here, there's no quiet. We can't join here, we just can't." Able stopped walking stared at the sidewalk.

Vic's anger boiled to the surface; he shook with it. Through gritted teeth, he said: "Tomorrow, we'll go tomorrow. You can manage that at least, can't you? We'll look for another place to stay tomorrow, maybe near a park, you'll like that, won't you? But we'll come back to find the special ones. It'll be dark when we do, so you'll like it better."

Vic took them back to the room, picking up a copy of the Vancouver Sun on the way. He had to find work to provide protective colouration. And he needed to be close to his hunting ground. Able would have to start adjusting to life in the city. After all, it was just a different kind of forest, a concrete one. This city, he thought, this is the best. No one pays any attention to anyone else. It's like the bush in a way. You're alone in the crowds the way we were in the trees.

Vic knew he'd have to leave Able on the outskirts someplace wooded and come into the city alone. It wouldn't be the same. It was a kind of fracture, and he felt anger burning deep inside him. He'd make it work alone if he had to. Meanwhile, he'd go looking. Then they would begin. They'd send the chosen ones over, begin their own transformation. If Able couldn't, Vic knew he'd have to find his own completion.

The room was too warm, but the window air conditioner was noisy enough to bother Able, so Vic had to turn it off. Able had curled up in a chair with the Nature channel. Vic checked the ads and his maps.

Not too far away, he thought, but not so close to the city that Able can't manage. Finding a regional paper to write freelance for again might be best. That way I'll be free enough. And there are parks all over the place. Stanley Park in the city, small for Able, but convenient. Above North and West Vancouver are foothills, and places like Capilano and the Lynn Valley have got deep ravines. The drive'll be longer, but there're logging roads, there always are. Able, he thought, will do better there. Maybe we can heal again somewhere like that, then take the city. He knew it was a pipe dream, but maybe, just maybe. Yea, the city for night hunts, and the bush for retreat and union. Vic smiled at the thought.

He spent most of the day preparing his resume and scouring maps for locations. He'd pick up a couple of topographical maps in a bookstore along with a few books on local trails and back roads that most maps didn't show. Between them, he'd narrow the area to maybe a section in the foothills.

Able had fallen asleep, the television showing a program on migration movements along the Amazon. He would have liked that one, Vic thought. He turned off the set, gently covered his brother with a comforter from one of the beds, wrote him a note, and left the room. He needed a hardware store first and a visit to Mountain Co-op next. He'd have to hurry. Rush hour started at about three, and it was close to that already.

Mountain Co-op was on Broadway out towards the university. It should have been an easy drive, but the traffic was thick and slow. Vic had to search for parking on a residential side street six blocks south, most of it permit parking. There was no parking on major streets after three, and he ended up in an alley jammed in against a fence.

A ticket was the last thing he needed right now. His plates were good, but tickets meant a record, and records meant a trail, and they didn't leave trails. The parking police had their hands full on the streets this time of day, so he thought the alley was about as safe a spot as he could find.

As he approached Broadway, Vic could see the long green awning on the building. Mountain Co-op ran for half a block along Broadway. Vic went through the front doors and stopped in the busy foyer. The store was huge, two full floors of stuff, and it was busy. This late in the season with the rains almost here, the crowds surprised him. Vic wandered about on both floors until he found what he needed. At the busy checkouts, he paid in cash.

When Vic returned to the motel room, Able was still sleeping, curled into a ball in the middle of the bed. He'd crawled under the comforter because he felt threatened. It always made Vic angry when he did that. He ground his teeth, shook his head. "I'll have to get him out of the city." As his anger grew, he muttered, "He'll learn to hunt with me, or I'll go on without him. This sickness makes us weak, and I don't want it. I'll get him his damned bush this time, but he'll have to learn, or he'll destroy us."

Vic took Able along Highway 1 to the Second Narrows Bridge. Once across, he drove up the Dollarton Highway to Deep Cove. The village straggled down a hillside on the edge of Indian Arm, a huge inlet of deep water that sliced into the interior part way along Burrard Inlet well before that one ended in the shallows of Port Moody.

Beyond the town center, Vic drove past large houses straggling along the steep shoreline. The road narrowed here to two thin lanes of blacktop and began to climb. Farther up the road, they passed through a small village called Woodlands named after the great drifts of Douglas fir that surrounded it. Higher up the foothill, they drove into Cascade, another small village perched on the steep slope. A stream plunged through the center of the village, roaring down steep rock steps, and after a long fall, plunging into the depths of Indian Arm.

From the edge of this village, a narrow dirt and gravel road led up the massive bulk of Mt. Seymour. Vic shifted into four-wheel drive to navigate the switchbacks. There were many, each one finding the easiest path around the heavily treed cliffs, each one revealing stunning views out over Indian Arm. The road led eventually to a small turnaround perched on one of the few flattish areas the mountain provided. A trailhead led into the depths of Mount Seymour Provincial Park.

These harsh slopes had been partly logged a long time ago. Second growth crowded bits of old growth right up to where the forest thinned as it rose into the permanent snow cap. The old logging roads were so overgrown they were mere tracks, many almost obliterated by the rampant growth and filled with so many fallen conifers they were impassable.

Vic parked the van in the turnabout and got out. Able tumbled out the other side and stood beside him. There was little to see even though they were very high. The tall trees rose everywhere, the wind whispering through the branches as if the trees were breathing. It was a familiar kind of quiet, soothing to both.

The trailhead was well marked, the trail itself near vertical from where they stood. Vic looked at Able and smiled.

"This is what you like, isn't it? None of the noise of the city. But the city's where we'll find them. We'll search here for a place. We can bring supplies. We'll have to prepare our base. Then, I'll return to the city, find them, and come for you so we can hunt. We'll mark them together just as we have before. We'll release them as we always do."

Able said nothing, just nodded and smiled. Vic watched his body language change. He became more fluid, as if he were suddenly released from something. Vic smiled back and nodded as well. He gestured toward the van, and they climbed back in. Maybe they could make it work.

"You watch from your side. You're closer. You know what to look for."

Vic kept the descent slow so Able would have plenty of time to study the forest. The few tracks in the upper regions were too precipitous and good only for all-terrain vehicles. As they passed into the larger logged areas, however, Able stiffened and pointed.

Vic stopped. They both studied the almost imperceptible trail. It appeared unused and overgrown, but it was worth a second look. Vic left the van as close to the inner edge of the road as possible, and the two walked in.

Within a hundred yards, widowmakers littered the ground, the massive trunks blocking any progress. The two men retraced their steps and drove on. They spent the rest of the afternoon investigating trails that were equally poor except for two farther down. Both were open enough to get the van through with a little work. But both were also trails that showed signs of use by ATVs. Neither was private enough for them.

At the last switchback before the village of Cascade, they found what they wanted. The old logging road could be navigated easily enough, and it was well hidden behind a natural looking wall of second growth. Vic and Able walked a kilometer in and had decided to use the road for a base when suddenly the roar of ATVs broke the silence. Six or seven of them rose up the ridge in front of them and came crashing through the undergrowth no further than a hundred yards away. Vic and Able couldn't see them, but they knew the road was useless.

"We can't use this place, Able, we can't get in far enough to avoid those machines, and we can't tolerate their presence either. We'll find somewhere else closer to the city, easier to use, and quieter."

Able slouched along beside his brother. Vic knew he'd have to leave the area entirely and thought again about Stanley Park. If they could find a quiet part, maybe it would work. It was on the city's doorstep, so close to where they'd hunt. They just needed enough cover. He turned to Able.

"We're going to the park, that big one I showed you on the map. It's huge, it's covered in bush, and it's surrounded by water except for where it joins the city. There are roads around the edge and trails people use, but there are large parts in the center that are just bush. We'll find a place there."

Able nodded glumly. "Do we have to go back? This is where we should be, here, not near the city. It's too big. Can't we look some more?"

Vic's anger surfaced and he shook with it. Able wouldn't look at him. "There's nothing that works without ATVs getting in the way. We need something better. The park is better; in the middle it's better. We'll look there. This place is useless and you know it."

Vic drove back through Cascade and Woodlands and took the Dollarton Highway back to Highway 1 and the Second Narrows Bridge. He turned west and left the bridge behind. He took Highway 1 to Taylor Way. Then Marine Drive took them east again to the Lion's Gate Bridge. They could see the great promontory of Stanley Park rising on the other side, rank after rank of conifers blotting out the city's skyline.

Vic turned off once he'd crossed the Lion's Gate and worked his way down the narrow road that followed the ocean's edge around the side of the park until he reached the lot at Second Beach.

He parked close to the road and glanced at his brother. Able's sullen look made Vic's anger flare again.

"At least give it a chance." He hoped that once he got Able off the main trails and into the bush he'd see the advantage of being here, close to their hunting ground but still isolate enough to perform their rituals.

Vic got out of the van and slammed the door hard. He went to pay the parking meter, read the instructions and cursed. He realized that he couldn't park overnight and had to input his license plate number to get a ticket. "Shit!" He kicked the base of the machine, then took a deep breath and tried to relax. Losing control wasn't good, not good at all.

He collected Able and they crossed the busy road, passed through the forest's edge on a path, and walked up a carefully maintained crushed-stone trail.

"We'll be alright here. We'll take Lee's Trail into the center, then some paths into the bush. We're like phantoms in the bush. You know that. We've been close to people before near the commune, remember? And no one ever saw us. It'll be the same here. You'll see."

Able shook his head. "No, it won't, it won't be okay. There're people all over the place and there're too many paths. It's too close to the city."

Vic took a deep breath, clenched his teeth, said nothing, and walked on, stiff with anger. Able followed glumly, occasionally shaking his head at the crisscross of paths.

Vic turned up a part of Lee's Trail until he found a side path that looked well used. He led his brother into the bush. After a while, the trail led to a couple of large burned-out stumps from an old fire. It widened here and circled the remnants of the great trees. Inside the hollowed-out stumps were bits of paper, discarded tissues, packets that had once held condoms and lubricants, and a torn white t-shirt. What the place was used for was obvious. Able just pointed to all the waste and looked at Vic. Vic turned and walked on.

Beyond the two stumps, several narrower trails led off into thick bush one way and into large stands of tall trees the other. Ferns and salal grew under the drifts of conifers.

The paths wandered off in various directions in the trees, most ending in swaths of downed giants, the trunks sprawled on the ground in random patterns like bunches of pick-up sticks. They were the legacy of a massive storm that had battered its way through a year before. There were areas of heavy bush, however, that were different. They were choked with shrubbery and young deciduous trees struggling against the competition. Here, the few paths disappeared quickly, blotted out by the rampant growth.

Vic led his brother into one of these, but it was too small an area and bounded by yet another of the tailored paths down which strolled a pair of young girls. Vic watched Able sigh.

The girls passed, chattering to each other, unaware of the eyes fastened on them. Vic prodded his brother, and the two crossed the crushed stone path and entered the bush on the other side. There were no trails here, the bush was virtually impenetrable. Vic smiled to himself. Taking the lead, Able seemed to glide through the underbrush leaving no trace at all. Vic followed, his smile deepening, his body free of its former tension.

At one point, they stopped in a mossy depression behind a huge decaying trunk, a natural place to center themselves. The two quartered the whole area until they were sure of its size and its remoteness from the general flood of visitors. They saw no one while they did this. They returned to the mossy depression and squatted. Vic nodded at his brother and got a reluctant nod back. He knew Able didn't feel as free as he'd like, but he knew his brother would soon adjust and recognize the value of this immense park on the edge of the city. They could live here, at least Able could. They could bring their catch here, and they could restart their process of renewal. Vic was pleased with the place, and he thought Able could learn to function here.

The last night in the motel on the Kingsway, Able watched Nature again while Vic planned another shopping trip. He wanted intended to set up in the park the next day. He'd leave Able there with supplies to prepare the site. He had most of what he required already, not all but most.

Morning found them out early. Vic parked a few blocks from Mountain Co-op and left the van with Able in it. Up the street on the corner, he bought a couple of egg sandwiches and some coffee from a McDonalds and carried them back to the van. Able wasn't exactly happy, but Vic didn't think he was as depressed either. A good sign given the situation. They ate and drank in the car as traffic built around them.

When Vic returned from the Co-op a short time later, he found Able curled up, his head squeezed down between the shift lever and the driver's seat.

Vic yanked open the door and said, "Get up, Able, there's no need for this. It's just a street, and you're not even on it. You're disappearing on me, moving away, and you can't do that and survive. You know that! Without me, you're lost. Get the hell up!"

"I hate this place! I hate the noise. All of it. I just hate it! I need to go home. Why did you bring us here? Why do we have to stay? Why can't we go home?"

"We can't go home, don't you understand that? We can't find them around Harbour City now. The cops are still hunting us. That's where they're looking, in the town, in the bush. They're not nearly as good as we are, but they have more people to look with. We have to hunt here in the city where we can disappear in the streets."

"I won't, I can't! I can't stay here! Take me back! I can't be here. I won't! I'll find my own way if you won't take me back."

"And how will you do that, Able, how? You'll have to depend on yourself and you never have, you can't. Without me, you can't exist. You don't exist. I am you. You're a part of me. You know that. So how, Able, how will you find your own way?"

"I can! I can exist without you. You're just saying that. You like it here, and you don't care about me. If you want to stay, stay. I'm going home where we belong. You're the one wants to be separate. I know, I've watched you. You don't blend with me anymore. We need to go home! We'll be alright if we go home. We need to go! You know that."

Vic stood on the sidewalk beside the car and watched his brother curl more tightly on the seat. The anger burned through him. He stood rigid with anger, then he smiled.

"Alright. If you won't hunt here, I'll take you home." Vic knew the severing had gone beyond repair, and part of him felt the loss. He knew he'd have to finish it. He felt as if he'd lost an organ as valuable as a hand or foot and he wondered if he could compensate, but he hid it from Able.

"We can scrap the park and even leave the city and go back to the island. We'll get the feeling back, you'll see. We'll be together again the way it used to be for us." That should reassure him, Vic thought. At least until I can get him in the bush.

He stroked Able's head slowly, gently, but his brother just curled his body more tightly. Vic walked around the van and climbed in the driver's seat, put his hand on Able's shoulder and waited.

Then he started the van and began to work his way out of the city. The island would be best. There was a kind of symmetry in that, he thought, to end where we began. He turned the big vehicle toward Highway 1 and Horseshoe Bay's ferry terminal. With luck, he'd make the three o'clock.

22.

The three o'clock ferry from Horseshoe Bay was crowded with students returning from a field trip. Two Greyhounds had already unloaded, and the walk-on area in front of the ticket kiosks was thick with girls in short, pleated skirts and teenage boys looking sloppy and acting sullen. A staccato of voices, mostly girls, filled the air, drowning out the raucous calls of the gulls that hung around the docks looking for handouts. Some of the crows in the trees near the beach were picking up snails, fluttering up high like little helicopters, and dropping them on the road to shatter the shells. Vic watched them until some large diesel rigs slid down the first lane nearest the town blocking his view.

Once the big rigs had disappeared under the raised ramps to wait for boarding, Vic shifted his gaze to the harbour. He saw the leading edge of one of the new ferries sliding into view past the headland. It dwarfed the Bowen Island ferry that was steaming in a long curve around it, slicing through the whitecaps.

Vic turned to his brother. He was staring vacantly ahead. Vic thought about what he'd do on the island. Where they'd set up. Too bad the cabin was too risky now. Damn detectives ruined that.

The ferry whistle cut through his thoughts, and he looked around. The students were gone from in front of the ticket booths, and people were streaming down the stairs from the overhead heading back to their cars, some with dogs, some carrying paper cups. Vic knew that most of them would join the long line at the main cafeteria on the ferry as soon as they were on board.

"It won't be long now, Able. We'll grab a coffee and come back down to the van. Maybe talk over where we'll set up. We've got an hour-and-a-half, plenty of time." Able nodded but didn't smile.

Down the waiting lines of cars, Vic saw taillights flash. He started up when the car in front of him began to move, followed it up the ramp onto the top car deck. They'd be able to see off the side of the ship all the way across.

"Let's go up now. Come on, you need to move around a bit."

Able sighed heavily, but he got out and followed his brother up the flight of stairs to the main passenger deck. Students cluttered the aisles chattering to each other, the girls giggling incessantly. Able shied away from them, hugging the wall.

At the counter in the coffee bar, Vic added milk and sugar to both cups of coffee, put on lids, and led Able back down the stairs to the van. His brother had not said a word. He'd followed Vic glumly, bothered by the crush of students and the growing line of adults at the entrance to the cafeteria.

Back in the van, he took sips of his coffee and stared out the window at the Salish Sea as if mesmerized by the flowing lines of whitecaps out in the bay. Vic waited. He knew when to leave his brother alone and when to try to engage him. But damn, he was sullen. Not for long though. Vic thought about that and relaxed.

He smiled as he thought how satisfying it would be to take another girl and how much it would confuse the searchers. They'd be running around in circles as they usually did. It's not a bad idea, Vic thought. Send another on her way, try another joining in a place that's home, at least for him. He glanced at Able still looking at the water. There was a kind of harmony in that, a fundamental symmetry. The crossing was uneventful, and they docked without incident.

The islands were covered in heavy rain. They could barely see the grey bulk of Gabriola Island as it loomed into view like the prow of a huge phantom ship. On the big island, they could see nothing of the town but hazy dark shapes and the bulk of the great hills that lay to the south and west of Harbour City. The ship's horn blasted into the sullen grey skies as the ferry reversed thrust and slipped toward the dock. The final mooring was smooth and efficient as always, and Vic had the van on Stewart Avenue minutes later.

He turned up Brechin Hill, following the line of cars heading for the bypass on the other side of the city. The posted route took tourist traffic north along the old highway through a three-mile strip of ribbon development. Vic, however, travelled north only a few blocks to Northfield Road like the rest of the islanders. That road gave him a direct route to the bypass highway, but instead of running with the traffic going north, he turned left at the light onto Bowen Road and drove toward the city center. He turned again at Wallace. Once down the hill, it became Victoria Crescent, their old hunting ground.

All the way in, the rain remained heavy. The stroll on Victoria Road was deserted, the few girls pressed into doorways waiting for a lull. Vic drove slowly up the hill on Victoria and watched Able. He saw his brother respond to the street, saw him struggle to regain a connection he'd lost on the mainland. This is where they'd hunted, here and in the great stands of fir and cedar along the Mist River that poured out of the mountains and ringed the city.

"Can we keep going? There's nothing here. I know the rain will make setting up harder, but can we? We're so close now!"

Vic smiled, his anger at the city and his brother tucked away. He had his plans. He picked up speed and within three blocks had left the stroll behind him. He drove the length of Victoria Road to join the highway south of town. He pulled into the Tim Horton's drive-through in the plaza just before the old highway met the new bypass and bought several sandwiches and more coffee.

"We'll get supplies tomorrow. These will do for tonight. When the rain lets up, we'll find a place. If it doesn't, we'll sleep in the car and start tomorrow. We'll go to the river where we're comfortable. We can begin again there."

Able smiled and nodded. "The river, yes, let's go there. We'll be home then, we'll be together again like before." Vic took out a sandwich, gave half to Able, and handed him one of the coffees. They ate and drank while Vic drove down the old highway a couple of blocks to Extension Road that led off to the west toward the Mist river. Conifers stood tall and thick all around them in the grey rain. A few new subdivisions had been cut into the forest, and a few small farms huddled near the road. Eventually, the road ran past a pair of narrow, overgrown, single-lane blacktops that led to the isolate evangelical commune where the brothers had been raised. At the first of these two roads, Vic slowed and turned in.

The rain was lighter now, the sky darker. Strands of fog crawled through the evergreens and drifted across the narrow road like long, hazy snakes. The greens of the conifers had turned almost black in the misty, failing light. This road was one of the two that ran off Extension Road at almost equal angles. The point of the triangle the roads formed a few kilometers in led to the tiny commune they'd called home for their first fifteen years. Beyond the point of the triangle, an old gravel track led to the eerie ruins of a colliery. Beyond that was only forest.

All through their childhood, the two had escaped their sadistic, fundamentalist father whenever possible and had run free in that forest. The man had often caught them, and when that happened, they'd been locked in the root cellar under the house. Sometimes their quiet, submissive mother slipped them food, but often they had nothing.

The floor and walls of that cellar were dirt that filled the space with the pungency of damp earth. There was no light at all. The two of them lived in total darkness save for the tiny scraps of light from either the day or the oil lamps that squeezed through the stout door at the top of the stairs. Their incarceration often lasted days since the duration depended on the whim of a sadistic man whose arrogance and religious fervor were shot through with visions of damnation and hell. What warmth there was came from their own bodies and from what clothes they still wore, if any.

Mostly in the forest, they were naked, and if they were caught before they managed to dress at the edges of the tiny village, they remained naked under the house. They often curled together on the floor in an intimacy of their own that grew stronger as childhood turned into adolescence. They developed their own perverse rituals in that forest and in the root cellar. Those rituals had changed them as thoroughly as the strange religious rituals of the commune had changed its inhabitants.

Vic stopped the van, turned off the motor, rolled down the windows, and they listened. It was evening now, the grey skies dark. Tendrils of fog continued to seep out of the black forest sliding slowly across the narrow blacktop. They were more numerous now and more substantial. From the circular meeting house in the center of the village deep rolling chants oozed out of the silent trees as menacing as distant thunder.

For the two brothers, it was a familiar sound. It had run through their young lives and was an intimate part of the private rituals that had made them what they had become. They listened for a long time, then Vic turned to Able.

"The city's full of prey, Able, and even though you think we belong here, we need the city to hunt in. Harbour City you know. You've been there, hunted there. We found the perfect ones there, the ones who needed us. We can do that again, hunt them in the dark. You can see that, can't you? Remember the last one, the one who ran? We'll find her again. She's still here, Able, still waiting. In Harbour City."

Vic watched carefully. Able had loved that one especially, spent a lot of time with her in the pit while she was sedated. As Vic had expected, Able sat up, smiling at the memory.

"We can find her? That one? Do you think we can? I'll go with you, and we'll bring her back. We'll need a new place, though," he said excitedly. "A special place for her. I'll make it that way, I'll be careful this time. She won't run again."

Vic smiled. "She's still there waiting. She wants to be found, you know that. All we need to do is wait for her where we waited before. Then we can give her what she really wants."

Able was more alive than Vic had seen him in a long time.

"Let's find that one, Vic. She needs us, she does! And I'll make it special for her. Let's go now, let's find a place. It'll be like it was. "We can be together again."

Vic smiled to himself. "Maybe on the far side, upstream past the Mist River gorge we'll find a place. We can hike in easily from one of the old logging roads. Lots of those lead back into the hills, into the old cuts.

As Vic swung the van around, heading out to Extension, he turned south on River Road along the banks of the Mist until he was close to the main highway. There were hydro gates on both sides of the road just before the gravel works that ate up most of the huge hill the highway went around. Those gates were always full of cars, some there for as long as weeks. Vic knew they'd be fine there. Nobody would roust them, not in a spot used by the locals all the time.

He pulled in as far as he could, and they sat talking about setting up. They had food and water; there were blankets and supplies in the back. The cars that were here now belonged to partying young people and to the night shift workers at the gravel works just downstream. A lot of the workers parked here rather than in the parking lot down in the pit to avoid the dust that seeped through every crack and covered the interiors of cars in a single shift.

Vic got blankets from the rear, a couple of pillows, some bottles of water, and opened the last of the sandwiches. They ate outside on a flat layer of rock, then settled into the van's ample rear cargo area for the night.

First light was slowly turning the sky brighter as Vic took the van up River Road. The clouds pale pink underbelly began to look more like cotton batten as the sun gained strength. The sky over the island was full of long rolls moving east, pushing against the thin strand of pale blue that rested over the Salish Sea. It wasn't raining yet, but Vic thought it might later on. As the sun rose above the cloud banks, their light underbelly suddenly darkened, then disappeared entirely as if someone had shut off a light. As the cloud banks coming over the mountains thickened, early morning began to look more like early evening. Vic smiled as he glanced up at the sky. Neither of us minds rain, he thought, not here. It's cooler now, but we don't mind cool either. We've lived in this bush most of our lives, it's home if anywhere is. So, it's good to come back, a kind of fitting finish of a sort. He thought about their time together, the girls, the rituals, the richness of blood, all of it good, all of it done now, then there'll be a new beginning in the streets of the city where I belong. He almost missed a turn and yanked the wheel to compensate. Able grabbed the dash and glared at him.

"It's all right, I was thinking about her, not paying attention. Relax, I'll watch the road."

Able grunted and leaned back. He seemed moody to Vic, but at least he wasn't strung out. No reason he should, Vic thought, he's here where he wants to be, that's gotta be good.

Vic took the van farther upstream until the houses were gone. This area was solid rain forest and mostly uninhabited, only the occasional cabin broke the forest. And the few there were, were close to the blacktop. After a while, even these disappeared. Then the road degenerated rapidly, quickly filled with potholes and turned to gravel.

They looked for old logging roads. Some were protected by gates even though they were unused, some were not. These vast tracts of property belonged to lumber companies, so logging roads were common. They were searching for roads that weren't gated, roads so old that they'd become mere tracks. There were only a few, all on the river side. At each, Vic pulled off the road, and the two of them walked in as far as the track allowed.

They spent the morning looking. Most of the tracks were full of widowmakers and too overgrown. And the pitch down the banks to the Mist River was always too steep and strewn with boulders. But on a couple of them where the bush allowed, they thought the van might make it.

They checked the river on both trails, looking for something fordable. Every spring, the river rolled boulders down its course and uprooted trees, creating new patterns in the river's bed and

walls of drift along the sides until the river eased into the coastal flats and became less angry. This far upstream, nothing remained as it had been the year before. On one of the two tracks they'd chosen, the river's bed looked acceptable. The water was fast, but shallow, the bed mostly boulders the size of melons with only the occasional large one sticking its head out of the current. Vic tried walking across, but the current was too strong. Instead, they studied the crossing as carefully as they could.

"I think there's enough room between those two big ones to make it across." Vic pointed to two boulders that seemed to block the shallow path. "The van's heavy enough the current won't be a problem, and it's got four-wheel drive, so that'll help too. That far bank worries me, though. It's steep and rock-strewn. We might get hung up there some. I need to get across and see how far in we can go before we have to walk."

"We can swim it farther up. See, there?" Able pointed to where the river pooled at a bend. "There's only one place that's got a strong current, and we can angle up there and get across. It's not far."

Vic studied the pool. "We'll get pulled down a bit, but maybe we can get over. Let's try it."

He got up and took off his clothes. He left his shoes on. It had been a while since they'd lived entirely in the bush, and their feet were a little tender. Able followed suit, then the two of them made their way upstream to the pool.

The water near the far shore was swift and deep and cut into the bank. They swam upstream as hard as they could, but the swift water shoved them down. They both got a bit bruised bumping over the rounded surfaces of the big boulders in the river's bed. The current threw them against a massive trunk along the shoreline with only stubs of branches. Grabbing a couple of these, the two brothers pulled themselves out.

"Let's hope we don't have to do that too often. Current's stronger than it looks."

Vic sat on the trunk, his feet pulled up, water beading and trickling down his flanks. Able sat beside him, running is fingers through his hair. They waited a bit to catch their breath, then worked their way downstream to the ford.

The track leaving the river rose steeply, but only for about twenty feet. It followed a low ridge upstream along the river and remained reasonably open until it turned away from the river into a ravine between two steep hills covered in thick stands of fir and cedar. There the track crossed an old rotted log bridge.

"We can probably get this far in. Maybe. This is possible. Let's see if we can find a place to set up."

Vic used the rotted logs from the base of the bridge to walk across a swampy area and followed the track up the ravine along the far side. Able was right behind him. About ten feet in, there was an indentation in the side of the hill where two great slabs of bedrock plummeted underground. It was filled with ferns and salal and was about the size of a tennis court.

Able knelt to study the base. "This is perfect. I can make a pit here, a good one. It's tight sand under the surface. If there's no water, we can make this work."

"There might be. We'll have to dig and see. Let's go back." Crossing the river at the pool was tricky. The current near the bank was strong, so they waded into the rapids above the pool, dove in, and swam hard.

Upper level winds had begun to shred the clouds into long strips of grey. The sun threw shifting patterns down the gorge, and light suddenly danced off the tips of waves in the riverbed. In the strengthening light, the river sparkled. Moments later, the same wind pushed heavier clouds over the hills and the river's deep water turned bluish green.

The brothers worked their way back to the road, walked across a flat ridge of rock, then down the shallow ditch. The rain would wipe out anything in the ditch and the flat rock would hide their tracks. From there on, the track was overgrown and virtually invisible unless you knew what to look for. Satisfied, Vic eased the van back onto the potholed gravel road, did a three-point turn, and faced back the way they'd come.

"We need a couple more tarps for the rain and maybe some fresh food. We got lots of freeze-dried. We can be back in before nightfall."

"I don't want to go back to town. I can stay here and get started."

Vic sat idling and thought about it. "We've got most of what we need in the back. Take in a shovel, one backpack, and a tarp and the tents, you should be able to get most of it done before I get back. I'll be a couple of hours, maybe more. If you don't dig too deep, the sand should hold."

He glanced up, watching the sky. The overcast was solid now, but no darker than it had been most of the day, so the rain would likely hold off. He helped Able unload what he needed.

By nightfall, Vic was on his way back from Harbour City, cruising slowly past the last of the houses looking for the old logging track again. When he found it, he dropped the van into all-wheel drive and gently urged it through the ditch, over the rock flat, and into the beginning of the track.

He drove in as far as the steep decline before the river, then walked back to the road and erased any tread marks. When he returned to the van, he studied the rock-strewn decline, dropped the van into low, and inched his way down. He had to fight the wheel. Once on the river flats, the van bounced its way slowly over the water-washed boulders as far as the edge of the river. Vic stopped here and got out. He studied the flow once again, working out just where he'd try to cross. Then he got back in, checked the shift, and eased his way in.

The current pulled at the van as it crept across. In the deep current, water ran across the floorboards. Vic felt the heavy van shift as it lurched on, pulled sideways by the force of the water on the side panels. But the deep-water passage was short, and he felt the tires grip near the shore. At the edge, Vic floored the van and rammed his way up the shale and boulders that littered the steep track. Once up the grade, he eased off and the van slithered into the turn along the rock ridge. The rest was easy.

And there was Able. Vic sighed. He felt again the void that had developed between them and the anger flickered inside. He tamped it down.

He left the van at the remains of the old bridge and hauled the supplies across the swampy area. Able had set up their little camp in the middle of the ferns and salal. He'd cleared enough space for Vic to unpack the gear.

"I'm gonna take the van back over before it's too dark and leave it in the scrub. You keep on with the pit." He was harsh in his delivery, and Able looked up, a little unsettled.

Taking the van back over the river, the swift water grabbed the vehicle before Vic was ready, and he nearly lost it. All that saved him was one of the two large protruding boulders. The van slewed around in the current losing traction and banged into the side of the huge rock. Vic felt the door panel give and knew he'd be jammed there.

The van was already in low in four-wheel drive, so he floored it and waited. He felt the shift as the wide tires found purchase. He bounced around on the seat when the back end caught and scraped along the side of the rock. As the vehicle righted itself and plunged ahead into shallower water, he eased off and crept along to the water's edge. Once out of the river and on the flats, he pulled up and got out.

About a hundred yards upstream, he found a shallow trench of water-washed stones defined by drift piled up on the river side. A wide swath of red alder overhung the trench and would hide the van. He drove in, got out, pushed a few saplings he'd knocked over as upright as he could. When looked back, he was satisfied that the copters the logging companies used wouldn't see the dark-coloured van when they were either carting crews or surveying.

Then he stripped and swam across, using the same pool they'd used earlier. This time, however, he swam upstream in the pool as hard as he could before the current caught him. When the swift water pulled him downstream, he was closer to the shore and caught a sapling at the water's edge.

Able had pitched the other tent and hung their supplies in a couple of trees. He'd laid out a rectangle about eight feet to the side and was already down four feet. It was still dry. Vic fished out some dry clothes while he watched Able. Between them, they finished digging about two hours later. The rest was dry and easy.

They hauled some fallen branches back to camp, stripped them, and roped together a small raft-like square that they secured as a kind of lid for the pit. Able wove the supple ends of fir branches through the grid so the top would stop a lot of the rain they knew was on its way. The bottom was a bit dampish, but the sandy soil had held all the way, so the sides were strong enough without bracing. Able had cut a number of small logs just in case, and these he lowered into the finished hole.

The night was uneventful, and the rain was light.

Late afternoon the next day in Harbour City, Vic left the van in the parking lot on Victoria Crescent across from the SHH Investigations office. Able was asleep on a bed roll in the back cargo area. The van was in behind the small fleet of white Mercedes Transit vans that were always there, so it wasn't noticeable from the street or, more importantly, from the office on the second floor of the old firehall.

He glanced up at the windows. Although it wasn't raining anymore, it was a dull day, so the lights were on, and he could see Harry as he wandered about. He knew Sabina had her own office on the side somewhere, but he couldn't see her.

Vic smiled to himself and thought, I'm right outside. All you have to do is look. But even if you did, you wouldn't see anything out of the ordinary. For one thing you're too slow, and for another, I'm too good.

Vic walked down the crescent, watching the street. It was early for the stroll to be active, but there were always a few who tried and a few who cruised for them. The two he spotted, he studied, then discarded. Neither had the aura he was looking for.

He walked past the so-called square where two streets joined and turned leaving a strange looking almost circular asphalt area. A square it wasn't, but it had the requisite coffee shop. A block farther on, the highway sliced through, cutting off the city from the crescent. Vic crossed and sauntered along looking in store windows. He glanced at the Serious Coffee shop, but there were no young women at the outside tables.

He passed the bank on the next corner and turned in at the Modern Café. Before he spent much time on the street, he needed to eat. Neither of them had had much that morning. Breakfast by the river had been a bit bleak. By late afternoon, Able was exhausted from working on the site, so when they set out for town, he retired to the rear cargo area for a nap. He was still napping.

Vic knew he had no need to find work this time. He wouldn't be around long enough to matter. One or two nights will do, he thought. Then maybe a couple more to get free. After that, I'll head back to the big city. Everything I need is there. Vic smiled as he waited for the waitress. Maybe, he thought, maybe she's still here serving, the one we lost. But the girl who appeared and took his order wasn't anything like her.

His dinner was excellent, better than he remembered, and the wine list had improved. The waitress who'd brought his food had been pretty enough, except for multiple rings in her ears and a stud in her lower lip. He'd never understand the attraction of that sort of mutilation. He preferred his own.

Over a final glass of wine, Vic thought about Able. They'd have one more tryst together, repeat the old familiar ritual. But he doubted it would have the same intensity. The estrangement was too great now. The power of the blood remained, but it was his, not theirs, not anymore. He thought about the others, the rituals of application, the necessity for it all. He knew his power had grown while Able's had withered; they were reciprocal now; one grew, the other diminished; one rose, the other fell.

Now his greatest pleasure lay in the warmth of blood, the ecstasies of touch. When they had sent them over together, they had felt them pass, the pleasure flowing through them, rippling along their bodies. They'd watched the girls' eyes, saw the terror, the acceptance, the passing. It was like smoke rising, evaporating in the air, like embers winking out, warmth dying. As life left the girls, it passed through them, enriching, fulfilling. That was what they lived for. But the husk that remained mattered as did the place of passage; both were powerful symbols of transformation, a mark in time, profound and magical.

He got up, paid his bill, and walked down toward the crescent. First, we'll find her, he thought. Then we'll see.

As he walked, he could feel his singularity, his aura stronger, more powerful. He marveled that the ones on the street saw and felt nothing. I'll be complete soon, he thought, Able after the girl, a second soul to feed me. The blood will be mine by right.

The day dragged slowly to a close, the sky a sullen grey. As the light began to fail, shadows devoured the street. The stroll would soon come to life, the girls rising in the dark like mushrooms. When we find her, we'll take her together. He sauntered up the hill to the van on Victoria Road.

23.

Harry wandered over to the office window. It had been a long day, and he was tired. Will and Rory were still working a case, a very nasty divorce and custody suit, and they hadn't found enough yet to satisfy the husband. Harry didn't understand that kind of vitriol. If you loved someone, why would you try to destroy her, why would you want to? Still, that sort of case was a big part of their income, that and stuff like the one he'd just finished writing up: yet another case of fraud. People seemed to think they had a right to pilfer, and some of them were damned good at it.

He leaned on the sill and looked out at the street. The day was overcast, threatening rain. It was dismal, but still dry. If it held off long enough, they could get dinner and be home. He saw a few people trudging along, looking sort of like he felt. And one who seemed more alert, more intense, walking up the hill on Victoria as if he had something to look forward to. He thought about Sabina still working the electronic stuff on the CEO case, and he felt a bit livelier too. She was something to go home with, that's for sure. Harry turned from the window and began to clear his desk.

Something about that one guy twitched, like a ripple in a pond that came from nowhere. Harry shrugged, maybe it'd come to him, maybe not. He gathered the report pages together, walked out to the reception area, and dropped the pages on Isabella's desk.

"What's this then?" She glanced at the papers Harry'd put on her desk.

"Harry, you need to be more like your partner in there, the one who does all the work? Nobody hand-writes stuff anymore. Here's an idea! You could use that computer she gave you and send it to me in print so I could read it. That'd save you walking out here too. Be a relief for both of us. I suppose you're done for the day since the donuts are gone."

"Izzy, my love, that's the most you've said to me in months! I know you think I'm the cat's ass. It's just that sometimes you have trouble getting it out."

"You got the ass part right."

"The clients, Izzy, what would the clients think? I know they're just words of endearment, but they'd wonder, now, wouldn't they?" Isabella looked around the reception area, stood up, and scanned the floor. "What clients? The few we get, you just seem to irritate, like you do me."

Isabella flipped her head toward Sabina's office. "If it weren't for her, you wouldn't make enough for donuts." She sat back down and looked up at him.

Harry frowned and said, "Speaking of donuts, we're out. Be terrible if we got one and had no donuts. Might just walk out. No pay for anybody then. You're falling down on the job, you are."

Harry didn't wait for a response. He ducked back into the office and watched Sabina working her computers. She saw him in the monitor's reflection and wriggled her fingers.

When things were slow, or he was as tired as he was now, he just watched her. There was so much pleasure in that. She was such a good thing to have in his life. And she was a whiz with the electronic stuff. Harry still couldn't believe his good fortune.

He leaned on the doorframe. They made a fine team, he thought, except for the mess they'd made of the ritual murders. That was a bit of tarnish. He thought again of the dead girls, of how close they'd come and how dangerous it'd been, especially for Sabina and Sally. Now, the killer was back. A new victim in Powell River, a task force set up. He wondered if they'd be invited in, sort of on the side like last time. He was thinking about their old case when Sabina's screens went black.

"Okay. Buy me dinner. You look like you could use some. We got an evening coming up all to ourselves, so you need to be prepared. There was a very subtle pun in there floating around. I hope you got it."

"I'm a master detective. how could I miss? Run that by me again?"

They left the office and walked down the stairs to the street. Isabella ignored their chatter. She was inputting Harry's scribbles. They turned down Victoria Crescent towards the main drag. Sabina grinned at Harry. "What'd you do to Izzy? She let us both out without a word. That's not like her. She usually throws a few barbs if we leave before she does."

"We were discussing handwriting versus more advanced methods, and she seemed somewhat unhappy with the former. Suggested I do something with a computer. Well, Sweets, we're here aren't we? And there's that pun you left hanging."

The discussion continued all the way to the Modern. Over dinner and a couple of glasses of a rather good Australian shiraz, Harry mentioned the walker he'd seen from the office window.

"He was just walking up the hill, you know, like everybody else, but there was something." Harry shook his head as he thought.

"Still bothers me, I guess. Like a hangnail."

"I've heard that a distraction will sometimes jolt things loose. What say we go home and try that? See what comes up."

They left the restaurant and cut across the steet, through the alley beside St Paul's Anglican Church and walked along Front Street. The harbour lay just the other side of Pacifica, the newish condo tower built along the seawall.

They could see the water and slices of the outer islands in the gaps between the tower and the two-storey office buildings along the way. They passed the old city hall and walked around the long curve that overlooked the tiny lagoon with its white-railed foot bridge. The lagoon hadn't changed, but the park surrounding it had. The city had spent a mint on new cobblestone paving and a bunch of sycamore trees.

Beyond the park, the inner harbour looked grey and uncomfortable, heaving slightly in the dull evening. They walked down the hill to Terminal, crossed the bridge over the Millstone River, and walked up Stewart to Kiyo's hair salon.

Harry opened the door on the far side of the front windows and followed Sabina up the stairs, watching the action. He opened the apartment door and stood aside. Sabina sauntered in, twirled around once, her short skirt floating up a couple of inches, and made for the kitchen. Harry heard her rummaging around in the cabinets and got the scotch from the living room.

The bedroom was next. Most distractions happened there, whether they jolted anything loose was moot.

Vic took his time on the stroll, waiting for darkness to take the street. He crawled along near the curb, stopped sometimes to watch the girls saunter along, skirts riding high. When they spotted the van, they wandered over and displayed themselves, legs stretched out hip shot. But they were the desperate ones, Vic thought, the ones who were needy and none too clean. They weren't for him. The night settled sullenly, the bellies of fat grey clouds hanging low, lit feebly by the few city lights. The rain held off, but the air was heavy and restless. It wouldn't be a good night, they both knew that. The girls would pick up on the coming rain. The short skirts and the legs and the heels would show, but the buzz wouldn't be there. The threat of rain tamped down the pleasure. Able sat beside Vic, silent and intent.

Vic sighed and considered giving up for the evening, but then he saw one of the tall ones sauntering down the hill. He pulled in on the other side and waited for her. He'd give it another hour or so. Able pressed his nose to the glass, staring intently at the tall blonde.

Vic watched her walk. She had the moves alright. She ignored the weather, no coat, no umbrella. She was taller than most, and her legs were long and inviting. Her blond hair was down and swaying gently around an exquisite face beautifully made up. She looked too good for this place. She seemed unused, unsullied, and he liked that. This one tweaked a memory. He thought he recognized her.

As she got closer, he remembered the night they'd almost

lost it all. He remembered the two girls walking up the sidewalk to the side entrance of the house on Hecate: That one and the blonde detective. He remembered the struggle, the tasers, those lovely loose bodies. And then that damned detective's partner and the cops. They'd dropped the girls, scrambled into the truck, and had only made it out of Harbour City by driving the truck along the railway tracks until they were clear. Damned near ruined their kidneys.

A setup, it had been a setup, and this one, this blonde one, had been part of it. They'd wanted the blonde detective especially. What was she called? Vic tried to remember. He and Able had watched the two of them together a few times. Listened to their chatter. The detective's name... Sabina, she was called Sabina. Harry was her partner, he remembered him.

No, he thought, we'll steer clear of the blonde for the moment. They'll both be here when we want them. Let's see what else the night brings out.

He drove on up Victoria Road and crossed with the light at Milton. Able sighed and slumped in his seat. "She was lovely, we could have had her."

"She's the one who kicked you, remember? We'll leave her for another time when she's with that detective bitch. Let's look for a while longer."

The upper part of the stroll usually wasn't as busy as the few blocks below Milton, but some of the better ones stayed up here, so Vic was hopeful. Able said nothing more and seemed to withdraw into himself. Vic continued to cruise, ignoring Able and concentrating on the street.

They were on the far end of the stroll now, up near the gas station at Needham. Beyond the intersection, the truck's headlights picked up a girl. She was slim, long black hair swaying seductively as she walked. Vic stopped at the corner as he studied her. He liked the way she moved, the way she walked, the way her body seemed fluid as if her bones were flexible. She wasn't dressed for the stroll, no short skirt, no tight top, nothing like that. She had on blue jeans and a light blue sweater, the kind you pull over your head.

Able sat up and hummed to himself, nodding, and Vic pulled across the intersection. Able rolled down the window on his side of the van, leaned out, resting his upper arms on the door and wiggling his index finger in the usual come here signal. And much to his surprise, the girl did. Able was excited and smiling as he spoke to her. He knew he'd have to be careful not to frighten her, so he asked her for directions to the university.

She stood in front of the side door looking up at him, smiled, and nodded. "All you have to do is turn around, take this street back to Fifth, and turn left. Just keep going up Fifth Street and you'll run right into it."

Able wasn't sure what to do next. She seemed so innocent. So he said, "My name's Able and this is my friend Vic. Can we give you a lift?"

She reached up and took Able's hand in hers. "I'm Mercedes."

She climbed up on the running board, reached in across Able, and offered her hand to Vic. Her sweater pulled tight and Able could feel her breasts pressing against his thigh. He breathed in, held his breath, and felt himself becoming aroused. He squirmed about a bit trying to hide the obvious. Mercedes didn't seem to notice.

Vic reached out, took her hand in both of his, and held it gently. "I'm very pleased to meet you Mercedes. You're a lovely young woman, and I'd appreciate it if you'd let us drive you to wherever you're going. After all, you've saved us a lot of time looking for the uni."

"Sure, I'd like that. I was goin' to see my girlfriend's new dog, but it'd be a lot more fun if we could drive around in your truck some. I never been in a truck like this before, and it's big. Can I sit between you?"

Able couldn't help himself, he giggled, pushed up against her, and ran his arm around her waist. She looked at him, smiled, and pecked him on the cheek. "You're sweet."

Able grazed the top of her head with his lips, rubbing his cheek on her silky black hair. "Let me get out and help you in," he said.

Mercedes stepped down to let Able open the door. He offered her his hand. She took it, and raising one leg to the running board, released his hand, glanced at him, smiled, and waited. He hesitated for a moment, then understanding what she wanted, placed his hand on her rear and pushed.

Mercedes giggled as she stepped up and squirmed across the seat. She smiled at Vic as she settled in and said, "He's a nice boy, isn't he?"

Vic wasn't sure how to handle this one either. Was she just some kind of innocent, maybe a little slow, a little out of it? Or was it an act and she was a pro?

Whatever she was, they had her. He thought about it some more as he released the parking break. No, no pro. She was too unaware of her own sensuality and too ignorant of how she affected men. Somebody looked after her, her thought, somebody made sure she was clean and presentable, somebody let her out on her own reluctantly, and somebody was a bit overly familiar with her, that seemed obvious. She was prefect. They could take their time her.

The streetlights were on now, and the one near them threw a gentle yellowish light across her silky black hair and the side of her face. These lights were old, on old poles, with incandescent bulbs hanging under corrugated shades that looked like circular crimped pie plates.

Vic put the Transit in gear and drove on out Victoria Road. He rejoined the highway at the new stoplight and drove down toward the plaza and Extension Road.

Just as Vic approached the lights at the plaza, Mercedes leaned towards Able, and said, "Oh boy, a Timmy's, let's get some doughnuts and coffee. Vic glanced at her. She seemed excited, sort of childish. He thought, she's an innocent, has no clue how her body lures men. But she could easily corrupt just like the others. And she'll be so much easier, he thought, she'll never realize. And her transcendence will be glorious.

Vic turned at the corner, drove into the drive-through, and ordered whatever she asked for. Mercedes was delighted. In the lot, Able helped her with her doughnut, gave her coffee, and slid his arm around her waist. She snuggled in close to him and lifted the doughnut to her lips.

"These are so good!" She grinned at Able, grains of sugar making her lips seem to sparkle in the lights of the lot. He nodded and brushed the dusting of sugar off her lips letting his hand gently caress her cheek.

Extension Road led off to the right, slid under the bypass

highway, and crept up the hill beyond the school. It ran through forest along the ridge. Below, the Chase River made its way toward the harbour. At this point, the river was broad and slow, meandering across a flat, grassy valley with the occasional house plopped down near the water. Beyond the valley, another forested ridge rose, sharp and high, so that the view was contained. Vic glanced at it out his window. He thought the small river originated back in the bush somewhere south of the road they were on.

Extension Road met River Road at an angled T-intersection. River Road, they knew, followed the much larger Mist River up toward its source in the mountains. River Road originally had been a logging road and had been paved in stages as the forest companies pushed farther and farther into the bush toward the river's source. At this point on River Road, the Mist was contained between two ridges. Vic couldn't see it, but he knew the river was narrow and fast, punctuated by long, steep gorges through which the water roared. He knew, too, that kids jumped from the steep rock walls into the river and were carried down to one of the many deep pools. Every summer, some of them were pinned against the rocks and drowned. There were little cairns built along the paths leading into the gorge, put there by grieving parents. The kids ignored them.

The old logging road lay a long way up River Road, way up past the gorges. This upper section of the river was swift, but had worn its bed through narrow, undulating valleys and was free of gorges. Vic knew he'd have to slow down when the road turned to gravel if they expected to find the trail. Able had hidden it so well even he'd have trouble.

Mercedes had finished the doughnuts and had settled into the seat. She didn't seem interested in anything outside the van, content to snuggle up to Able and rest. Vic glanced over at her and discovered she'd gone to sleep.

Full night had settled in now, and the forest was a black mass either side of the road. The van's headlights punched a cone of light through the darkness that spread and weakened as it extended outward. At the edges of the cone, the dark mass of the forest waited, rising into the night sky, brooding, oppressive, blotting out the stars.

Vic stared straight ahead, searching for his logging road,

trying to ignore the sense of pressure flowing in from either side. The forest was their home, not something set against them, he thought, but this night, he felt its force, and it wasn't welcoming. He glanced at Able, but his brother was smiling down at Mercedes, unaware of anything but the girl.

Vic slowed the van and studied the ditch along his side, looking for the marked logging road. Able was so into the girl that he'd be useless. Vic sighed. I'll need my wits about me just to find it. That old tree limb Able draped across the shoulder should be easy enough to find even in the dark, but there's so much down. I'm gonna have trouble finding anything.

Vic slowed even more, barely crawling along. There were broken limbs all along the road, the products of a short-lived, heavy wind that had crossed through earlier that evening. Vic muttered to himself, "I can't find the damn road." He stopped the car, reached over, shook Able gently, and raised his eyebrows. Able nodded and began to concentrate on the ditch.

Vic edged forward slowly, threw on the high beams, then took them off. They didn't help. He drove another couple of hundred yards, then stopped again. He looked at Able, who nodded again, then turned the van around and started back.

"There." Able said suddenly, and Vic turned toward the shoulder. He watched Able slide the sleeping girl's head to the seatback and climb down quietly. He pulled the branch out of the way.

The ditch was easy to cross, but the surface rock on its far side was more difficult, and Vic didn't want to wake the girl. He slipped into four-wheel drive and slowly climbed the rock into the beginning of the old logging road. He glanced at the side-view mirror and watched Able hide the opening once again. Vic stared out the windshield and began a slow drive down the track, pushing over the small saplings that had grown up in the middle. As he drove, he felt it again, that strange pressure from the bush, as if something dark and brooding lived there.

The forest around him seemed unfamiliar, dangerous. For the second time in his life, the forest seemed implacable. Vic had never felt uncertain, but he did now, and that unsettled him. He thought about that moment in the bush near

Hammil when he'd felt so similar. This is my home, he thought, this has been home for both of us all our lives. I shouldn't feel like this back here, not here. He tried to shrug it off, but the feeling persisted. Able followed behind the slow-moving van, pushing the saplings back up to hide any trace of their passing.

Vic concentrated on the trail, passing as gently as he could over the humps of bedrock and the boulders that lay in his path until he reached the top of the steep decline that led to the river itself. He stopped and waited for Able. The oppressive sensation niggled away at him. Vic ignored it and watched for Able. Mercedes slept on, her head now snuggled in against his shoulder.

As the two brothers sat in the car discussing how to get the girl down the decline and across the river, Vic felt the oppressiveness seep away and marvelled at the change. He breathed more easily, the bush and the river returned to normal. The dark, brooding sensation had gone like mist rising from water.

He turned to his brother and smiled. "We'll use that fallen cedar you found upstream, but Mercedes won't sleep through all that, so…"

Able studied Vic and shook his head. "We could use the Taser, but I don't want to. I don't want to hurt her before you know, what we have to do." He looked down and began to stroke the sleeping girl's hair. He looked up at his brother tentatively, hoping he'd agree so they could find another way.

"We don't have a lot of choices," Vic said. "If we don't use the Taser, we'll have to sedate her, and to do that, we'll have to wake her and feed her a sedative. Then we'll have to keep her mind off where we are until it takes effect. That won't be easy, Able, she'll want to go back most likely. She won't like it here. Right now, she's sleeping, and it'd be good if we could keep her like that. The Taser won't hurt her much and it'll keep her out."

"It will too, you know that!" Able gently shifted the girl. "You know it hurts, not for long, I know, but it hurts a lot for a bit, and I don't want to hurt her even for just a little while until it's time."

Vic sighed. He knew he couldn't shake Able's concern for

the girl, so he compromised. "There's some Coke in the back, a couple of bottles, and I've got some sleeping pills in the glove compartment. I'll have to mix them in, so slide her over here again and get one of the bottles. You'll have to wake her and keep her happy for a few minutes."

Vic popped the cap, poured the Coke into one of the paper coffee cups, dropped in three of the tablets and stirred until they dissolved. "Okay, wake her now, do it gently, and give her the cup and that last doughnut."

Able put his arm around the sleeping girl and kissed her gently. She reached for him, still drowsy, and kissed him back. He stroked her hair, ran his fingers across her lips, talked to her, told her he had something for her to drink that she'd like, and kissed her cheek.

Vic watched his brother. His gentleness surprised him. So did his dedication to the girl. He was usually far too hungry by this time to care about anything but placing the girl in the site, arranging her, and watching Vic apply the patch saturated with Sux.

Able held the cup to the girl's lips, and Vic saw her swallow. Watched her snuggle once again into Able's shoulder and in a few minutes drift off. That had gone far better than he'd expected. She hadn't really woken up before she drank the coke. She seemed to be content just to be with his brother, to feel his warmth. There was something innocent and sensual about it, something purely animal. That, Vic understood and so did Able.

Now, he thought, came the hard part, getting the girl over the river in the dark, finding the prepared site, then arranging her. Vic remembered the others, images passed through his memory: the sensual pleasure of the brush over skin, the power of the emerging symbols so necessary for transformation, then the opening, the blood spreading, pooling, the feel of it, the rich coppery taste of it, the fecund odour of it engulfing them, uniting them, leading finally to their own union and the power the blood lust gave them. Vic shuddered, felt the currents flowing through him. He reached for the girl.

Mercedes didn't really wake, she just came closer to consciousness, floated near the surface for a while before sliding into the depths. Able watched his brother remove his clothing, revealing the cursive patterns running across his chest and shoulders and down his torso. He handed the sleeping girl to Vic and prepared himself. Once he'd stowed all the gear and retrieved his buckskin waist pack, Able took Mercedes in his arms once more and began to descend the rock-strewn path toward the river. Vic followed, amused by his brother's gentle handling of the girl.

The flood plain was more difficult, the water-ravaged shrubs and the floor of rounded boulders the river had thrown up made progress slow. Mercedes slept on, however, and the brothers reached the great cedar log spanning the river that Able had found upstream.

They paused here while Vic considered how to get her across. There were the handholds Able had created from the stubs of branches the river had left, but they had the girl to carry, and the tree trunk, although wide, was rounded and slippery. Finally, Vic led, helping Able across while he concentrated on the girl in his arms. Mercedes helped too. She was still below the surface of consciousness, but aware of Able's arms around her. She snuggled into him in a kind of loose way making his progress easier.

The stone circle was just upstream, a flattish area under some young firs that formed protective arms along the sides of the site. Able lowered the sleeping girl gently to the ground, removed her clothes, lay the girl carefully in the center of the stone circle, smoothed her hair, and spread it around her lovely face. He sat back.

Vic opened the small pack Able carried and took out his brushes and the ink, a thick green-blue substance he'd made mostly from grass and blueberries. The substance was needed to carry the symbols her crossing required, and Vic carefully used his index finger and a stubby stick to create the intricate patterns across her body.

Once finished, Vic took out the patch saturated with the Sux he had found on the net and ordered from a source he'd never heard of. Both knew that once it was applied, the drug acted swiftly, paralysis running rapidly through the body.

Now they watched her breathing slow, her eyes suddenly snap open. They saw her fear. They saw her eyes change, saw the terror, then the acceptance as the life force began to leave her. Quickly, Vic took the knife and began the ritual that excited them both. Mercedes' heart had already stopped. She was gone, so the blood flowed copiously but there were no sudden arterial spurts, just the blood flowing, the thick coppery smell of it, the warmth of it running over his hands. Able slid his hands into the opening and shuddered in a kind of ecstasy. This was their moment, the beginning of their own transformation. They closed their eyes and lost themselves in the pleasure.

Their pit lay a little down river where Able had set up camp, a shallow replica of the root cellar of their youth, rich with the fecund smells of moist earth. In this pit, Vic entered his brother. As their union became complete, Vic slid his hand around his brother's neck and applied another patch. Startled, Able turned toward Vic and for the briefest of moments, saw the mixture of rage and pleasure that lay in his brother's eyes.

Able reached for the patch, his fingers passing through air and falling to his side. Vic watched his breathing stop, watched his eyes grow very large, saw the horror, then the loss of everything and emptiness replace it. He took the knife from its leather scabbard and began to cut. He was gentle at first, then as the fever took him, cutting turned to slashing. Vic ripped with the knife over and over, caught in a frenzy that engulfed him. As his vision cleared, he looked down at what remained of his brother and felt both appalled and elated. He embraced the carnage, wrapped his arms around the bloody remains, and lay still until he felt complete again. Then he stood, looked down at the carnage, frowned, climbed from the pit, and cleaned himself in the river. He watched the blood curl away in eddies and slide in sinuous threads downstream. When he'd finished, the walked back to the pit and began the task off filling in his brother's resting place.

He struck camp, gathered all the gear, threw everything they'd brought into the pit, threw in Mercedes' clothes as well, and began to shovel. He returned the site to what it had been as well as he could. It took most of the rest of the night. When he'd finished, he crossed the river to the trail up the hill and reached the van. The sky showed a pale suggestion of light in the east, overhead shimmering stars still covered the blackness. He stood beside the Transit, breathing deeply. He found his clothes inside and dressed. He turned the van, drove back to River Road, and then toward the main highway. He drove under the highway on the long cloverleaf, emerged on the other side, and drove north to the Duke Point ferry road. At the end of the road, when he entered the ferry terminal, he could see the huge dark bulk of Gabriola Island on the far side of the channel that led to the Salish Sea and the mainland.

The great city across the water waited for him, its treasures now his alone. Vic smiled and settled in to wait.

24.

Alan and Spence caught the ferry from Saltery Bay to Earls Cove on the south side of Jervis Inlet. The highway along the coast took them through Sechelt and south to the docks at Langdale where they waited for the ferry to Horseshoe Bay and the road to Vancouver. It was late evening now, and raining once again, the sky black with dark grey clouds floating over the water like fat dirigibles.

"You know," Spence said, "those guys in Hammil and the ones from Powell River've got a good grip on what went down at that site. After Jake and Larry got there, and we went over the files again, we got some good forensics and some good stuff on that farmhouse. I'm happy we went and that Jake and Larry saw the sites. They've never seen one before and they needed to. These are definitely our guys."

"No question, they're our two alright, but keeping the task force in Vancouver was the right decision. We've got Jake and Larry to thank for that one, not that we didn't think the same thing. The Hammil guys seem relieved, don't you think?"

"Jake and Larry took that float plane from the lake, didn't they? Then they'll beat us in. Until we get another one, Brian's gonna put those two on other things and that'll leave us pretty much free to refresh your murder book. Me? I'll stick to computer notes. Hey, that hotel wasn't bad, was it?" Spence leaned on the railing and studied the barnacles on the huge support pylons that lined the berth.

"I loved that lobby, especially the old guy, Burl. The whole thing looks like it was ripped out of the 1920's and plopped down in the hills. Breakfast was good too. That gal Agnes sure knows how to make pie. Mine are never like that. Wonder how she does it."

They watched the ferry slide into the dock, water boiling up around the ship's bow. Well, the bow now, but as soon as they sailed it'd be the stern. These ferries were double ended. They waited in line for the boarding call, moved onto the ferry's lower deck, then left the car and went upstairs for coffee.

By the time the ferry reached Horseshoe Bay, the rain had tapered off to little more than a soft shower, but the cloud cover had deepened and seemed to them lower than ever. They could see only a part of the high ridges surrounding the terminal and only the lower part of the town. It looked like something out of one of Edgar Allen Poe's gloomy tales. The dark facades of buildings on the side of the hill pushed out of the dark mist like black teeth. Spence shuddered when she looked at the town as they disembarked.

"Jesus, that's depressing. The place looks eerie, buildings stickin' up out of the fog like that. Gonna be a bitch of a drive back."

She took the car up the long hill out of Horseshoe Bay, plowing through the substantial walls of mist and passing a line of tractor trailers before the road joined the highway to Vancouver. The cloud bank held until they got to Taylor Way and the streets leading to the Lions Gate Bridge. They could see the whole arch across the harbour through a mist that was rapidly dissipating. The other side of the bridge plunged them into the dark mass of Stanley Park before disgorging them onto Georgia Street and the lights of the city. By this time, the rain had become drizzle, then even that stopped. The ceiling remained low though, just above the high towers. The city lights turned the bellies of the cloud banks a silvery grey.

"You wanna stop at the station?" Spence worked her way up Georgia.

"I guess we better. Let the guys know we're back or leave a message if they're out. Then let's head home. It's been a long day and we'll have to get the task force set up here tomorrow, at least the com section."

"Okay, then let's head out and find a place to eat, save us from cooking anything. I'm too wiped to cook."

Spence grabbed the next left, shot down to Hastings and headed east, cursing the buses that clogged the narrow street. Passing two of them and barely missing a couple of night people shuffling into the street, she made Main, turned left to Cordova, then right, hitting the garage entrance too fast as usual.

Larry and Jake, who had indeed arrived earlier from Powell River, were out somewhere. Alan left a quick note on Jake's desk and joined Spence again in the garage. She peeled out, leaving a pair of black streaks on the ramp, and turned down Cordoba.

"Take it easy on the stroll. Let's see what's going on if anything. Then maybe head up to Broadway on Clark, and we'll try the Cactus Club.

"Long way round, but it'll be sorta fun on Clark, what with all those big rigs lumberin' along."

"Just try to get us there without creating a mess so we can relax a little." Alan let out a slow breath and watched the blur of buildings slide by on the sides of the street. It was better than watching the road.

The office was humming when Alan and Spence got in the next morning. Jake and Larry were off till the four o'clock shift, so they looked for the conference room that had been allocated to the task force. Inside, they found a couple of techs setting up computer stations.

One of them at a desk on the side wall turned. "Hi, I'm Ted, this one on the floor is Ron. You the guys runnin' this thing?"

Alan pointed at Spence. "Spence Riley and I'm Alan Kim. Yeah, we're runnin' this thing. You guys gonna be finished soon?"

Ron grunted from under the desk and said, "If we can get this damned stuff wired, yeah."

"Tell us if you need anything else, and we'll get it for you. Big budget on this one. Good thing too since we've gotta link Harbour City, Powell River, Hammil, and us. That's phones and secure computers."

Ron slid out and grinned at Alan. "You got that kind of clout, get us a couple Asus laps, hell, get three, and a couple routers and.... Look I'll make a list, alright? Just give me a minute. Phones are okay. Who's got a pen?"

Ten minutes later, Alan was in Brian Stevens' office with the list. Brian grunted, frowned, but signed off. Alan grabbed the papers and Spence, dropped the orders off at Requisitions with a rush attached, and the two of them hit their desks to go over all the reports one more time.

"We were just stoppin' in, what the hell're we doin' here?"

"Finishing up. We gotta get all this stuff organized. Then we head back to the conference room, see if we can find out how staffing's going to work."

Alan flipped over another report, then said, "You know, if our guys spread this mess out even more than it is, the task force is going to be huge, and we both know that won't work. We're centralized here, and I guess that's best, but the crimes now cover a lot of territory. I guess if we can hold with the guys we have and keep the brass out, it might work. Call the thing a task force if that's what it takes to keep it simple."

Spence sat back and sighed. "You know damned well the brass'll be all over us. The bigger it gets, the more they'll wade in. They'll want multiple reports, probably daily, and some asshole'll screw up the budget. It'll be a mess. Too many guys and it'll be useless. But you're right, if we can keep it the way it is, just reps from the cities, maybe we can get somewhere. Depends where our nutcase hits next."

Alan looked at Spence who was leafing through one of the forensic reports from Powell River. She was calm enough, given the situation, and he hoped it'd last. Neither one of them had been in quite this situation before, and the stress and frustration were going to build, something Spence didn't deal with well. She'd get restless and want to do something other than yap. Alan knew he'd have a hard time tamping her down once she got started. He shook his head and sighed. They still had no idea who these two were. They only knew their victims.

"Why don't we get out of here, grab some coffee, and talk about the case, see if we can figure out where to go from here. The reports help, but we need a strategy since we're the leads. First though, let's get back to the conference room, see who we've got now, and set up a staffing list."

Ted and Ron were still messing with the computers, monitors, and the wiring for a large projector. Ted stuck his head out from behind a monitor, "Hi guys, we'll be done in maybe an hour."

Alan nodded. "You guys are assigned to us I'm assuming, so we need to know how to keep this place staffed twenty-four seven. We have to have an operator in place all the time and an office manager to coordinate stuff."

"We got all that covered as far as tech goes," Ron said. "We'll split the shifts on the board. There are three of us, and Brian's already assigned a manager who'll put it all together and prepare reports, so you guys just need to catch this creep. Guy's name's Herb, the manager. Been around the place forever, and he's a wiz at keeping things organized. He'll be in when Jake and Larry are on, so you can get all that set up then. We'll be done for sure in a couple of hours, then we're heading out for eats and we'll be back for the four o'clock changeover. Any luck on the computers?"

"The requisition's in. I don't know how long it'll take from there, but you got what you wanted. We're getting out of here too. Thanks for what you've done. See you at four."

They left the room, hit the stairs to the garage, and took off for the Cactus Club over past Main.

Four-thirty found Alan and Spence, Larry and Jake, and a scattering of other people including Ted and Ron in the conference room. The table in front of them was littered with coffee cups and wrappers from the snack machine in the hall.

"Okay, let's get down to it. You all know the case, and you'll all have duplicate reports from Herb soon."

A tall thin man with a fringe of brown hair dressed in jeans and a white t-shirt raised his hand. "I'm Herb and I've got the paperwork with me. Jodi and Helen here will man the phones and fill in wherever needed." Herb looked at Alan and hesitated. "How about everybody pick up packages when we're done here?"

Alan nodded and smiled. "Okay, we have our techs, Ron and Ted and?" Alan waited, and a hand shot up.

"Roger. I'm with Ted and Ron." Roger was a portly guy in a suit as rumpled as Larry's always was.

"Okay," Alan said. "And we've got Herb as case manager. And we've got the four of us as detectives. You all know Jake and Larry. I'm Alan Kim and this is Spence Riley, my partner. We'll likely have a couple of detectives from Powell River join us and maybe one or two from Hammil. The most recent murder is inland from Powell River, close to Hammil, so they have an interest too."

Alan looked around the room, but no one had questions.

"There's also Josie Atardo in Harbour City, our boss. She'll assign whoever we need there. We're connected electronically with all of them, thanks to Ted and Ron and Roger."

Alan paused for a moment, considered bringing in the two privates, Sabina and Harry, and decided against it.

"Alright, let's get organized. Herb, make sure everyone has a file. We'll meet again at eight tomorrow morning. In the meantime, familiarize yourselves with the data, and update through Ted and Ron. Any suggestions go to Herb. The search for the name of the latest victim is ongoing, so feel free to pursue that as well."

Jake raised a finger, and as the group broke up the four detectives retired to Jake's office.

"Okay, we've got our group, as spread out as it is," Jake said once they were seated at their desks. "But that really doesn't get us very far. We have all the data from the island murders, and we have the latest stuff from Hammil and Powell River. We also have the Powell River coroner's suggestion about the method these guys may have used to commit their crimes. None of that gets us any further than we already are. Until we get another victim, god forbid, we've got bloody little. And when we do get another, it'll be the same: no clothes, no forensics to speak of, no nothin'. You two are the leads, how do you want to proceed while everyone gets up to speed?"

Alan nodded. "We've got to find out who the latest one is. We need a name. If we manage that, then we do deep research on her. We need her background, everything about her. That'll help us understand how and why she got taken. We've got a lot of stuff, but we have no way of using it yet. We need, just us four, to concentrate on that. Find the girl. Get her background. We'll feed it to the profiler and see what she thinks."

"We've got urgent mispers out all over the place already," Larry pulled at his necktie and shoved both hands in his jacket pockets. "I don't understand how she can't be missed by somebody. I mean, she was well fed, in good physical shape before our guys got to her. So she wasn't indigent, homeless, a druggie. Why the hell can't we find her?"

"Dental records?" Spence asked.

"Taken and distributed around the province. Every dentist. The next step's country-wide, and that's in the works now. The records've gone to every force and from there to every dentist. It'll take time, and I don't think we have much of that. All we've given them is a rough time frame and the xrays. Unless we're lucky and somebody misses her, I think we're screwed."

Jake leaned back in his chair, raised his eyebrows, and looked at Alan. "So, what else, or do we just twiddle our collective thumbs?"

Alan shrugged. "We've done everything we can. We've been over the files a dozen times. Um... I probably shouldn't even say this, but I think we need the privates. At least, they'll give us a different slant on things. Maybe we've missed something somewhere. Those two are sharp, and they've got contacts we don't. If we keep quiet about it, why not use what we used before. There's no need to go through SHH Investigations, we just set up with them privately and compare notes."

Spence sighed and shook her head. "I hate involving those two and she bugs the hell out of me. They shouldn't be a part of police business, even if they have been hired on two of the cases."

She shook her head some more. "But I gotta agree with Alan here. We need them. They have contacts we can't get. You know I've already been in touch. We've got a heavily encrypted link established, thanks to Sabina. That puts us in a very secure loop with them, and we know that she's got links to Chinatown's fat lady who's just up the bloody street."

"We're the glory boys around here now," Larry said, "what with the creep in custody and the three girls safe, but there ain't no way we can do anything shady in the office. So, if you guys got a secure link, can you get us in as well, maybe at your place or Jake's? He's got nobody in his life except me, so his place is practically empty."

He grinned at Jake and yanked at his tie some more. The top button of his shirt was already undone, the tie now halfway down his front.

"We're getting nowhere sitting here," Spence said, "Let's get the hell out and grab some eats, talk this mess over, and set up a plan. We gotta be back here at eight tomorrow, and it'd be nice to have something to contribute."

The four of them went to a restaurant on Water Street in Gastown. It was a quiet place with booths along one softly lit brick wall and tables in the middle. Jake took a booth in the rear of the room and the four of them sat. The waiter took drink orders and left them alone. He was used to cops, Larry said, especially them, and wouldn't come near them until called.

Spence sighed and looked at the two across from her. "Okay, this rehash is going nowhere. Let's talk about a hookup. Jake, since you're a lot closer than we are, if we can set up a computer in your place where you two can get at it, then I can send a note to Sabina, see if she'll get you into our loop. It's private, heavily encrypted, and you'll get what we do when we do. You good with that?"

Jake nodded, "Sure, I'm close, so we can go over after we eat. I've got a couple of Apples, not new but not old, so you can use one of those."

"One thing," Spence looked at Jake. "Sabina's shifty. She'll get into your computers and raid 'em. But she's kosher, she won't reveal anything, she just collects. If you're good with that, we can get a text off to her once we're done here."

"Let's order, I'm famished." Larry signalled the waiter who glided over. Jake frowned after the orders were in. "How deep does she go? I mean how much personal stuff is at risk here?"

"Nothing's at risk. All she's interested in is the case. She won't touch personal stuff. So relax. What you got on there that's so personal?" Spence grinned at Jake.

"Stuff it, Spence, I got my secrets." Jake grinned back.

Their orders came and they ate in silence. After coffee, they paid up and walked to Jake's place three blocks away.

The apartment was in an older building, one that had been refurbished carefully. The old lobby held a couple of guilt mirrors, a pair of loveseats bracketing a square, heavy-looking coffee table, and a pair of real palms in large, green pots. The elevator lay behind this ensemble. A pair of brass doors with one of those old floor dials above it was set in a stone wall. Stairs with an ornate cast iron rail stood on the right-hand side, curving gently upward.

Larry hustled over and hit the button. The car arrived silently, and they climbed into a brass-walled cab with a mahogany hand- rail about waist height. The cab rose silently for a couple of moments, opened just as silently, and all four stepped out into a corridor with a barrel-vaulted ceiling and a ton of crown molding. The walls were papered in a rich flock paper rather than the usual paint, the carpet a thick-piled Persian motif over dark hardwood. Jake led them down the corridor to the end unit, unlocked the door and stood back, as did the others. Everyone looked at Spence.

She didn't know what to expect after the elevator and the hallway, so she took one step and stuck her head in and looked around. The place was so ordinary she chuckled and shook her head.

"You had me goin' what with the elevator and hall, but this I get." She stepped in and the others followed.

The apartment was painted the usual beige, but Jake had negated that effect with some local art. He had a couple of Brent Heighton street scenes on one wall and a series of Hobson's paintings of the west coast of Vancouver Island on the other. They dominated the room, and he'd played to that with colour and shape: neutral loveseats with colourful accent cushions and carpets picking picking up and echoing the strong colours of the artwork.

"The den's this way," Jake said from the hall, and after a quick look around, Spence and Alan followed him down a short hall. This room was all business: filing cabinets, a working desk, and a library table with two laptops open on its surface.

Larry was already there, his suit jacket hanging lopsidedly from the back of the desk chair, but he remained standing. His attention was focused on the two computers both of which showed the Vancouver Police crest on a blue background.

"We're already linked to the office and all that other stuff. I hope that's not going to be a problem with your hookup,"

Spence pulled out the chair and said, "Not a problem, let me get this thing set up. Go sit down or something. Stop hovering, for god's sake."

Jake shrugged, "Just tryin' to help, moral encouragement an' all that." He sighed heavily and shuffled over to another chair and sat, head bowed.

Spence looked at him and said, "Jesus, gimme strength." She turned back to the computers, hit some keys, asked Jake for a password. Then she began keyboarding.

"Okay, I'm in and I've sent an email to Sabina askin' for a link to this computer. Now we relax for a bit. She'll answer for sure. It's still office time. If she's not there, Isabella'll forward the stuff. Got anything to drink around here?"

Jake had a wine cooler in the kitchen, and they all sat around with a glass of good Pinot Grigio. Every ten minutes or so, Spence checked the computer she'd carried out of the den office and plugged into a kitchen outlet. That bottle an almost a second had disappeared before she got a response.

"Okay, I've got Sabina, and she's setting up a secure connection with her own brand of encryption. Won't take her long." Spence closed the lid of the computer. "Any more left?"

Jake cracked a third bottle, put out cheese and crackers, a bowl of nuts, and leaned against the counter watching the other three. He looked at Spence and asked, "Once she's done, are we gonna be able to reach you two as well?"

"Yup, what we'll have is a closed loop independent of anything else you use the computer for. We'll be linked to her and each other. Be careful, though, she's probably got her own little spiders or somethin' stuck in our machines, 'cause she sure knows too damn much about too damn much."

"If it's private, we've got nothing to lose and a lot to gain." Jake offered more wine. He held up the bottle, but they all shook their heads. As good as it was, three glasses were more than enough.

"Okay, let's go see what we've got." Spence propped open the computer. Jake walked over and watched over her shoulder. On the computer's screen was a graphic he'd had never seen before.

"We're in," Spence said. "Let me check for mail." She hit a couple of keys and looked at the text.

"She's got nothing concrete to offer yet, but she thinks that the body up in Hammil isn't going to be the last and that we can expect more soon." Spence read on. "She's convinced she says here that bodies can be expected in the city or even back on the island." Spence turned the computer so everyone could read the text. Jake stood back a bit to give them room.

Larry straightened up, tugged at his tie, and shoved both hands in his pants pockets. "In the meantime, she got anything we can actually use?"

Spence shook her head. "She'll keep us informed, but there's nothing solid there yet. I gotta say, though, that she's rarely wrong. I don't know about the island bit, though, seems pretty far-fetched, that pair'd be crazy to go back there."

"I'm not so sure she's wrong on that one." Alan had straightened and had also stepped back. "Psychopaths are notorious for playing with their pursuers, so it's possible. If that happens, though, it'll sure screw up the task force."

"Okay, let's add it in the morning for what it's worth so everybody knows. If we're set up here, let's get back to work. Evening shift's already out." Jake tapped his watch.

In a half hour, all four were back at the station and working out the night's duties.

25.

Gena walked slowly along Hastings, her high heels emphasizing the smooth rotation of her hips. She knew she was different from other girls, better walk, willowy, and, she thought, far less trashy looking. She wore a short red skirt, a matching lacy top, and black, patent leather knee-highs. Her hair was long and black and worn in a braid down her back. It swayed back and forth as she sauntered along, emphasizing her natural grace. Her makeup was light, only some blush and lipstick. She didn't need anything else. Didn't even need that.

But it wasn't the clothes, the high heels, or even the suggestive saunter that attracted men. It was all that, sure, but she had that sensual almost tactile aura that filled the air around her, like the subtle aroma of expensive perfumes. Men were drawn to her like moths to the streetlights. She could pick and choose, and she did.

Part of the choosing was the car. She knew the BMWs and the Saabs, the Mercs and the Jags, the caddies and the Lincolns. And she had a well-developed sense of how much the drivers were worth. It wasn't their clothes especially. It was an attitude they exuded, and she read it very well.

She hadn't been on the street long and wouldn't stay long either. This was a way to avoid her violent boyfriend. Well, maybe boyfriend wasn't the right term. More like keeper and provider. If she did what she was told, he wasn't likely to beat her. He was worth a lot, had all the right contacts in the rarer atmosphere of old, established money. And he knew the more unsavory areas of prostitution and drugs. He knew the crime bosses, what they controlled and how, and he had enough on them to keep himself clear. She'd met him at a lavish party over a year ago now. She knew he was a sociopath, charming, successful, dominant, and explosive.

One night a week ago when he was at a meeting, she packed a few clothes and left. She'd be leaving the street in a few days because if she didn't, he'd find her. He had the contacts. She knew when he did find her, there'd be a beating she'd likely not survive. She knew too much to let her live.

She thought about her current plan: to move to the north of Vancouver Island and set herself up in a town like Port Hardy or even Sandespit or Charlotte, up in the Queen Charlotte islands. The islands had some whacky Indian name now, Haida something. She figured the tourist trade in the summer would be enough to keep her going. Or maybe, she thought as she walked along, she'd go to the Sunshine Coast. Lots of fat wallets around there.

She turned off Pender onto Campbell, walking down toward Prior Street and the big park that lay on the far side. She knew there was a little mom and pop place that sold good coffee and decent sandwiches just a block this side on Adanac Street.

Behind her, a Transit panel van crept slowly along the street, apparently looking for an address. On the side of the van was an abstract logo in a bluish green colour that formed a large circle with intricate curvilinear designs. Gena noticed it as it passed her, mostly because of the design and because it was going so slowly. Ahead of her, the van pulled to the side of the street and sat there idling.

Don't like vans, she thought, maybe this one's on a delivery, maybe not. Guys hide in those things looking for easy targets. Haven't seen any around here. Not like in LA. where guys snatched girls for the trade or for fun with vans like that. Got the buggers with mace once and ran my ass off.

Gena sauntered on, hand in her purse wrapped around her spray, passed the van, turned at the corner, and walked up Adanac. Delivery, I guess. She let out a long breath and crossed the street, admiring the Victorian houses, the many trees along the street, and the front gardens.

She reached the small store, a house front really with an attached awning like a verandah of sorts where people sat at tables protected from the weather. It even had heaters for the cold. Inside, all kinds of groceries sat on shelves along the side walls, and a kitchen rectangle sat in the center of the store where the lady owner served hot food. An open refrigerated section against one wall had salads and sandwiches in it along with blocks of cheese and other stuff.

When Gena approached the store, three old men were sitting at one of the outside tables with coffee, a couple of dogs beside them. A scruffy, grey cat she'd seen every time she'd been there wandered among the tables looking for whatever dropped. The dogs didn't seem to mind the cat, and the cat ignored them and everybody else.

It got quiet when she walked under the porch roof, and she got stared at as she knew she would. She went inside, looked in the refrigerated unit, and bought an egg salad sandwich and a bottle of orange juice.

Back outside, she smiled at the men under the porch roof, unwrapped her sandwich, threw the wrapper in the bin by the door, pinched a bit of egg out and dropped it for the cat. Then she walked toward the little park a half block away.

When she reached the corner, Gena turned with the street and walked along the sidewalk beside a series of two-story town houses all painted dark green and all joined together. As she passed each, she peered into the sunken areas that had been carved out between the house walls and the street's sidewalk so the cellars could be made into apartments. In each area, the owners had put in gardens or had created little patios with deckchairs and plantings. She thought she wouldn't mind finding a place like that when she got where she was going.

She sauntered on, eating her sandwich. On the other side she saw an older woman with two dogs come out of the park. For some reason, a murder of crows followed her, dancing along on the tops of cars as she walked along the street. Gena stared at her curiously and didn't notice the van with the circle emblem idling along behind her.

Between two of the parked cars, Gena finally understood. The woman reached into her large cloth bag and threw handfuls of breadcrumbs along the sidewalk and into the spaces between the cars. When she did that, the crows converged, a fluttering mass of black wings. As she moved on, the crows danced along behind her, hopping from car top to car top. Gena, who'd been standing watching this strange behaviour, chuckled to herself, took a last bite of sandwich, and opened her orange juice. She took a sip and wandered on, heading for Campbell Street and back to Pender.

The van with the circle emblem passed her as she turned the last curve of the U and pulled into the curb on her side half-way up the block in front of an old double store front that had its front windows painted the same yellow as the walls. Gena watched the driver get out, turn towards her, and take the cement stairs to one of the two-storey Victorians down the short street on slightly higher ground than the sidewalk and road. The van sat idling.

Gena hesitated, sipped some orange juice, and watched the van's driver, a young guy in a brownish uniform with a small parcel in his hand. He was on the large veranda pressing the doorbell. She had a healthy distrust of vans and drivers because of her own experiences, but she thought this guy was legit. She sauntered on.

Just as she was passing the van, the guy hurried down the stairs. Gena began to turn and reach for her mace, but the guy was on her too fast, his arm reaching around her. He had something in his hand. Gena registered that much before a searing pain in her middle doubled her over. The last thing she saw before she lost consciousness was the sidewalk coming toward her, the curled leaves reaching up.

The van with the circular logo slid away from the curb and moved slowly down the street to Campbell where it turned toward Hastings, made a left at the light, and moved off towards town.

Back near the Victorian house, in the dead leaves at the edge of the sidewalk lay an orange juice bottle, fluid dripping from its open mouth.

The church in the east end stood on a corner surrounded by old maples. They were plentiful around the area between Heatley and Glen as far down as Strathcona park and as far up as Hastings. It was autumn now, the trees losing leaves, lifting crooked fingers into the rain-filled night. The streetlights in the neighbourhood were as old as the church with incandescent bulbs throwing a weak, amber light in misty arcs across the wet pavement and along the dripping side walls of the church. The feeble glow barely reached the two arched wooden doors in the front façade. The gloomy, indistinct building façade looked more threatening than welcoming.

The deconsecrated church had been abandoned for years. In the past, it had served as a youth center, a Montessori school, a day care, and finally a drop-in needle exchange. When the roof began to leak seriously, the City had closed it down.

Now it sat here, the old pews stacked in a corner near the main doors. The altar and the rose window were still in place, but the open nave had been cut up and walled off until the last tenant left. City engineers had removed all the partitioned spaces when they sent their report to the City, so the church looked more like a church, but old, hollowed out, empty, derelict. And it seemed to be filled now with something that shouldn't be there as if the air itself were pushing down.

The few who managed to get in by forcing the one basement window and spent some time in the nave felt a heaviness in the old place, muted but there, like a disturbance in the high open space. Not many stayed for long, not even the occasional religious ones. But now, with the cold rains, those few who wormed their way in tried hard to last the night even if the place seemed spooky.

Roger and Carol were cold, and wet, and hungry, and more than tired. They had been on the road from early morning, spent most of it on the shoulders, trying hard for rides and getting few.

It was raining hard when they'd gotten out of the back of the stake truck at McGill and Highway 1 after crossing the Second Narrows bridge. The canvas top was old and hadn't done much to keep them dry. Neither one of them had eaten much, only a couple of energy bars. They hadn't been warm for days. The bush was sopping, so no cooking and warmth. Hoping for some relief in the city, they had decided to press on.

Now here they were, walking on Hastings toward downtown. When they tired of the constant traffic, they walked in a block. They ate Salisbury steaks in a greasy spoon on Franklin, a side street near Commercial running parallel to Hastings. At that time of night, the place was almost empty.

While they ate, the counterman lit up and leaned on the far end of the counter's smudged top reading a ratty looking newspaper. Roger nudged Carol and said: "Place looks like a Hopper painting; you know, the one of the all-night diner "Nighthawks"? This one's maybe dirtier, but it's just as lonely."

"That guy with the empty places, you mean? I remember one called "New York Theater". You know, the one of the inside, where the girl usher sort of looks at nothing? Yeah, you're right. An empty loneliness. Sorta like this place." Carol smiled at Roger and sighed. "We gotta find something out of this rain."

They used the dirty washroom for the necessities and to change into whatever they had that was drier than what they were wearing. They left the restaurant, walked back up a block to Hastings, crossed over, and wandered around side streets. The rain seemed lighter but just as cold.

As they walked, they stood in doorways and looked around. Across the street at one of their stops was a church. Roger crossed to look and waved at Carol, then he worked his way around the walls. He found the one basement window, forced it by kicking hard on the wood frame. Carol was a tall, slim blonde, so it was she who went through first. Roger handed their packs in, then struggled through himself.

Once inside, they felt their way out of the furnace room into the old parish hall, up the stairs, and down the corridor that ran alongside the choir loft. The door at the end of that hall led them into the right transept of the church. It was pitch black, so they stopped and listened.

 Carol edged up against Roger who slid his hand back along her side, a protective gesture. They stayed that way for a while. They heard nothing and started to creep noiselessly into the nave. Then they moved slowly toward the locked front doors and a pile of pews on the side. Their eyes adjusted to the dark slowly, but there was little they could see.

A subtle odour hung in the air, and when they reached the pile of pews, they crouched into the corner next to them where they huddled together.

They'd almost decided to find a more comfortable space in another room when they heard a soft noise, a kind of sibilance in the air. They stiffened, listening. Roger shifted Carol behind him and crouched low, creeping forward slowly into what was once the center aisle. There was virtually no light, just a feeble glow from the great rose window at the back of the church above the altar.

Roger felt Carol touch his back, hold his jacket. They barely breathed. They heard another soft hissing sound, and Carol's hand tightened as they both sensed something stirring in the oppressive darkness. Then it stopped.

The strange odour didn't stop. It got stronger. It triggered something in Roger and raised the hackles on the back of his neck. He could feel Carol clinging to his sleeve. He pushed her back and told her to wait in the corner. She was too frightened to do anything but obey. Roger, alone now, began slowly to crawl up what would have been the center aisle.

"That damned slaughterhouse," he whispered to himself. He inhaled and remembered that hellish summer between his third and fourth year at university. He smelled blood. The coppery, unforgettable effluvium he'd carried with him everywhere. He'd never gotten used to it like the others had. He'd carried it home every damned day. He remembered the showers, the scrubbing until his skin was raw, how he avoided his friends and even his family. The smell clung to him. He had never got free of it. That odd memory consumed him so completely that he remained on all fours in the center of the nave.

Roger had no idea how long he stayed that way, but he came back slowly to the darkness around him, a strange pressure in the air. He moved up the nave on his hands and knees until he rammed his fingers into the bottom step that led to the choir loft.

The pain was enough to clear his head. He cursed under his breath. Then, startled, he heard something. He turned to find a terrified Carol right behind him. He reached out and touched her face. He felt the steps again and whispered for her to stay put. He climbed slowly.

The odour was much stronger up here. He could sense the raised floor of the choir stalls on either side as he moved up the center isle to the base of the altar. Here, the air was saturated, heavy with that coppery stench.

Roger felt in front of him and reached the bottom of the altar. He ran his hand up the decorative column at its side, felt it slide in the viscous fluid that dribbled down.

His heart thudded as he slowly stood up. The light that passed through the grimy rose window did little more that lighten the darkness. But it was enough.

On the top surface of the altar, bathed in that soft, hazy half-light from the dirty rose window above him, lay a girl. She was naked, her eyes staring emptily at him. Her pale face rose out of a pool of blood. Roger's eyes followed down her body, saw the horror of her midsection, the raw gaping slash, the loops of entrails arranged like a frame around her. Then he saw the stab marks all down her sides, the slices the knife had made on her legs. Her whole body was raw with slashes, only her face was untouched.

Roger stood in front of the girl, her blood still dripping down the altar. She seemed peaceful, at least her face did; there were no signs of damage there. It was as if she had just lain there dreaming while the atrocities were visited upon her.

Roger watched her eyes film over.

That broke the spell and he turned and pushed back from the altar. He heard Carol calling him softly. He tried to speak out to reassure her, but he had no voice.

He worked his way down to the nave and with Carol grabbing his coat, walked back to the stack of pews. There was no need to be quiet now. Whoever it was had gone. All that was left was the strange heaviness and the acrid, coppery smell of blood.

Roger wiped his hands on the sides of stacked pews, then reached into his pack for one of the cloths he carried for cleaning up. As he cleaned his hands further, he talked softly to Carol, his voice reassuring and calm. He had to get her out of here, and he had to call the police. He feared that call would drop them both into a quagmire of suspicion, questioning, and probably incarceration. Still, he knew that was what he had to do.

His greatest worry was Carol. She didn't handle stress well and was subject to panic attacks. And this mess, he thought, would definitely put her through a few of those. Roger put his arms around her, held her close, told her what was on the altar, and explained what he had to do. Carol wrapped her arms around him and began to sob.

26.

The rain was still coming down when they left the church by the same basement window. It got heavier as they searched for a telephone a few blocks away from the church. They could see lights and hear traffic nearby and went in that direction. Cell phones were a luxury they couldn't afford.

They found a small convenience store with cluttered, dirty windows on Hastings at the corner of Heatley. Roger's enquiry for a phone was met with a shaking head and a finger pointing at the door. They left.

Farther down the street past a construction site squeezed in between a place selling commercial kitchen appliances and another specializing in restaurant supplies, Roger spotted a lit front. He headed that way, Carol following meekly behind. It was a bath house, one of those places that catered to men and maybe hookers if they had private rooms. He left Carol outside and went in.

He asked the attendant, a young Chinese guy behind a counter piled high with rolled white towels, if he could use the phone. Roger felt he could trust this guy with more information, so he told him about the church and the body. No details, just the basics.

"You're jokin', right? A body? Where? Holy shit!" He handed Roger his cell.

Roger told the 911 operator about the body, told her where it was and where he was, and was told to wait at the store. Roger handed the phone back to the excited young guy and explained that he had to wait.

"Sure, man, sure. A body? You're not shittin' me? The cops are comin' here? Hope nobody comes up from downstairs. That'll scare the crap outa them, I mean cops and all. They'll think it's a raid like we used to have sometimes, you know? Haven't had one of those in years, but our guys are mostly old, so they'll freak, you know? You want a coke or somethin'?"

"My girl's outside, can I bring her in? Maybe get her something to drink?"

"Sure, man, sure. There's no room to sit or anything, you know, but sure bring her in. I got some cans back here. Got a chair in here, so she can come back here and sit 'til the cops get here."

Before Carol had opened her coke and settled in her chair, they heard sirens. Two cars slammed into the curb, blue and red flicking around the inside of the small lobby.

Two constables came in, one slim and young, the other more beefy and older. By the stripes, Roger knew the older one was a sergeant. He saw no sign of anything but suspicion in those eyes. He knew these guys were patrol and hoped the Ds would come soon.

The young one was being trained, Roger saw, and he would mostly watch. Roger'd been interrogated by an older guy like this one once before, and it hadn't been pleasant. He didn't expect the sergeant to be any different.

In Roger's experience, these older ones were street smart, acted like they'd heard it all before, didn't believe anybody, and didn't give a shit. He knew he wouldn't get roughed up, especially not with a trainee on board, but he'd have a hell of a time convincing this guy that he'd just found the girl. There was blood under his fingernails, blood in the fine lines of his hands.

"You the fella found the girl?" the older one asked, looking straight at Roger.

"Yeah, my girl and me. We were in the church tryin' to get dry for the night, ya know, and we heard something, smelled something. I left her at the back and I felt my way up to the big window and the altar. Couldn't see a thing. I was tryin' to see with my hands, you know, no light in there except through the grime on that window, and one hand slid up the carved altar spindle, you know, at the side, and it slid through blood. You could smell it too. When I got to my feet, she was on the altar, blood everywhere. She'd been sliced up pretty bad. She's dead, couldn't be anything else lookin' like that."

"Got any ID?" The older one held out his hand, glanced back at the girl behind the counter, nodded to the rookie, and waited.

Roger dug in his pocket and hauled out his wallet, extracting his social security card and his license. As he handed them to the sergeant, he watched the rookie go behind the counter and begin questioning Carol.

"Sit over there and don't move." The sergeant pointed to the one foldup chair the Chinese attendant had brought out, waited until Roger complied, and scanned the room as he gave instructions to the rookie. Then he left for the first cruiser.

Roger saw the sergeant talk to the two constables in front of the building and point to Hastings Steam behind him. Then he watched the sergeant walk back to the second cruiser, get in, and run the license. He watched one of the uniforms take the front door of the steam bath, the other the only open establishment on the block, the convenience store on the corner.

While the rookie constable waited with Roger and Carol, he glanced out the front window often. Roger understood why. He was waiting for the homicide detectives to arrive.

Moments later, a black SUV double parked by the first cruiser, grill lights flashing, and four suits got out. Roger watched the door as they came in.

Alan went straight for him, introduced himself and Spence, and asked for the story. Spence nodded to the boy and stood with Alan. Larry and Jake went back out to talk to the sergeant still in the second cruiser.

"Yeah, as I told the sergeant here and the station when I phoned in, that big church at Heatley and Pender. The front doors are chained, and we needed to get dry. There's a basement window on the side. The girl's on the altar at the back. There was something, someone or something, freaked us out. That's why I was up there, at that end."

"We know about the church, we got cruisers there now," Alan said. Give us the rest of your story. Details on how and where you got in, all about that window and where you were in the basement. Then go through the rest and don't leave anything out. Take your time but be as precise as you can."

Roger went through how they got in, where that window was, their climb up the stairs and down the side aisle, how they entered the transept, and what they felt.

Alan stopped him there, took him back over the sensation they'd experienced, then let him tell it all.

When he'd finished, Alan turned to Spence, raised an eyebrow, got a headshake. He told Roger, "We're going to take you two over to the church now. We've got a lot of people coming and we need you to walk us through everything before the place gets busy. You up for that?"

Roger nodded and pointed to Carol behind the counter. "I've got my girl here. She's gotta come with us. She didn't see the altar stuff, the dead girl I mean, but she was in that church too.

Carol joined the three of them. Larry had come back in and had stood just behind Alan and Spence, listening to the story. He looked at the two kids.

"Get in the black SUV you two. We'll drive you over." Larry turned and walked out with Roger and Carol. Alan and Spence got them settled in the back and Spence stayed with them. Alan joined Larry in the front. Jake drove.

The church's bulk loomed over the forensics trucks nosed in toward the steps on Pender. Next to the trucks, cruisers sat with their light bars flashing, throwing red and blue steaks crawling over the houses on Heatley and Pender. Just as they pulled up in the SUV, high intensity lights went on inside the church, adding to the light show.

"Let's get those cruisers shut down first, not that it matters much now. They always do that, and half the street's here before we are." Larry cursed, got out of the SUV after Alan, and talked to a constable standing near the cruisers. Before he got back, the light bars were off.

After signing in with the uniform controlling the scene, all four detectives followed the kids around the side of the church, saw the window where they'd gotten in, and marched them back to the great front doors that now stood partially open. The chains had been cut by the forensics crew.

Alan looked at Roger, cocked a finger, and pointed to the front doors.

"We'll go in here, take the side aisle on the right. That'll take us to where you came into the transept and won't disturb the techs. You take us back from there and walk us through what you did. Don't leave anything out. When we get to the back of the nave where the pews are, where you rested, you wait there."

Jake and Larry stayed behind to talk to a forensics tech to get what they could so far and to see if they could view the body. The tech was a tall redhead and he looked a bit frazzled, sounded it too. "You can't get anywhere near the altar, not yet anyway. You gotta wait for the boss if you wanna see anything up there. We're still processing, so the site's locked. And there's nothing to tell you yet either, so you'll have to wait on that as well. I gotta go." He moved off up the side of the church and into the left transept.

After Alan and Spence settled the kids in the corner, they joined Jake and Larry and waited for the chief of forensics. As he came down the nave, Jake recognized him. "Harvey, glad you're on this one. Let me introduce you. This is Alan Kim, he's one of the leads on this one. And this is Spence Riley, she's the other lead. They're both mounteds. Spence, Alan, Harvey Couch, head of the forensics crew. How about it, Harvey? We get to see the body anytime soon?"

Harvey shook his head. "I knew you'd wanna get up there as soon as, but it'll be a while yet. The boys are still processing the body and the coroner has to pronounce, then you're good to go. Might be able to sneak you in in between if he's late getting here, but not all of you."

Harvey raised his hand in a salute of sorts. "Good to know we got someone from your side of the fence on this one. No offence, I hope."

Spence grinned. "None taken, this time at least. You know where the hell the coroner is?"

"Been called, should be here. Give me a minute. Harvey left for the altar and was back in a couple of minutes. Pretty close to his estimate. "Good to go. Be careful though, don't even breathe up there. Two at a time." Harvey nodded at Alan and Spence. "Wait another mo, I gotta make a quick call."

ENDGAME

Harvey took out a cell from his overalls and hit a couple of buttons. He smiled apologetically and walked out the doors. They could hear him talking to somebody. Then he returned and said, "Okay, coroner's gonna be late as usual. Go for it." He pointed to the altar end of things. "Follow the red markers up the left side aisle. That'll keep you clear. Take a look, but follow what the tech says, and don't get too close! I guess you leads'll wanna go first. Jake and Larry? You two go up when they get back. Me, I gotta get back to the van. Don't take too long or the coroner'll spot you and blow a fuse!"

Alan walked over to Roger and Carol to remind them to stay until he'd finished at the altar. "Don't leave, don't get in the way, and don't talk to anyone. When I get through, I'll find you a place for the night."

Alan and Spence followed the markers, Spence leading. They watched themselves on the steps to the choir loft and stopped about three feet away from the body at the last marker. Two light stands set either side about ten feet away lit the scene.

"Jesus, look at that mess. She's ripped to bits, multiple cuts all over except the face, that's perfect. No shoulder signs I can see in that blue-green stuff our guys use, so much blood though hard to tell. Look."

Spence stepped back carefully, and Alan edged by.

"I'm not sure either, the marks, maybe, on the shoulder. But this is savage, not like our guys unless they've lost control. Even then, I wouldn't expect this level of violence. But no clothes, entrails arranged around the body. Face untouched. Could be them. Wasn't there something the privates had in a church? We used that animal thing as a precursor if I remember. Didn't the profiler suggest that was a link? Maybe they're decompensating, regressing."

"We need to check the photos and sketches. Who does them here, do we know? We should be able to see if there are marks. They'd let him closer than we can get. We also better check with Harry and Sabina, given the altar thing, maybe get them over here somehow without anybody getting excited. What d'ya think?"

Spence craned around Alan's shoulder. "No arterial spurts, no spatter, just lots of blood. Done on site or they brought her here still breathin' then finished her off. That's just like the others even if the slashing isn't."

We'll check with Harvey, see who did the photos. I'm done. Let's get back so Jake and Larry get a look, then we'll put our heads together."

"Jesus, we gotta stop these guys. Bodies pile up around the city and we're all gonna be in deep doodoo. The brass'll go apeshit when this gets out." Spence turned carefully and started back.

"The sooner Jake and Larry see this, the sooner we can decide how to react. Check with Harvey about the photos, will you? I gotta talk to Roger again." Alan followed Spence watching where he put his feet. Two more light batteries came on. The place was lit like a movie set.

Alan and Spence worked their way back to the church doors. Spence went to see Harvey, and Alan, after sending Jake and Larry on their way, walked over to the pile of pews and knelt beside Roger.

"Okay, how're you two holding up?"

"We're good, I think, just tired is all. It's pretty late now." Alan smiled at Carol then turned again to Roger.

"Let's go over your movements from here up the nave to the altar. Everything you can remember. Take your time, but don't leave out anything, noises, feelings, that smell you mentioned. Give me everything, okay?"

And Roger did. It took him a good ten minutes. "Okay. I've taped what you've said on this little guy." Alan drew a small digital recorder out of his pocket. "It's tiny, but ultra-sensitive for statements and you're going to have to make a formal statement, probably tomorrow. But for the rest of the night, the little that's left, let's get you somewhere dry where you can change, get some warm food, and rest."

Alan stood. He motioned to one of the constables near the door and said, "Can you find these two a place to stay for the night and get them some food? Maybe somewhere near the station? We need them close, but they need some comfort."

"I'll talk to the desk, sir. We'll find them something. Nothing else for me to do here now. If they're ready, I'll get them settled."

Alan watched as the constable led the pair out to a cruiser. They looked pathetic, he thought, dragging along with one knapsack each. Food and rest, that'll do them good. Tomorrow, we'll see about getting them on their way. He turned once again toward the altar and watched the crew. Spence joined him and told him that the photographer was back in the forensics van and would talk to them anytime.

Larry and Jake were just coming back down the aisle. Both looked a little green.

"That's one hell of a mess. My god, is that how your guy did the girls on the island? She's been eviscerated, bits of intestine lying around, but the face, that's perfect. I've seen violence, but not like this frenzied mess. And the face. Jesus." Larry shook his head. "I'm gonna take a breather." He walked out the front doors and stood on the steps, his fists jammed into his jacket pockets, pulling the fabric down so much the back panels slid down past his shirt collar and stretched taut over his shoulders.

Jake had been looking at the floor, but now he looked up at Alan and Spence. "That's brutal, up there. Larry's right, the face gets to you. I can't remember anything around here as vicious as this one." He glanced out the doors at Larry's back. "It really threw him, and it takes a lot to do that. He'll be alright in a few minutes. We should get back and decide how to handle this. I hate playing catch-up."

"One thing we know from the island murders, these guys always come back to see if we've messed up their scene, so they can fix what they see as disturbed. Those pricks could be out there in the crowd watchin' this circus, gloating over how stupid we are. I hate these guys." Spence turned abruptly and walked outside stopping next to Larry.

"That's the coroner's ride, he always drives that thing. Let's get out of here." Jake walked out to join Spence and Larry. Alan watched a tall man get out of the massive black SUV and hurry up the steps to the church. He nodded to the detectives who ignored him and hurried inside.

When Alan joined the others, no one said a thing. They left the church, walked down the steps past the growing crowd, and piled into their unmarked for the ride to the station. Jake drove.

No one spoke till they were on Hastings heading toward

Main.

"When that place dies down and the damn crowd's gone, we'll need to find some way to cover it. They'll come back, they always do, and we've never seen them, not at the church when they were doin' animals, nor at the sites in the bush. And we looked, hard. Maybe we left too soon, but when we checked later, they'd been back. So they'll be back here too, and we need to find a way to set up surveillance they can't spot."

Spence stopped, looked at the others, shook her head, muttered something to herself, crossed her arms under her breasts, and sat. Impatience steamed out of her. Alan could almost see it. He smiled to himself. She was something. She was beautiful when she got like this. He could feel the tension in her. He knew she'd explode if anyone talked. He'd learned that much over the two years they'd been partnered.

Jake drove the unmarked into the underground garage off Cordova, and the four of them took the stairs to the homicide office. The place was almost empty, just two detectives in a couple of the cubicles, sitting in front of computers, pecking away. The little space the four of them had on the far side of the room overflowed with paper. It covered all four desks with more stuck haphazardly to the walls. But there was an order of sorts, and all four knew it.

Jake took a long look before turning to the others. "Let's take one of the conference rooms. Anybody need anything out of here?"

"I need the murder book," Alan said. "I'll meet you over there."

The conference room Jake chose was next to the one the task force used. It was smaller but had comfortable padded chairs and a small round table they could all sit at. A coffee machine that made individual cups from pods sat on top of a small fridge.

"This one's really for Brian's meetings. Let's grab a cup and get started. It's damn near morning, and we need to plan what we're gonna do."

"What we're gonna do is saturate that place with surveillance the creeps can't spot. We need to be invisible. They're good." Spence carried her cup over to the table and sat. "We haven't talked to the photographer yet, and he's expecting us, but it can wait until we get the forensics tomorrow. He probably knows we got a lot to do and just forgot."

"We can talk to the neighbours that back onto the church lot, see if we can get permission to use their back rooms." Larry slurped coffee. "For the rest, we can take cars from the impound, ones seized in raids. Staffing's gonna be a problem because of budget."

"Brian's given us the okay on that. I called him from the church. It's gonna be twenty-four seven for us. Any suggestions?" Jake looked around the table at the team. "We're too tired for this now, so we need fresh bodies. We gotta get some sleep or we'll be useless. But in a few hours, I think we should be the ones out there watching."

"When's shift change? Maybe we can syphon off some of the guys for surveillance?" Alan glanced at Jake then Larry.

"You're the boss, Alan, you get whatever you want. You gotta talk to the day supervisor, get him on side. I can help by being with you when you do. He knows Larry and me well enough, so he'll trust us on this one."

Jake shoved a list over the table to Alan. "The guys on the list are cruiser guys. Stan won't spare many, but if we get four for the cars even for a few hours and some of our guys for the back rooms of the houses, we can get everything started. Stan's always early, so he might be in now. Let's go."

"I'm draggin' my ass here, so me and Spence are gonna sack out in the dorm for a few hours. You should too. No sense tryin' to get home. We gotta be back here early so Stan can get his guys back for their shifts an' we can take over. We got his and hers up there and showers, so we'll be good." Larry walked off.

The dorm was a pair of rooms on the third floor, each with showers and cots separated by flats. Six cots per room. The rooms were there for times like this when shifts of officers were needed and the department was short staffed. Which was almost always.

Jake and Alan gathered up the paper, threw out the garbage, and Alan slipped the murder book under his arm.

"Let's see Stan, get that part set up, then join them upstairs for a couple. We'll need night guys too, so we'll leave Brian a note asking for six of our crew to help out. If there's enough bitching at the top, we'll get everything we need. Lead the way, Jake."

Stan was sitting in his tiny room sipping coffee. Jake introduced Alan as lead in the task force and stood back.

Stan nodded at Alan who started right in, "We've gotta cover the church murder that happened tonight. We need to watch the scene twenty-four seven for a day or two and we need to start now. Can you spare four men for say five hours to sit surveillance? We'll supply the cars and lay out positions. We need to cover the streets, but we need to be invisible. This is no notice, I know, but everything hit the fan at once as usual."

"Gimme ten, where you gonna be? Four right? Five hours only. I get 'em back then?"

"We'll be in the homicide office. Five hours only, and you get 'em back. We appreciate anything you can do."

"Wait for the call. I'll get 'em, just have to rearrange some things."

Jake and Alan backed out of the tiny space and went straight to the office. Jake sagged in his chair.

"Jesus, I'm beat. Stan'll come through. If we get five hours, we'll be good to go. Why don't you go up. I'll wait for the call. No sense both of us doggin' this."

Alan nodded. He didn't need to be told twice.

27.

It was after seven and the SHH Investigations office was still open. Isabella had long gone, but Harry had reports to finish, and Sabina was busy with her Vancouver hacker, Jim, and the computers at Horseshoe Bay. Something was going on, Harry knew, but he kept his nose out of the cloud stuff. Horseshoe Bay belonged to Mamma Jing, the matriarch of Chinatown, a woman who had her own army and meted out her own justice whenever she felt the authorities either couldn't or wouldn't.

Over the last year, Sabina's pile of electronic material had grown, and her U-shaped office was jammed with monitors, towers, and a plethora of cables and black boxes. Stuff just replicated in there, Harry thought, and smiled at the idea.

He swiveled toward the window in his office chair and started thinking again about the fellow on the hill. There was just something about the way he moved, like he had a purpose, was determined. Harry sighed, frustrated.

He turned back toward his desk. Replicated. He smiled. I'm gonna slip it in over dinner, see if she notices. He looked down at the paper on his desk and the screen on his computer, which for him was just a kind of typewriter. Harry sighed again. I'll just do a couple more pages, pile it all on Izzy's desk, and head for dinner. Get a bottle of that lovely Australian Shiraz the Modern has. He glanced up at the ceiling: The English say anyroad, I read that in a mystery by an English guy named Robinson. Maybe that's the original and we just switched it around. He continued typing and away.

He finished the reports, then levered himself out of his chair, leaned over his desk, and watched Sabina stare at a screen. She twirled a bit of hair around a finger, then attacked her keyboard. Harry sighed happily and muttered, "Life's good. A bit unconventional, sure, but good. She's great with clients, demure and all that, but at home and around town she's something else. Turns a lot of heads, and she knows it. She's perfect, even if she does kinda straddle the line."

Harry called, "Hey Sweets! Gonna be long? I'm expiring here. Donuts're gone, and Izzy's unavailable for more. We could hit the Modern and enjoy some good stuff."

"Relax, H, almost there. This is Mamma Jing through the Horseshoe Bay computers, so I gotta be thorough. There's also this email from Alan and Spence. They've got a body, a new one." Sabina did some rapid keyboard work and shut down. All the monitors went black at the same time.

Sabina stood and stretched. She wandered over to Harry's desk and said, "Atta boy, H, you got that lot done. Izzy'll be happy. Let's blow the place."

The Modern Cafe sat on one side of the central square that kind of anchored the downtown, its red neon sign reflected on the paving stones that joined the three streets feeding the square. Most of the shops were down Commercial a bit, the square being taken up with real-estate offices, restaurants, and boutiques. The SHH Investigations office where they were, however, was on the second floor of an old firehall that raised its crenellated red-brick bulk part way up the hill on Victoria Crescent. Terminal, the name of the highway that ran through the center of the city, tended to cut off the strip of shops on the crescent from the rest of downtown.

Harry and Sabina walked down the hill to Terminal, crossed at the light, and wandered up Commercial. Harry dawdled as he usually did, looking in store windows and wondering again, how some of them survived, given the stuff they sold. Sabina was strangely quiet.

Harry glanced at her, noticed her preoccupation. "What's up, Sweets, you managed Mamma Jing's query and that should make you at least relieved if not happy, so what's got you twitchy?"

"The matriarch of Chinatown, she'd twitch anybody. She's not satisfied. We're getting nowhere on Mary Chang's case, H. We don't even know where the hell her clothes are let alone where that pair of psychopaths is."

They entered the restaurant and took a booth by the back wall. Dina, the beautiful Native girl from their recent big case involving the two psycho brothers, was on tonight. She'd been entombed in their root cellar and escaped barefoot through the bush before swimming down a river. Kylie Wingate and Mary Chan hadn't been so lucky.

Dina smiled at them. Harry smiled back and as always looked where he shouldn't. Dina played to that, so flirting with her was fun, even if Sabina kicked him under the table. They both liked the girl.

"I'll have whatever she's having," Harry said, nodding at Sabina but smiling at Dina, "and a bottle of that Shiraz you keep hidden for me. At least I think you do, because nobody else seems to get any."

Their orders in and the wine served, Sabina and Harry sipped and relaxed.

"Okay H, here's the thing. This email from Alan and Spence in Van. They've got a body, it's in town this time, but cut to bits, not like the Hammil one. It's on a church altar. That ring a bell for you? Remember father whats-his-name? Grimson, something like that? Remember that church way out in Cedar somewhere? Bunch of animals carved up and left on the altar? Never did find who did it and we looked. Sent one of Rory's operatives out there for four days and got nothin'. After that human bodies started turning up butchered the same way. The profiler was sure they were related, the animal carcasses and the bodies. Now we got it again."

They took a sip of wine.

"I'm into the servers at police headquarters in Vancouver, so that's done. And I've got Spence and Alan and the two Vancouver dicks on a closed loop that's encrypted, so we can talk to the four of them without anyone else knowing. That's where the latest came from, their loop, and we need to talk about that."

Sabina leaned in towards Harry and continued, "Alan and Spence want to get together with us about that new one. But they need to be discreet, of course. So maybe we shift over there for a while, use the Gastown apartment. Bike's still there, so we got wheels."

Once the food arrived, they concentrated on eating until they were on coffee and dessert. Tonight, it was a sticky cake that Harry loved. The Australian cook who worked the grill most days made them when he had time. Dina always put most of the cake aside for Harry when she could, and he always bought as much as she could save. It never lasted the night.

"Well, if we go to Vancouver and hook up with the cops, we've also gotta set up with Will and maybe Sally to help Izzy keep things rolling. Not that she'll want any help. Adding Will and Sally's doable, and they won't replicate efforts, not with Izzy around."

Sabina looked at Harry. "Replicate? You been into that dictionary again?"

"The dictionary's there just to hide the scotch as you well know. I know a lot of stuff, so words come easily."

"Well that one didn't. You meant duplicate. What we need is to set up in Gastown at my place, and to do that I'll have to either carry a lot of gear over or buy some spares. I'll take my laptop, so I've got the links, but I'll need a day and a trip to the Apple store."

Harry groaned. "You know we don't make a thing on this one, don't you? It's gratis unless Mary's sister, Olivia, coughs up again. And why should she? We pretty much blew grabbing Mary's killers."

"As far as Gastown's concerned, I'm gonna need what I'm gonna need. We gotta be equipped over there. It's gonna be our second office anyway once we extend ourselves. You'll just have to suck it up, H." Harry sat quietly for a moment, sipped his coffee, then sighed.

"There's some scotch we need to use up at home since we're gonna be away, so let's finish our coffee."

"Atta boy, H. I'll even make out with ya if I get some new gear out of it."

"Then we'd better hurry." Harry paid the bill and they walked to Front Street and the seawall. The night was quiet on the wall, the water dark and heaving gently. Rigging in the marina pinged softly as they passed.

Lights from the houses on Protection Island seemed to follow them, wriggling in fractured streaks across the harbour. Red and green channel markers blinked on and off in a kind of syncopated harmony.

They took their time and watched the harbour defined by the two islands, Protection and Newcastle, the first bearing houses the latter a provincial park.

At the largest of the three marinas, Harry and Sabina turned uphill a short block to Stewart and their home. Their place lay above Kiyo's hair salon in a two-storey red brick building with the three arched windows of Harry's living room running along the upper façade. Harry unlocked a stout, banded oak door just past the salon's double front window and followed Sabina up the staircase. He always did that, and she knew why.

They went to the kitchen overlooking the harbour, the floors of waxed oak hardwood mellow in the light from the dimmable pot lights Harry had installed the previous summer. He always left them at half-mast. A small rectangular table covered in a light taupe cloth rested against the wall opposite the counter with enough space for the two of them to get comfortable.

Sabina leaned against the rear wall by the kitchen window looking out at the end of Newcastle Island and dark waters of the harbour. A small gaggle of Canada geese floated near the marina's last dock, lit by the feeble glow of the safety lights strung along its length. She turned when she heard Harry enter.

He carried two shot glasses and a half-full bottle of Glenlivet, a reasonable single malt. He poured each of them a double, raised his glass in a salute to her, and took a sip. Sabina joined him at the table.

"We've been thinking about setting up over there for a while, that's why you kept your place in Gastown, so I guess this is as good a time as any. We haven't got much going for us on the case, though. We've got the two unsolveds here, Mary and Kylie, and now the new one up in Hammil. If I heard you correctly, we just got another one in Van. We'll need to see the gang of four before we get much further."

"Yeah, H, that's already in the works. They'll be expecting us sometime tomorrow. Alan and Spence are leads on this one, and they have the two local dicks, Larry and Jake. I'm linked to all four in that closed circuit I told you about. And now there's a task force. Brass's getting jittery what with memories of that pig guy, Pickton, and all the media attention they're starting to get with this latest. The Hammil thing's still a bit of a secret, but the last one's already leaked."

"You know we can't be seen around those guys. Remember what happened here when we lost those two nutcases? Alan and Spence got seriously yelled at, we got blackened by the media and lost our status with the cops, and all just because we got caught working together. Now, there'll be serious scrutiny."

"Everybody's aware of that, H, but we're in. We just need to stay invisible, that's all. I've got my encrypted linkup, and we'll have our office set up in the apartment. We'll be close enough physically, just a few blocks down the street from the station, so the guys can drop over for meetings."

"Best we stock it with a few bottles of this stuff. We're gonna need it. I'll pour us another. Gimme your glass."

By midnight, the bottle was low, and the two of them were exhausted and mellow. Little had been decided, except that they were going tomorrow. Harry killed the lights and with his arm around Sabina, they managed the bedroom with most of their clothes still on.

Harry stood by the kitchen window while the coffee perked. The morning was overcast with a fuzzy mist over the harbour. The islands looked more like huge phantom sailing ships what with indistinct grey. He had coffee and toast on the table when Sabina wandered in with a towel wrapped around her head.

"Good on ya, H. I need this. Last night was a little kinky, even for you." Sabina lowered herself into a chair and sipped contentedly.

"It was the scotch and the Vancouver mess that did it. Of course, you helped a good deal."

"Eat your toast, we gotta get going soon." Sabina yawned. "Bring the pot over will you? Aren't you the least bit hung over? How can you look like that this early?"

"You young'uns never get the hang of single malts. Although I must say you tried hard last night. Here, have another cup."

An hour later, they were on Stewart in the car heading for the office. The lot across from the old firehall was almost empty, the white Mercedes vans that stood in a couple of the rows every night and most days were gone. Harry had two reserved spots farther in, but he left the car as close to the office as possible.

He glanced at Sabina. "Don't know what you're gonna bring, so closer is better. Hope Izzy's not in a mood. Let's get in there, beard the dragon in her den. What's that mean anyway, bearding dragons? I mean, I use it because it's there. You young computer hacks probably have stuff like that all figured out what with those games you play."

"You mean the games you won't try but always gripe about? Yeah, they do have lots of dragons and dens, but bearding them anywhere is beyond even my skills. Maybe it's somethin' old in a book. You should be good at that, you look at them enough, especially the one in the scotch drawer. One thing, though, Izzy's not gonna be happy we're this late getting in."

"Probably got stale donuts. She gets them early just to frustrate me. Let's go, Sweets. We got lots to get done."

Izzy wasn't at her desk. Harry peered around the door into the office, spotted her at the coffee machine in the alcove, grinned at her as she turned and said, "Izzy, darlin' you make that just for us? You got donuts?"

"Well, well, the two of you finally arrive. Forget your string and get lost again? Tricky tellin' clients like the two you had this mornin' that you're a touch late because you're wandering around in a field. They won't be back. I set up the contracts but they won't be back. I sent them to Will who works. Grab a cup and check the copies on your desk, for all the good it'll do."

Isabella'd been hired just after the new office opened and ran the place like a well-oiled machine. She was good with clients and caustic with the two partners. But she loved them both, considered them her wards. She also knew they were damn good, especially the girl, Sabina. Harry'd told her about finding her on the stroll in Vancouver's East End during the last case. Isabella knew Sabina was a programmer of some note, had made a lot of money, loved the action of the business, and had good connections.

"While Izzy's out front and occupied, let's grab the donuts and a coffee and get organized. She'll be impressed that we're prepared and off on a case in the big city."

"There isn't much on this end that needs doing. Let's list her instructions vis a vis Will and Sally and leave it at that. She'll cope, probably better than we will. Where's the ferry schedule?"

When they'd finished the list, and Sabina'd got what she needed, they were ready for the 12:30 ferry. They talked with Isabella, headed down the stairs, grabbed the car, and drove down Stewart to the ferry docks.

28.

They were both quiet on the ferry, thinking about the mess they were jumping into in Vancouver. They knew they had to be careful with the case what with the media and the politics. It wouldn't do to be found out. They were still on the books for Mary Chang, though, and could justify any action if they had to, could even bill for it. Sabina flipped open her laptop and began typing. Without looking up, she asked, "We'll be in when?"

"We need an hour and a half and a bit to get across the Salish, maybe twenty minutes to get off the vessel, so we should hit downtown Vancouver somewhere around three, three-thirty if the Lions Gate doesn't jam."

"The Lions Gate always jams. Let's say quarter to four to hit the apartment and prepare a bit. Shift change over there is at four and then there's the task force meeting, so we'll meet them say at five-thirty in the alley behind my place." Sabina typed in the instructions and shut down. "If that doesn't suit, I'll hear back before we dock. Now, what's our plan?"

The sailing was fully booked, the passenger deck crowded, so they'd grabbed one of the small round tables in a corner near the snack bar.

"H, we need to think this through a bit. I gotta have a day to set up what I'll need for one thing, and we got diddly on what's happening with the homicide dicks. So, big boy, you're the boss, as you often say, and bosses make up plans all the time. What's yours?" Sabina smiled sweetly, twirled a bit of hair around a finger.

Harry shrugged. "We've got two bodies, albeit in different parts of the province and in vastly different shape, a whole bunch of people involved, mostly cops of one sort or another, and a task force growing like a cancer. Then there's the two of us, and some coroners pitchin' in with suggestions. Shouldn't be hard to make a plan out of that. Oh, and there's Mamma Jing and the boys. She probably knows more than the lot of us. Let's tell the four homicide dicks we have no idea how to proceed and could use their input if any. How's that?"

"Aren't you the vaunted private dick everybody raves about? That's it?"

"Partners share. Let's put our heads together. So, Sweets, what do you think?"

"If they're in the city, and that's a given, they're gonna kill more girls. They're also losing their cool and escalating if the condition of the last vic in the church is any indication. That'll help us and hurt them. So the plan should have something to do with all that."

"Agreed, Sweets. If they're beginning to lose control like Roberta, the profiler, predicted, they'll start making mistakes. We know they revisit the kill sites, so if they still do that, we should be able to find some way to monitor them without spilling the beans. We know they're more capable in the bush than we are. But in the city, we're probably better."

"We should be, but we're still playing catch up. We'll have to do better than that, and the only way that's gonna happen is if we catch them on a return to a site. Let's talk to Alan and Spence, see if that's being considered here. Maybe we can help with that."

The ferry blasted one short blast that filled the cabin as it approached the Horseshoe Bay dock. Everybody started moving for the stairs. In about ten minutes they'd be ready to disembark. Sabina closed her laptop. Harry turned to watch a gaggle of girls rush by, then the two of them hit the stairs to the car deck, waited patiently for the ferry to complete the docking, drove up the hill in the scrim of cars and trucks, and headed for Taylor Way.

The Lions Gate was indeed jammed with a waiting time of about twenty minutes. Cars from two different two-lane roads merged at the bridge entrance, feeding onto it one at a time. Usually, that went smoothly, but sometimes everything would snarl. Sabina sat muttering to herself behind a black Porsche that kept revving its engine. Fortunately, the driver restrained himself, and traffic moved slowly forward.

Once across the bridge, Sabina drove through the long blur of Stanley Park's green trees. She hit Georgia at about a quarter to four, close to what she expected. The apartment in Gastown was only minutes away.

Sabina parked the car in the narrow side alley close to the shed that held her bike. Then they walked around to the building's front. It was one of the originals, and there were only a few of those left. The front façade was three storeys high with ornate cornices and articulated panels of what looked like terracotta tile adorning the brickwork. The ground floor front held two shop windows with a heavy, glass-paneled oak door between them. Sabina hauled out a key, unlocked the door, and they walked up to the third-floor landing. There was another deadbolted heavy oak door here, solid oak, no glass. Sabina fished out another key and unlocked her door.

Harry remembered the room they entered, but he stopped anyway. It was impressive. On the floor lay a large silk Persian carpet in intricate patterns of subtle blues and reds, the silk glowing with the soft light thrown into the room by the long narrow front windows. The room was sparsely furnished, the wood pieces all a rich mahogany, the upholstery in neutral shades. The few lamps, Harry knew, would create an intimate, mellow ambience when night fell.

Sabina marched into the bedroom and after a few moments, Harry followed. The large room housed a king size bed with smaller Persian carpets strewn around. The dresser was massive and mahogany and served as the only storage space. Beside it stood the door to the bathroom. Sabina dumped the laptop and their bags on the floor near the dresser and flopped on the bed.

"We got maybe an hour and twenty, H. Wanna cuddle?"

"We start stuff like that, an hour and twenty'll just frustrate both of us. You ought'a know better. Once you're back in the big city, you just revert to stroll mentality. Not that I find fault with that, mind, but we gotta meet the dicks in..."

Harry shot a cuff, looked seriously at the watch on his cuff but couldn't keep it going, and dove for the bed. Sabina shrieked, rolled over, and they ended in a tangle of limbs.

An hour and twenty later, they were downstairs in the alley waiting for the four cops.

"We haven't got much to offer, have we?" Harry looked around.

"Not much, no, but we do have the similarities with the markings, the stones, and with this one, the altar. Even in the church, there were a few symbols."

"A few marks that may be intentional on her shoulder. Nothing in the blood. But the damage was so damn severe it's hard to tell from the photos you downloaded, at least the ones we've got so far. Maybe when they're all posted, we'll see something. I don't think Alan and Spence have connected this one with the animals on the altar in that church in Cedar, but the patterns in their blood, the circles of intestines, all that is suggestive. Those altar killings were pretty primitive given what those guys progressed to, but this church thing has similarities."

Sabina thought for a bit, twirled a ribbon of hair around her finger, the tip of her tongue peeking through her lips.

"I wonder if the church connection is intentional. I mean, are they taunting us? Would they do that? Is the excess violence intentional, a prod just for us? Maybe they're not losing control, maybe they're setting us up, pulling us into something, but it's hard to figure what that would be. Oh, here they are!"

Alan and Spence appeared around the corner, followed by Larry and Jake. Spence smiled at Harry, glanced at Sabina.

"You two set up here yet?" Spence eyed Sabina's short skirt.

"Just got in, really, but by tomorrow evening we'll be rollin'. You gonna introduce us?" Sabina stretched out a leg, shot her hip, and smiled at Spence.

Alan pointed to a heavy guy in a wrinkled suit. "This is Larry Sharp and the tall one's Jake Kenney. These two run the case with us. Brian Stevens put us in charge, but these guys know the city, the east end especially. Without 'em, we'd be nowhere."

Both men nodded, shook hands with Harry and Sabina, and waited. Sabina turned toward the rear door, a flat metal thing with no handle painted into the wall, hit the button on a remote in her hand, grabbed the now open edge, and looked back.

"We're three floors up, no elevator, guys. But we got refreshments, liquid ones at least, so let's get friendly and relax a bit. Been a long day for all of us."

The four cops bunched up in the doorway on the third floor, gawked at the room, and slowly walked in.

"I don't believe I've ever been in one of the old ones. This is beyond stunning." Jake smiled appreciatively.

Larry slipped off his shoes and ran his stockinged feet through the Persian carpet and groaned. "I could sleep on this if it weren't so damn fine. It's silk, right?"

"Yeah, it's silk, don't know the exact origin, though. Saw it at a Maynard's auction a couple of years ago and couldn't resist. Come on in guys, grab a seat, and let me get you all drinks."

Sabina opened the doors on an antique mahogany sideboard on a wall perpendicular to the windows, exposing a loaded bar. "I've got ice in the kitchen. We're havin' a nice single malt if that's of interest, otherwise, I've got just about everything."

Larry grinned and leaned over the chesterfield he'd burrowed into. You got any cold beer, maybe a Corona?"

Jake shook his head. "I'll go for the scotch. I can get beer anytime."

Alan and Spence both spoke at the same time and asked for the same thing. Sabina grinned.

"Cold beer, any kind." Spence nudged Alan and smiled. "We've been together on this one for so long, we've started to blend. Beer would be really good."

"Grab a seat and gimme a minute."

Sabina rummaged in the sideboard, selected a bottle. Spence unloaded her briefcase on the table and began to sort.

"I've to the profile for reference, the cult stuff from Dr. Spencer at SFU, the autopsy reports from Hammil and here, all the forensics for the two murders here on the mainland, and the photos and sketches for both. The church is our guy, no doubt about it even if it was messy. Take what you want. There's six of everything."

Sabina brought in the drinks on a large tray, set it on the other end of the coffee table, and sorted a pile for herself and one for Harry who was talking to Jake. Once Spence had settled next to Alan on the sofa with her beer, the others got their drinks, and they began.

"Okay, if you look at the photos from Hammil, you'll see the body's laid out just like the ones on the island, Mary Chang and Kylie Wingate. We don't know yet who the girl up there is. The chief of police, Herk Berman up there, along with Gordie Parker from the detachment in Powell River will both be down here with the task force tomorrow. We'll see what more they've got." Spence looked up to see if everyone was following and continued.

"We need to get these pricks, and now they're in town maybe we will. We gotta be better here than they are. We know the city, they don't. We have more people and we're better equipped. We can go over the reports and the site photos, but we're still playing catch-up, and the immediate advantage rests with them. Until we find a body, we're blind. Even when we do, we're still behind them. All we really have going for us is the possibility that they'll return to the kill site to check that nothing's been disturbed. If they do that, we'll get 'em. Jake and Larry have some ideas."

Jake nodded to Larry who set his beer down on one of the reports and leaned forward.

"What we need to do is saturate the area around the church with cars from the impound, stuff seized in raids, nothing these guys could suspect. We'll staff them ourselves when we can, the eight of us, twenty-four seven. We think they got into the church through the basement window, so we'll have that covered as well as the front and sides. We've also got permission from two house owners whose houses back onto the church grounds to use their back rooms for observation. We'll have those staffed as well. If they come back, we'll know."

"Are we on that already?" Sabina asked. "Because if we aren't, it's probably already too late."

"Everything's in place and staffed, right now by constables until we get all our guys here. We'll spell most of them tonight and by tomorrow, the Hammil and Powell River guys will cover it. But you two can't be seen to have anything to do with this operation. You gotta stay low."

Larry looked at Harry who shrugged.

"As far as we know, we're clear so far. And we can stay that way. Of course, there's always the possibility that we'll be outed by somebody. Task forces leak like sieves."

Alan sat forward and pointed at Harry. "This one won't. I can promise that. We're tight, all of us, including the help. We all know what's at stake. We're all aware of the scrutiny the task force faces. Nobody wants a leak."

"Good, neither do we."

Sabina yelled from the kitchen, "Any markings on the girl or in the blood at that damned church? Anything in the autopsy report?"

"There's nothing in the blood except for the marks the young guy who found her left, and they're only on the altar post. The rest was clear. On her shoulder, though, the coroner's report says there's something, a smeared streak or two of a blue-green substance. It's been sent for analysis. If there are symbols in the marks, they're not obvious. Forensics calls them smears, and the coroner agrees. It fits with the decomp that seems to be goin' on."

Spence drained her bottle and set it down on the floor.

"If we're not part of the surveillance, what do you want us to do?" Harry looked around the group.

"We thought you needed to be here when we find these guys. And I'll admit that we hoped Sabina'd keep tabs on Chinatown. If these guys do slip up, I promise you'll be there, right in the middle of it. For now, we do the scut work, you two gather data. We meet here every day after the task force meeting and talk it out, maybe come up with something to improve the odds."

Sabina had come in from the kitchen and stood at the foot of the sofa. "There are no stones, no marks, no anything in the church for them to come back to, and the body's been removed already, so why are we watching, what's the rationale?"

"We're not sure they will come back, but it's a pattern. It's all we have. We gotta cover it." Larry scratched his neck, pulled at his tie, and leaned forward again.

"Any chance this increased fury is intentional? Maybe they're not escalating?" Harry said, "Maybe it's a ploy to pull us in?"

"We haven't considered that at all. Maybe they're counting on the media to create a real stink, get us all pumped, then move on. Make us look like jerks." Alan looked at Spence.

"I don't know, I really think that's a bit off. They're losin' it, and that's our big break. They gotta make mistakes now. Look at the sloppiness, the viciousness. They gotta be getting more and more irrational," Spence insisted.

"Let's leave it there. We gotta get back. We have to replace some of our homicide guys who relieved the constables this morning. It's our turn. We'll be at it most of the night."

Jake stood and glanced around one last time. "This is pretty damned special, and we appreciate it. Thanks, you two."

"See you all tomorrow. I'll lay in some fixins so we can all eat while we talk. By then, I'll be set up and mining whatever I can get my hands on." Sabina nodded to Alan and Spence as they all made their way to the apartment door. Spence nodded back but muttered something under her breath. Alan looked at her carefully, grinned at Harry, and went through the door after her.

Sabina walked over to one of the front windows. "That went well, wouldn't you say, Sweets?"

"You bug that woman something fierce. And Alan's beginning to like it. Must be your skirt."

Harry came around to Sabina's side, slipped an arm around her waist. "What say we turn the mattress or something, get comfortable."

"Jesus, H, again? How about we eat first. I got something frozen that'll do." She left him at the window and went into the kitchen.

"Any scotch left to go with it?" Harry yelled.

He looked out at the street for a moment, watching the traffic, then turned, and walked to the kitchen doorway. Sabina had her head in the freezer, one long leg stuck out behind her.

Midnight found them sleeping curled into each other, the light from the street sliding across the sheets and up the far wall.

29.

Vic was enjoying himself. It had been such a pleasure, better than before, better than his brother, the blood richer, the feelings incredible, and the moment of blood and release extraordinary.

Vic parked behind a black BMW and waited, windows down, birdsong flowing through the old Transit van. He didn't know when classes might let out, given the numerous programs and varied lecture times, but there were bound to be streams of students returning to their cars during the day. He'd stay and watch.

After an hour of sitting quietly, watching a dribble of students return to their cars along the narrow two-lane blacktop that slid down behind the gardens and ran along the bluff above the Fraser, a road students used to avoid the hefty parking fees, he spotted a black sedan moving slowly down the road behind him. Not a cop, he thought, university security.

Vic grabbed a novel from the passenger seat, got out, and walked up the road toward Marine Drive and the university buildings. He watched the car make the turnabout, come back, and pass him again. He ignored the two in the front as they ignored him and kept walking: just another student making class. At the turnabout at the road's end, he turned, waited until the car was out of sight, and walked back to the van.

He sat listening to the birds in the botanical gardens, mostly raucous crows with a few songbirds sliding notes in between. He felt good. He thought again about the altar her naked body, the blood flowing, running down the altar's columns, the visceral pleasure rippling through him as he slashed at her over and over until finally, the release came thundering through him.

And now he sat anticipating more pleasure. Couples and singles straggled down the road at various times, cars drove off, the road began to empty. He was in no hurry. He knew if nothing appealed, he'd cruise the grounds of the university later that night. He'd find what he was looking for.

He decided to find a place for the night not too far off. He checked in at a hotel on Granville down near the bridge over the Fraser River that carried traffic to the airport. The hotel, if a little down-at-heels, was convenient for him, reasonably quiet, and the bar food was good. He passed the early evening there, listening, watching, waiting. Not one of the many women was alone. Not one had that quality that marked her.

At eight as the light began to fade, he drove back up Marine Drive to the university grounds and started a slow grid.

By nine, the light had failed. The streetlights made round patches of light at regular intervals, but they were ineffectual against the mass of darkness. Vic parked on the busiest of the university roads near a late-night eatery and watched. Students moved in and out of the restaurant, wandered along the road, and dawdled off across the grass quadrangles.

An hour later, the traffic was down to occasional couples and infrequent lone stragglers.

Then he saw her. She was wearing a black skirt, flats, a pale-coloured sweater. Her blond hair was pulled back into a ponytail and trailed along behind her swinging slowly from side to side. She sauntered along the edge of the road, her movements fluid and graceful even with the slouch of her shoulders. She looked only at the ground in front of her as if she were struggling with some weighty issue.

Vic tracked her first through the rear-view mirror, then the side, then the windshield. He checked the road, saw no one else, got out, and under the arching branches of a willow at the roadside spoke softly just behind the girl. She turned, looked up, and smiled. Vic Tasered her slid his arm around her as she fell and dragged her to the van. There was no one to notice. Once he had her inside, he drove down Marine Drive to the cut behind the botanical gardens. The sign at the beginning of the drive, warned him that the road was closed at eleven every night. So he drove down the road to the turnabout, then came back up slowly. There were only a few cars left, and all of those were on the water side, drawn up along the woods. The botanical gardens, tumbling down a steep slope on the land side of the road, were covered here mostly in heavy bush, all of it on the other side of a six-foot frost fence. Perfect cover. At least it would have been if he'd had another hour or so and some way to get through the fence.

Vic turned the van back to Marine Drive and took the divided highway back toward the city, turning right into the exclusive Shaughnessy enclave. He drove slowly along a narrow two-lane road, looking at the old mansions on his left, most already renovated, others currently in the process. There were no new builds. The two-lane ran along the edge of the old neighbourhood: the left side filled with the massive houses, the lots narrow but deep; the other with a dense stand of trees and a deep ravine.

That ravine effectively separated the mansions of Shaughnessy from the slovenly houses of the reservation on the ravine's far side. Vic scanned the heavily treed area. He noted the stream that ran along the bottom. It was deep and dark enough, but too close, he thought, too many eyes. He stopped, turned between the stone pillars of one of the great houses, backed out, and took Marine Drive into the city.

Down near the Fuzzy Arms, Vic parked beside a rail line on a short side street that paralleled Granville. It was dark and lonely, the houses facing the street blocked by large trees. He slapped a DMSO patch containing a strong sedative to the girl's arm near her shoulder, then he drove on.

He had plenty of time now. He decided to take his time driving along West Marine Drive to Boundary, past Central Park to the cloverleaf to Highway 1. He crossed Burrard

Inlet on the Second Narrows bridge and turned left Narrows bridge and turned left on Main. He took Mountain to Fern, and worked his way around to St. Denis Ave, a side street that ran along the banks of the Lynn River.

Parking at the end of the street, he cut the engine and sat listening to a silence broken only by the whisper of the river's gentle rapids. There were no houses or lights this far down, and the van was well hidden by the brush at the side of the road.

Vic looked at the girl in the back and thought about the van. After this, I'd better get a new ride. A pickup? One of those V8s with a heavy-duty suspension and grille bars, so I look like a local redneck. Lots of those around.

A path ran along the river from the end of St. Denis all the way up to the Lynn Canyon suspension bridge and on into the mountains. The first part of that path had been a service road at one time, but it had been abandoned years ago and was now used only by dog walkers and people out for daily strolls. At night, no one used it.

Vic turned off the interior lights, opened the rear door, and slid the girl out. He threw her over his shoulder, walked down the path a few hundred yards, then turned down a steep incline to a hidden rock ledge close to the water. Here the river was wide, shallow, and swift.

Vic had discovered this ledge one afternoon when his brother was holed up in the motel watching the Nature channel. Vic grimaced as he remembered that night. He began muttering, "That blonde bitch detective. The bitch. Almost had them. So damn close!" Vic felt the anger rise. His stomach churned. She'd pay alright. Damn bitch, he thought. She was the cause of their severing. His brother was never right after the island. Damn her! Now become prey!

He slowed his breathing and thought about how he'd lure her. This time she'd provide the blood he craved. There would be glory for him in her passing. She'd discover the trail of bodies he displayed just for her and her partner. They'd already found the bloody altar and now there'd be today's little gem here by the river.

She'd follow, he was certain of that, and he'd take her, send her over, tear her flesh, give the empty carcass back to her hubby and the stupid cops. He was so much stronger, more adept, smarter.

The damned blonde! She'd caused them to lose something visceral. In the streets and alleys of Vancouver, a kind of sickness, black and bitter, had eaten away at their bond. He'd had to take his brother back to the island, back to their old hunting ground, back to the darkness of the pit where they'd found their union. After Mercedes, in the rich, earthy darkness of the pit that his brother had dug, Vic had cut him away from himself, slashing in a delirium of bloodlust until he'd obliterated everything, every known contour, from his brother's groin to his face, slashing over and over until the frenzy climaxed, until his breathing slowed, and he felt both emptiness and release. But she had caused that! Finally, the black emptiness in him was gone. He was floating free, his mind clear.

He felt strong now, powerful. He knew his need was greater now, but it was his alone and he revelled in it. There had been the church, now there was the river. He knew this one's blood would be his alone and he smiled. Her passing would enrich him, fulfill him. He felt his pleasure mount as he carried the girl down the bank to the hidden strata of rock.

The boulders rose like black threats on either side, blotting out the night sky. Between them lay a gently curved depression covered in a litter of fallen leaves, edged by straggly bushes, mostly salal. Even the soft whisper of the river was muted. This place would be his own sacred point, would create a powerful crossing, the blood rich and fecund.

He removed the girl's clothes, watched her for a while. The pale moonlight washing her body gave her a soft ethereal presence, like something out of a story by Poe, paler than human skin should ever be. He opened the pouch and quickly and roughly applied the great symbols that would link the two of them. He sat back, feeling the flow begin.

He reached into the pouch once more, pulled out the patch saturated with Succinylcholine. He waited until the girl showed signs of recovering, then laid the patch on her naked shoulder just below the symbols. As she began to struggle to consciousness, he watched her, his anticipation burning through him. Her eyes flew open. She lay still for a few moments, then, her eyes filled with horror as she felt the paralysis travel through her muscles.

She tried desperately to breathe, her eyes wide now and terrified. Slowly, so exquisitely slowly, all expression softened, as if she had recognized the futility. Vic felt the difference, a profound shift in the ether.

Her passing swept through him. He withdrew the knife and began the incision. Blood pooled under his fingers, rich and dark, and the hunger took him. The knife rose and fell, rose and fell. Blood splattered across his chest as he slashed at the girl's abdomen. Severed entrails slid through the blood, down her side, lying like thick worms beside her. Once the fever climaxed and fell, he stopped. He slid his hands into the warmth, and breathed in the rich, coppery smell. He stayed that way for a time. Then he began again, lost himself in a bloodlust more powerful than he had ever known. He felt the surge and tore at her viscera, then he took the knife again, slashing, until exhausted, he lay beside her remains breathing deeply.

30.

Early morning light saw dog walkers on the wide path. Several of them paused when they picked up the unpleasant smell and noticed the spiral of turkey vultures circling above the river. A woman in her late seventies turned to her elderly companion who held the leads of two small, fluffy dogs.

"George, what's that smell?"

"Somethin' dead acourse."

"Well, find out what!"

"Fer chrissake, Moira, I'm not goin' down there!" he said, nodding toward the river.

George looked as if he might manage a few steps down if he took his time, but only a few. He was tall and very thin, dressed in shorts that revealed spindly legs, slightly bowlegged, and a light, short-sleeved cotton top that hung loosely on his thin shoulders. He had on sensible walking shoes with red ankle socks. He towered over his wife.

Moira was tiny, mostly wrinkles, at least what could be seen of her. Her hair was almost white and fell straight to her shoulders. She wore a long, flower-print dress, a broad-brimmed summer hat, and a pair of those sensible shoes, black ones with thick heels.

"I'll go!" said a young man on a bicycle who'd also stopped because of the vultures.

"Could be somethin' maybe drowned."

The man, no more than or twenty, wearing cycling shorts and a bright green short-sleeved shirt, hopped off his bike, handed it and his helmet to Moira with a grin, and dropped out of sight down the bank. Others walking by lingered, curious, and eyed the vultures.

He was gone a long time. When he finally came back up, he was as white as the proverbial sheet. He looked stunned. He said nothing, just pointed behind him, bent over, and puked. When he straightened up, he reached for the bike Moira was still holding, fumbled around in a side panier, and yanked out a cell phone. He hit a single button and listened for a moment.

"There's a body down here cut to bits. Jesus, it's a mess. You better get down here.... What? Oh, off St Denis on the path near the Lynn River. I'll wait here. But I'm not goin' down there again."

George and Moira simply stared at him, their shock obvious. Others who had stopped popped out questions all over the place. The cyclist sat at the side of the path and refused to answer other than to say it was a body and it was all cut up. Others in the growing group listened, glanced at each other, and as if a signal had passed between them, made for the bank in a group, some were young, some middle aged. George yelled at them.

"Hey, that's a crime scene, you better stay the hell out! Cops're on the way. They won't like anythin' buggered up by a bunch a hoodlums."

The lot of them paused for a moment, looked at each other, then began to move forward again. They all heard a siren scream at them from the end of the street. That stopped them in their tracks. They glanced up at the flashing lights and filtered back into the growing crowd.

A cruiser rammed its way down the short street, red and blues throwing streaks of light despite the early morning sun, braked to a hard, dust-filled stop, and disgorged two uniforms. The taller of the two, a sergeant by the look of him, made for the group. A younger uniform opened the cruiser's trunk, grabbed a roll of yellow tape, and followed.

"Right then, who's the one phoned it in?"

"That'd be me."

The cyclist stood, and the cop walked over.

His partner kept the crowd at bay, pushing the leaders farther away so no one could hear the conversation. A second cruiser tore down the street, skidding in beside the first one. It too disgorged two constables who took over crowd control while the first taped off the area.

"I'll need your name and some ID." The sergeant took out a small, black notebook and waited.

"Randy, Randy Jarvis. Hang on, my wallet's in my panier."

He picked up his bike, now lying on the grass beside him where Moira had lain it, and dug in the panier for his ID. He turned to look at the sergeant, "I can tell you where to look, but jeez, I don't wanna go back down there."

"Let's have the ID son, then we'll see."

Up the street, just where it turned to follow the river, a large black SUV appeared, grill lights flashing. It pulled in beside the cruisers. Four occupants got out, three men and a woman. All four wore suits with white shirts, the men dark ties. The woman was small but seemed to radiate energy and anger. People near her stepped back a little.

The crowd eyed them as they walked up to the sergeant. The woman turned, then looked back at the crowd, held up one hand, then pointed over their heads. The uniforms began to push everybody back.

Jake and Larry looked at the sergeant and pointed at Alan, "He's the lead."

"Alan Kim. What've you got?"

"Sergeant Strangelove... don't ask. I got the kid's name and address. He found the body. Says it's a girl, young, naked, slashed up a lot. Haven't been down, been waiting for you. Scene's pristine except for what he touched. Forensics on the way?"

"They've been called, but I'd like to get what I can from the kid. Then my partner and I will look."

Alan spent a few minutes with the young guy who found the body. He didn't get much but now he knew how far the kid had gone and what he'd touched. He nodded to his team. "We can go down to the edge of the big rocks. The guy's touched everything that far. It's steep, how about in twos, take a quick look, wait for the techs. Take Spence. We'll follow when you're back."

Larry yanked his tie down a couple of inches, sighed in relief, and waved them off. The sergeant stood uncertainly, unsure of his place. Jake called him over. "Get someone at the top of the bank for sign-in, use one of your guys, set it up so he's not in the way when forensics gets here, but tell him to get everyone. No one who doesn't belong. You know all that, so get it done."

Alan and Spence waited beside the path. They'd seen Jake talk to the sergeant and point in their direction. They waited while the sergeant signalled a constable and pointed, waited while he rushed over with a clipboard. They signed in and began working their way down the steep bank, following the scuff marks left by the cyclist's shoes. They stopped at the edge of the little clearing, the huge boulders creating a kind of flat indent in the bank.

"Shit! Look at that mess!" Spence leaned in further. "That can't be our guys. They're meticulous with the cuts. This is pure savagery. Hard to tell it's even human except for the face. That's left perfect."

Alan leaned over her shoulder. "Look at her upper arm, those markings, you can barely see them for the blood. That's their signature, And the stones, look at them. They're losing it, but it's them."

"This's worse than the church. It's fucking savage. But you're right, at least I guess you're right. You can hardly see the ink marks or the stones for all the body parts lyin' around. And those marks, they're rough, sort of slathered on. That's more than anger, that's.... I don't know what the hell that is!"

"Let's get back up, give Jake and Larry a chance to see what this guy does up close. It'll be their first real look at one in a natural setting like we had on the island. They know about grisly; they saw that body in the church. They need to see this, and we need to find Roberta Cannon, the profiler. Maybe get her back here, get her take on this mess."

"They're gonna hate this. Be like that pig guy Pickton all over again, only worse if they keep goin' like this. Okay, let's get up." Spence stood, turned, and began to climb. Alan followed.

Jake and Larry stood a few yards away with the sergeant talking to the forensics crew. Spence could see their van pulled up close. The crowd had been pushed way back to the end of St Denis, and the uniforms had strung a huge loop of yellow crime scene tape from the street end to about fifty yards past the site. Jake glanced over and waved them in.

"Alan, Spence, you remember Harvey Couch, head of forensics. Harvey? Alan Kim and Spence Riley, Harvey, these two were assigned to us from Harbour City. You guys met at the church."

"Sergeant, see if you can organize some way to send that crowd on its way, get them out of here."

Jake turned again to the forensics chief. "Seems that the two guys who operated on the island are now here, so we need everything you can get from this one. Everything."

"Got us a tiny task force." Larry said, hands emerging from his sagging suitcoat pockets and hitting the air a few inches apart.

"Mostly it's ours, so no sweat, but any results come down, get 'em to Alan here or Spence. Like Jake said, they're the leads on this one. Here, call us, we got our own phones and everything. Even got us a manager, he's on there too. Whose doin' the shots?" Larry held out a business card listing all the task force members with one central phone number. He'd written Alan's and Spence's personal cell numbers on the back.

Harvey glanced at the card, stuck it in his pocket, nodded at Alan and Spence, and turned to Larry.

Harvey was six-two at least and had to look down. He was dressed as usual in blue scrubs and desert boots with soft crepe soles. His hair was a light-brown halo around his ears but lay flat on the top of his head. He had a large, hooked nose. His smile was little more than a slight upward turn of his thin lips, but his eyes were a bright, inquisitive blue. He led the best forensics team in town.

"I got Bart LaJeunesse. Came in with us, he'll be goin' down now, getting his stuff organized." Harvey glanced back at a man with a camera bag slung over his shoulder just approaching the riverbank and waved him over.

"Bart, Alan Kim and Spence Riley, leads here. You know these other guys." He nodded at Jake and Larry. Alan and Spence shook his hand.

Alan glanced at the bag slung around Bart's shoulder. "Pretty small bag. You got a mirrorless in there?"

Bart grinned, "Fuji XT3. Fast, pretty good in low light, and I use an OIS zoom lens. Can't do better. I'll do the sketches as well, be done in an hour. Let you know."

Harvey nodded, and Bart walked to the edge of the bank, suited up, signed in, and started down. The others watched.

"We'll go down, take a look when he's done." Turning to Alan and Spence, Jake said, "What do you guys think?"

"It's our guy, we're pretty sure, but he's getting vicious. Lotta blood and he's slashed everything to bits, pulled out organs, left everything spread around. It's pretty bad. Worse than the church, so be prepared."

Harvey shook his head. "I'll never understand these freaks, never, it's as if they're not human." He shook his head again and sighed. "I gotta supervise the collection setup and the lights. We'll be here until we're finished which likely won't be until tomorrow sometime. We'll let you down before that of course, but let's get the basics done, and then the coroner can pronounce. Path'll be marked for all the good that'll do, but the scene's marked off, so no touching. Sorry, habit."

Harvey turned to Alan. "Coroner arrive yet?"

"He's not here yet, but we expect him any time." Alan said. He looked at Jake.

"He's been called. We've got a new one, name of Wainsbury, I think. Should be along shortly."

Harvey nodded, shook his head again, and turned toward his team. They all watched him go.

"It'll be a while before Bart and Harvey're done, so let's get some coffee. It's gonna be a long day." Alan glanced at Spence who was staring moodily at the river.

She turned and glared at the lot of them. "That creep, there's gonna be more. It'll be like the island: first a church altar, then the bloody bush, not a damn thing at the site and no clothes. At least this site's more civilized, not way back in the middle of nowhere…Yeah, let's get coffee, lots of it, and sure, lunch. Might as well eat while we can."

Spence turned toward the mobile lunch truck now parked at the near end of a long line of cruisers, black SUVs, and forensics equipment trucks that stretched from the end of St Denis almost as far as the dump site. Alan, Jake, and Larry followed.

Like the island murders, Spence and Alan both doubted they'd ever find either the clothes or the actual murder sites. For all the bloody body parts spread around, they had seen no arterial spurts on site and that meant that the girl had been murdered somewhere else and transported. Either that or they were looking at death at the site by some agent they hadn't yet identified.

In her report, the coroner had written that the drug left virtually no trace in the bloodstream and was impossible to find, and that testing for it was expensive and inconclusive and therefore rarely used. She'd concluded that she had indeed tested for it and had found nothing. But she insisted that that did not mean it hadn't been used, only that the test hadn't found any trace.

Spence drifted back to walk beside Alan. Jake and Larry gave them room. "You know what we're gonna get at the site, don't you? Same thing we got on the island, nothin', no clothes, no trace to speak of, no defensive marks, no bloody nothin', shit!"

She slid between Jake and Larry, stomped up to the truck, banged on the side, apologized to the woman operating the kitchen, and ordered coffee and whatever else she had that didn't taste like blotting paper.

The woman grinned, leaned over the drop-down counter, and said, "Don't tell the techies, but I got some good roast chicken. No sense wasting it on them, they can't taste anything anyway. I'll run you all up a pair of sandwiches each while you have a coffee. I'll whistle when they're ready."

Alan, along with Jake and Larry, looked around and spotted a couple of old bleached logs lying along the side of the path. They parked themselves on one of them and waited. Spence got four cups of coffee, shoved sugar packs in her pocket, stuck a carton of milk under her arm, grabbed the cups with both hands, and gingerly back to the others. All four sat on the log and sipped.

"Let's call the Powell River coroner to find out more about that sux drug she mentioned in her report. Won't do us much good, but at least we know the murders can occur on site rather than somewhere else. Otherwise we have to look for kills sites that aren't there."

Alan leaned across Spence to include Jake and Larry. "I think we have the name of that drug somewhere in the reports. But even if we do focus on this site, we're not gonna get much. It'll likely be just like the island cases. All we got going for us is that they're losing control, at least the dominant one is, and they might have made a slip. If they have, and they're bound to eventually, we'll get them."

"There's also the fact that these guys return to the site,"

Spence added. "We gotta make sure we cover the place without being seen. And that's a problem with these guys. They're good. We know they go back, because we've seen signs of site repair in the cases on the island. But we've never seen them or found any sign of how they got there either initially or on a return visit. Tryin' to cover this site's gonna be a problem in a lotta ways. It's even worse than the church."

Larry tugged at his tie. The thing looked like something dead just hanging there. His shirt, a wrinkled mess to begin with now carried a couple of coffee stains near the buttons where it bulged out. He sighed heavily, rubbed his head, and said, "If we can't do it manually, can we maybe rig the damn place with cameras or something, catch 'em that way?"

"They're too good for that. Only thing might work is a drone or two, way up? I mean the site's been full of people every day, so they might not notice any surveillance, but I wouldn't count on it. Maybe drones would work." Alan rubbed his face with his hands, his frustration evident. "And that's only if they come back. Given the mess down there, their control's gone to hell and their rituals may be broken too. We gotta do somethin', but what'll work is anybody's guess."

No one said anything for a while. Only the sound of the river and the occasional yell from the park area on the far side disturbed the quiet. They all turned as a sharp whistle sounded behind them.

"The eats, I'll go get 'em. You guys sit some more." Larry got up, brushed off the seat of his pants, and walked off toward the truck, waving to the woman leaning on the counter. They all watched as he felt around his pockets looking for his wallet. They saw him slap some bills on the counter and watched him gather up four white paper bags and turn toward them.

Once they were eating, Spence asked Jake and Larry, "We got any idea yet who the first one was, the one in the bush near Hammil?"

"We got requests out all over the country now, so we'll know soon. We got a meeting at four today, maybe the techs got somethin'."

"Young girl like that, somebody shoulda missed her, Jesus." Spence lifted the top of her sandwich, checked it, and took a big bite, chewing thoughtfully.

"You'd think so, wouldn't ya. But we've had paper all over the place, even Ontario and Quebec, nothin'." Jake rubbed his head again, picked up another sandwich and sat looking at the river. They ate quietly for a while, all of them looking at the river, waiting for the crew to finish collecting trace from the site.

They all heard the siren chirp and watched a large SUV clear the road end and lumber down the path toward them.

"That'll be the coroner," Larry said, munching on his second sandwich. "He loves those bloody big things. Owns three of 'em. Drives the black one to sites. That's what I've heard anyway. Only been at two city murders with him myself. He's fast, though, so we should get down soon."

The coroner climbed down from the driver's seat, threw open the hatch, and pulled out his bag. He was tall and so skinny he looked like a modern version of Ichabod Crane. In keeping with the image, his suit was dark, his shirt white. He had a full head of black hair, long sideburns, and an extraordinary nose much too large for his face.

Behind him came an ambulance, moving slowly down the path, lights flashing. It pulled in beside the coroner. Two men emerged, opened the rear and took out a stretcher and body bag. They joined the coroner and all three started toward the forensics collection tent that had been erected close to the bank and the path.

"Harvey'll let 'em down to pronounce once he's done with the preliminaries and it looks like he is. He's in the tent. I saw his head. Damn coroner's almost as tall as he is." Jake finished off the last of his lunch, wiped his hands on his pants, and stood up. The others followed suit.

Jake glanced at his watch. "Meeting's at four. Why don't you two get on back, we'll look and follow you. Won't be long. The coroner's just gone down. I'm not sure I wanna look, but Larry and I have to see at least one I guess."

Alan nodded and he and Spence left the scene. "You know, Alan said, "those bloody drones might just work."

Spence grunted, grabbed the door, and climbed in. Minutes later, they were crossing the Second Narrows bridge.

31.

Once over the bridge, Spence slipped onto McGill, then drove the black unmarked SUV along Nanaimo to Dundas and Powell. Down a few blocks on Powell, the traffic began to bunch. Spence thought about cutting over to Franklin on Victoria, but that'd only dump her on Clark, and she'd have to swing down under the elevated, leading to the docks and pick up Powell again. Wasn't worth the effort, she thought, so she sat in the now stalled traffic, fingers drumming on the edge of the wheel.

"What the hell's the holdup? You'd think with two bloody lanes these goons could at least move."

"It's the Commercial light. Except for rush hour, you can park along the curb lane, and some of these yoyos park right next to the light, so no one can get by if a driver's turning left. We've got lots of time."

Alan glanced behind the unmarked and saw a line of cars backed all the way up the grade to the Nanaimo intersection. He thought to himself that Spence should have turned up Victoria to Hastings and scooted over to Clark. But she was Spence, so telling her anything, especially in traffic, was not a good idea.

Alan was reaching for the phone to call in when he saw Spence's hand flash by. He felt the jolt and heard the siren as she ripped the unmarked out of her lane into oncoming traffic. Grill lights flashing, siren screaming, she hit the light at Commercial, swung a left, and hurtled up the divided street to Hastings. She threw a right Alan was reaching for the phone to call in when he saw Spence's hand flash by. He felt the jolt and heard the siren as she ripped the unmarked out of her lane into oncoming traffic. Grill lights flashing, siren screaming, she hit the light at Commercial, swung a left, and hurtled up the divided street to Hastings. She threw a right, slowed, and killed the siren and lights. She grinned at Alan who shook his head and kept quiet.

"Won't be late now. We'll have time for a Starbucks too. There's a place just down the street."

"There's nothing before Main. The one you're thinking of is farther on and there's no drive through. Street's a mess, and you can't park anywhere."

"So, I'll double park, hit the lights, you run in, grab a couple, and we're good. I need another coffee if I have to sit through a bloody meeting, especially a task force even if it is ours."

Spence took the unmarked across the Main and Hastings intersection. It was always depressing. The corner was the center of the infamous East End. There was at least one mission in that block and a food dispensery in the old bank building on the corner. An amorphous crowd of derelicts floated around like a thin roiling storm cloud at any time of day. Added to that menagerie, there were the truly damaged, and, always, a splattering of druggies still tripping. This was drug central. You never knew what would cross the street in front of you.

Alan tensed as Spence scooted across the intersection and relaxed only when her progress was blocked by a bus.

The street changed in a single block from derelict storefronts, depressing old theater marquees with tattered remnants of posters still up, and sleazy hotels with ratty neon signs, to upscale restaurants and shops in refurbished buildings with restored facades. The Starbucks was a couple of blocks away, right in the middle of the Gastown district near the steam clock on the corner.

Once the bus had moved on, Spence slid quietly toward the row of parked cars in front of the store, left enough room for Alan to squeeze out, hit the flashers, and grinned. "Get big ones will ya, and maybe a sandwich or two. There's nothing remotely edible in those bloody machines at the station. And that cart Jake and Larry love is obscene."

Alan got out and hit the store's glass doors. The line was mercifully short, the orders quick for Starbucks, and the barista cheerful. He was out in no time.

Spence killed the grills and the flashers, and drove sedately down the street to Cambie, hung a right, drove a block, hung another right, and took Cordova back to the station at Main.

Conference 1, the room assigned to the task force, was full. The techs seemed to have added more computers, and there were now two young women on the phones, constables Argos and Titles, according to the tags. He bent over, introduced himself and discovered that Argos, the dark haired one, was Jodi and the blonde was Helen.

"Anything on the body up near Hammil yet? Do we know who she was?"

"Nothing yet, sir, and we've had no luck with the calls. Herb had us check as many stations out of province as possible just in case. We're already linked to the ones here. The techs have that one." She nodded across the room where Ted, Ron, and Roger were messing about with keyboards and a small army of monitors. Alan had no idea what they were for.

Spence was already there talking to Ron. She looked up, shook her head, and turned back to the techs and the monitors.

Their own workstation was close to the tech table. They had their own laptops, good ones provided by Ron and the crew. The two sandwiches and coffees Spence had brought in with her sat on the edge of the table. It was obvious the techs had already eaten: cartons and runched up paper littered the floor around their station, close to but not in the wastebasket.

Alan and Spence ate and sipped, watched the techs messing about, and waited for Jake and Larry. While they drank coffee, Herb Chase, the case manager, came in, spent a minute with the women on the phones and the techs before grabbing a chair near Alan and Spence.

"We've spent a chunk of budget looking for that girl up in Hammil, but nothing, no missing person that fits the description here or anywhere else. I don't understand. Somebody must miss her somewhere. I mean she was well nourished according to the coroner's report, so she wasn't derelict or homeless. How'd the new one look?"

"Brutal, worse than the church." Alan said, "but we need to talk about that one as soon as Jake and Larry get here. There're some markers we need to discuss, some links to the island murders. But there's also a lot of difference." Alan looked at Spence who nodded.

"It's beyond brutal, it's a bloody hack job, but we think it's our guys."

The conference door flew open and in came Larry, balancing two paper cups and a couple of dogs from the cart out front.

"Jake'll be along, he's with Brian for a mo. That was unpleasant, that was. But you're right, we had to see her. So now it's two, what with the church. We still on surveillance there or what?"

"We're gonna discuss that one and the one by the river. We wanted you to see one outdoors, because we think there's some parallels with our island girls, some stuff not in the reports." Alan finished his coffee and threw the cup in the wastebasket.

"There's a lot that's different, that's for sure, but it's our guys. And we need to talk to the privates. They're still active on the two cases over there, and they know as much about the church murder as we do." Spence looked questioningly at Larry.

"Yeah, we can fill 'em in later. At least Jake will. He's got all the reports so far, he'll tell you what all came in when he gets here... and here he be."

Jake came over and picked up his coffee.

"We've got a problem. We gotta pick up Herk and Gordie at the airport, they're flyin' in early courtesy of our budget. We gotta be out there at seven. So we let the privates know we'll be over after that. And I think we all four should go, find a spot out there, get 'em up to date, then get back to the Gastown apartment. By the time we're done over there and get back here, Herb here will have things sorted, files for each of us, chores laid out."

"Brian getting leaned on any harder?" Larry bit into a hot dog, mustard dribbling down his chin. He handed the other dog to Jake.

"He'll handle it and he'll keep it clean. Let's get at it, Herb."

Herb stood at the head of the table, looked around to make certain everyone was seated. "Okay, people, let's get started. This is the second murder in a couple of days, and we need to move on it. Let's have the reports on this one. Helen, Jodi?"

"We don't know who the Hammil girl is yet, and we've covered the country as far as the east coast. And we don't know who the church girl is either. Again, we've covered the province and extended to all jurisdictions." Helen looked at Jodi.

"Okay, we've got better news about the river girl. She's been gone two days now from a dorm at UBC, and her roommate got worried enough to call it in. When she didn't come home the first night, the roommate figured she had a date that turned into, well, you know. The roommate's name is Heidi Stillman and the vic's is Janet Bergson, twenty-three, major in Fine Arts, 110, 5'6, blue, brown. Brian's trying to reach the family now. Hometown is a place called Port Perry in Ontario. It's reasonably close to Toronto so we can orient ourselves from that. She did her undergrad at U of T, was doing research in a graduate program here."

"Alan, Spence?"

"We've had the church under surveillance since the night of and have nothing to report, no sightings, no activity of any sort. We've thought about that, and we think there's nothing left in the church that they'd return for. All that's left is the blood, body and parts have been removed. We've pulled the surveillance and we'll concentrate on the Lynn River site since that one's outdoors, and there's a lot at the site for them to return to. I'll let Jake explain what we're going to do there." Alan looked over at Jake.

"What we're going to do is use high altitude drones, about a half dozen of them. As I understand it, the feed'll be directly to this room. Brian's okay'd the expense, has ordered the drones and given the whole thing priority. Our techs'll have the feeds." He nodded at Ted, Ron, and Roger.

"We know from the island cases that these guys return to sites that are outdoors, so we expect them to do the same here. But we do have differences. These girls have been literally slashed into bits, eviscerated. There's a level of violence that's missing from the island murders and from the one in Hammil. But the leads, Alan and Spence, who've been all over the island ones and ours here, think these murders are by the same guys. I'll let them explain."

Spence cleared her throat. "We're relying on the profiler's report and her belief that these psychos'd lose control in time and become far more volatile. We think that's what's happening now. Our best bet is to go with the drone surveillance and watch for their return to repair the scene. That's part of the ritual they follow, checking after we've left to make certain the ground hasn't been disturbed and to make corrections if it has. That suggests that the site has some fundamental importance to them, much like a highway memorial where people put flowers. We're not sure what that significance is, but it has something to do with transference, movement from this world to the next, a kind of crossing that's accomplished only by the blood of their victims. The sites of the murders are sacred places.

"Everybody should be familiar with the profiler's report. There are copies on the table. Something else to remember. The girls are dead before the mutilation, perhaps on site, that's what our profiler thinks, or before they're brought to the site. And that goes for the two bodies we have here and the one in Hammil. We're inclined to believe what the profiler suggests: that the girls are murdered on site because that's where the transfer occurs. Doesn't make any sense to kill them elsewhere and transport them, not if the transfer of the girl's spirit or whatever it is makes the sites important."

"Okay, thanks Spence. Everyone should read that report. Ted, Ron, Roger?"

"We've already got the feed directly from the drones. They went up about an hour ago. That's spitfire fast, so somebody's got juice. Anything appears, we relay to the unmarkeds that are scattered around. We've also got a pile of cruisers on standby pretty much all over the area. That means Highway 1, North and West Van, and surrounding neighbourhoods. But the priority is to get any movement from the drones to the four homicide Ds so they can roll quickly."

Herb stood and looked at the group. "Okay, we all know what's happening. I need you to know that we'll have two more members, Herk Berman from Hammil, he's the chief up there, and Gordie Parker from Powell River, he's homicide and has been on the Hammil case."

Herb picked up a pile of papers from his desk. "These are the autopsy reports, one from the church, it's final, and one from the river, it's preliminary. Copies for everyone. Read them through, if anything clicks, feed it to me."

Herb looked around the room. "Okay, tomorrow at four as usual. Get to work and good luck."

Larry had finished his hotdog and was working on his coffee. "So we go get that pair from up north now, then head to Gastown?"

Jake took a last sip and tossed the cup at the waste basket, watched it bounce off the rim and go in. "Let's all four of us go out there, fill them in. I've got copies of the reports they can read later. It's rush hour, so by the time we hit the domestic terminal, they'll have arrived. Right, let's move."

Main Street was jammed from Hastings all the way up the hill. Spence, who was driving, looked over her shoulder at Larry who was in the back of the unmarked SUV. "We got any way out of this mess, or do I just hit the lights and siren, move the bastards over."

"Won't matter what street we try, they're all jammed, lights and siren won't help either. Streets are full both directions. Inch along as best you can, I guess."

"Screw that, I'm gonna goose it some." She hit the lights and siren, swung into the opposing lane and began forcing cars aside. When she couldn't get anywhere there, she swung back and took the sidewalk, pedestrians flattening against the sides of stores until she swung back into the road. She got quickly to the Main-Broadway intersection where everything jammed.

"I know you love this shit, Spence, but there's no need, and you're scaring the pedestrians. About six of those people were glued to store fronts, the rest were damn near on the road tryin' to get away without bein' squashed. Road's the safest place, nothin' moving there. Larry leaned over the back seat of the big SUV. "But damn, that was fun."

"If you wanna beat the worst of it, you should slide over to the side streets, they're narrow, and you can't get up much speed, siren or no, but it's less frustrating for you. And we're less likely to pee ourselves." Jake still held the little handle above the rear door, both feet pushed forward on phantom brakes.

Spence sighed heavily, shook her head, and tapped the siren to move a driver into the curb. "You guys really don't care when we get there, I'll do the sides. Takes forever, but saves the seats, I guess."

She swung right at the first descent looking cross-street, which was 41st. She ripped across to Oak, turned left and ran down to Marine Drive West. She crossed the Arthur Liang Bridge, flipped the lights again, and passed everything on the road. Spence left the SUV in the taxi lane at the domestic terminal, badged the security guy who was coming to move them on, and all four went in.

The flight had landed on time and most of the passengers were massed around the baggage ramp like pigs at a trough, grabbing bags as they circled. Only two of them seemed not to care, so Alan walked over and shook hands.

"No bags?" she asked.

"No need for anything more than these." Gordie said. Herk just nodded. Both men had small tote bags on wheels but they were carrying them and Spence hadn't noticed.

"Okay, let's get out of here, unless you guys want a coffee or something."

"We filled up on the plane, so we're good." Herk looked questioningly at Gordie, who shook his head.

The terminal wasn't busy, just a few people lined up outside the waist-high stone wall near the carousels waiting for the next flight. A handful moved down the escalator that formed a half circle around the huge totem, heading for the arrivals taxi line or the terminal parking lot, a separate three-storey bunker on the far side of the road.

The SUV had three rows of seats when necessary, so all six of them fitted nicely. Spence took the airport access road and fought her way downtown. They hit the office again to see what if anything had transpired and introduced Herk and Gordie to the gang. Herb had them booked into a motel up Main on the hill south of Broadway because it was close to the station. All of them spent a good two hours together, answering any questions Herk and Gordie might have. Jake and Larry decided to stay on with the techs and monitor the drones. By eleven, Spence left for the car.

After talking to Jake and Larry, Alan followed her down the hall to the basement parking area. They walked over to her Camaro. A thin blanket of dust thrown up by the constant traffic in and out covered the once shiny red car. Spence ran her finger along the front fender and mumbled something Alan didn't catch. She turned to face him, folding her arms under her breasts.

"What'll we do with those two northern guys? They can't really help with anything. Besides, there's nothing much we can do except wait for another bloody body and have more bloody meetings."

"At least we get up to date on what's come in."

"I know they're necessary for a whole lot of reasons, but all we do in there is drink coffee, rehash everything, and divvy up useless jobs. At least on the church surveillance we had something to do besides sit. Well, not much I guess. Jeez, one break, just one, and we'd get these pricks."

"Let's get out of here, maybe stop at Starbucks, get something to eat and a coffee. We're too tired to start cookin' stuff, and we have to be back early morning, pick up Gordie and Herk at the motel and take 'em around to the church and the river. They're good guys. And given they've got one up there, they deserve to be in on the chase." Alan leaned on the car's front fender.

"Jake and Larry comin' with us? We need to take that damn big thing out again? It's like drivin' a tank."

"Not the way you drive it, but I talked to Jake in the office, and they'll gladly leave that part to us, so you get to drive whatever you want. After the airport drive, Jake's a bit gun-shy, I think."

"Okay. Let's get goin'. What about that place on the turn into Powell, it's just down the road."

"If not, there's the bar at Victoria. They've got eats, and I know they don't close until late."

Spence revved the engine a few times before she peeled out and shot down Cordova toward the turn. She caught the first light, drummed her fingers on the wheel, took off on the orange, and fudged the next one. The Starbucks was closed.

"Shit, I need good coffee. The bar'll do, but if the coffee's lousy, I'll probably drink something harder. You too. Make us a bit sleepy maybe."

Powell was almost clear that time of night, so she got the light at Clark, and tore down to Commercial. She waited for the light, shifted and revved some while waiting. She hit the brakes at Victoria, slipped around the corner, and jammed the Camaro in between a black SUV and a Jeep.

"You ever noticed there're too many stoplights? Can't get a decent stretch anywhere. Maybe tomorrow we'll hop up to Horseshoe Bay after the river. Got a Starbucks up there too, and it'll be open."

Alan looked at the bar on Dundas. "This place won't be too bad. It's had some good reviews, so we should be fine."

Victoria Street was poorly lit, the road made of reddish paving stones, many of them chipped, some of them gone, leaving black holes like missing teeth. The street heaved here and there, rolled a bit like a swell in dark water. The few trees did nothing to dispel the gloom. The whole street was like that all the way up the slope to Hastings. In the dim light, cars sat against both curbs like dark beetles.

As Alan stood by the car for a few more moments, he glanced toward Hastings. "Looks like the end of a nightmare. Let's hope the food's better."

Spence shrugged her shoulders, made no comment, and started for the light at the corner. Alan followed.

The Victoria Bar and Grill was just what you'd expect. Maybe a little nicer than you'd expect, but basically, it was just what it advertised: a bar with a fast food grill. They entered directly into a room splattered with those Canadian maple tables with turned legs that everybody used to have in his dining room. Booths ran along the side wall behind the tables. A very shiny dark-wood hulk of a bar ran the whole length of the room, black-topped old-fashioned swivel stools marched along its length. Behind the bar rose the usual mirrored wall with glass shelves filled with the requisite assortment of coloured bottles. A hall ran into darkness in the middle of the back wall.

Alan and Spence took one of the booths and waited for the waitress who was kidding around with a couple of guys who looked like truckers. They were probably bikers of some sort, Alan thought, as he watched them. The leather jackets bore no insignia, just a crest he didn't recognize.

Spence was about to get up and grab the waitress when she turned and ambled over. She was easily in her forties and obviously tired, but her uniform was neat, clean, and wrinkle free. It made a swishy sound as she walked. She dropped a couple of menus on the table and asked, "What can I bring yous?"

"The coffee fresh?" Spence asked

"I'll make fresh, you don't want stuff's been sittin' around. Check the menu and I'll get at it. Cream?"

Both Spence and Alan shook their heads. "Just black is fine."

With another swish of nylon, the waitress turned, made a beeline for the kitchen pass-through, and shouted, "Hey Joe, make a pot will ya?"

She returned to the trucker-bikers and flirted some more. Alan watched her. She kept her eye on the booth in between laughs. There was no one else in the place.

At the sound of a bell, she turned toward the pass-through, picked up the pot, ran a finger through a couple of mug handles on a shelf below the opening, and approached their booth.

She set the mugs on the table, poured, and looked questioningly at Spence who took a sip of the hot coffee and nodded, "I'd like a burger and fries, side salad if you've got one, and more of this."

"Dressing?"

"Whatever you've got. Maybe blue cheese?" The waitress nodded and turned to Alan.

"Double that, skip the salad and add some pie, apple if you've got it. And more of this as well. Good coffee. Thanks."

While they waited for their orders, they sat quietly, sipped, and relaxed. It'd been a long, frustrating day, and they felt pretty much used up.

Alan loved to watch Spence when she was quiet. She was such a feisty, impatient, beautiful slip of a girl. A very generous slip, he thought, and she did things to him, even more since they'd been living in the apartment. Right now, she was like a damped fire, a bundle of curled up, sleepy energy. He felt a warmth spreading through him and he smiled. He was content just to be near her.

When another ding sounded, the waitress left the guys at the bar and picked up the food, plates balanced along one arm, the other hand brandishing the coffee pot. She slid the plates onto the table, refilled the cups, smiled at them both, and sauntered back to the now empty bar.

After the first bite, both Spence and Alan realized they were very hungry. They finished quickly and sipped their coffee. While they were eating their burgers and fries, the waitress had appeared with the pie, slipped the bill on the table, and added coffee to their cups. She returned to the bar and the barkeep who was washing the last of the night's glasses.

Spence took a final sip of her coffee, smiled at Alan, stretched her arms above her head, and let out a long sigh. She pointed at the plate with the bit of top crust sitting on the edge. "If you're done with that, let's go home."

As Alan was paying the barkeep, the kitchen went dark, and the waitress began stacking chairs on the tables. He returned the change, then followed them to the door, pulled it open, and said, "Have a good night, you two, come back anytime." Alan heard the door lock click behind them.

"Bit of a bum's rush, wasn't it? How the hell late is it anyway?"

Alan looked up at the night sky. "At least one or so."

"How can you tell from that?" Spence looked up at a dark, silvery grey sky, city lights bouncing off the night's cloud layer.

"Internal clock. Don't need the sky really."

"Horseshit!" Spence punched the stoplight button a few times, ignored the red, and started across. Alan watched her go, shook his head in pleasure, and followed her to the car.

Spence backed the Camaro around the corner into Powell, saw the light change, and gunned it up the street. Alan saw a street sign flash by and realized that Powell had already changed into Dundas. At the intersection, Spence took Nanaimo up toward Hastings, and two other rights took them home into the alley behind their building.

Alan turned toward her. She smiled at him, ran her hand down the side of his face.

"Let's go up. Lemme get the bathroom first okay? Won't be long. Then you can join me if you'd like."

"Like, very much like. Let's go."

"Don't get carried away, it's just a bathroom."

"Yeah, but it's your bathroom."

Alan opened his door, walked around the car, and opened hers. Spence sat a moment, looked up at him, and sighed. "Sometimes, you get so eager it's frightening. All right, let's go."

The stairs were steep to accommodate the porch floors, and they were breathing hard when they reached the top. She dropped her bag on a kitchen chair, flipped on the lights, and headed for the bathroom. "Gimme two, then come in."

She shed clothes as she went, and by the time she'd reached the bathroom, there wasn't much left to get rid of.

Alan watched her go, kicked off his shoes, slipped off is tie, looked at the clock, measured off three or four minutes. He went into the bathroom himself, the door partly open, steam curling out along the ceiling. He could hear the blast of hot water running in the shower. Alan slid back the curtain and stepped into the cloud.

By the time the water shut off, the hall ceiling and walls were damp, the bathroom itself dripping. Alan and Spence were wrapped in one of the big beach towels they kept for showers, and there was movement under it that had little to do with drying. Finally, Spence slid out one end and walked slowly toward the door. She glanced back at Alan and said, "Don't say a thing, you, not a thing."

"I can admire quietly if you like, but my god that's a beautiful ass."

"You're so full of shit, you know, but I sort of like it every now and then."

Spence disappeared around the door, and Alan heard her bedroom door open. He didn't hear it close.

32.

When her phone rang at five a.m., they both reached out, Alan to air, Spence to where her phone sat on an end table. "Wha? Shit! When? Give us twenty, we'll take Second Narrows and meet you at Main."

Alan sat up, wiping his eyes. "What?"

"He came back. Drones picked him up. Get up, we gotta move." They both threw on the clothes they'd dropped a few hours before, hit the stairs, and were out of the alley in minutes.

Spence floored the Camaro down Nanaimo, blew an orange at Dundas, and took the sharp turn onto McGill too fast. She heard the rear end scrape the yellow cement safety blocks before she pulled the car back into the turn and rocketed down McGill to the long curve that fed onto Highway 1. She slowed slightly, was still too fast, and felt the rear end jittering again.

She powered up the bridge incline, hurtled over the top, the car lifting slightly, and ran down the far side. She slowed for Main at the bottom of the bridge, swerved right, and pulled over. One cruiser sat on the shoulder, engine running. Spence could see another coming fast and quiet. Otherwise it was strangely silent.

In the Gastown apartment two cell phones went off together. Sabina stuffed her pillow over her head with one hand, reached out with the other, found her cell, and pitched it across the room. Harry sat up abruptly, reached for his, and answered.

"Wha?"

"What? When?"

"Shit! Wake up S, we gotta go, now!"

Sabina burrowed more deeply under the pillow, and Harry slapped her ass. She yelped, threw the pillow at him, and slid out of her side of the bed. Muttering curses, she plodded naked to the bathroom and slammed the door.

Harry slid on his pants and yelled, "We gotta go, Sweets. No shower. Somebody tripped the drones."

It took a few minutes, but in ten, they were on their way down the stairs and out the back door. Sabina unlocked the shed, pushed out the red Yamaha, threw a helmet at Harry, and kicked it to life.

She went down a block to Powell like any ordinary person, then let out a yell and hit the throttle. The front wheel lifted, slammed down hard, and she was gone, the bike's high-pitched roar racing them down Powell, passing Clark to Commercial.

A red there slowed her down slightly, then she was off again. She blew through the Victoria light and the next, made the turn at Nanaimo on a yellow, took the curve onto McGill, the bike almost horizontal. She straightened, gave the bike its head, flew around the long, lazy curve onto Highway 1, belting it up over the Second Narrows bridge. She braked hard at Main and slid to the side of the road behind the red Camaro, a cloud of dust sliding up the side of the car.

Harry was off before she could park the bike and leaned in the window on Alan's side of the car.

"Anybody on the river yet?"

"Jake and Larry. They parked a street over out of sight. They walked to the river across backyards. The cruiser's got 'em on a remote, we've got one, and here's one for you. It's a discrete channel nobody's on but us. We gotta move the cars over to theirs when they tell us. Leave the bike. Too noisy."

"Speaking of noise, those guys are gonna know something's going on." Harry looked up. "Highway 1 blocked? It's so quiet it's freaky. They'll be long gone."

"Apparently, that's the plan. Block everything, force 'em to run. They got nowhere to go. Then the troops tighten the noose until they're isolated. Everybody's armed."

Sabina joined Harry and asked, "Where're the blocks on the highway?"

"One's at the Hastings cut-off, just before the tunnel. Routing everybody up to Hastings and through town over to the big bridge. The others are up the big hill and at Taylor Way where they're turning everybody down to the Lion's Gate. Every other exit's blocked by cruisers."

Harry's secure mobile vibrated.

Spence grabbed hers, listened, then started the Camaro and yelled, "We're on, guys. Get in the back. We're joining Jake and Larry's SUV. This thing's got a map, a Google app. Or try Waze."

The car was throaty. Spence drove through the residential area a lot more slowly than she would have liked. She'd barely parked on Dollarton when they got the sign.

She floored it to the Seymour Highway, hung a left, then a right on Keith. She searched the side streets until she saw the big black SUV on Orwell. She idled up the block, slid in behind it, and killed the motor.

The silence was deafening.

"Any chance to get out and stretch? It's like a sardine can in here."

"We're supposed to wait. That's what the remote's for, to let us know when to move. But feel free to get out anytime." Spence rolled her eyes. Alan caught it, smiled, nudged her, and got a grunt in return.

Sabina swivelled, stuck her feet out the window, and dropped her head on Harry's lap. "It's comfy enough in here if you get a bit inventive."

Spence squirmed, muttered "Jesus!", and drummed her fingers on the steering wheel.

The call came at 6:03. Every remote in every car vibrated. On the screen was one word: "GO!"

The four in the Camaro heard sirens start up everywhere, so Spence started up as well.

"What the hell does "go" mean? Where the hell is it?"

"Head for the river, let's get over there fast."

Alan buckled up and leaned forward just as Spence rammed the car into gear and peeled out.

Orwell Street, where she'd parked behind the SUV, dead-ended a few houses down. Spence did a 360, tires screaming, rubber hammering the road, and took off back the way she'd come.

The turn onto Keith was sharp and Spence took it too fast, lost the back end, recovered, and shot up Keith to the St. Denis turn, which was gentler. Still, she took this one too fast too and had to manhandle the Camaro all the way down the short block to the end of the pavement. She didn't stop there. She shot around the steel post and rammed the car up the path, sliding in beside the big logs where the catering truck had been.

Dust roiled around the car and drifted on up the wide path, a ground level fog of dirt. Spence spilled out her side of the car, Alan right behind her from his.

Sabina still had one foot out the window and was trying to get it in and peel herself off Harry's lap. Harry had lunged for the door on his side but couldn't get out from under Sabina. He'd gotten the door open, and as Sabina disentangled herself from the car, managed to throw himself out on all fours.

They grouped together by the great logs and looked around. There was nothing: no Jake, no Larry, no anything.

Sirens sounded everywhere but upriver. "Shit! What now?"

"They must have cut back through the yards to the truck. Let's get back there. Go! I'll call."

Harry grabbed his cell as the four of them threw themselves into the Camaro. He tried to reach Jake. Two remotes went off at the same time. Sabina grabbed hers.

"What the hell do I do with this thing?"

"Black button on the side. Push it, talk, and let go."

Alan leaned into his door as Spence took the corner onto Keith. He hung on hard.

Spence slowed at Orwell. "Nothin' down there. SUVs gone. I'm headin' back."

Sabina had opened her mouth and was about to push the button Alan had indicated when Jake's voice came over the intercom.

"I see him! Big pickup, black, looks like he's takin' 1. He's on the Highway makin' for the turnoff. I'm in pursuit. Oh crap, he's really fast!"

"Shit! I'm goin' back." Spence floored the Camero, tore down Keith, took the one-way circle around the Holiday Inn the wrong way, hit Mount Seymore, rocketed down to Riverside, and did lose it when she got to Main. The Camaro spun out on the shoulder and braked hard at Sabina's bike.

The remote squawked again. "Got 'im boxed. He's gonna take the feed to Fern. He'll try for Lillooet Road, but it's closed.

Cruisers coverin' both lanes. I'm on 'im."

"I know where that is. I need the bike. Lemme out! Damn it, Harry. Lemme out!"

"I'm comin' with you!" Harry yelled. But Sabina didn't wait. Either she didn't hear over the roar of the bike as she kick-started, or she ignored him. She left Harry beside the Camaro, flipped the bike sideways to avoid bombing him with gravel, and took off back up Main to Riverside, made the turn, and disappeared.

Harry could hear the bike revving, hitting high, downshifting for a turn, and she was gone.

"Holy shit!" Jake's voice came over the intercom. "He creamed a cruiser. He's comin' back! Watch it, watch it, he's by both of us. Somebody get on 'im. I'm comin' round."

"He's gonna try to cross, can't do it, guard rail's too high, he's comin' east, wrong side, he'll try for Main. He's past Main, he's gonna try for the feed onto the bridge," yelled Jake.

"Harry get in! He's comin' right here. We'll be on him like poop on a blanket. Get the hell in!"

Harry threw himself into the back seat. The Camaro took off, throwing crap from the shoulder and leaving rubber. Spence hit the east-bound lanes just as the pickup streaked by. She followed close. She was on him, but the pickup slowed and turned, rear end snaking across the lanes. He made the edge of the feeder road and was gone.

Spence missed it, going too fast to make any kind of turn. She hit the brakes, spun hard, and clipped the high curb on the bridge approach. She fought for control, the Camaro slipping sideways toward the feeder. She made the curving two-lane and accelerated.

Main Street was empty, the pickup gone. Spence hit the brakes, listened for the truck's engine, heard it west of her, up the grade near Bridgman Park.

Two cruisers coming fast roared down the feeder. The first swerved around the Camaro, braked hard, turned, and careened up Mountain. The second cruiser caught the side of the Camaro, the jolt sending both cars off the road, the cruiser into a ditch and the Camaro up on the divide and into a pole. Air bags exploded before either had come to rest.

Alan and Spence fought their way out of the passenger side door, shaken but unhurt. Harry crawled out of the rear, his head covered in blood.

"I'm alright, I'm alright, who hit us?" He struggled to his feet wiping his eyes. Alan reached for him, pulling a handkerchief out of his back pocket. Harry brushed it away.

"It's nothing, nothing. Cut my head on the seat bracket after I got free of the airbag."

Harry looked around. Spence was across the road helping the cop out of the cruiser.

"Nobody hurt much, then, we good to go?" Harry looked at the battered side and front of the Camaro. "Guess not, shit."

Alan wiped the side of Harry's face and Harry let him. "It's not too bad, maybe need a couple of stiches. Up near the hairline. Here, hold this, it'll help stem the bleeding at least. Head cuts always bleed."

Spence and the cruiser cop were about to cross the road when the black SUV pulled up behind the Camaro. Larry stuck his head out. "We heard the crash, cruiser had his mike open. Everybody okay?"

"Good to go, all of us. Where'd the truck get to?" Alan answered. Spence walked up to Larry's door. "Camaro's a mess. I'll get it later. Let's move."

We got 'em trapped, sort of. Truck's way up Lillooet, along Lynn Canyon Park, probably up near the suspension bridge. Cruisers're on their way up Lillooet, but it's slow with those damned speed bumps every hundred yards. That pair can't go anywhere. We got cruisers comin' up Lynn Valley Road on the far side. They'll go all the way to the Lynn headwaters in the park. We'll have 'em boxed."

Larry leaned out the passenger window, looked at the three men getting in the SUV. "Jesus, Harry, what the hell happened to you? You all right?"

Harry took the blood-soaked cloth away from his head and nodded. Larry smiled. "Okay, get in. We're gonna follow Lillooet up this side and find that truck."

Spence and Alan got in and then Harry and the constable got in the back. Harry leaned over the back of the seat in front of him between Alan and Spence. "Any of your guys see Sabina? She's on that damned bike, took off up Riverside aimin' for the truck, must have at least made it up the side of the park."

Larry leaned over the seatback, looked past Alan, and glared at Harry: "You two were supposed to keep a low profile, very low, so what the hell's she doing goin' after these guys? Look, we've been focussed on that truck. Reports say one occupant, not two, so we got problems. One of them may be loose. I'll check on the bike, but it's not a priority right now!"

Larry was angry, and Harry knew he had a right to be. Last time they'd been involved, it'd cost Spence and Alan big time. The brass did not like privates mixing with their officers. He hoped this wasn't a repeat. The brass were also onto every move the task force made; they'd be right on top of this chase. Every cruiser had video, all of it available. And the media would love it. There were enough leaks to guarantee they'd know about it."

Harry took the cloth away from his head carefully and waited a bit. No more blood ran down his face.

He turned to look at Larry who said, "Okay, none of the chase cruisers has seen the bike. I talked to one makin' the turn onto Lillooet, he hasn't seen her. And nobody on Lynn Valley Road has seen her either. Good, we're maybe gonna be alright. She's a smart girl. She'll know to keep low. We're goin' up there now, so we'll meet up somehow. Relax, Harry, she's alright."

By now, the SUV had left the best part of the street and was on the long narrow road up the side of the park, flying over the speed bumps and setting down hard. Jake was aiming for the dead end farther up past the suspension bridge.

Alan and Spence braced themselves and sat quietly, Alan holding on to the strap above the door, feet braced against the SUV's speed. Spence grinned and watched Jake maneuver the big SUV. Harry still dabbed at his head. The constable just sat.

Ahead at the suspension bridge, two cruisers were nosed in, light bars flashing, with the uniforms gathered around bridge entrance.

Jake slowed long enough to see that all they were doing was guarding against the possibility the perps would try to cross there, even though the pickup had long passed the place. What logic there was in that escaped them all.

Harry craned his head looking for the bike and Sabina.

The constable simply sat.

Jake accelerated and barrelled by, making for the road end. Something glinted through the trees, he thought. Chrome, maybe, from a big black pickup. He hit the gas, hit a few more bumps, and slid into the parking lot at the road's end. No pickups, just a few SUVs and sedans.

33.

Vic's pickup had very little damage given the mess it had made of two cruisers. The fenders were a bit buckled, but the heavy grille bars on the front had saved the rad and engine. He had left the chase cruisers behind easily, saw that he couldn't climb the cement safety divider on Highway 1, passed the Main Street turnoff, then hit the Second Narrows bridge.

He slammed the big truck around and ran the wrong way down the bridge approach road onto Main. There he sped up Mountain, turned on Fern, and powered up Lillooet. He flew over the speed bumps, came down hard each time, fought for control, and kept the accelerator floored. He was belted in, but he still had trouble as he bounced around.

He heard a roar but couldn't see anything. He concentrated on the road. Then he saw a flash of red, high up on his right on a path that paralleled the road. The bike shot ahead at times, dropped back at others.

Vic glanced over as often as he could. The damn thing was pacing him. He had an idea who it was; he knew it wasn't any cop. It's gotta be her, he thought, grinning to himself, it's gotta be the bitch detective. He muttered, "Oh god, let it be her, let it be the bitch. I need it to be her. In the bush she's mine, take my time with her. It's gotta be her!"

As he hit the last of the bumps, he slammed the truck around the curve and saw the parking lot ahead. He hooked a sharp left, took some blacktop down to a park building, and plowed through a restriction gate, hitting the gravel path that led to the head waters of the Lynn.

He could hear the bike. "Still comin'," he thought. "Good. I'll take her into the mountains, trap her there." His mind buzzing with the idea, he took the last hill too fast and slid down towards the bridge.

Vic hit the brakes. He felt the rear slip sideways. He pointed the front end toward the trail leading into the mountains and hit the gas. Gravel spewed from the fishtailing back end as the oversize tires caught.

The front grille bars hit the eight-by-eight cross beam blocking access to the trail. The grille hit hard. Instead of splintering wood as he expected, the truck's big bars slammed back into post. The truck bucked, tail end whipping up, then coming down hard. The engine stalled. All the air bags blew.

Vic couldn't believe it. He'd already taken out a couple of these things with no trouble.

He unbuckled, wormed his way out of the truck, dusted off the air bag powder, spit, and walked around the barricade. It wasn't level anymore. It canted backwards, and there were splinters in the crossbeam itself, but it had held.

Then he saw why. The damn thing had been reinforced with large quarter-inch-thick steel plates. He cursed, turned, saw a party of three Asians on the bridge looking at him. He realized that he couldn't hear the bike anymore.

Then he caught the sound of sirens screaming. They were close and coming fast. He turned and ran up the trail toward the mountains. This was a popular hiking area, but he saw no one ahead of him.

"If the bitch follows, I'll lead her into the bush", he thought. He ran faster.

Sabina had been close behind the truck all the way and had kept pushing the bike hard. She'd had some trouble at the parking lot when the path suddenly turned down toward the road. She took out a bit of fence, slid into the ditch, and hurt her knee. But she'd made it.

Now she roared down the black top, missed the bits of gate the truck had hammered through, and hit the trail not that far behind him.

The dust was a problem. She couldn't avoid it, and there was no way she could take the bike off the trail. Too much stuff in the way, one side damn near straight down, the other straight up. As long as the trail stayed reasonably straight, she thought, she'd be okay.

She heard the crash even over the bike's roar. She cut her engine, coasting down a long grade. When the bike stopped, she heard nothing but cooling pings of engine parts and the hiss of escaping steam from the truck.

She got off the bike, stashed her helmet, and worked her way through the bush above the trail.

When she reached the top of the hill, she stopped, braced herself against a big spruce, slid forward and glanced down. The truck was rammed into a crossbar, the front pushed in, the grille pushed back. Looked like the bags had exploded. She watched carefully. There was no one, no movement. No one near the truck, no one on the bridge.

She could hear the scream of sirens and then saw one cruiser ripping up the grass toward the bridge. The driver managed a skid that threw turf around like buckshot and missed the bridge by inches.

Two uniforms got out but neither one approached the truck. They were waiting for backup, she thought, safety in numbers. So where was he?

Up the trail or down the river? Up gave him miles of bush and steep cliffs. Down gave him more bush, but a difficult crossing even if the water was shallow, and a lot of cops. It had to be up, she thought. Sabina knew she had to get on that trail without being spotted. If those cops saw her, they'd stop her. She mumbled, "I gotta get that bastard!"

Sabina made her way down the slope, slicing away from the beginning of the trail, moving back into the bush and trying for the trail farther up. It wasn't easy going. Her knee will still sore, but at least she was dressed right. Her dark pants were tight enough, and her top was long-sleeved and dark. Cycle gear was perfect for bush like this.

She slid down a steep, dry, eroded part of the incline she was working her way across. She ended the slide against a large chunk of rock, slid around the edge, and worked her way down to the trail. She was up far enough to be invisible from the bridge and far behind her quarry. She also knew he wouldn't stay anywhere near the trail, that he'd head inland into the mountains.

Sabina stopped suddenly, just on the verge of thick bush. She knew the trail was easy for hikers, but only for a few yards. After that, it was either damn near straight up a mountain side or up the deep ravine cut by the river. And that ravine, she knew, was nothing more than a large dent in the side of yet another mountain. It was steep and dangerous. There were debris chutes all over the place. Then, too, there were other trails branching off. The Lynn peak route was the closest, and that would take him up about a thousand feet. If he kept going another four hundred feet, he'd reach the needles. But he'd need gear, and he had nothing. So maybe not that way.

If he reached the third debris chute, he could cross the river, work his way up Kennedy Creek to the lake. The lake watershed area was restricted, no one allowed in, so that would suit him. And it was close to Grouse Mountain. If he went that way, he'd have a chance to get out. That's what I'd do, she thought.

Sabina decided on the Kennedy trail and started up that way. Then she realized she had no water. But neither did he, she thought, so it'll be the river and the creek.

She ran hard toward the debris fields on the trail. The river was over to her left down a steep bank covered in forest and salal. She knew that when she got as far as the river she'd have to stop. She knew the rangers were hooked into the search. Maybe copters and dogs too.

Sabina ran. This part of the trail was steep but reasonably clear. She needed to make up time. Her knee still hurt but she ran. If he crosses that damn river, he'll disappear, she thought. We know from the island that he's great in the bush. I gotta get this guy before he reaches the debris fields and the river. And before the cops. I want him for what he's done, for Kylie and Mary and the three over here. My kind of justice for this shit. No prison is brutal enough.

She ran on, alone and fearless and armed with just her knife. She saw a kind of poetic justice in taking him as he'd taken them.

Vic smiled to himself and kept pace in the bush near the trail. He could hear Sabina running, he could see flashes between the trees.

Something bothered him. He'd stop for a few moments, listening. Something raised his hackles, shivered up his skin. But then the running girl grabbed his attention again and he resumed running.

Vic had a spot etched in his mind. It was only another few yards up the trail. She'd have to slow down and take the turn around the outcropping. He touched the pouch containing the knives and the inks. He'd added the taser that morning.

Vic smiled. She'd give him great pleasure. She had power, and he'd absorb it all. He'd be sure to leave her face so Harry'd recognize her. Vic smiled again as he ran.

Three more cruisers grouped themselves around the entrance to the bridge like piglets at a sow's belly. Red and blue streaks flashed across the trees and flickered over the tips of waves in the fast-moving water upstream. The constables moved up to the bridge. They eyed the truck but didn't approach. Forensics would skin anybody who screwed up a crime scene.

Three forest rangers who were assigned to the rescue unit sat with maps at a table on the grass to the constable's left. Below the bridge, the flat area had been tailered. Fresh green grass mowed regularly and lots of picnic tables scattered about. The rangers were working out possible routes and how to cover them.

All of them, constables and rangers, turned as the big, black SUV lumbered down the hill on the trail the other side of the bridge. Jake hit the brakes as he neared the bridge and stopped just short of the ruined truck. Harry was the first out.

"Where's Sabina? Where'd she go?"

One of the cops said, "We were here before anyone else except for the driver of the truck. We haven't seen anyone, certainly no girl."

"She's not a bloody girl, she's a private detective chasing a killer, and she had to come by that truck. She was chasing it, so who the hell's seen her?"

Harry saw heads shaking. He cursed. He took off across the bridge, passed the truck, and took the trail toward the mountains, leaving Jake and Larry standing by the SUV. Nobody said anything.

One of the rangers crossed the bridge and ran to the truck and the big black SUV. He held up his map and raised his voice: "No sense just runnin' off up the trail like that. Listen to me! We know this area like the back of our hands, and we know how to stop him. If you give us a chance, we can show you."

He kept waving the paper map around above his head, and the rest of them gathered round.

Alan raised his voice above the hubbub. "First off, call in and close the park, both the main gates on the residential side and the trails on the Lillooet side. Keep the press out. Call forensics and let them know we're here and that we've taped off this site. Once you've called, get busy and tape the site off. Start up the damn hill and down to the bridge. No one gets in here. This truck's a crime scene, you guys should know that. Everybody move back to the other side of the bridge. Site's fucked up enough as it is. If you Ranger guys know how to organize a chase, tell us. Spence and I are leads here, and we'd sure like to know."

They all walked down the hill and across the bridge. Once on the grass on the far side, the ranger with the map unfolded it on one of the picnic tables and began to explain how to trap their man.

Harry ran. It wasn't easy in his suit and leather loafers. Still, he ran as fast as he could. He passed the first two debris chutes and ran for the third. He couldn't tell if Sabina had taken to the bush at some point, so he ran. There was nothing else he could do.

As he ran for the third debris chute, his left foot caught on something on the trail. He fell heavily and lay winded for a minute. He got up slowly and studied the area around him.

He saw the vines that had been tied to the trunks of young trees on either side of the trail.

His heart sank as he realized that the vine rope had been for Sabina. He must have her. "A fucking vine rope," he mumbled. "Shit."

Harry studied the edge of the trail near the vines and saw where Sabina had been dragged into the bush. He followed but soon lost the trail.

He remembered how on the island these guys never left a sign. No one could ever find how they had gotten in and out from anywhere. Never a trace, not even at the dump sites.

Harry's heart raced. He made himself stand very still.

Maybe Sabina would make a noise, give him something to follow. She couldn't be far. There hadn't been enough time.

He took a few more steps, stopped again and listened. He could hear the breeze slipping through the trees. He could hear the susurrations of the river. He could hear distant voices. Over it all, the immense silence of the forest hung on the air. His heart hammered.

Then there was something close, something like a low murmur, maybe a groan. He listened hard for a similar sound. Then he heard it again, soft and low-pitched.

Suddenly he knew that Sabina'd been hurt by that madman. That was her he'd heard, he was sure of it. She was alive! Thank god! She was alive!

He pushed his way through the bush, stopping every few steps, listening. She's alive and she's close. He kept moving, stopping, listening.

From less than thirty feet away, Vic watched him.

He'd find her. Vic had made sure of that. He'd left enough sign for anyone to follow, even someone as clumsy and thick as that guy was. He needed Harry to find her. And watch her die. He'd left her breathing still, if only for a while.

Vic smiled as he watched Harry search. He wanted to see Harry's face when he found her, steep himself in the pleasure. Savour it. Because they deserved it. She'd stolen his home, driven them off the island. And then she'd poisoned them, turned their union black and dangerous, a cancer metastasizing until Vic had cut it out to survive.

ENDGAME

She'd killed them. Had forced Vic to leave the remains of his brother in the forest that was his home, in a pit like the ones they'd grown together in.

Harry'll find her, he thought. Then he'll know what it feels like to lose yourself.

After that he'd move on across the river to the Kennedy Lake Watershed, a no-entry reserve where he'd lose the pursuit. Then he'd move toward Grouse Mountain and the road out.

The rangers had briefed the group and had established their approach. They'd mount a pincher movement, one arm moving in from Grouse Mountain, the other sweeping up the river and bracketing the Kennedy Reserve. Then it'd just be a matter of closing the jaws until they'd force him out. The rangers believed there was no other way for him to go. The hiking paths led only into the mountains. The elevations were high, the cliffs steep, the cover scanty in the higher reaches. After the Seymour Valley Trailway, which they had fully covered already, there was nothing but forest. If he cut south, there was only Indian Arm, a body of water that shot up into the land and cut him off.

The ranger explained that even a qualified woodsman could not make it over The Needles or Coliseum or Burwell mountains, not without serious gear which they knew he didn't have. So, he'd choose the Kennedy Lake Watershed, a restricted reserve, and Grouse Mountain. Crews were already in place at Grouse and were moving toward the Reserve. Their crew would head upriver, then curve in toward Kennedy.

The head ranger looked at Jake and Larry, Alan and Spence, and said: "You four'll have to wait here. You've got nothing with you, and we haven't any gear to spare. They're flyin' drones high over the river and the Reserve, and they're equipped with serious cameras. The monitoring point is setting up here in the park. The chief'll soon be joining you. Stay here and you'll see everything we do. Okay, guys let's move."

Harry stood still. He'd heard nothing for the last few minutes. He made himself stand and listen even though he was shaking with the urge to run and find her.

He tried to control his breathing, so he could hear better. Nothing. He wasn't sure that what he'd heard before was human.

He was shaking with fear.

Then there it was again. A low sound, almost a murmur. But it wasn't natural. Harry pivoted, listened, and pushed through the bush to his right.

In a slight, concave hollow in the forest floor lay Sabina, her body clothed only in panties, her center nothing but red. On her shoulder were the familiar blue-green marks, but this time, there were no symbols, only streaks as if the killer had had neither time nor interest in careful calligraphy. The whole scene was a mockery of the other deaths. It was as if he were saving this one was just for Harry.

Harry dropped to her side, his eyes riveted to her face. The low moaning continued.

He couldn't breathe.

He snatched up his cell and hit 911. Thank god there was coverage and the answer was swift.

He gave his location, gave the operator body and blood details and was told help was on its way, to stay on the line. Harry brushed hair away from her face, kissed her mouth, and steeled himself to look at the damage. He moaned; tears streamed down his face. She'd been cut from pubis to sternum, skin parted, intestines gleaming and strung about on her panties, some still partly in the body cavity. Blood was pooling everywhere.

Harry screamed, "You son of a bitch! I'll find you! No fucking way you live! You hear me! I know you're out there, I can smell you, you bastard!"

Harry stopped, breathless. Suddenly he remembered the closed-circuit mobile in his pocket and yanked it out.

"Anyone, just answer, anyone. I've…"

The voice on the mobile cut through Harry's yelling. "Who is this and where are you?"

"Harry. Get me Alan or Spence. Hurry! I've got a girl badly wounded by that bastard. We've gotta get her out fast. She's still alive, needs a medic now!"

"Harry, Alan. Where are you? Is it Sabina?"

"He got her, Alan. She's bad. We're thirty meters in the

ENDGAME

bush, off the path just before the third debris chute. There's a huge rock you gotta go around. You'll see a bunch of vines on the path where that bastard set a trip. She's bad, Alan. Really bad. We have to get her out now!"

"Hang on, Harry. We have a big four-wheel ATV on the trail past the gate. Paramedic's ready to go. Hang on."

Harry tossed the mobile on the ground. He stroked Sabina's forehead. "You'll be okay, my love. I'll make sure. Everything's going to be fine. You'll see. I'll never leave you." He choked, trying to fight the tears and keep his voice soft and smooth.

The futility of it all threatened to undo him. She couldn't die, he thought, she couldn't. Harry raised his head and howled in anguish. Then the tears came hard.

Vic watched it all, smiling, a sweet pleasure filling him.

He shivered with pleasure. He could almost feel her power crossing to him. She was close, and her soul would pass soon. Her power would course through him. He'd be complete then. And more powerful than ever before.

Vic listened to Harry pleading, whispering empty promises to her. Then he moved off quietly into the bush, heading for the river and the Reserve.

Harry heard the ATV roaring up the hiking path, heard it brake at the rock, heard the engine shut off. He heard the yells of the crew. He stood up and hollered "Help" again and again until he got a yell back.

Two medics burst through the surrounding bush and knelt quickly beside Sabina. Harry stepped back. He heard one medic say, "Jesus, she's been gutted. Christ, get a drip in, I'll call it in."

He heard the call go through, the urgency in the medic's voice. Then he saw Alan pushing his way into the little clearing.

"Harry, my god!" He touched Harry's shoulder.

Right behind Alan came two more medics, a stretcher between them. They flipped it open and conferred with the two on the ground.

Alan led Harry away, back toward the trail.

"They're the best, Harry, let them do what they have to. Give' em room to get her out."

"I'll kill that fucker, I'll kill him. That bastard, he was there, you know, he was there watching. I know it, he was there, that prick. He was close. I'm goin' after him."

Harry turned and started back. Alan grabbed for him and missed. "Oh god, what he did, my poor girl, what he did, a profanity. I'll kill him! He doesn't get to be captured, promise me, Alan! He gets what he's done. He gets what he's fucking done!"

Harry tore through the bush, back to Sabina and the medics. They had her on the stretcher now, one of them in contact with the hospital relaying vitals, taking direction. The four pushed past Harry, ordered him out of the way, shouldered him aside. They were running now, as much as that were possible, the stretcher bucking dangerously at times.

Alan reached him and tried to talk him down. Harry wasn't listening. He wanted to give chase and kill the bastard. And he wanted to go with Sabina. He shook with anger, a steady low-pitched growl sliding from his mouth. He was beyond reason.

Alan remembered how he had felt when his sister had been attacked years ago. He didn't hesitate. He tackled Harry, took him down, held him, and said over and over, "You can't go after him. You can't go after him, you know that. You can't. We'll get him, we will."

Slowly Harry's struggles became less severe. Then he began to cry. Alan held him, just held him. There was nothing to say, no words that meant anything. He knew where Harry was, helpless, enraged, hurt beyond pain.

He keyed his mobile, ordered a forensics crew to the scene, and gave directions. Then Alan led Harry away, his arm under Harry's shoulders, leading him to the trail, whispering platitudes: "She's a strong girl, she'll be okay, she's got the best help, we'll get him Harry, I promise you, we'll get him."

Vic crossed the river easily. He'd seen the drones high above the river's bed and knew he had been seen. But he didn't care. He had the power, the strength from that bitch. Nothing could stop him.

He smiled, pleasure rippling through him. He ran. He moved into the Reserve quickly, like a flickering shadow, like a phantom. He was in ecstasy.

When a sharp weapon hit him, he felt no pain. When he felt a thud of a short spear in his chest, saw his blood streaming down, he was fascinated by the flow. He stopped walking. That was the last time he moved. He could hear and feel the impacts in his flesh, his thighs and his groin. Swarms of them. One hit his left eye, another buried itself in his open mouth. Vic slid down quietly, sat on his thighs on the forest floor, then his head slowly dropped, and he toppled forward.

34.

The ranger, who was one of the two who led the crews, glared at the chief of police. "We've been at this all day. We covered and recovered the area after we followed him across with the drones. We know he's in there, we know that, and he's not getting out. But we haven't found him yet, and the light's fading now, the crews are tired. Replacements have arrived at Grouse and here at the headwaters. We'll hold until morning. He can't get out, no way. He's boxed. We'll get him in the morning."

Jake and Larry were with the chief along with Alan and Spence, the leads in the murders. Around midday, Brian had Herk and Gordie driven to the site to join the four principals and get caught up. So they all stood around when they'd all rather have been in the bush looking for the killer.

Alan and Spence felt they should be at Vancouver General with Harry, but they were stuck in the middle of this mess, trying to placate both the brass and the crews and failing miserably at both. Herk and Gordie simply watched, amused at the bickering. Everyone else was angry; everyone pointed a finger; nobody listened. It was a typical task force fuck up.

While they were all arguing with each other, a cruiser slid onto the grass near the monitors, and a constable approached the group. "We got press comin' out of our..." He saw the chief. "We got press bunched up at the park entrance. They want info and they want in. We hold or what?"

"Press officer'll go down with you, give 'em what we've got, which ain't much!" The chief glared at the ranger, then turned to the constable, "You keep 'em there, all of 'em. Who you got anyway?"

"Looks like everybody. I only saw the vans: CBC, the Sun, Global, CTV, but there're loads more. They're backed up on the street far as you can see. Copters are overhead, you can hear 'em."

"Press rep's got a prepared statement for them. And I'll talk to them in the morning."

The chief turned his back and looked up at the sky. The press officer handed a sheaf of papers to the constable. "Get these out to everybody. You got enough people to do that. I'll ride to the entrance with you. See what's goin' on".

Everybody watched them go. Nobody said anything. Rotor noise from the copters floated around overhead slicing up the silence.

"Can't we get those damn things out of here?"

"I'll phone it in, Chief, threaten charges, see if we can get them to move. Free press an' all, though, probably tell us to shove it."

"Fuck 'em. They interfere with this investigation, and they are, charges'll stick. Get 'em outta here and keep 'em out."

The chief turned abruptly and marched to his limo. The chauffeur turned the black Crown Vic around, cleared the grouped cruisers, and headed slowly out.

The police captain the chief had spoken to spent some fruitless minutes yelling on the phone, sighed heavily, and shook his head. "Ain't gonna happen, not from here anyway. Big guy'll call in some favours. Watch, they'll be gone, at least from overhead. He's gonna be royally pissed once he reaches the press mess and has to bull his way through, so he'll make the copters pay, you watch."

And they did. Gordie and Herk got themselves some coffee, sat at a picnic bench with Jake and Larry and listened while the two detectives from Vancouver homicide explained the operation and filled them in on events so far, including Sabina's injuries.

"You got sixty or so guys out there in the bush looking? This is pretty rough territory looks like." Herk looked at

Jake.

"Yeah, it's rough and with only sixty or so and an area that size, chances are slim they'll find the bastard. The ranger up there talkin' to the chief says otherwise, but I think he's just coverin' his ass. It's a kind of pincher movement, so the rangers think they can find him, especially as they wade in deeper. I don't know. Hope it happens."

Gordie leaned forward, rested his coffee cup on his thigh, looked at the monitors, and shook his head. "We got pretty rough stuff up around Powell River, and we've had to try to cover that by copter. Pretty useless. But we had to do it what with the brass an' all. Here, I dunno. Doesn't seem likely to me they'll catch this guy. But those rangers know this park backwards, so maybe they're better judges. I'm just damn glad we're not out there trampin' around in that stuff."

Twenty minutes later, the copters withdrew, formed a kind of circle some distance out. A half hour later they were gone, and the night sky deepened. Stars appeared over the mountains, sparkling in the clear, black sky.

There was lots of coffee and sandwiches for the night crew. There were two food wagons in the park now and another two over near Grouse. The control group settled in, watched the monitors. The drones stayed up. Everyone except Alan and Spence, Jake and Larry, and Herk and Gordie took off.

"We're not doing any good here, won't be any forensics to speak of until morning and even then, there won't be much. We've been through both sites for what that's worth. Forensics is finished with them, and we've got what we always get with these guys: nothing. Let's head for the hospital, talk to Harry, see how Sabina's holding up." Alan looked at the others. They all nodded.

"We'll do that, then we gotta get some sleep. Be back here at daybreak wastin' more time pissin' around. Jesus! I hate task forces."

Spence stomped off toward the big SUV and waited. The others followed. Herk and Gordie decided they'd grab a cab at the hospital and head for the motel. Burnaby, Coquitlam,

Maple Ridge, and Mission all moved over when the SUV roared by.

Vancouver General sprawled along Twelfth Avenue from Oak all the way to Cambie. Larry went in on Powell to Main, then up to Twelfth. There was little traffic this time of night. Herk had already called for a taxi, and it was waiting at the emergency entrance.

Jake leaned over the front seat. "We're gonna be here a while, but we'll have to go back to the site by morning. We'll pick you up when we leave here. We can all grab a bite before we head out. At least you guys'll get a couple of hours sleep."

"Sounds good. We'll expect you early then. Restaurant's probably closed but the coffee shop's open all night. We gonna be joining the line, you think?"

Jake shook his head. "The leads are, for sure. We'll probably sit on our asses again until they find this guy. The chief won't turn up again until then, so there'll be a lot less tension. Once they have him, though, we'll all be involved."

Larry parked near the emergency entrance and Herk and Gordie climbed into their waiting taxi.

The four rushed through the doors. When they turned the corner of the long, wide hall, they saw Harry sitting on a chair off to one side. His head was down, elbows resting on his knees. He looked as miserable as it was possible to look.

Alan muttered, "That doesn't look good."

Spence pushed past, marched down the hall, sat next to Harry, and bent her head to match his. The others hesitated, then as a group, walked slowly down the hall and joined them.

"She's in surgery, she's been in there all this time. She's still in there. I can't find out anything. When I can stop her, the nurse just says she's still there. That's not good, is it? People don't walk here, they hustle all over the place, doctors, nurses, nobody even slows down. I can't get any answers. She's been in there all this time." Harry shook his head, didn't look up.

Spence with her head next to Harry's saw a tear drop hit the floor, a little wet spot between his shoes. "Harry, it's good she's still in there. It means she's getting the best care she can get. They have a lot to do, the doctors, and they need the time. She's gonna be okay, Harry, you know that, you just need to wait. We'll stay with you until she comes out."

Spence put her arm around his shoulders and tipped her head against his. "Don't cry, Harry. She's gonna make it. You gotta know she's tryin' hard. And you gotta give her that. We're all here to cheer her on. Give the docs a chance to help her."

The night crew was restless. They all knew they were spread too thin. The ranger who led them felt discouraged and tried hard to keep his crew confident and charged. It was always money, he thought, the bloody politicians slash budgets and expect miracles. He checked his watch again. Three in the morning. Pale light trickled through the great trees coating the forest floor in a patchwork of silvery grey. No colour yet, that would come later. Sunup was still distant.

He stretched, glanced along his line, shook his head, and picked up his glasses again. That son of a bitch could slip through. We've got night vision and he hasn't, but that doesn't mean much if we're too thin and can't cover ground. And if we find him, we've gotta hold him, and that won't be easy, not with this line. We could see him, raise the alarm, and still lose him. Bloody holes all over the place. And this guy's supposedly good. We're too bloody thin now. If we bunch, we leave open ends. We keep the spread, we're like a bloody sieve.

The light grew stronger, suggestions of colour began to appear. The ranger slipped the com from his pocket, made two clicks, got replies along the line, and spoke one word: "Go."

The commotion was subtle but noticeable as the line began to move. Early birdsong ceased for some moments, then began again. A nasty tell, the ranger knew. He had more than thirty men. They were good, but not that good. If the bastard heard, and he would, he'll be on the move, probably toward one end or the other. The ranger nodded to himself. He'll discover there really isn't an end, we drew both lines together top and bottom, more a circle than a pair of lines.

Moving made everyone feel a lot better. But by eight, the ranger was worried. They'd closed the circle by half and still no sighting. We should have him by now, he thought. I hope to god he didn't keep moving last night, he might already be outside. Shit!

A sharp whistle broke the silence, then another. The ranger held his breath, let it out slowly. That's it, he thought, we've got him.

He broke into a careful run, tried to avoid the worst of the forest floor, and aimed for the sound. About two hundred yards ahead of him, he saw a few of his men standing at the edge of a slight but large depression. In the center under one of the great firs, he saw something lying on the ground. As he approached, he saw that it was a body, a bloody one, surrounded by a circle of stones.

That's been staged, he thought. If this is our guy, he's been carefully laid out. Where the hell are his clothes? He's bloody naked. Who the hell could have done that and when? And where's the guy who did this? We had the place pretty much blocked.

"Don't touch anything," he said. "Everybody back off fifty feet or so and hold."

The ranger glanced up as his double appeared, raised his hand in greeting, and held up a finger while he called the leads, medics, and forensics. Then he joined his double and stood with him under a neighbouring fir and considered what had happened.

"Somebody else in here, that's for sure. I doubt they'd hang around, not with that lying there."

"That's a setup for sure and look at the damage. Jesus, there's a lot of blood. Looks like he ran into a bunch of barbed wire, he's cut all over, I mean besides that big bloody hole in his chest. That's just nasty, that is."

"We didn't hear a thing. You'd think with all that, we'd at least hear something. How could you do that amount of damage without making some noise?"

"Probably more than one too. There's too much for one guy. And why didn't our guy fight back? At least yell or something."

"No idea. But we've got him, at least I hope it's him, and he's not gonna cause any problems for us, not in that condition."

"You think? Who's gonna get blamed for his condition? We were supposed to capture the guy."

"Well, we did, it's just that he's dead, and we don't know how... Shit, you're right, we're gonna get hung out to dry."

"You think whoever these guys were, they got through our lines last night?"

"Had to, and if they did, we're gonna take the heat for that too. Shit! We had the whole place locked down, a little thin, maybe, but not that thin."

"Well, they didn't disappear like morning mist, did they, and they're not in here now, so they had to get by us. That's what the boss'll think and so will everybody else. I can take the boss's yelling and the reprimands. It's the jokes. We'll never be bloody rid of the jokes."

The two of them stood there waiting, and none too happy. It wasn't twenty minutes before they both heard somebody plowing through the bush. Two medics appeared complete with cases, and right behind them, Harvey Couch, head of forensics. Both rangers knew him from a previous body-in-the-woods incident last year.

"Rick, Don, you two on this thing?"

"Yeah, we're the leads here, but the homicide guys run the operation."

"They're on their way. My crew's comin' in. We'll mark off the site. You can clear your guys out. Anybody been near the body?"

"We looked at the body, but nobody's been closer than about ten feet. Nobody touched anything, and

"Okay, less than perfect, but at least we got ten feet clean." we backed everybody off quickly, fifty feet out at least."

"Can't blame the guys really, they damn near tripped the body. We've got over sixty men involved in this over operation, bloody lucky some of them didn't step on it."

"Okay, okay, didn't mean to cast blame. We just need to know how much contamination to expect, is all. Not blaming you guys." Harvey glanced up, saw his gang approaching, and excused himself.

"That wasn't so bad, was it? But you can see how it's gonna play, can't you." the first ranger said.

"Yeah, so it's a bit of a fuckup. At least we got him, and that's gotta count for something."

"Well, somebody got him, that's for sure. Wasn't us, though."

The two men moved off, rounded up their troops, and began the trek out. One crew went back to the Grouse Mountain staging area, the other to the bridge at the Lynn Headwaters Park.

Emergency had filled up. People were scattered all over the place, asking questions, waiting impatiently. It was a big city, and like all the other emergency rooms, this one was crowded.

Harry still sat with Spence beside him. She didn't want to leave him until he seemed a little less shaky. Jake and Larry, though, were getting restless, fidgeting in their seats, wandering around looking at art on the walls, leafing through magazines. They were driving Spence nuts.

A doctor pushed through the door, spotted Harry and came over. "You're the detective she came in with, aren't you?"

Harry looked up. "She's gonna be alright, isn't she?"

"She was in surgery a lotta hours. She's in intensive care now. I just talked to the surgeon, and he thinks maybe she'll pull through. She lost a lot of blood, and the procedures took a long time. There was a lot of damage. Between blood loss and the surgery, she's critical. You can see her, but she's in an induced coma so she has a chance to recover. Elevator's that way. Room 312." The doctor pointed down the hall and went back through the door he'd come out of.

Spence watched Harry carefully. He seemed better now that he'd learned how Sabina was, but she'd walk him up there. She glanced at Jake and Larry both of whom had been listening.

"I'll go up with him, make sure he's alright. Then we'd better get back and see how the search is going."

"I've called in a few times," Jake said, turning toward Alan. "They haven't found him yet. The crews're staying on it. Night crews've been in place for hours. Seems the press've been a bit of a nightmare, but the chief reamed them a new one. The usual press release stuff's been put out, so we're good till morning. He knows we're here, expects us back early, especially you and Spence. Brian's on top of things. Knows where we are, so all's copacetic."

Alan nodded to Spence and joined her and Harry.

"Harry, we'll get you up there, set you up with a cell. You stay with her as long as you like, okay? We'll be with you till morning, then we take off and cover the search. We'll get him, maybe not today or tonight, but we'll get him. There's nowhere he can go. He's in the Reserve somewhere. He's trapped."

Harry turned on Alan. "What he's done, you don't take him in. You know what that'll mean, delays, lawyers, court case. He doesn't get any of those. He gets what he gave, he gets what he's done. You two fix it, you can make it look good." Harry looked from Spence to Alan, shook his head. "No way you take him in."

He turned abruptly and marched down the corridor towards the elevators, Spence and Alan trailing.

Larry and Jake watched their three friends reach the elevator, watched Spence push for the car, watched the door open, and watched them disappear inside. Then Jake looked around.

"There's gotta be somewhere around here to get some rest. Too late to go home, besides we gotta stay until Alan and Spence get back. All four of us need to stay together, get back out there at first light. We can't do anything tonight anyway. Let's find a lounge or something. We gotta get some sleep."

"And some eats. Shit, it's been a full twenty-four, and I can't remember when we last ate." Larry waddled down the corridor, heading for some machines he could see in a little alcove near the elevators.

35.

Outside, morning light coated everything in a silvery grey. It was still early. Once outside the hospital doors, Larry stopped and looked up at the sky, saw dull grey clouds tinged with pale light, and said, "Gonna rain soon, that'll screw things up."

He glanced around looking for Jake, spotted him near the SUV, and hurried over.

"Don't know why you're so anxious to get back. All we'll do is stand around with whatever brass is left, and watch monitors that are already bein' watched. We gotta wait for those two anyway. And you know that when we get back, we can't do a damn thing."

All of this came out as he opened the driver's door and climbed in. He looked over at Jake. "You look pretty beat. Whyn't you grab some winks in the car while we wait for Alan and Spence. Then I'll get us back to the motel, pick up those two from up north. We can grab a quick bite and head out. I got this beast."

An hour later, Larry watched the hospital doors open.

"Here they come draggin' their asses. Must be hard for 'em to leave. Harry's a good friend of theirs and he's sure hurtin'. It'd help if we got some good news about Sabina. I'll drive over."

He started up, swung the big car around, and braked right in front of Alan and Spence. Once they were in, he revved the engine a couple of times, grinned at them, yelled, "Hold on!" and shot out of the lot.

The motel on Main was quiet this early. Larry pulled in and parked while Jake went to the office and had the clerk phone Herk and Gordie. The coffee shop off to the side of the lobby was open, the smell of fresh coffee filling the space. Jake breathed in gratefully and turned as the two northerners appeared at the door.

Behind them Larry, Alan, and Spence hustled into the lobby. They were all eating eggs and toast when the call came through. Half-finished plates and empty coffee cups were strewn across the table. The six of them ran for the car.

"Can you drop Gordie and me at the task force? We've got a lead on the girl in Hammil, and we'd like to follow it up before joining you guys. We'll pick up what we can and drive ourselves out." Herk looked a bit apologetic, but he was determined not to forget their own murder.

"I'll swing by the station. You guys hop out. Good idea if you kept on top of your girl. Maybe at least one of them'll make some sense."

Larry took a left out of the motel lot, cut across three lanes of traffic, and swung down toward the station, ignoring the multiple angry horns. He dropped Herk and Gordie and took off.

Traffic was early-morning strong, so it took Larry time to clear the city, make the run-up Highway 1, and reach Lynn Valley Road and the headwaters. Even with the grille lights on as they approached the park entrance, it took time to wade through the press vans, show their creds to the guards, and stop again at the sign in.

Larry shoved the SUV between two cruisers, killed the lights, and the four of them walked over to the monitoring station near the trees just down from the bridge. The cloud cover was now solid, the light of early morning struggling to get through. Larry looked around for the foodie, spotted the van over near the park office, and went for coffee for all of them.

Alan and Spence left the monitoring station, found an empty park bench, and sat. Jake joined them. They were all tired, but the coffee perked them up. As she usually did, Spence lifted the lid on hers and studied the contents.

"It's one of the forensics foodie trucks. Tastes okay anyway." Larry took a slurp of his coffee.

Alan's cell chimed. He listened for a few moments, ended the call, and looked at his friends. "Forensics has already gone in. We'll catch them up. They found him somewhere in the bush. He's dead. Or somebody is. The way in's posted, so let's get at it."

Alan stood, tossed his cup in the trash barrel, and started for the bridge. On it, a lone man waited, another park ranger. The four detectives joined him.

"You guys ready to go? Sign-in's been established the other side of the river. Medics and forensics went in about half an hour ago." He looked at Alan. "You can move the sign-in if you want. This way."

The trail in wasn't easy. They had a steep bank and the river to cross, then a tramp through heavy bush. The river was okay. Someone, probably a ranger, had strung a rope across, and there were enough large stones above the rapidly moving water to allow passage. But the bush was another matter. At the edge, just beyond the river's flood plain, the sign-in constable waited. Everyone signed, and Alan checked who'd already passed.

"Keep on here. Nobody else needs to be here, so keep 'em out. That means everybody except the coroner and whoever's with him."

"Forensics and the medics went up already, you're close behind. Harvey said to tell you he's got supplies up there for you."

"Good, we came straight from town."

The trail in had been carefully marked with tape tied to shrubs and trunks, so the party had few difficulties. Heavy material on the forest floor that created hazards had been moved off except for the fallen trunks of conifers, of which there were many. Those, they had to go around. The forest floor itself was another matter. It was rock-strewn and uneven, coated with the usual detritus and clumps of salal and sword fern.

Alan, who was leading the group, could see men in small groups standing around talking quietly. They were the remnants of the search parties. He approached a ranger sitting on a log and suggested he move his men back to the staging areas at Grouse mountain and the headwaters park.

Spence had gone on ahead to the beginnings of the crime scene where she identified herself and Alan to another sign-in constable.

"Spence Riley. And my partner is Alan Kim. We're the leads on this case."

She flipped open her credentials, looked back, and pointed at Alan. "That's Alan Kim. Harvey's obviously still in there. I can see him. And I can see the techs and the collection site. But we need to get in there ourselves, and we need to do it before the coroner gets here. Any idea when Harvey'll be done?"

"No ma'am. He's been in there about a half hour though. If you'll sign in, you can talk to one of the techs."

Spence could see the marked path from the collection tent up to the center of the depression. She skirted the site, and walked over to the collection tent, careful not to disturb the path the techs used. She'd get her booties later. Right now, she needed to know when they'd be able to study the body. Maybe it was their guy. But the way the body was displayed, it was probably someone the psycho had murdered. If that were the case, she thought, their killer was long gone.

This was a restricted area, so it probably wouldn't be some hiker or camper who strayed. The Reserve was well posted. It'd have to be a deliberate act, coming in here. And if it was their guy, as unlikely as that seemed, who the hell had gotten him and arranged him like that? Bloody strange.

"Spence Riley, I'm one of the leads here." She didn't know this tech, so she showed him her ID. "Any idea who that is in there? Any idea when we can get in ourselves? Sorry, I should have said. That's Alan Kim, my partner." She turned and pointed to Alan. "We've been chasing this guy a long time. Two murders that we know of on the island and three here. So we're a bit anxious to see what's over there."

"Ted Green." He pointed to himself and smiled. "We're still collecting trace, if you can call it that. Not much of anything near the body. No clothes either. Photos are done, and the photog's over with that bunch." He pointed to a small group of searchers still standing around despite

Alan's order. "I think it's Bart Lajeunesse, same guy did the body at the river and the one at the church."

"Yeah, I know him. I'll go look. You'll let me know when you're done?"

"Yup, I'll talk to Harvey and catch you soon as."

Spence looked at Alan who was looking at her, pointed to the small group, and walked over. Alan joined her. "Everything look the same as far as you could tell?"

"Yeah, looks the same, probably someone our guy got. If it's our guy, who got him? And where are they? It's creepy."

Spence tapped Bart on the shoulder, and when he turned, said, "How ya doin' Bart? This another one?"

"It sure looks like it. On the surface, everything seems the same right down to the stones, but it's not. I've got photos and sketches, and I've been comparing this set to the river ones. There's lots of mutilation, but it's a different kind. The main cut is in the middle of the chest, more like a puncture wound, then the incision like the others. The rest of the body's got strange puncture marks all over it, and the head on this one's a mess. The face has cuts. At both the church and the river the heads were perfect, about the only things that were. So, I dunno. This is just different. Maybe more like the photos I've seen from the island murders, maybe not. It's just that there are some things that're similar, a lot that aren't. Here, I'll show you guys what I got."

Bart opened his case and handed Spence the photos he'd printed on a portable printer. Alan leaned over her shoulder.

"These are weird, Alan. The posing's right, the site too, but the damage to the head. We've never seen that before. And Bart's right, the main cut's different. This isn't like the island murders or the freaky slashing we've had here. No clothes, though, that fits. Then again, there're no markings on the shoulder or the arm. None of this makes much sense. If it's our guy, there should be a different kind of damage, not these weird puncture wounds, look at this one. There's something not right about the top end of the incision. There's something there I can't make out."

Spence shoved the photo at Alan and waited. She looked back at the collection tent then up at the darkening sky. The clouds were heavier now, the bottoms bulging downward like heavy bellies.

Rain was imminent. She saw the techs looking up as well. One of them ducked into the tent, took out another tent, and took the path to the site.

Alan looked up from the photo. "There's some strange stuff goin' on with this one, you're right. That cut's odd."

He glanced up at the sky then over to the site. "As long as they get it covered, we should be okay. Any idea when we can get in?"

"There's not much trace. Soon I expect. Harvey's still there, but I'm told he hasn't found anything significant yet. God, I hope he'll hurry up and leave, I don't want to go over that site in the bloody rain, tent or no tent."

Anybody heard from the coroner yet? Is it that lanky guy we had at the river, the one with the special car and the Gucci shoes?" Spence smiled at the memory.

"That's the one, I think. And he should be here by now. Maybe having trouble with the river and the bush since he's a city guy. He'd hate natural stuff like this. Reminds me a bit of old Harding on the island except Harding wasn't as elegant or as quiet."

Alan nodded toward the site, and he and Spence moved over to the ten-foot restricted area and watched Harvey work while they waited.

They saw Harvey stand up when a rumble of thunder rolled over the bush. A sharp, cool breeze pushed through, lifting the tent tops and bending saplings as it went. Then the rain came hissing down, hard and cold. Neither Alan nor Spence had rain gear, and the specimen tent was out of bounds. In seconds, they were soaked.

"Well, shit! Just what we need, a bloody cloudburst. And it's cold. We gotta get this done and get out of here. Catch our death if we don't. How much longer is he gonna piss around in there?"

As if he'd heard her, Harvey turned and left the covered site, moving quickly to the specimen tent. Alan and Spence moved over to him.

"We good to go, Harvey?" Alan's hair was plastered to is head as he leaned into the tent to grab two sets of booties. They'd wait till they were under the site tent before they'd put them on. Their latex gloves were already in their pockets.

Harvey turned toward Alan. The little there is useless. Again, as usual. No clothes though, and the stones are there, so maybe it's another victim and your guy's gone. But if that's what it is, he's reversed himself. This one's not the carnage the other two were. It's staged the same way, but it's cleaner. And the vic wasn't killed in this spot either. It's like the ones on the island and unlike the two here, so you need to search in the Reserve for the kill site."

Harvey turned toward the specimen tent and called, "Good luck finding anything besides the oddities. You'll see those right away. Hard to miss. Oh, and grab some coveralls from the box there. You don't want to get any wetter."

Spence rolled her eyes. Alan grabbed a pair of suits, and they ran to the site tent.

In the tent, they struggled into the protective coveralls and booties, hard to do when you're as wet as they were.

"You know, that's the first time I've ever seen Harvey smile. I could kill him for that!" Spence cursed as her foot caught on the leg of her suit. She hopped about on one foot till Alan grabbed her shoulder to steady her. "Thanks, I got it now, bloody thing's like pullin' on a wet rubber, and you shut up, you!"

Alan grinned and pointed to the body. "You think this is our guy or another victim? Gonna be damned hard to tell. Whoever it is, it looks like he ran into a bunch of barbed wire. Look at all those cuts. And what the hell happened to his face?"

Spence poked her head around Alan's side and studied the body. "That's weird. But the major cut's clean. It does look like the ones we had back home on the island. It can't be a new victim, though, he couldn't revert like that, could he? I mean he's losing it, he's vicious now, out of control like Roberta said he'd be. He can't suddenly go back to bein' neat, can he?"

"You're forgetting Sabina. She was cut the same way, and it was clean. No question it was our guy. So maybe Roberta's wrong, and he can revert."

Alan bent closer. "Damn face is a mess, but I think I've seen it somewhere. There's something familiar about it."

Alan pointed to the body and leaned over even more. "There's so much blood I can't see clearly, and his mouth's badly cut, and that eye. Something, though. Maybe when he's cleaned up, I'll remember."

"Well, we can't touch him now, although I've never understood why not. I mean the coroner's just gonna say he's dead and then cart him away, so why not clean him up a bit and take a closer look while we can?"

"Why don't you take a really close look now and see what you think. I know this guy from somewhere, I'm sure of it. If I could just see his face without the cuts."

Spence slid around Alan, bent over as close to the body as she could, and studied the face carefully. "Yeah, you're right, we've both seen this guy somewhere. Maybe when he's cleaned up as you say. Maybe we'll have to wait for the autopsy. He'll be cleaned up then for sure. Who's the coroner, do you know?"

"I'll ask Jake. Whoever it is, with this backlog and cutbacks, we'll be lucky to get to an autopsy in a week. Unless somebody pulls strings."

Spence glanced back toward the small group still standing around at the collection tent trying to stay dry. Jake and Larry were there along with the coroner, a tall, skinny guy with a large nose. He was wearing his usual suit, and this one looked sodden. She saw Harvey point and the coroner look up and nod.

"Here comes Ichabod. Let's clear out, let him pronounce, maybe get the medics to let us clean off some of the blood when they transport. What the hell's his name, do you remember?"

"Wainright? Wainsboro? Wainsbury! That's it! You're right, he is an Ichabod." Alan stepped out of the site tent, and he and Spence passed the coroner on the marked path. The man nodded, smiled, and said nothing.

At the collection tent, Alan looked for the medics who'd transport the body. The rain was still coming down, quite a bit lighter, but still cold. Now a ground mist was creeping in. Nobody was dry. The tent was small, and the group had to squeeze together to get any relief from the incessant rain. Alan cornered Jake and asked who the chief coroner was and when they could expect an autopsy.

"The guy's a bit of a hardass, but he's good. Name's Bartlett. James, I think. He'll have the body today, but an autopsy? Who knows. That place is always full. But I'll bet this one gets priority what with the press and the brass all over it."

"The medics are comin'."

Jake pointed toward the trees, and Alan saw two men emerge from the mist like dark floating shapes, their legs hidden in the ground fog. Everyone watched as they passed the tent and followed the flags to the coroner and the body.

A minute later, they reappeared, the coroner in front, the medics following, hauling the body on a stretcher. It looked like a funeral cortege of three. No one in the collection tent said a word, and the trio passed silently. Everyone watched them disappear slowly, as the ground fog and the rain ate them.

Larry broke the quiet. "Well, that was fun, weird but fun. Spooky too."

The rain suddenly slowed, then stopped altogether. The fog grew thicker. The conifer limbs, heavy with water, sent huge glistening drops into the thickening ground mist. There was no wind now, and tentacles of the fog slithered across the forest floor, followed by a low, thicker bank of the stuff.

Without much to say, the group of techs and detectives filed along after the medics, picking their way carefully through the fog, trying to stay on the marked path. Two stayed behind with Harvey to remove the collection tent. The site tent would remain until the site was no longer needed.

In less than an hour, the forest was silent, the ground fog a blanket of white, undisturbed by any movement. The fog made the river crossing difficult. It was hard to see the crossing stones and they had to feel for them. Once across the river and up to the trail, however, the medics from the coroner's office easily walked the body down to a van that had been backed up to the beginning of the river trail.

Alan and Spence had given up trying to get the face cleaned up when they'd seen the body bag zipped tight.

The four detectives and the forensics techs walked back to the headwaters park where their transport waited. There wasn't much talking, everybody was too wet, too cold, and too tired.

Herk and Gordie had been waiting most of the morning, thankful they'd been forgotten in the rush to get to the body. They'd had plenty of coffee, had talked about their case in Hammil and the girl who had still not been identified. They'd watched the rain approach, spent the duration of the downpour in one of the SUVs, and were now under the tent that protected the electronics and the crew that monitored the drones. The drones were still up, but they'd been moved over to the site where the body'd been found. They'd remain there as long as needed on the off-chance the killer might return.

Gordie saw the group of men coming down the trail near the bridge and nudged Herk. "That's gotta be our guys in that bunch. Let's go see if they know who the dead guy is. Maybe it's our killer."

Herk stepped out from the protection of the tent and raised his hand. Gordie followed. He saw a hand go up in the group in return. The four detectives separated themselves from the techs and walked over to meet them. The six stood around one of the picnic tables and talked.

"We don't know who the hell it is." Larry stuck his hands in his jacket pockets, making the material sag with the weight. "Might be our guy, might not. The body's just strange, and it's male not female. There are deep cuts all over the place, some even on the head like he ran into barbed wire or something. But you got the rocks all around him like you guys had and like the one at the river."

Larry glanced at Alan as he spoke. "But at the river, we had that body like the church, slashed all to bits. This body's not like that, at least not the torso. The head's another matter."

Spence broke in. "Yeah, if it's our guys did the killing, and I don't see how it could be given that the body's male like Larry said, but if it's their kill, they're reverting. The main cut's clean. No mutilation like the other two. And our profiler said that's not possible. Once a psychopath starts to lose control, he can't get it back, and our guys sure as hell lost control two bodies ago. Larry's right, we got ourselves a puzzle."

She ran her hand over her wet face. "Right now it looks like it's not our guys. If one of our guy's the body, who got him?"

Spence looked at Alan and shrugged. "There's the fact that this body's been staged like the ones on the island and the one up north. And he wasn't killed where we found him either. Maybe there's something in that. But with all that damage and that straight cut and the fact that it's a male, it's confusing. If it's our psycho who got it, I sure wanna know what the hell happened to him and who took him down."

"He's familiar, though, I've seen him before." Alan thought for a moment. "Spence thinks she's seen him too. We just don't know where. Maybe on the island. Wasn't here, we'd remember. Problem is his head's so messed up it's hard to tell."

"I know I've seen him before. Alan's right. Had to be on the island. I just can't connect him with anyone. Maybe it'll come to us later, maybe at the autopsy when they clean him up. We couldn't touch him on the site, not even to check his face, so the autopsy's our best bet. Problem is, we don't know when that's likely to happen, and we need to know now."

Spence glanced at each of them, the question in her eyes. "If that body is our guy, it gets even more intriguing. Because then we need to figure out who got him and how. That damn Reserve was really covered with cops and rangers. If somebody in there got him, where'd he go?" Nobody said anything.

After a moment Herk said, "We don't know much. I think Spence and Alan are right, we gotta wait for the autopsy. And both of us would like to be there. We called the task force guys a few times while you were in the bush, and nobody has anything to add. They're still looking for who the church girl was. Sor far nothing on the killers. They've been in touch with the hospital, though, sort of on the sly, and Sabina's still the same, in a coma to protect her while she recovers. I gotta say, that doesn't look good. She must be pretty bad to have to be in a coma to do that."

"You've all seen what these guys do to the girls they take, and they were dead before he sliced. But Sabina was alive. So the damage is more severe and harder to fix. Then there's the shock. Maybe that's why she's still in an induced coma. At least the doc said she's stable. That's good news." Alan wasn't so sure himself, but he refused to be pessimistic about Harry's girl and wanted to reassure the rest of them at least a little so they'd concentrate on what they needed to.

"Look, we're doin' fuck all here," Spence said, "so why don't we go back to the hospital and see for ourselves how she is. We gotta wait till we hear about the coroner's schedule, so we got little else to do now except paperwork." Spence looked around, the others nodded, but nobody moved.

"Okay, I'm drivin', any of you comin'?" She marched off toward the row of SUVs that sat in the grass near the bridge. The others watched for a moment, then followed.

Alan knew there was no sense trying to change her mind, not when she got that look. "Take it easy going out."

"Yeah, better do that, Spence. When we came in, the street was solid with those vultures. And there're still a lot of vans and stuff out there. They've pretty much blocked the street. Some stayed all night, I guess. Bloody persistent, the lot of them." Gordie leaned over the back seat to make sure everyone heard him.

Spence grunted then hit the lights and siren and once on a solid path, floored the SUV, spraying path gravel in an arc across the grass.

There was still a token sign-in constable at the gate. For some reason, the press had stayed out, maybe because of the constable. She ran the gamut of press vans, damn near caught some guys moving too slowly and careened down Lynn Valley Road toward Highway 1.

She made the cloverleaf turn with difficulty, fought the big car straight, hit the gas, and tore down the long hill toward the city. Stuff moved out of her way all along that hill. By the time she hit the Second Narrows bridge, traffic had cleared a lane and she took full advantage.

Spence ran down Powell and up Clark. She killed the siren once she was on Twelfth approaching the hospital, but she kept the lights until she hit the emergency lot. She slid into the closest spot, killed the engine, and climbed out without a word. Jake, Larry, and Alan followed.

Herk turned to Gordie. "We gotta try the task force again. Maybe Herb's heard about our girl. I can't understand why we haven't heard. We've got stuff all over the place, even up in the territories. It's been almost a week since we found the body. Besides, here we're intruding since Sabina's still in a coma and we don't really know her."

"You'd think he'd let us know if anything came in, wouldn't you? Give Herb another call if you think it'll do any good. Me, I'm goin' in with the guys, see if I can get a lead on the autopsy. You hear anything from Herb, come get me." Gordie climbed out and followed the others. Herk watched him go, shook his head, and took out his phone.

This time when Herk called, Herb had better news. "A call's just come in from Ontario's OPP. One of their missing girls fits the description of our request for information. It looks like your girl, Herk, the description fits. Seems she's been on a cross-country trek with a boy named Jason Sanders. The roommate reported her missing when Jason showed up for classes and she didn't. Her name's Jasmine Holmes. Parents deceased, no sibs. Full data on her is being sent now."

"Look, I'm at VGH tryin' to get into the morgue. We might be able to identify the killer if we can get the body cleaned up without waiting for the coroner, at least Alan and Spence think they can. If that happens, we can get our end settled. I've gotta talk to Alan and Spence, find out how Sabina is. I'll call you when we're done. Can you book us a flight for the AM, maybe send us a cruiser later when I call? We gotta get our stuff from the motel, check in with you, and get back north asap."

"Done, call when ready."

Herk sighed happily. They'd soon be back where they belonged, where the pie was excellent, and the town manageable. He didn't much like this town, too much goin' on, too many crazies on the streets, cars everywhere day and night. Herk sighed again, locked the SUV, and headed for the hospital doors.

When the elevator doors opened, he saw Alan and Spence

in the hall talking to Jake and Larry. Harry was just walking up to them. Herk didn't like the look on his face. He was stressed, sure, but that look, that was murderous. Gordie was nowhere to be seen. He joined the group.

"She's being brought out of the coma slowly," Harry said. He nodded to Herk. "The doc says he's watching for infection. That's the big thing now. The incision was deep enough the liver got nicked and the intestine was cut in places. She lost a lot of blood. He said she's not responding to the medication as well as he'd like. He's concerned about the possibility of peritonitis. Thinks maybe they'd missed a nick or something given how she's doin'. I'm gonna be here for a while until I know she's alright for sure."

Harry glared at Alan. "You guys got that murderous bastard, didn't you? Tell me you got him! You did what I said!"

"No, Harry, we didn't do what you said, but somebody got him. And we're not sure who this is. What we've got is a dead body laid out like all the victims on the island, clear depression in the bush, circle of stones, no clothes, big cut down the front, all that. Somebody did that to this guy, we don't know who yet, but we will. Spence and I think we might know who the dead guy is, so we're tryin' to get into the morgue to see if we can get him cleaned up enough to try for an ID."

Alan laid a hand on Harry's shoulder. "Why don't we find a place to sit down so we can talk. There's gotta be a lounge or something on this floor."

With some guidance from the nursing station, they found a conference room with some upholstered chairs, a round table, and a three-seater chesterfield in a dismal cherry colour. Lots of black metal shelving held journals and piles of paper. The floor was the usual grey industrial carpet, the walls a soft green. On one wall were a series of prints, mostly Group of Seven and Emily Carr. There were enough chairs for all of them.

Harry was barely seated when he started in on Alan. "So who the hell is this guy you think you know? He's gotta be one of the guys murdered Kylie and Mary on the island and a bunch over here. Whoever got him has my blessing. Just how the hell would you two know him anyway? I gotta know for sure. I gotta know who damn near killed my girl!"

"Easy, Harry. Look, he's cut up some, especially his face. One eye's gone and there's so much blood we aren't sure. We gotta get into the morgue, see if we can get his face cleaned up before the autopsy. This city's huge, and there's a ton of bodies to get through before ours, so we have no idea when an autopsy's gonna happen. If we can get in there, clean him up a bit, then we'll know. Spence and I are both sure we've seen him somewhere, we just don't know where. It's gotta be on the island."

Larry nudged Jake. "Don't you know one of those guys who help out, you know, some kinda morgue tech? Don't those guys clean stuff up before the coroner starts? Maybe you could get your guy to speed that up some so Alan and Spence can get a look. You know who I mean, that little guy, baldish, dark, funny little mustache on his upper lip, bit of hair on his chin tryin' to be one a those what-you-ma-call-its. You used to take him out for drinks now and then if I remember right."

"You're thinkin' of Mustaf, yeah. Haven't seen him in ages, haven't thought of him either. It's a long shot. Lemme check." Jake worked his way around the table and hit the door.

"Jake used to know lots a guys around here. Used to work the Eastside on patrol, tons a bodies back then, three, four a night. He knew everybody. Had to go to autopsies all the time." Larry tapped the table and nodded to Harry. "He'll find somebody if that guy's not here anymore. Jake's good at that kind of thing."

Larry looked around the table. Nobody said anything. Everybody looked too tired to talk. "Jesus, we gotta perk up some. You guys look dead. How about I go round up some coffee, maybe somethin' to munch on." He checked out the table, grinned, and pushed himself up. "Back in a jiff, don't go anywhere."

None of them had slept much in over 24 hours, and they all felt dragged out and dirty. All the adrenalin hype the chase provoked was long gone. Spence groaned and lowered her head to the table. Alan sat back and closed his eyes. Harry seemed worse off than any of them. He looked drugged he was so tired, like he'd been on the street for days. He just sat there, gone somewhere else. Herk and Gordie were the only ones who'd had anything resembling sleep, so Herk just watched the others. He felt as tired as they looked, and he'd been far less busy. He jumped when the door opened and Gordie peaked in. He saw Herk point to a chair and slid in.

"I found the morgue, ran into Jake in the hall. Damned thing's in the basement. Jake's lookin' for some guy he used to know, gonna try to get us in. Place is a labyrinth, corridors all over the place, got lost twice. Jesus, everybody looks dead."

Herk rubbed his chin, then the rest of his face as if he were washing it. "It's been a hell of a night for them, and we had some rest. These guys haven't had any, and they've been at it for more than a day. I'm surprised they're still upright."

"They're not, they're flat on the table. Bet half of 'em are asleep."

"Larry's gone for some coffee and eats. He gets back, they'll perk up some. I talked to Herb. We know who our girl is and where she came from. He's bookin' a flight back for us in the AM. Once we get an ID from Alan and Spence, we can go home and put ours to bed."

"And she's who?"

"Oh, sorry, name's Jasmine Holmes. Been travelling the country with a boyfriend named Jason Saunders. Didn't turn up for class at the University in Toronto when he did. Apparently, they'd had a fight and split up somewhere on the island. Roommate phoned the cops, cops alerted the OPP, OPP called us. That's all I've got so far. But it's our gal for sure, so we need to get back."

36.

Jake had been about to enter the morgue doors when he saw Gordie coming down the hall. He waved, stopped, and waited for him.

"I've gotta find a tech to let us into the morgue. We're gonna try to identify the body, at least Alan and Spence are. They're are up at ICU in a conference room. If you join them there, I'll get back with some information as soon as I can." Jake looked hopefully at Gordie. He knew the guy had a rep for going his own way, which, Jake thought, he was doing now.

Gordie rubbed his head. "If I can find the damned thing. Been lost at least twice so far. This bloody place is huge, hallways all over the place, red lines, blue ones, yellow, you're supposed to follow them, but that didn't work, so I've been takin' whatever came up. Okay, I'll grab an elevator and get up to ICU. See you up there."

Gordie turned, retraced his steps, and punched an elevator button. Jake watched him. Gordie waited impatiently, hit the button a dozen times, kicked the door softly a couple more, and turned to see if anybody'd seen him. Jake grinned, waved, and turned toward the doors leading into the morgue.

He looked into the morgue through a glass wall and saw a long line of stainless-steel coolers. It was huge room with a dark red floor and cream walls. There were side rooms for storage and other things, like instruments. Jake wasn't sure what some of the rooms were for. He'd only been in the main one for autopsies and once or twice in the teaching space, another separate room. He could see several autopsy tables, so presumably there were several coroners. The Chief Coroner, James Bartlett, was difficult, Jake knew, so he was hoping the guy was away at a conference or something and that the tech he knew from his patrol days was still around.

Jake was still looking into the morgue when the door opened and one of the techs came through. "Anything I can help you with?"

"I was wondering if Mustaf is still on staff here. I knew him from my patrol days. Used to spend too much time in that room." Jake pointed through the window.

I don't know the guy. He's not on staff now, I'm sure of that. So, can I help you? Name's Bond, James Bond.... Oh god, I love sayin' "that. You should see the look on your face! Really, though, that's my name. Call me Jimmy." The tech grinned and waited.

"Thank you for that. Levity's always good, and given the night I've had, it helps. Yeah, you can help me a lot. I'm part of the team that got the psycho who killed those girls you've had in here, and we need to see his face cleaned up some. We think we know who he might be, at least two of our team think so. Any chance you can help us out?"

"I can see who's assigned the body, check when the autopsy's scheduled, maybe that'll help."

"Appreciate any help you can give."

"Just a mo, then." The tech turned, went back through the door, and Jake saw him enter the morgue proper, check the freezer cabinets one after the other, open one, check the toe tag, close the door. Several minutes later he returned.

"You guys must have some pull. I checked the paper and the autopsy's scheduled for today, but not by the chief, so you're doubly lucky."

"When today?"

"Within the hour. Everybody's up top at a meeting. Four scheduled for now, yours is one of them. Fortunately for you, I'm the tech, so you get special treatment. And you're lucky it's not the Chief Coroner who's doing it. From him you wouldn't get anything, and I wouldn't be helping. Coroner's named Gibson, not Mel, that'd be too cute. It's George. George Gibson. Where are you guys? Got a cell?"

"We're up in ICU. A friend of ours got mixed up with that creep and got cut. Here's my cell." As he scribbled his cell number on the back of a card he asked, "Can I get four of us in there? We're all leads on this one."

"George's pretty easy, but I'll check and let you know. You just want a look at the face, that's it? You don't wanna stay for the rest?"

"It'd be good if we could stay. Maybe something else'll turn up we can use."

"Let you know."

The tech turned suddenly and walked back into the morgue, leaving Jake standing looking through glass. He stood for a few minutes, remembering other times, and then he walked toward the elevator to return to ICU.

The room was quiet when he entered, everyone either folded over the table or bent over in chairs. All of them were asleep, even Herk and Gordie. Alan lifted his head and squinted from his place at the table as did Spence. Jake nodded to both and pointed to the door. They met in the hall.

"Autopsy's scheduled for today. All I'm waiting for is a call from the tech and the four of us can attend. The coroner's lenient, I'm told. Harry's not gonna want to leave Sabina, so we can fill him in later. If we get an ident, we can lock this one up."

"Herk's got an ID on his girl," Alan said, "and he and Gordie want to get back. If we get him an ID, he can wrap up his as well. That leaves us with only one girl we can't identify yet, the one in the church."

"We still don't know anything about who got this creep and if it's him." A chirp came from Jake's phone. He yanked it from his pocket, listened, and smiled.

"We're in. Let's get Larry and go down. Autopsy's in thirty minutes and the four of us are authorized to attend. I think we can stay for the whole thing. Might learn something about this guy."

"That'd be good. We know he's been staged just like the girls, cut just like 'em too, so whoever got him's gotta know a lot about the case. That should tell us something." Spence looked worn, Jake thought, but she still had a bit of bite left.

The autopsy room was busy. There were three autopsies running in the main room. George Gibson's autopsy table was at the far end. Jake saw James Bond roll the body from one of the coolers to George's table. Then he lifted the body, placing it on the autopsy table with its head raised on a block with a curved surface.

The four detectives, Jake, Larry, Alan, and Spence, all gowned up, gathered round the table's end so they wouldn't get in the way. George nodded to Jake. "Just stay on that side, please, and we'll get started."

"Okay, James, you got the x-rays up?"

George and his tech took a step toward the light boxes and studied the three plates. "Looks like the heart cavity's been broached, probably what killed him, but we'll wait on that. Nothing else of any significance that I can see. Okay let's get him ready."

James used a suspended hose and carefully washed the face and body. He was careful to do only superficial cleaning and not to disturb the wounds. George stood by and addressed the four homicide detectives.

"Anyone here who's never been to an autopsy? Just so you know, I'm a forensic pathologist as are all the guys here.

'So what's a forensic pathologist, then?" Spence glared at the man.

"An MD who's trained in death investigation and autopsy pathology. All the coroners you see at a murder site are like us.

We all work under the Chief Coroner.

"Okay, here we go. All this goes on tape, by the way, and is filed with CCMED, that's the Canadian Coroner and Medical Examiner Database in case you need to know… This is the body of a male Caucasian, circumcised, 180 centimeters, 72.52 kilos, no amputations. Identity is unknown, date and place of birth unknown. The subject was found naked, so there are no clothes and therefore no papers or other identifications available. Age is estimated at between twenty-five to thirty years. The eyes are blue. Hair is dirty blond cut short. No scars or tattoos visible, no physical abnormalities."

The pathologist paused here to add what he'd found to the body diagram, then continued.

"Okay, James, let's start at the top. Injury to the left eye from a sharp knife-like instrument. Depth is, let's see, five centimeters, nature of cut, double edged short instrument, unusual shape. Mouth is badly cut, several teeth broken. Looks like a similar instrument was used. Lot of force. Damage is severe, deep cuts to the lip on the left side, cuts to gums and tongue also on left. Incisor and two molars damaged.

"Now the body, and god knows what the hell happened to that. On the front of the torso there are six wounds, one very deep chest wound, and it looks like it's three-sided. That sort of wound might be caused by a hunting arrow. But there's no way to be certain what the weapon was.

"The deepest wound is the chest wound which is likely the cause of death. The incision running down the torso is not as deep and was made by a sharp blade, different from the chest wound which pierced the breastbone and the heart. The remaining body wounds were caused by that same sort of double-edged weapon that was used on the face. Depth is roughly the same in each, approximately five centimeters. There are similar wounds on the legs and thighs: three on the left thigh, one on the left leg, four on the right thigh, and two on the right leg."

Again, the pathologist paused, made notes on his body chart, looked at James, and said: "Okay, let's turn him over."

Alan stepped forward before the two men began and studied the chest wound. The pathologist looked up quizzically. "You got something to say?"

"They're all the same, and I think you'll find the ones on the back are too. The weapons are usually called shurikens. They come in a lot of shapes, but the circular ones with three or four pointed, double-sided blades are the most common."

"And how would you know just from the wounds?" The coroner was curious and a little taken aback.

"I'm Korean, belong to a martial arts group, and we use

these things in training. I know the shapes and what kind of marks they make. If you'll let me, I think I know what the chest wound came from."

"Hey, the floor's yours. We've turned off the recorders."

"I think the chest wound was caused by a bo-shuriken, a short spear. The tip's steel, the blade about eight to ten centimeters long, but sometimes longer. It's very sharp, and often three-sided. That's the only weapon that makes sense, given the other wounds."

The pathologist looked more closely at the chest wound, then back at Alan. He nodded, obviously interested. "Who'd use them?"

"I'd guess someone trained in the martial arts that use these things. The clubs are fairly common."

Spence leaned close, looking over Alan's shoulder. "I know this guy, Alan, you know him too. That's Martin, that bloody reporter."

Alan leaned forward and studied the face. "You're right, it is Martin. I was looking at the wounds, but you're right. That's Martin."

"So you got a last name for this guy? Be nice if I could list his identity." George looked from Alan to Spence.

"He's a reporter in Harbour City, or was, I guess. Maybe the paper knows his last, I don't. He was freelance, I think."

"Let's turn him over and finish the examination. James, gimme a hand." The back of the body was riddled with wounds, all very much the same as the front. George looked at each and measured the depth and looked thoughtfully at Alan. James photographed the wounds. Then George looked back down at the body, flipped the recorder on again, and continued.

"The wounds on the back are the same as the others. There are twelve wounds distributed across the upper and lower back and two in the buttocks. Two on the left thigh, none on the right. Legs are clean. The weapons used to inflict the wounds are unknown. All are serious but not life threatening. Cause of death was a chest wound caused by an unidentified weapon with a tripartite blade that pierced the heart. Manner of death, homicide."

George stopped the recording and looked at Alan again. "You seem pretty sure about the weapons, but I'd need to see them to know if you're right, hence the unidentified verdict. And I'd need more than your thinking you know this guy. I need some verifiable paper on him. All I've got now is your guesses. I'll eliminate them from any official record, but I'll keep notes on what you said. The rest of this autopsy gets messy. We're gonna do a Y cut, look at the organs, measure, weigh, take our samples. Then we'll study the brain. None of that should matter to you, so if you'd like to get out of here, we'll finish. Or you can stay, if you like."

"We've got a lot to sort out ourselves. Thank you for the chance to watch you work. It's given us more than we expected." Alan looked at both George and James as he spoke, motioned to the others, and they all filed out. The four men gathered in the corridor beyond the morgue doors. Larry and Jake said nothing, just looked to Alan.

"Spence and I do know the man from the island. There, he was a reporter for the local rag, but freelance. We don't know anything else about him."

"Except that he was a pain in the ass." Spence added. "He was always hanging around the station, and he tried to get to the privates, Sabina and Harry, but never got by Isabella, their secretary. I can't believe we knew him all this time. Shit!"

Spence shook her head in disbelief, then she got angry. "That fucker and his pal killed two women at home and left them to rot. Then he got three more over here and really messed them up. That one up in Hammil, she was cut like the island ones, wasn't she? We gotta talk to Herk and Gordie. See if they had a reporter doggin' them. They're still upstairs. Let's go get 'em."

Spence left them standing together and marched up the hall toward the elevators. Alan looked at the others, shrugged and followed. Jake and Larry brought up the rear.

Upstairs in the lounge, Herk and Gordie had been busy. They'd reached their respective offices and updated their subordinates. Celia, Herk's go-to girl, updated their files and checked the reservation the task force manager, Herb Chase, had already made. Then she began to trace the route that Jasmine, their murdered girl, had taken with Jason

Sanders. Herk knew that'd keep her busy and out of his hair for a while.

Gordie reached Frank Miller, his partner, and updated him, giving him the name of the girl murdered near Hammil, and asked him to follow up on her and her companion. They were still on their respective phones when the four detectives arrived. Herk and Gordie finished their calls and looked questioningly at Alan, who was first through the door. Spence was right behind him.

"Did you have a reporter up in Hammil who appeared around the time of your murdered girl? And if you did, what was his name?"

"We had a new guy in town. Been around a few weeks, working freelance for old Manchester who runs the local paper. This guy had a brother who wasn't all there, we didn't think. The reporter called himself Vic. Called his brother, uh wait a minute, I know the name...can't remember. Vic used to hang around the office and flirt with Jenny tryin' to dig out stuff on our body. Able, that's it, the brother's name. Why?"

"Because we had a reporter too, pushy prick, used to hang around the station, covered a lot of stuff, worked freelance, called himself Martin. Didn't see a brother, but we know our psycho had an accomplice.

"We think now that Martin was our killer, and we think he was yours too. We both just identified him downstairs. It sounds like your Vic and his brother fit the profile. We'll know for certain if you come downstairs and tell us if your Vic is our Martin."

Alan pointed toward the door and said to Herk, "Let's go down and see."

"We'll stay up here with Gordie," Jake said. "No sense all of us traipsing back down there. You come back up when you're done, and we'll compare notes."

Larry sank onto a chair and sighed. "Bloody hot up here." He yanked his tie down, unbuttoned the top button on his shirt, spread his legs, and turned to Gordie. "You know, the two girls we had murdered here, we only know the name of one of them. The one from the river that started all this. The church one, we haven't a clue yet. Sort of like your girl up there. But you finally got her pegged, and that's good.

Our two leads think they may have psycho pegged too. Problem is, even if Herk confirms, we got diddly. Two first names, no lasts, both phony. We all got a lot of diggin' to do."

In the morgue, George was about to remove the skull cap when Alan and Herk, barely gowned, were led back into the room by a tech who had just seen them leave. The forensic pathologist turned off the saw, placed it beside the body, and looked up, eyebrows raised in question. He looked squarely at Alan. "What now? Thought you had things to do?"

Herk leaned over the body while the coroner looked on, obviously annoyed. "This is Vic, no doubt in my mind. So now we know. The bugger lived with us for weeks, and we hadn't a clue."

Herk stepped back, turned, and left the room. Alan apologized and quickly followed. George shook his head, sighed, and picked up the saw. The buzz of the Stryker filled the room.

Upstairs, the five homicide detectives and Herk sat around the table. "Okay, we know what exactly?" Gordie looked around questioningly.

"We know that the reporter in Hammil and the one on the island are the same guy. We also know with fair certainty that he's our killer. What we don't know is his real identity."

"We don't know bloody much then, do we?" Gordie looked around the table. "Are we certain this guy's our killer? Okay, he used different names in both places, and he was in both places at the right time. But so far, that's circumstantial. We can't charge with stuff like that let alone get it to the crown attorney."

"I'm bloody sure about this guy and I know Alan is too. Okay, we can't prove he's the one, but he fuckin' well is. There's no doubt in my mind, and I don't think there's any in your minds either." Spence glared at Gordie ready for a fight.

Gordie raised his hands in surrender. "All I'm sayin' is we gotta be more certain. Same name, same place isn't enough, and you all know it. I don't want an unsolved any more than you do, Spence, but it's gonna happen that way unless we can find more."

"Then there's his brother and accomplice. Where the hell's he? Why isn't he around? We haven't seen or heard of him since we started getting murders down here in the city. He was around on the island and he was around in Hammil, but not here." Alan glanced at each of the others, and each of the others shrugged.

Herk picked it up. "This body is likely the killer, I think we all agree on that. What we don't know and what irritates the hell out of me is who killed him and why in that way? It's poetic justice I guess, but who did it? I know we should be more concerned with identifying this guy properly, but it's just as important to know who this new killer is. Rather than prosecuting him, I'd like to give him a medal if I could find him."

There was a long silence as everyone stared at the table. Alan ran his hand across his mouth. "Has anyone checked to see if forensics has submitted its report yet? And has anyone run the prints through RAFIAS? I have a hunch Harry'd know who killed him, but I'm equally sure he wouldn't tell us."

"What's RAFIAS?" Herk looked at Alan.

"It's a big name for our local fingerprint ID service. Regional Automated Fingerprint Identification Access System. Forensics usually does this stuff, checks for prints on the body, any weapons, of which there were none, of course, and no clothes either. It's unlikely, but let's check with Herb."

Alan took out his cell and pecked out the number. Spence looked exasperated. She was a hell of a lot faster.

"Herb, Alan. Have we got the forensics report? Yeah, we're all still at the hospital, been down in the morgue for the autopsy. We know our psycho's dead, killed with some antique weapons. I'll explain when we're back at the station. Fingerprints. Anything yet?" Alan held up his index finger asking for quiet. Everybody shut up, even Spence. "Okay, thanks for that."

"Forensics report is in. It's about as useful as the ones on the island. The body's prints were submitted. He's not in the data base. Didn't think he would be. This guy's a mystery. He's not anywhere: no phone records, no computer activity, no permanent address, no credit card data, no passport, no social insurance number, no nothing."

Alan shoved the phone back in his pocket, shook his head, and rubbed his face some more.

"As I said, we don't know bloody much, do we? And it sounds as if we won't get any more from the sites than we already have which is zilch." Gordie looked around waiting for comments. There were none.

"You know what? I don't give a shit! The fucker's dead, that we do know. And that submissive sidekick isn't gonna do anything on his own. Our profiler, Roberta Cannon, said that and Dr. Spencer did too. The psycho ran things, it was a cult of two, and he's dead. I don't care if we ever learn who he is, and I don't care who killed the psycho, and I'm sure as hell not gonna try to find him. We need to wrap up what we can. So we got an unsolved, who cares! We got our killer." Spence glared at everyone. Nobody said anything.

Alan stood and said, "We need to get back to the station and deal with the paperwork. And trust me, there's lots."

Spence rose and picked up her phone off the table. "We need to check on Harry and Sabina before we leave. So why don't we do that now. Then Herk and Gordie, you two can head back to the hotel and get ready for your plane, and we can get back to the task force."

Alan looked around the table, got some nods. He walked to the door followed by Spence. The others followed her. In the hall, Herk took Alan aside.

"We're goin' back to the motel. There's nothing we can do here, and a lot we need to do up home. I wanna thank you for keeping us in the loop. You didn't have to, and we both appreciate it. Anything that still needs to be done can be done by email. I'm sure the brass'll be holding press conferences for a week or so, and that should keep 'em off all our backs. Herk turned to Gordie. "Got anything to add?"

"I'm good. We do need to get back, though, as soon as we can, and Herk's right, there's nothing we can do here that matters, and a lot we need to do there."

Alan extended his hand, and they shook. He thanked them for their patience and said: "I'll make sure you guys get copies of all the reports for your files. The task force will look after all that. And any personal stuff that comes my way, I'll get to you pronto."

37.

In ICU, Alan and Spence and Jake and Larry found Harry pacing in the corridor, so preoccupied he didn't see them. Spence walked up to him, tugged at his arm. Harry turned toward her and the grief in his eyes shook her. "Jesus, Harry, what's happened?"

"They took her back in. They won't tell me what's wrong, just said they had to operate again. Oh, god, I'm afraid she'll die. She was so peaceful in the room, I could sit by the bed and be with her. Now, I don't know, I don't know."

"Come on, Harry, let's sit over there and we can talk. I'm so sorry. Come on, let's sit and talk." Spence led him over to one of the chairs along the corridor wall. Alan and Jake and Larry remained standing in the corridor, watching.

"Do we know anything, Harry? Anything at all?"

"She was fine. Suddenly things started to beep, all those machines. A crew came in, grabbed her bed and all those bottles and wires and stuff and ran down the hall with her. A doc came back and told me she started bleeding again. They had to go back in and find it and stop it."

Harry shook his head, tears streaming down his face. "He said she's got a lot going for her, she's young, she's strong, and she's a fighter. He said all that matters a lot. If they can stop the bleeding. He said he's hopeful. But you should have seen her, Spence, she looked so pale, so broken, I don't know if she'll ever come home. I can't lose her, I can't."

Harry looked broken himself, Spence thought. She put her arm around his shoulders, pulled him close. Jake and Larry and Alan watched, feeling helpless.

Jake said to Alan, "We need to get back, we're useless here.

Come with us. We need one of you. Spence can stay with Harry, she seems close to him, and she can help him cope."

Alan nodded, "Let me talk to Spence so she knows."

As the three detectives walked down the hall together, Larry turned to Alan: "There's your connection with the reporter and Herk's with his reporter, and you're both certain they're one and the same. It's not much, but it's what we got. We can't prove the body's our killer, and we can't prove anything about who killed him even if you have some ideas. So we're gonna have a lot of flack comin' down the shute. It'll be interesting to see how the brass spins this one."

"They'll spin it alright. And the press won't hear about the internal squabbles or our unsolveds if the brass have anything to do with it," Jake said.

"At least the death certificate'll be definitive. No question about the manner or cause. Still, it'll list homicide as the manner, and that'll bring us grief if we can't offer anything more definitive. It's a mess." Alan sighed, and they kept on walking.

The task force was still functional, the techs still gathering data, the phones still manned, and Herb was piling reports on the table s they entered. But the buzz had gone. It was like the aftermath of a party, empty plates and dirty glasses, and the cleanup crew doing what they do. Herb came over when he saw them enter the room.

"Okay, we've got everything we can get. Forensics is in on the latest for what it's worth. What I need now is whatever you got written up. We've still got no ID on the church victim. By the way, another body's turned up on the island. Pretty badly decomposed, but they're definite it's a female. Same sort of arrangement: little clearing, circle of stones. The autopsy's scheduled for today. Mispers have been checked, nothing there either. Josie Atardo wants you two back to work it. Where's Spence?" Herb glanced worriedly from Jake to Larry to Alan. Am I missing something?"

"Spence is with Harry. Sabina's been taken back to surgery. Spence stayed behind to help him. I can call her back."

Alan looked at Herb and then went to the table, "We've gotta get the paper done at any rate. And we have to arrange a search of the Reserve to look for the murder site. Half the Reserve's already taped off, no one in or out except we okay it. With all this rain, though, we're not gonna find anything worthwhile. Still it's gotta be done."

Alan looked at Jake and Larry, his face scrunched up as if he were in pain. "We'll coordinate with the rangers again and start tomorrow. Herb, you'll have to arrange for that. Same crews if you can get them. They know the place best, know where they've been and where to look. Have I missed anything?"

Jake thought about it. "We can cover everything here. But you two remain the leads, they're your bodies. We can also arrange for you to remain in the city until our work on this case is complete. Your body over there can wait, the cooler's gonna keep it fresh, so-to-speak. That way, we can all get some rest before we dive into this mess." He tipped his head toward the table.

"I'll call Spence. You call Brian and set it up, and we'll tackle all this stuff tomorrow. In the meantime, Herb, you can get that useless search going. We'll look into our new case on the island, get the forensics and autopsy reports at least. Not that they'll be worth much."

Alan stretched his arms and neck. "Get some sleep, start fresh tomorrow. You guys good with that?"

Larry grinned, yanked at his tie, already at half mast, and nudged Jake. "We got a date with the foodie outside. Then we're gonna hit the road. See ya in the AM, but not too early. I'll bring coffee."

Alan glanced around the room, nodded at Herb, and pulled out his cell.

"Close it down, Herb, regular hours beginning now. We'll finish tomorrow. Disband after the paper's filed. So round table at ten for any loose ends. I gotta make some calls."

Early evening light poured through the bay window into the front room of the apartment. The reds and blues of the Persian carpet glowed because of the silk threads. Spence had found the carpet in a shabby store full of what she called junk in the east end of the city and brought it home one night proud as punch at how little she'd paid. She'd spent an hour telling Alan how she'd gone into the store, haggled, gone out, gone in again, haggled some more and had beaten the store owner down so he just gave in to get rid of her. Alan smiled at the memory.

He stood looking out at the traffic that ran up and down Nanaimo in a steady stream, the lights of the cars making undulating ribbons of red and white light. The windows were double glazed, the traffic noise a low-pitched growl of sound, not at all unpleasant. He turned as Spence entered the room and pointed to the street. "Come and watch the traffic, it's relaxing."

"I don't wanna relax, not with all the damn reports on the screen. We gotta deal with this mess, and we gotta do it tonight if you wanna get out of here sometime tomorrow. We do have to go back, you know, and we've gotta pack, arrange shipping for all this, and set up a sublet. We can do all that in the morning, early, but we gotta do the reports now. The sooner we get back to the island, the sooner we'll get this whole thing wrapped up if it can be wrapped."

Spence scowled at Alan and glared even harder when he chuckled and shook his head. "Okay, okay, you're just so damn cute when you get going."

"You stuff that, you, and get serious. Look, we've got no car anymore. Mine's totalled, a write off. That hit bent the frame, and insurance is dragging its feet. Plus, we gotta drive that damned unmarked piece of junk until we get back home. So the sooner we get through all this useless paperwork, the better. We got that damn meeting tomorrow, and we've got nothin', less than nothin'. Jesus, this is a bloody mess! All this stuff and we can't close anything. We don't even know that the body's our killer. Let alone the girls he's killed."

"Okay, no traffic watching. But let's start with some coffee, then the paper, then how about a late dinner out somewhere quiet, with a bar, a good one. We can forget about the mess for a bit."

"Coffee's already down, so grab a cup and let's get at it. Dinner out sounds good. If we finish before bloody midnight, we can do that."

Spence turned, sighed heavily, and went back to the computers.

Alan got a mug out of the cupboard in the tiny kitchen, poured a cup, looked around the place and sighed. It'd been home for a while and he'd miss it. He sipped quietly enjoying the silence. He topped up his cup, then walked back to the spare bedroom where the computers were.

It had been some time now since Spence had stopped sleeping in it. He stood in the doorway and watched her. She was muttering under her breath, hitting the keys hard, and Alan had a pretty good idea what that was about. He joined her.

"You working on the final report on our guy?"

"I gotta soften it somehow, make it seem like we have what we haven't. It'll maybe keep the brass happy if nothing else." Spence paused, looked at the floor, then grinned at Alan. "I can lie like a trooper and still sound reasonable. But in the end, we got a bunch of unsolveds. If we can't prove that that body is our killer, and we can't, we can't close a damn thing. Trust me, Josie'll go through the roof when she sees this. Read it over and see if you can add anything."

Alan read and could add nothing to what she'd written so far. "You're doing a great job on this. I almost believe it. Josie'll have to at least give us some slack."

Alan went to stand behind Spence and rubbed her neck. "Why don't we call it a night, go get some eats, have a couple of drinks, get a bit mellow maybe." He began to massage her neck and shoulders. "Maybe we'll even get some sleep. Then we can face tomorrow when it gets here. The meeting'll just be a formality with lots of paper. We all know we're stuck with a bunch of unsolveds officially, but we all know we got the prick, or somebody did."

Spence groaned in appreciation. She was starting to relax, and Alan kept working at it. "Harry and Sabina, you and me, we know even if we can't prove it. The fat lady in Chinatown said she'd deal with Mary's killer if we didn't, and she's got her own sense of justice. Those weapons are her trademark."

Spence raised her arms and stretched. She sighed deeply. "Who cares if nobody but us knows. We'll file tomorrow and then get home...That feels so good. You ought to get a license and start a practice. Now get away and let me finish."

In Chinatown, three men slid into an old storefront on Pender. In an open space at the rear of the store, they faced a very fat woman in an ornate dragon chair. Two of the men lowered their heads. The third one spoke, then lowered his. A smile creased the fat woman's face, but there was no warmth in it. It was not a smile anyone would welcome. She studied her men, then nodded and muttered, "He take from me, I take back."

At Vancouver General, there'd been a code blue. A lone man sat in the corner of a room, his head lowered, his elbows on his knees, tears running down his face and dropping to the floor between his feet. In the center of the room against the far wall, lay a bed with crumpled bloody sheets. The mute machines beside it no longer measured out a life. Half full bags held high on stands dangled useless tubes that told their own story.

Acknowledgements

Only a few people helped on this one and I wish to thank Solveig Farquharson for proofreading the manuscript and Debra Bodner for proofreading and providing research time in Vancouver; Karl Rainer for proofreading and for his suggestions for improving the story; Dr. K. T. Houghton for providing medical advice; Renee Mallinson for editing, marketing, and support during the long process of writing this novel; and finally the two cats, Figaro and Kiyo, for providing comic relief when needed.

About the Author

Gar Mallinson lives in a small cottage in downtown Nanaimo on Vancouver Island with his partner, Renee, his cat, Kiyo and, until recently, his English foxhound, Scarlet. His novels are set on the east coast of Vancouver Island and in the city of Vancouver. He writes short stories and mysteries. Check his website www.garmallinson.com.

Also by Gar Mallinson

The Fraud Murders

Bloodlust

Made in the USA
Columbia, SC
08 June 2020